HAVE YOU READ . . .?

IN THE EVENT OF MY DEATH

There were once six teenagers in Wheeling, West Virginia. They called themselves the Six of Hearts. They knew how to have fun, and get into trouble. One night things went too far and a girl died. The rest swore never to speak about what happened. Until, thirteen years later, one of the remaining Six is murdered.

TONIGHT YOU'RE MINE

Fifteen years ago, Nicole and Paul had the perfect life. She was a university student, he was a concert pianist. They were deeply in love and passionately happy, until one violent night changed everything . . .

Also by Carlene Thompson

CARLENE THOMPSON

Don't Close
Your Eyes

HODDER

First published in Great Britain in 2013 by Hodder & Stoughton
An Hachette UK company

1

A CIP catalogue record for this title is available from the British Library.

Book ISBN 978 1 444 77871 7
eBook ISBN 978 1 444 77872 4

Printed and bound by Clays Ltd, St Ives plc

Hodder & Stoughton policy is to use papers that are natural, renewable
and recyclable products and made from wood grown in sustainable
forests. The logging and manufacturing processes are expected to
conform to the environmental regulations of the country of origin.

Hodder & Stoughton Ltd
338 Euston Road
London NW1 3BH

www.hodder.co.uk

*To all my dogs, who have given me joy,
inspiration, and unconditional love throughout the years*

Thanks to my patient and supportive agent, Pamela Ahearn.

Special thanks to William E. Johnston, D.V.M., for technical advice and excellent care of the Thompson animals.

I

SATURDAY NIGHT

Tamara dried the last crystal wineglass, held it up to the fading summer light shining through the kitchen window, and nodded. Spotless. She hated spots on glasses, particularly crystal. Tomorrow night, when Warren came home from his conference in Cleveland, they'd share a bottle of Château La Tour Blanche on their sixth anniversary. Tamara was not a wine connoisseur, but he'd assured her the Latour Blanche was expensive and should be properly appreciated. When she'd fussed about spending a lot of money on a bottle of wine, he said it was a gift from a patient. Tamara knew better than to ask which one. Warren was a psychologist and never discussed his patients.

Tamara looked around the pristine kitchen. The whole house was spotless. With no children and no job, she had more than enough time to keep the house perfect.

Tonight, however, she had nothing left to clean. She'd even reorganized the kitchen cabinets and put down fresh shelf paper. She could work on her latest quilt, the lovely one with the hummingbird design she'd created, but she wasn't in the mood. She could drop by the headquarters of the suicide hotline Warren had forced her to organize, but tonight she didn't want to hear any sad stories. She didn't enjoy Saturday night television and she felt too restless to read. Usually she took an evening walk, but a storm was predicted.

Tamara looked out the window and sighed. Daylight Saving Time extended light until nine o'clock. So far it was a lovely evening, a bit cloudier than usual, but still nice. Surely the storm wouldn't hit for over an hour. That left plenty of time for a walk.

She grabbed an old white sweater off the coat tree beside the back door. It was mid-June, but Port Ariel, Ohio, sat on the edge of Lake Erie, which sent cool breezes off its water all year. The comfortable temperature was what drew so many tourists to the beach area every summer. Warren hated tourists, but Tamara spent most of her time at home and rarely had contact with them. Besides, they were good for local business and therefore good for her twin sister Lily, who owned a successful antique store downtown. Tamara was making the hummingbird quilt for Lily's shop. "People like old furniture but not old bedding. Only bedding that looks old," Lily always said. "I could sell three times the number of these gorgeous quilts you make!" Tamara was pleased by their popularity, but she never increased her production. Haste made for sloppy work.

As she automatically locked the back door and descended the porch steps, Tamara glanced at her watch. Eight-thirty. Warren always called promptly at ten when he was out of town. She frowned. She mustn't be late for the call. Things were rocky between them. Warren had been irritable, quiet, and aloof for months. Tamara felt he was disappointed that she hadn't been able to give him a child, although he never mentioned it. Lily contended that Warren didn't *want* a child—not everyone did. Tamara told her sister she was being ridiculous.

To be twins, they were so different, hardly like sisters at all except for their looks and their love for each other. Lily wasn't even religious in spite of their strict Catholic upbringing. Ignoring Lily's good-natured skepticism, Tamara had begun attending mass every day, praying for the child that would draw Warren back to her. Now she knew her prayers had worked. Her periods were always irregular, but this time she was over a month late. She'd taken a home pregnancy test this morning and she had wonderful news for Warren, which she'd save until tomorrow evening when he returned.

Humming beneath her breath, Tamara crossed the lawn and walked down Hyacinth Lane, a wide dirt road running north through a wooded area. She delighted in the towering oaks, locust trees, and scattered dogwoods and crab apples. When the dogwoods and crab apples were in bloom, this place seemed like a fairy world.

She took a rubber band out of her sweater pocket and pulled back her long blond hair in a ponytail. Delicate silver filigree earrings set with amethyst stones swayed in the breeze, tickling her neck. She tilted back her head, closed her eyes, and drew a deep breath. Clean, clear air tinged with the scent of approaching rain and the water of Lake Erie filled her delicate nostrils. When she was young, she and Lily had spent countless hours on the lake in their parents' cabin cruiser and their sleek twenty-foot inboard motorboat. The girls were excellent water-skiers. Warren went out with the family sometimes on the cabin cruiser, but he always stayed on board. He didn't even fish.

Something rustled in the underbrush. Naturally timid, Tamara grew motionless, her gaze scanning the sides of the road. She knew the sound probably came from a small animal. Most of them were perfectly harmless except for poisonous snakes, although there weren't many of those around. Besides, a snake wouldn't make so much noise and it certainly wouldn't attack unless threatened.

Her mind knew this. Her body didn't. She felt cold, imagining a sleek head rising up to bury venom-filled fangs in the skin of her ankle.

The rustling grew louder. Tamara stiffened. She was ready to turn and dash for home when a large dog burst from the greenery on her left. It bounded to her, panting.

"Well, hello there!" Tamara exclaimed, laughing in relief. This was the fourth evening in a row she'd seen the dog on her walk. It had wiry black-and-tan hair, mostly black, and seemed to wear a perpetual smile. She called it "Happy Face." Showing no fear of humans, the dog approached her on slender tan legs with white paws, its curled tail wagging. Tamara bent to pet it. She had no idea what breed it was, but she thought it would be beautiful if it were bathed. Instead its hair was matted and slightly oily. It wore no collar, and a fresh scratch ran down the right side of its tan face.

Poor thing, Tamara thought. She'd love to have the dog, but Warren had firmly pronounced they could not take it in. He didn't like animals. The dog was so endearing, but it was getting thinner. She decided to buy dog food tomorrow. At least she could keep the dog well fed even if she couldn't give it a home.

Happy Face walked beside her for a while, glancing up as if for approval. Wild violets grew along the edges of Hyacinth Lane. Tamara stooped and picked a few while the dog waited patiently. A slate-gray catbird emitted its lonely mewing call to the evening. A few ambitious fireflies were already hard at work, blinking gaudily against the darkening sky.

Tamara looked at her watch again. 8:45. She should return home. She could be bathed and ready for bed by the time Warren called. She smiled. When she was ready for bed, Lily would be ready for a night at trendy Panache. Their old friend Natalie St. John was back in town and Lily wanted to show her a good time. She'd invited Tamara along, but Tamara declined, telling her she would be waiting for Warren's call. "You're hopeless," Lily had teased. "I might get married some day but I'll never be as settled as you. Hovering around the phone at ten for a *husband*?" Apparently Lily thought hovering only justified in cases of handsome, unpredictable boyfriends.

The dog looked up at her expectantly. She'd forgotten their game. "Okay, Happy Face." Tamara bent and picked up a stick. The dog shifted from paw to paw in anticipation. Tamara threw the stick far into the trees. The dog shot after it. Usually it returned in less than a minute with the stick, which it dropped at her feet. This time Tamara heard it barking. The barking grew fainter. Obviously it had spotted a rabbit and was giving chase. At least she hoped it was a rabbit. She didn't want to be greeted by a dog reeking of skunk.

She stood on the road for a few minutes. Up ahead reared the remains of Saunders House built back in the early nineteenth century when Port Ariel was called Winthrop. When the senior

Saunderses died, their beautiful daughter Ariel became the lover of Captain Zebediah Winthrop, whose father had founded the town. Ariel was labeled a "scarlet woman" after she gave birth to Zebediah's son Thaddeus out of wedlock. In his youth Zebediah had been forced to marry a homely crab of a woman inaptly named Mercy. While Zebediah sailed Lake Erie, Mercy and her pious friends delighted in wreaking petty vengeances on Ariel and the baby, terrorizing the young mother. Then, when Thaddeus was barely one year old, Captain Winthrop's ship, the *Mercy*, caught fire and foundered on the shore near Ariel's house. Ariel had spotted the wreck from her widow's walk and rushed to the rescue, single-handedly saving two injured sailors and her beloved Zeb from drowning.

Mercy died shortly afterward, mostly from bitterness and jealousy and pure meanness, people claimed. She was barely in the ground when Zebediah married Ariel. Most citizens had forgiven her in light of her bravery and did not object when Zebediah changed the name of the town in her honor. Together they had two more children. Zeb died long before Ariel and she had a large monument built to him in the town square. Although she lived to be eighty, she never remarried.

As children Tamara and Lily were entranced by the story of Ariel who had lived alone on the windy shore of Lake Erie, tormented yet strong and loving. They thought she was beautiful, wonderful, courageous, and all that a woman should be. Unbeknownst to their parents, they used to dress up and play for hours in the Saunders house, taking turns at pretending to be Ariel. Sometimes Natalie St. John played with them. Tamara had seen pictures of Ariel and thought that with her long black hair and dark eyes, Natalie made the best Ariel, but she never told Lily. Natalie was the only one of their friends with whom they shared the secret of the game. Natalie could always be trusted with a secret.

For just a moment Tamara had an impulse to forge ahead and take a look at the decrepit house. Then she glanced up. Dark clouds billowed. The summer storm was blowing in faster than she'd expected. She had no time for exploring now. She'd left several of her windows up and her new car in the driveway beneath a tree instead of in the garage.

Tamara turned and took several hurried steps down Hyacinth Lane. Tree limbs swayed and creaked. A silvery shaft of lightning ripped the gray sky. Tamara's ponytail blew wildly in the wind and a piece of dirt flew into her right eye. She stopped, rubbing at it gently. Damn. It had lodged under a contact lens.

A tear ran down her cheek. Lord, it hurt. She shut her eye and took a few more hurried steps. A scrabbling sound pulled her up short. She jerked her head to the right. What on earth was *that*? It sounded as if it were *rushing* at her.

"Happy Face?" she called. "Happy, is that you?"

The rushing sound stopped. Now there was silence, but a sinister silence. Something was *watching* her. She could feel the gaze running up and down her body. Her hands turned icy. She took a deep breath. Don't be silly, Tamara, she told herself sternly. What would be watching you? A chipmunk? A squirrel? Still, a dark wing of fear fluttered inside her. "Happy Face?" she called again, hopefully, uncertainly.

But it wasn't the dog. Suddenly footsteps pounded through the underbrush, snapping vines, then smacking against the bare dirt. Tamara whirled blindly, not sure in which direction to run. It didn't matter. In a flash an arm shot out from a slick, dark mass. Some kind of plastic coat. Tamara yelped in fear as the arm clenched around her neck and yanked backward. She dropped the violets she'd picked earlier. Her heels dragged the ground. She clawed uselessly at the sinewy arm locked directly under her chin. Her neck felt as if it were going to snap. Her eyes bulged in fear and shock as she gasped for air. "Wha—"

A long steel razor with a bone handle flicked open. In one cold, frozen moment Tamara saw the blade glint in a flash of lightning before it slashed viciously across her throat and around her neck, cutting the vocal cords, severing the carotid artery. Blood spurted straight out, then cascaded down, drenching the sleeve of her white sweater.

"Their throat is an open tomb," a voice whispered caressingly in her ear as Tamara's slender body jerked grotesquely in its death throes.

The arm released Tamara. She fell in a heap, still twitching, her eyes wide, her blood soaking the dirt. The figure kneeled beside her and tucked a note into the fold of her sweater. Then it stood, bowed in a grotesque imitation of servitude, and wafted silently back into the dark, swaying forest.

Rain had begun to fall when the dog returned five minutes later. It loped toward Tamara, then abruptly stopped, dropping the stick. It whimpered unhappily. Finally it warily approached the body of the woman who earlier had greeted it so joyously. When it smelled blood, the hair on its back stood up and it crouched, half-crawling to Tamara. It stared at her with warm amber eyes, the smiling look gone from its face. Gently, almost reverently, it lay down and stretched its sleek neck across the gaping slash in hers, protecting her from further harm. As rain poured, the dog howled mournfully into the lonely night.

2

1

SUNDAY MORNING

Natalie slowly opened her eyes. Morning sun filtered dimly through delicate willow-patterned curtains. A beautiful green coverlet lay over her drowsy body. She drew a deep, lazy breath, then shot up in bed, her dark gaze frantically searching for the clock. Nine! She was due at Anicare an hour ago. She was on the Sunday morning shift. What had happened to the alarm?

Reality rushed back. She closed her eyes in relief and leaned back against the pillows. She wasn't at Anicare because she was officially on vacation—on vacation from her job, on vacation from Kenny Davis. She was back in Port Ariel in her old room and unless her nose deceived her, she smelled bacon and eggs frying.

Natalie stretched, yawned, considered going back to sleep for a few minutes, then thought of the breakfast being prepared for her. Under normal circumstances breakfast consisted of a bagel or an English muffin eaten on the run.

She was swinging her legs out of bed when her father yelled, "Natalie, breakfast! Hurry up before I eat it all!"

She smiled wryly. He'd been saying the same thing since her mother left twenty-three years ago when Natalie was six. He'd always seemed to think cooking breakfast for her could make up for any emotional trauma—a runaway mother, a faithless lover.

"Be right there, Dad," she called, looking around the room for her robe. It lay on the white bedroom chair, a beautiful splash of pale green-and-pink silk. She wished desperately she had brought another robe. She'd grabbed this one because it fit neatly into the suitcase, but just looking at it caused her pain. She'd been so touched when she'd opened the package last Christmas morning and found the exquisite kimono-style robe she'd admired in a store a month before. She didn't think Kenny had been paying attention.

Tears pressed behind her eyes. "Stop it," she told herself firmly. "You're not going to sit around weeping and wailing all day."

She shrugged hurriedly into the robe and brushed her long, black hair back into a ponytail that hung halfway to her waist. A close inspection in the mirror showed that her large dark brown eyes—the eyes with the slight almond slant she'd inherited from her Eurasian mother—showed tiny red lines. She reached for the Visine. Just four margaritas last night at Panache with Lily Peyton and now she had bloodshot eyes. Four *was* over her limit. After her second, though, it had seemed so good to see Lily again she didn't want the evening to end. After the third, she'd reached the maudlin stage and began describing in what she now realized was excruciating detail the demise of her relationship with Kenny Davis and how she'd come back to Port Ariel "just for a couple of weeks" to get her bearings. Natalie shook her head. What a thrilling night for Lily, but she'd understand.

"Everything is going to be ice-cold if you don't get out here," Natalie's father threatened.

"*Coming!*" Natalie rushed from her bedroom into the roomy country kitchen filled with morning light. Sunshine bounced off the copper bottoms of cookware hanging above an island range, and plants cascaded from pots sitting around the many windows. Exercising his amateur interest in architecture, Andrew St. John had designed the house for his bride Kira and had it constructed on a beautiful piece of land running down to Lake Erie. Natalie had always loved it. She thought it reflected her father's personality—big, strong, open. The place was built of solid stone to stand up to the heavy northern winds, and glass expanses showed off the spectacular lake view. When she'd first left home and begun living in apartments, she'd felt as if she couldn't get her breath.

"Sorry, Dad," she said, taking her seat and picking up a glass of fresh-squeezed orange juice. "I'm not used to being served breakfast."

"That boyfriend of yours not willing to cook a simple meal now and then?" Andrew asked, scooping up scrambled eggs.

Natalie set down her glass, groaning silently. Her father had never liked Kenny Davis with his golden blond hair, movie star features, and easy charm. "He's too slick," Andrew declared after one brief encounter. "I don't trust him." She'd dismissed her father's assessment. What was it based on? she asked herself then. Nothing but the fact that Kenny was handsome. Now it appeared that Andrew had been right—Kenny wasn't trustworthy. She wasn't ready to capitulate to Andrew's judgment, however. As angry as she was with Kenny, Natalie still felt compelled to defend him. "Kenny is very busy, Dad. He is a brilliant veterinarian," she said as Andrew set a plate heaped with food in front of her.

"Yes, a *vet*, not an M.D."

"Dad, *I'm* a vet."

"Who should have been an M.D."

Natalie sighed. This was an old argument. Old and impossible for her to win. Years ago Andrew had decided his daughter would become a surgeon like him. She'd balked. She had wanted to be a veterinarian since she was twelve, and she'd done exactly as she pleased. Andrew had not been happy about her career choice. He hadn't been happy about the most important romantic involvement of her life, either.

"Dad, I love animals and I love being a vet," she said patiently. "And as for Kenny, he didn't cook breakfast for me and I didn't cook breakfast for him. Anicare is the biggest animal clinic in Columbus. We were both on the run." She was determined not to belittle Kenny in front of her father even if he was the reason she'd dragged her hurt and embarrassed self back to Port Ariel.

Her mind drifted to three days ago when she'd come home

early. Walking in on Kenny passionately having sex in their bed had destroyed an already eroding relationship. She'd suspected infidelities, but suspecting and actually seeing were different. She'd never felt such shock as she had when confronted by the sight of Kenny in flagrante delicto. She'd stood frozen in the doorway until the sweating pair finally noticed her.

"Natalie!" Kenny had exclaimed, his blue eyes flying wide beneath his tousled hair. "This isn't—"

"What it seems?" she asked, amazed by her calm voice when her entire body seemed to be quivering. "What *is* it?"

"Natalie, shut the door. Go downstairs and—"

"And let you continue?" She'd glared at the flushed young redhead wearing diamond stud earrings and nothing else. "I've seen you at the clinic. You have that white poodle Snickers. What a ridiculous name! He has a horrible disposition." Natalie couldn't stop babbling as the reality of the situation fought for acceptance in her mind. "No wonder he's always irritable. You drag him in constantly and there's nothing wrong with him. Now I know the reason for your frequent visits."

"Natalie, please don't turn this into some ridiculous farce," Kenny said in a controlled voice as the woman fumbled frantically for the sheet to cover herself. "We'll talk later."

"I think not," Natalie had replied coldly. "I don't think we will ever talk again."

With that she had descended the stairs of the townhouse, crossed the small foyer, and walked outside. As soon as she closed the door behind her and heard the lock click, she remembered her purse. Her purse on the hall table holding her wallet and keys. The keys to *Kenny's* condo as well as her car keys. She was not only stranded without money and transportation, she was also denied access to the place she'd called home for the past eight months.

Oh, dear God, she'd thought in despair. Could this get any worse? Humiliated, she had rung the doorbell repeatedly until a blazing-eyed Kenny swung open the door wearing only an old pair of jeans. "Why are you doing this?" he'd demanded.

"My purse." Natalie wanted to cry. Her throat was tight and the words grated. She blinked frantically. "Just give me my purse with my keys so I can leave. I'll be back this evening to pack."

"Nat—"

"My *purse!*"

He'd turned away from the door as tears spilled from her eyes. He retrieved the purse, handed it to her, and watched her stalk to her car.

She'd gone to a good restaurant not crowded at such an early hour, and cried in the restroom for a good twenty minutes. Then she'd applied a lot of powder around her red nose and swollen eyes and sat in the darkened bar for the next three hours. She felt like getting drunk, but the objective part of her knew oblivion wasn't the answer. Instead she'd slowly sipped two small glasses of Chablis and wished she had a friend to talk to. For the first time she realized she had no really good friends in Columbus. Kenny had monopolized her time. No, she'd let him monopolize her time. She hadn't made close friends here because they might interfere with her time with Kenny. Her friends were back home in Port Ariel. Her very best friend from childhood, Lily Peyton, was there. Suddenly the place Natalie grudgingly visited only twice a year was where she wanted to be more than anywhere in the world.

When she'd returned that evening, Kenny looked miserable. "Now you can explain," she said.

"I can't. I mean I don't have a good explanation. I guess I just panicked. We've been in this semi-marriage situation for months and I got scared. Commitment. The old phobia."

"Did you hear that on a morning talk show?" she'd asked scornfully.

"No. It's the truth, Nat."

"How many times, Kenny? How many times in the last eight months have you gotten scared and done something like this?"

"Never."

He was lying. She'd stared at him for a moment and walked upstairs. He followed, watching her desolately as she began taking her clothes out of the closet. "Stay with me, sweetheart," he said softly. "We love each other. We'll get engaged."

She had glared at him. "You've just told me you're afraid of commitment, you spent the afternoon in bed with another woman, and now you're asking me to marry you?"

"Yes. I'm serious."

"I don't want to hear it," she'd snapped, throwing another blouse into the already overstuffed suitcase. "My father was right about you. I should have listened to him."

"You did," Kenny finally shot back furiously. "Your whole life is about defying him. I always thought half of your attraction to me was the fact that he couldn't stand me."

Now, sitting across the breakfast table from her father, Natalie wondered if Kenny was right. She gazed at Andrew with his husky build, his thick white hair, his piercing dark eyes. He'd lived in Port Ariel all his life and been an admired surgeon here for thirty years. The townspeople's respect and affection for him only increased after his flighty wife Kira ran off to join a California commune in the late seventies and left him with a young daughter to raise. He'd devoted himself to Natalie. She loved him. He loved her and clung too desperately, fearing he'd lose her just like he'd lost Kira. He was strict, unrelenting, smothering. He'd wanted her to be perfect. And docile. Natalie was anything except docile and his attempts to turn her into a sweet, spun-sugar concoction of a little girl only made matters worse. They'd argued incessantly since she was six. She'd never been able to please him. She'd never stopped trying.

"Are you thinking about Kenny?" Andrew asked abruptly.

"No," Natalie answered truthfully.

"You won't tell me why you're really here, but I suspect you two had a real blow-up."

No, she hadn't told him the truth behind her visit. It was too humiliating. Besides, she wasn't sure she would not be able to forgive Kenny and return to him. She didn't want to give Andrew any more ammunition to dislike him if that were the case. Besides, she didn't think she could discuss something so personal as Kenny's infidelity with her father.

"Dad, I just wanted to spend some time back home."

"Then why hasn't Kenny called?"

"He did. Yesterday when you were out," she said, feeling no necessity to tell him she'd slammed the phone down on him. This was none of Andrew's business and she shot him a look that told him so.

He relented. "Eggs okay?"

"Great." Except I don't want them, Natalie thought. I'd rather have a bagel. I'm not used to all this heavy food in the morning.

Andrew was having no trouble with his. He ate like a lumberjack and never put on a pound. All the outside work he did, Natalie thought. He always had some project going. If he wasn't improving his property, he was helping someone else.

"Try that bacon. Thick-sliced. Really good," he said.

"I don't eat meat."

"A little meat isn't going to kill you."

"I don't *want* to eat meat so please get off my back. After all, you don't drink."

"Alcohol is bad for you. Meat isn't." He looked up. "And speaking of alcohol and those bloodshot eyes of yours, did you have a wild time with Lily Peyton last night?"

Here we go, Natalie thought. Still the judgmental father chastising the forever-child. "We had *fun*, not a *wild time*. We went to Panache. I had alcohol and lived to tell."

"Humph." The famous, disapproving *humph*. "How is Lily?" Andrew asked. "Still got that store downtown?"

"It's called Curious Things and doing very well. So is Lily."

"A hellraiser. Her father let her get away with anything and her mother was too meek to object. I always wished you'd been closer to Tamara."

Natalie put down her fork. "Lily is not and never was a hellraiser. She just likes to have fun. Tamara is more sedate."

"You mean boring."

"I mean *sedate*." Her father didn't look at her. He simply made pronouncements like God on high and never saw the need to justify his remarks. Natalie felt her back stiffening with the old tension, then forced herself to relax. I will *not* be baited into an argument that upsets me a hell of a lot more than it does him, she vowed silently. Taking a deep breath she said, "Lily and I are going to lunch today. Want to go with us?"

Andrew looked up, his eyes widening as if she'd just invited him to a slumber party. "Lunch! What in the world would I have to talk with you two about?"

"Oh, I don't know," Natalie said airily. "Boys. Makeup. Curfews. Our paltry allowances. The usual things twenty-nine-year-old career women discuss."

Her father stared at her for a moment before a grin cracked the stone of his face. "Okay. I keep forgetting you're not thirteen."

"I noticed. And thank goodness I'm not. My teen years were miserable."

Andrew shoveled in more scrambled eggs. "Don't be silly. You were the smartest girl in your class, the most popular, and the prettiest."

Natalie burst into laughter, almost choking on her orange juice. "Dad, being the smartest girl in your class isn't a plus when you're a teenager." She dabbed at her mouth with a napkin. "I was popular with girls but *not* with boys, and as for being pretty, I was skinny and I had braces. You wouldn't let me have contacts and forced me to wear those glasses with the horrid blue frames. I was a geek."

Andrew shook his head. "Never believed in contacts. And you've always exaggerated. You were lovely. You looked just like your mother when she was your age."

Her mother, who had never even allowed her daughter to call her "Mom." She was always "Kira." And she had left both of them. One day she was there, the next she was gone, off to join a commune. They hadn't heard from her for over six months after she left. "Don't *ever* compare me to that woman," Natalie said with quiet venom.

Andrew's white eyebrows slammed together. "That *woman* is your mother," he said fiercely.

"Being a mother involves a hell of a lot more than giving birth, so don't tell *me* about how much respect I owe Kira St. John, no matter where she's living with and with what man—"

"Do *not* say *anything* else!" her father erupted. He took a couple of deep breaths and looked out the huge kitchen window at beautiful Lake Erie beyond. Last night's storm had left the surface littered with leaves and twigs, but the smooth water reflected the sun and puffy clouds. Harvey Coombs from next door already sat in his rowboat, fishing diligently, stained canvas hat jammed on his bald head. He'd once been a brilliant chemistry teacher. Then alcoholism had taken control of his life.

"Kira has always been the flashpoint between the two of us," Andrew said finally.

"Which would please her because it means she's the center of attention. But, Dad, I really don't want to talk about Kira. I want you to understand about Lily. No one else had a mother who ran off to join a commune. The other kids teased me mercilessly about my crazy mother. Lily defended me like a pit bull. She's always been my best friend and she always will be."

"She encouraged you to sneak out your bedroom window at night and roam around with her."

"All we did was go to The Blue Lady and work on our music."

"The Blue Lady Resort!" Andrew looked appalled. "I had no idea that's where you went. The hotel burned down!"

"Not the dance pavilion. We thought it was romantic. And the acoustics were great."

"Acoustics? Who cares about acoustics? It suffered damage from the fire. It's not safe. It should have been condemned years ago."

"It's still romantic."

"A long time ago it was romantic. The hotel was lavish. The pavilion was beautiful, built out over the water. Some of the biggest bands in the country played there. Quite the tourist draw. Then there was that awful business in 1970."

"In the hotel, not the pavilion. The hotel is gone."

"I don't care. The pavilion is a wreck. A danger. It should be destroyed."

"It should be *restored*. You're handy with a hammer and nails. Maybe you should do it. It would give you something to fill up your empty life."

Andrew scowled. "I don't have an empty life."

"I know you have your medical practice and your gardening and fishing and those civic clubs you belong to, but I'm talking about a *real* life."

"Define real life."

"Companionship."

"I see Harvey Coombs next door regularly."

"A wonderful companion. When he drinks too much he thinks you were CIA operatives together."

"And many dangerous missions we worked if you'd only give him a chance to tell you about them."

"Harvey should have written novels, not taught chemistry. I'm serious, Dad. You should see someone romantically."

"I did. Viveca Cosgrove."

Natalie rolled her eyes. "Three years ago and not for long, thank goodness. Oh, I know she's beautiful but she's *such* a snob and she can't seem to stay with a man. She broke things off with you so she could date Eugene Farley who was too young for her."

"And I thought I was the judgmental one," Andrew said dryly.

Natalie ignored him. "He was completely out of his depth with someone like Viveca and look what she did to him."

"You didn't even know Eugene Farley," Andrew said quietly. "And his death was not Viveca's fault."

"Not directly, but she was the root of the problem. Thank heavens she's ancient history," Natalie said briskly. "What worries me is that you haven't dated anyone since her."

"Who says?"

"Come on, Dad."

He drained his coffee mug and pushed his chair back from the table. "I happen to be seeing someone now."

Natalie's eyes widened. "What? *Who?*"

"I'm not telling you. You'll be driving past her house, asking your friends all kinds of personal questions about her, maybe even dropping by her place to offer free veterinary service to her cat just to get in the front door."

"I wouldn't dream of prying into your life any more than you'd pry into *mine*," Natalie said slyly.

Andrew rose, gathered his dishes, and carried them to the sink. "You have many wonderful qualities, Natalie, but subtlety isn't one of them. You'll find out about her when I'm ready for you to. That is if you stay long enough."

"Oh, Dad, that isn't fair!" Natalie exclaimed. "A bribe to get me to stay?"

"I like to look at it as an incentive."

"You think you're pretty smart, don't you?" Natalie asked. "Well, don't be too pleased with yourself. You've already given away something about her."

"And what would that be, Detective?"

"She has a cat."

Andrew smiled. "Good luck tracing her in a city of twenty thousand people with *that* piece of vital information." He turned on the faucet, drenched his dishes in water, and looked up at her. "I have work to do. Enjoy yourself today and Natalie, for once, *try* to stay out of trouble."

II

Lily was picking her up at twelve-thirty for lunch. Dinner and clubbing last night, lunch today. I'm turning into a regular party girl, Natalie thought. Well, what better way to get over a broken heart? Except that this round of socializing couldn't go on forever. She needed to make a decision about Kenny.

Natalie shook her head. She'd promised herself a week of relaxation with old friends. *Next* week she'd try to figure out the rest of her life. Right now all she needed to figure out was whether to wear a chain of silver or gold with her pale blue blouse. Silver. She tossed her long hair to one side and fastened the chain. First major decision of the day. "Natalie, you're making fantastic progress," she told her reflection in the mirror as she applied sienna-colored lipstick.

The doorbell rang. Her father claimed he had errands before rounds at the hospital and had left over two hours ago. Natalie thought he'd taken flight because he feared she and Lily might drag him to lunch. No matter. It was better to have Lily to herself. She might be able to find out something about Andrew's mysterious new girlfriend.

When she opened the door, Natalie marveled as always at Lily's youthful appearance. Her long blond hair hung thick and straight to her shoulders with a fringe of bangs across her forehead. She wore tan linen slacks and a matching jacket over a green silk shell. Her large hazel eyes sparkled. She'd pushed her designer sunglasses atop her head and she flashed an impish grin. "How much trouble did you get into for not coming home until one A.M? *Drunk*."

"Dad pretended to be asleep, but I know he wasn't. Still, he didn't rise to deliver a lecture. He doesn't want to drive me away in just three days, so he's going easy."

"That won't last long. Your father is a good man, Natalie, but he never did cut you much slack. Hey, are you *starving*?"

"No," Natalie said as she stepped out on the porch and pulled the door shut behind her. "Dad fixed me a huge breakfast."

"He *is* working hard to keep you here. I live alone so I had a stale doughnut and a cup of lukewarm coffee. I could eat one of the hamburger deluxe platters at The Hearth. And a big piece of cheesecake with raspberry sauce."

"I will never understand how you and Tamara eat so much and stay so thin. What are you? One-ten soaking wet?" Natalie asked, climbing into Lily's red Corvette. Ever since Lily was twelve, she'd wanted a red Corvette.

"One hundred and fifteen," Lily said. "My sister, however, has dropped at least five pounds. Maybe more."

Natalie picked up the serious note in her voice. "Are you worried about her?"

"A little. She is *so* obsessed with pleasing Warren and she thinks he's unhappy because she hasn't gotten pregnant."

"Does he really want a child?"

Lily shrugged. "I don't know. I've never seen him display any fondness for children, but something's wrong with him. He's irritable and nervous." They roared out of the driveway and shot away from the house. Lily drove like a professional race car driver. "Warren Hunt wasn't my choice for my sister. He's too controlling."

"Tamara isn't as independent as you. I think she likes his domination."

"Maybe, but he's not my cup of tea."

"Which is good because he's married to your sister."

Lily threw back her head and laughed. She had a deep, hearty laugh that always made Natalie smile. Lily slid a CD into the player. In a moment the speeding car filled with the sounds of Nine Inch Nails.

"Ah, still a lover of the classics," Natalie said. "I made the mistake of mentioning to Dad this morning that we used to go to The Blue Lady to practice our music at night."

"That was so much fun. We were going to call our band 'Fetish.' " Lily giggled. "We thought the name was so shocking! Poor Tam fretted over it for days. She was afraid Mom would have a fit. Like we would have *ever* made it in the rock world. You were the only one with any talent. When you left Kenny's in a whirlwind, did you remember to bring your guitars?"

"One. Toting it around is second nature to me."

"I'm glad you never stopped playing music like Tam and I did. Speaking of Tam, I've got a great idea. Warren is in Cleveland at some conference. He won't be back until tonight. Why don't we go by and pick her up for lunch? She'd love to see you, and you're not going to die from hunger before we get to the restaurant. I know she's lonely."

"I'd love to have lunch with her. It'll be like old times."

"I'll give her a quick call on the cell phone. She hates being taken by surprise. You know how structured she is."

Lily turned down the music and called. She waited a few moments, then frowned. "No answer."

"So much for lunch. I'll have to see her another time. I won't be leaving for over a week."

Lily slowly put down the phone. "Maybe we should go by her place, anyway."

"But you said she hates surprises."

"She does, but something isn't right. Even though she'd already turned me down about going to Panache last night, I called right before we left. I thought it was worth one more shot. No answer."

"Maybe she went to a movie."

Lily shook her head. "When the great Doctor Warren is away, he always calls at ten o'clock. I called around ten-fifteen from Panache. Still no answer. I know I sound like a mother hen, but I need to see about her."

"You have one of your bad feelings, don't you?" Natalie asked. "One of your twin feelings."

Lily looked slightly embarrassed. "Well, I *am* worried, about these unanswered phone calls, but yes, I do have one of my feelings. You probably think I'm crazy, but . . ."

"I do *not* think you're crazy," Natalie said as Lily turned right, heading away from the business district and toward the lake. "Even if I hadn't read so many articles about this mysterious communication twins have, I've seen it in action with you and Tamara."

"We're not as phenomenal as some of the people you see on television, but there have been a couple of spooky times."

"Like when we were twelve and no one could find you. Tamara insisted you were at Ariel Saunders's house. You were—with a broken leg. Everyone assumed Tamara had guessed where you were because we went there sometimes, but she told me she actually *saw* you in one quick flash lying at the foot of the staircase with your leg twisted under you. She made me promise not to tell anyone about her vision."

"She felt odd about it. She was afraid people would think she was strange. I had a couple of visions about her, too." Natalie noticed that they were going faster—too fast for these roads, but she didn't ask Lily to slow down. Clearly she was worried about her sister. "I'm not having any visions now—not of Tam, at least. But last night I kept dreaming of a dog howling in the rain. It probably had nothing to do with Tam, but every time I woke up from the dream, I'd go back to sleep and dream it again. Anyway, I *do* have an uneasy feeling. It's probably based on absolutely nothing except that I can't reach her on the phone." She turned a slightly tight smile on Natalie. "Thanks for indulging me, though."

"No problem. If she's home, we might stand a better chance of dragging her out if we approach her in person, right?"

"Right," Lily agreed, her smile broadening.

Natalie looked out the car window. The storm seemed to have blown the atmosphere clean. The sky was cerulean blue with a few clouds hanging like puffs of cotton candy. A light breeze ruffled tree leaves that still bore the fresh green of spring. Cooler temperatures around the lake always resulted in later blooming than in the middle of Ohio where Natalie lived. Although it was June, a few stubborn forsythia bushes held yellow blooms to the sun. On a glorious day like this, she could almost forget her hurt over Kenny Davis. Almost.

"That's Tam's and Warren's new house," Lily said, pointing ahead to a large Cape Cod painted pale yellow with slate-blue shutters.

"I didn't realize it was out of the city limits. It's so near Ariel Saunders's house."

"That place is falling to ruin. It's a shame."

"Why hasn't the County Historical Society done something?"

"Don't you remember that Viveca Cosgrove is Ariel and Zebediah's only surviving descendant? She owns the house. She *should* donate it to the Historical Society but she wants to *sell* it to them for an outrageous price."

"That sounds like Viveca."

"Exactly. She's still holding onto that piece of property The Blue Lady is on, too, although Dad tells me she's thinking of selling it to someone who wants to rebuild the hotel."

"I'd love to see the hotel rebuilt!" Natalie paused. "So she's still dating your dad?"

"For a year. I think that's a record for her. Tam and I are *not* happy about it, but Dad is just over the moon about her."

"Viveca strikes again. I'm glad my father didn't fall for her. At least I don't think he did. How's her daughter Alison?"

"Crazy as a loon, but I'm not supposed to say so." Lily pulled a face. "She's a patient of Warren's. She used to see some psychiatrist in Toledo, but for some reason she switched, even though Warren is a psychologist and can't prescribe drugs, which I think she needs." Lily slowed down and pulled into the driveway of the Cape Cod. Ahead of them sat a new blue Ford Contour. "That's Tamara's car, but look at it. It's covered with twigs and leaves. They must be from the storm last night. Tam wouldn't leave a car, especially a new one, sitting beneath a tree in a storm. She'd put it in the garage."

"Maybe the garage door is broken," Natalie suggested. "That happened at Kenny's condo one time. A cable broke and he couldn't get the door up."

"I don't know," Lily said doubtfully. "If that were the case, she would at least have moved it from beneath the tree where a limb could have fallen on it." She got out of the Corvette and headed for the front porch. "Here's the morning newspaper. Tam *always* reads the paper while she drinks her morning coffee."

Natalie followed Lily across the lawn. Although the sun shone brightly and the temperature was in the mid-seventies, the ground still felt slightly spongy. The rain had lasted for hours last night.

"And look at this living room window!" Lily called, alarm edging her voice. "It's raised about three inches. The sheer curtains are water-stained. Tam would never leave a window up during a storm."

"It's just one window." Natalie tried to sound calm although her own nerves tingled. "It's easy to forget a window."

Lily had backed off the porch and stood on the lawn looking upward. "There's another open window upstairs. It's her *bedroom* window. Don't tell me she forgot that one!"

There was nothing else comforting Natalie could say. Clearly something was wrong. "Okay, what do we do first? Call the police?"

"The police?" Lily shook her head. "No. Sheriff Purdue would have listened to me, but we've got a new guy from New York City."

"New York City? Here?"

"Yeah. His name is Meredith and he left New York because of some tragedy involving his wife. Anyway, he goes by the book. He'll say Tam hasn't been gone long enough to be declared missing or some damned excuse for not doing anything." She ran her hands through her hair. "Tam usually takes a walk after dinner. Maybe she fell."

Natalie glanced up and down the street with its scattering of large, new houses. "Which direction did she walk?"

"Not the street. Tam walked Hyacinth Lane that leads to Ariel Saunders's house." She walked out onto the lawn and pointed. "Maybe Tam walked all the way to the house. Maybe now *she's* lying hurt in that house and I didn't sense it because I'm so wrapped up in myself and—"

"Lily!" Natalie shouted, hurrying to catch up with her. "Let's just keep calm until we search the lane and the house."

"And if she's not around?"

"We'll call Warren."

"I don't know where he's staying."

"There can't be that many psychology conventions going on in Cleveland right now. We'll find him."

"And if he didn't talk to Tamara last night?"

"Then we'll have to call your jerk of a sheriff. But let's not go off the deep end. Getting hysterical won't help us find Tamara."

Lily drew a deep breath. "You're right. You were always the

voice of reason. It's just that Tam has seemed so unhappy lately, so vulnerable. If only I'd paid more attention to her—" She broke off. "What is that noise?"

Natalie had been vaguely aware of the noise for a few moments. Leaves brushing together. Twigs snapping. They both stood still. Everything went quiet. Even the birds stopped chirping. A line from a Keats poem floated through Natalie's head: "And no birds sang."

"Something's in the brush," Lily hissed.

"I know." Natalie kneeled. "Come here. Come to me. It's all right."

"What are you doing?"

"Lily, be quiet for a minute." Natalie peered into the dense undergrowth. "Come." She held out her hand, palm down. "I won't hurt you," she said in a gentle voice. The words weren't important but the tone was. "It's all right . . ."

More rustling. Then she saw the head. Long snout, mostly tan. Small ears, brown. Black body. "Come." The dog came to Natalie at a crouch, as if it expected to be struck. When it finally reached her hand, it sniffed twice and whimpered.

"The dog in my dream," Lily murmured.

"I thought in your dream you only heard howling."

"I did, too, until I saw this dog." Lily's voice rose. "Nat, it was *this* dog howling in the rain. What kind is it?"

"Mixed breed." Natalie stroked the head, then rubbed the ears. The dog rose a bit, losing some of its fear. "I'd say part Airedale." She bent her head. "Female. She's never given birth." The dog now stood at full height. "No collar. Long scratch on the face probably from a locust tree branch."

"It must be a stray," Lily said.

Natalie massaged the dog's neck, noting that its already wiry hair was even stiffer there. Oh, please don't let it have rolled in some foul-smelling dead thing, Natalie prayed. She brought her hands away. They looked reddish, rusty. She sniffed them, then looked at the dog. It whined. Her heart beating faster, Natalie placed gentle hands on either side of the dog's head and tilted it. She wasn't surprised at what she found.

"What is it?" Lily asked. "Your face is pale."

Natalie swallowed. "Lily, this dog has dried blood all over its neck but there's no sign of injury."

"Which means?"

Natalie didn't want to explain how a dog or wolf might try to protect another's neck. She stood up. "Lily, maybe the dog knows where Tamara is. Maybe it's seen her."

"How do we know that?"

"We don't, but let's walk and see what happens." Natalie turned to the dog. "Come." She tapped her thigh. "Come!"

The dog hesitated for a moment, then came forward. She understood basic commands. Natalie noted the protruding ribs and the paws with broken nails and small lacerations. This dog hadn't had an easy time of it lately.

"Lily, start walking. Keep your voice calm. The dog is frightened."

Lily blurted, "The *dog* is frightened—"

"Lily," Natalie said sternly, "I think Tamara is hurt and I think this dog has been with her. Now do you want it to run off because you're scaring the hell out of it or do you want it to lead us to Tamara?"

Lily nodded. "All right. I'm sorry. I'm just so nervous about Tam."

"I know. Let's walk." They started down the rutted lane. The dog hovered behind them. Natalie turned and smiled. "Come," she coaxed.

The dog approached Natalie, who patted it on the head. Reassured, the dog bounded ahead. In spite of its neglected condition, it looked strong and graceful.

Lily glanced around. "I don't see any signs of Tam."

"The road is so rutted and the brush has grown up. It didn't look like this when we used to ride our bikes up here."

"I hate to depress you," Lily said, "but we haven't ridden bikes up here for thirteen years."

"Hard to believe it's been so long." The dog broke into a run. It stopped about a hundred feet ahead where an oak limb that had been struck by lightning lay across the road. The limb was covered with honeysuckle. The tiny white and yellow flowers emitted a strong, sweet scent. Hundreds of bees drawn by the scent emitted a loud, threatening buzz.

Abruptly the dog began to bark. Short, sharp bursts of alarm. It ran back and forth in agitation.

Lily and Natalie stopped as oak leaves and honeysuckle rustled. Black wings appeared on the far side of the limb as a turkey vulture rose slowly, looking at them with tiny, conscienceless eyes encircled by red skin. Another followed. The dog looked up at the ugly carrion birds, barking furiously. Hair stood up along its backbone. A corresponding shudder ran through Natalie.

"What is it?" Lily asked in a thin, unnatural voice.

"I don't know yet," Natalie said. "Stay here. I'll go see."

Lily clutched Natalie's arm. "Nat, I feel sick." She had turned parchment-white. "I . . . I think I know what it is."

Natalie prized loose Lily's fingers. "Stay here."

If only Natalie felt as strong as she sounded. The day might be sunny perfection, but this place felt dark and cold. Wrong. Natalie had walked out Hyacinth Lane a hundred times and never experienced this feeling. She seemed to be in a totally unfamiliar, hostile place. An evil place.

She crossed her arms over her chest in an unconscious gesture of defense. Suddenly she became aware of the dog. It had come to meet her. Hair still stood up on its back, and it let out a little whimper of distress. Oh, God, no, Natalie thought. The closer to the honeysuckle mass they drew, the louder the bees sounded. Another vulture rose with frightening speed and size and flapped above her like something from a horror movie.

Natalie slowed and almost stopped. The dog crouched, whining. "Natalie?" Lily called weakly. Natalie didn't answer her. Chills running over her arms, she forced herself onward to the mass of oak leaves and honeysuckle vines. Getting as close as she could, she leaned forward, swiping at bees and a mass of black flies, peering into the brush. Then, amid the shiny green leaves and tiny fragrant flowers, she saw the side of Tamara's face. At least part of it.

The vultures had gotten the rest.

3

1

"Natalie, is it Tam?"

Hot water flooded into Natalie's mouth. As a veterinarian she had seen some gruesome sights, and the fact that she'd been looking at animals instead of humans had not made a difference to her. Until now. Before her lay the ravaged remains of a beautiful young woman. Not just any young woman—one she had known for over twenty years.

"*Natalie,*" Lily repeated, coming forward.

Natalie waved her away. "Stay back!"

The dog cowered and Lily froze. "It's Tam," Lily said in a flat voice. "She's dead."

Natalie closed her eyes. "Yes, Lily. She is."

The dog whined as if in sympathy. Natalie opened her eyes and looked at Lily. Lily and Tamara. Two faces, mirror images. Now one remained lovely while the other had been rendered grotesque.

"Are you sure she's . . .?" Lily asked hollowly. "Maybe she's just unconscious or something."

The eyes were gone and the remaining flesh of the face too white for life. "Lily, Tamara is dead."

Lily came to her and Natalie wrapped her arms around Lily's stiff body. "I'm *so* sorry," she said softly.

"It's all so strange," Lily mumbled. "My dream. The dog. I saw that dog in my dream. It was howling." She took a deep, shuddering breath. "That's Tam's blood on its neck."

"Probably."

"All night she was lying out here in the rain. I was having fun at Panache, then I went home and slept like a log in my nice, dry bed while my sister lay out here with only that dog trying to help her."

"It's not your fault. You couldn't have known."

Lily's voice rose. "If the positions had been reversed, Tam would have known."

"Maybe, maybe not." Natalie held Lily away from her and looked into the hazel eyes that didn't seem to be quite focusing. She started to say they had to go back to the car and call the police. Then the image of the turkey vultures flashed in her mind. She couldn't leave Tamara to a renewed assault, but she couldn't make Lily stand guard over her mutilated sister, either. She didn't want Lily to see Tamara. "Call the police on your car phone," she ordered.

Lily blinked. "You want me to go back to the car by myself?"

"Yes. I need to stay here with Tamara. Please, Lily."

Abruptly Lily turned and headed back down the road. Natalie watched her, hoping she wouldn't faint. Her legs moved quickly and firmly, though. The reality of Tamara's death probably hadn't hit her.

Natalie looked down at the dog. "Did you see what happened? Was Tamara killed by the falling tree limb?" The dog turned its head, listening intently. Natalie braced herself and walked back to Tamara. Only her face was exposed. The tree limb, leaves, and masses of honeysuckle covered the rest of her body.

She looked back at the dog, thinking. It had gotten the blood on its neck from Tamara, but only her face was showing. There was no sign that the dog had trampled over the honeysuckle to reach Tamara. The dog must have been around the body—the bloody body—before the limb had fallen. Tamara was already dead when the limb fell. Could she have been struck by lightning?

The dog came to stand by her, making an occasional noise that sounded like an attempt at speech. Natalie kneeled and took the dog's face in her hands. "You tried to help her, didn't you? You tried to help the pretty lady—"

Natalie's voice broke. Tamara was a pretty lady no more. Dear Tam who was kind and gentle, who had always tried so hard to live up to everyone's expectations. And this is how she'd ended. It was beyond unfair. Natalie felt like screaming her rage, her frustration, her shock. But she had to stay in control for Lily's sake. She could do nothing for Tamara, but she could get Lily through the horror.

Natalie paced back and forth. Shadows fell on her. She glanced up. The vultures circled overhead, waiting for her to leave their feast. She wanted to throw up. She could not look at Tamara. She felt small and cold and helpless and she wished her father were here. He was always a rock in an emergency. She hadn't really thought about that before. She'd only thought about how exasperating his iron control could be, not how comforting it was at the right time. She needed it now.

It seemed as if Lily had been gone for an hour, but when Natalie saw her coming back down Hyacinth Lane, she glanced at her watch and saw it had been only minutes. Lily didn't move as quickly and purposely as she had when she left. Her gait had a slight wandering quality. Please let her hold on for a while longer until Tamara can be taken away from here, Natalie thought.

"Did you get the police?" she called before Lily reached her.

"I got some deputy at first. He seemed to think I was joking. Some joke," Lily said roughly. "Then Sheriff Meredith got on the phone. He didn't ask a lot of stupid questions. He said he'd be here immediately." She stopped in front of Natalie, white to her lips as if every ounce of blood had drained from her usually vibrant face. "And I called Dad."

Oliver Peyton was a descendant of Port Ariel royalty. He'd inherited money, but it hadn't stopped him from pursuing his law practice with a vengeance. He had a reputation for being frighteningly intelligent and a dreaded opponent in the courtroom. Natalie remembered him as slim, dapper, and haughty.

"Is your father on his way?" Natalie asked.

"He was out. The housekeeper, Mrs. Ebert, went to pieces,

but I told her she had to pull it together and locate Dad and Warren. She thinks she knows where Warren is staying in Cleveland." She raised her hands helplessly. "I feel like I should be doing something else for Tam."

"There isn't anything else to do. You've called the right people and you're staying with her."

"I haven't even looked at her."

"You don't need to."

"Is it that bad?" Lily's eyes met hers and Natalie nodded reluctantly. "The vultures?"

"Yes. But she was dead when they came. She didn't feel them."

"We can't be sure of that. We can't be sure of anything." Lily's bleak gaze trailed the length of the thick limb covering her sister. "Tam hated storms. Why would she stay out here until the lightning got close enough to strike the tree?"

Natalie didn't want to bring up her theory that a falling limb didn't kill Tamara, and raise questions she couldn't answer. "You know how fast storms come up around here."

"Not so fast Tam couldn't get back to her house. It's nearly in sight."

"I don't know, Lily. Maybe she went to Ariel Saunders's house, stayed too long, and got caught in the worst of the storm."

"The worst of the storm didn't hit until around ten. She would have been home waiting for Warren's call."

"We were in Panache. We don't know exactly when the storm was at its worst here."

"But—" Lily broke off and her face crumpled. A long, racking sob shook her. Natalie rushed to her, catching her before she fell, and gently lowered her to the ground. Another sob tore at Lily's throat. "Oh, Nat, I can't believe it. My little sister. She was three minutes younger, you know. Three minutes . . ."

"I remember," Natalie said gently, rocking Lily's shuddering body.

"We were more than sisters. We knew what the other was thinking, feeling. We knew when the other was in trouble. At least Tam knew when *I* was in trouble."

"You knew about her, too. You knew something was wrong last night. That's why you kept dreaming about the dog."

"But I didn't see Tam in the dream!"

"You can't tear yourself apart because you're not completely psychic. And Tamara probably died instantly. You couldn't have saved her."

"You don't know that!"

Natalie felt huge relief when she heard sirens. Thank goodness help was coming because she didn't know how much longer she could keep Lily from getting hysterical. A police car was first to arrive. Lily must have given them precise directions because they pulled onto Hyacinth Lane, not Tamara's driveway. An ambulance followed close behind.

"I don't think I can talk to anyone," Lily quavered.

"I'll handle it." Natalie watched a tall, slim man with black hair emerge from the police car. She stood up as he approached.

"Miss Peyton?" he asked in a deep voice.

"No, Natalie St. John. This is Lily Peyton." She motioned to Lily sitting limply on the grass. "She's not feeling well. I found Tamara."

His deep blue eyes flashed to Lily, then back to Natalie. "How long ago did you discover Mrs. Hunt?"

"Around twenty minutes."

"Did you touch anything?"

"No. She turned and looked at the tree limb. The dog sat beside it as if on guard. "She's partially under there."

"Is that your dog?"

"No, it's a stray. I think it found Tamara last night . . ." She trailed off, not wanting to explain about the blood on the dog's neck. "We're trying to locate Mrs. Hunt's husband."

"All right." He looked at Lily and said in a gentler voice, "I'll have to ask you a few questions later, Miss Peyton." Lily nodded. He turned to Natalie. "Will the dog bite?"

"I don't think so, but I'll call it, anyway." She whistled. The dog responded hesitantly as the sheriff, a deputy, and emergency technicians headed for the body. Natalie sank down on the grass beside Lily. Another police car arrived. More deputies spilled from it. She stroked the dog's head as they watched the police peer through the leaves and the honeysuckle. Someone began taking photos from all angles. Natalie pictured exactly what they were seeing. Thank goodness Lily couldn't.

"I wish Dad were here," Lily said dully. "He always knows what to do. I'm no help at all."

"Even your father couldn't help, Lily. It's all up to the police now."

"But this isn't really a police matter. It was an accident. I don't understand why they're taking all those pictures."

Because they aren't sure what happened, either, Natalie thought uneasily. "The police come even if it's an accident. Besides, they have to retrieve Tamara's body."

"What's goin' on?"

A strikingly good-looking boy of about twelve stood in front of them, balancing his bike beside him. Natalie hadn't noticed his arrival.

"There's been an accident," she said. "You really shouldn't be here."

"Is someone dead?" the boy asked, his dark eyes snapping with excitement.

"Yes. Now please—"

"Jimmy!" A woman strode down the lane. Jeans covered her ample thighs and her denim shirt hung free. "I told you to stay away from here."

"Mom, someone's dead!" the boy called.

"Dead! Oh my!" She halted. She had a tired prettiness with dark eyes like the boy's, only hers were surrounded by faint shadows of fatigue. She looked at Lily. "Tam—no, Lily?"

"Yes, Beth." Lily turned to Natalie. "This is Beth Jenkins, Tam's neighbor."

"What's wrong?" Beth asked, coming toward them. "Jimmy said someone's dead."

"It's Tam," Lily said shakily. "She's under that limb."

"Mrs. Hunt?" The boy's face blanched, the excitement fading from his eyes. "Tamara?"

"I'm afraid it is," Lily said.

Beth's hand flew to her mouth. She looked fearfully at the police gathered around the site. "What happened?"

Before anyone could answer, someone called out, "Do the Hunts have a chain saw in their garage?"

Lily shrugged. "I don't know."

"We've got one," Jimmy Jenkins said. "I know right where it is."

Sheriff Meredith glanced up. "Hello, Jimmy," he called. "Sure your dad has a chain saw?"

" 'Course I'm sure. Are *you* sure that's Tamara? I mean, she's too young to be dead. And too nice. Maybe it's somebody we don't know," he ended hopefully.

"Jimmy, we'll worry about positive identification later," the sheriff said with a trace of sympathy in his voice. "Let's get that chain saw now."

He spoke to two deputies, who immediately walked toward Jimmy. "Follow me," Jimmy directed unnecessarily and he took off on his bike.

Beth twisted her hands together. "Lily, what can I do? Bring you some tea or lemonade? It's getting hot and you look like death. Oh!" Distress flashed across her face. "I didn't mean that. You look lovely. Both you and Tamara are such pretty girls. She came over yesterday and she was positively glowing. Oh! I can't say anything right!" A tear ran down Beth's right cheek. "I'm sorry. I just can't believe this. She was so kind. I'm so busy with the other kids. Jimmy was always dropping in on her. She gave him lemonade and cookies and talked to him and never complained about him being a pest. I think he had a crush on her. Oh, this is awful!"

Lily said gently, "Why don't you go home and help Jimmy find that chain saw, Beth? Natalie's with me and Dad will be here soon."

Natalie saw emotions tugging behind the woman's distressed

eyes. She wanted to be of service, but she also wanted to escape the terrible scene. The latter desire won. "Well, if you're sure."

"I am. Thank you, Beth."

The woman turned and nearly ran down the dirt lane toward the street. Lily shook her head. "Tam really liked Beth. And she thought Beth was so lucky—she has four kids. Jimmy is the oldest. Tam wanted children so much." Suddenly she moaned and buried her head in her hands. "I was devastated when Mom died. Now I'm glad she's gone. This would have hurt her so deeply she would never have recovered. Dad is stronger."

Men returned with the chain saw. Jimmy was in hot pursuit, but they stopped him before he could get near the site of Tamara's body. He stood, balancing his bicycle beside him, watching the activity. Someone revved up the chain saw.

Lily closed her eyes. "It's bad enough that she's dead, but to be trapped like that—" A shudder ran through her. "My sister wasn't supposed to die this way."

The roar of the chain saw ripped through the beautiful after-noon. "Watch it!" a man shouted. "You don't want to cut off her legs!" Lily leaned forward as if she were going to faint. "Please tell me this is a nightmare and I'll wake up."

"I wish I could."

"I'm not going to face it now." Lily clambered to her feet and began pacing around. "No, I'm not going to face it now. I *can't*."

"Lily, please sit down. You're so pale."

"I *can't*." She wrapped her arms around herself as she tram-pled aimlessly through the tall grass and weeds at the side of the dirt road. "I just don't understand. This doesn't make any sense. Tam wouldn't have stayed out in a storm . . ." She frowned, then bent down to pick up a piece of paper.

"What is it?" Natalie asked.

Lily looked at it for a couple of seconds and said in shock, "What in the world?"

Natalie came to her, holding out her hand. Lily gave her a piece of white paper, blistered from water damage. On it was typed in blurry letters, THEIR THROAT IS AN OPEN TOMB. The right side of the paper bore a red stain.

"It was under those leaves. Where do you suppose it came from?"

Natalie looked at the red stain, then at the site of Tam's body. Forty to fifty feet away. She knew. "It's probably nothing," she said carelessly to an already distraught Lily, tucking the note in her pocket.

"Why are you doing that?" Lily demanded. "It's wet and dirty. You think it has something to do with Tam, don't you?"

"Probably not." Natalie looked up. "Thank goodness. Here's your father."

Down the lane Oliver Peyton climbed out of a black Lexus. His silvering fair hair shone in the light, perfect as always, but as he drew closer Natalie saw that his face was almost as gray as his expensive suit. His eyes had a wide, staring quality as if he'd just seen something startling. Natalie had always thought he seemed like the coldest man she'd ever met except when it came to the girls. He'd been an adoring and indulgent parent, and Natalie had envied the twins' easy relationship with their father. It lacked all the prickliness of hers with Andrew. "Lily," Oliver called, his usually precise voice reedy and unsure.

"Dad, I'm so glad you're here."

Oliver stopped in front of her and took her shoulders firmly in his hands. "Lily, Mrs. Ebert told me you called. She said Tamara is dead. She's obviously mistaken. Now I want you to tell me calmly and clearly what is going on."

Lily gazed up at him. "Dad, it's true. Tam is dead."

"No, no, that can't be right," Oliver insisted. "Now think about what you're saying—"

"She's *dead*!" Lily blurted, tears spilling over her pale cheeks. "Tam is dead."

Sheriff Meredith appeared. Oliver Peyton was only about five foot ten and Meredith seemed to tower over him. "Mr. Peyton, your daughter *is* dead," he said quietly. "I'm very sorry."

"I want to see her."

"No, sir, you don't."

"Why?" Oliver demanded. "You don't even know if it's my daughter."

"It is, Mr. Peyton," Natalie said. "I saw her."

Oliver looked at her indignantly. "And who are you?"

"Oh, Dad, it's Natalie St. John." Lily sounded as if she were reaching the end of her endurance. "She says it's Tam and her body is not in good shape. You see, there were these vultures—"

Her voice broke. Oliver's smooth face blanched. Sheriff Meredith's eyes flashed sympathy but his manner remained businesslike as the chain saw continued its relentless grinding in the background. "Mr. Peyton, we don't know exactly how your daughter died. It looks like lightning struck a limb and it fell on her." Natalie's gaze cut to his. He paused for a couple of seconds, then went on. "Why don't you take your daughter home? We'll be here a while and then we'll take the body in for an autopsy."

Oliver and Lily winced. Natalie glared. Did this guy have to be so brutal? Lily was right—he *was* a jerk.

"I'm not going anywhere," Oliver announced.

"Dad, please," Lily said weakly. A sheen of perspiration covered her ashen face and her hands trembled. "I have to get away from here and I can't drive."

"Oh, darling." Oliver seemed to really see Lily for the first time. "I need to stay. Can't Natalie take you home?"

"No, Dad, I need you. I want to go to your house—our house. Please. There's nothing we can do here." She handed a set of keys to Natalie. "You can drive my car home."

Natalie nodded although she couldn't drive a four-speed. She didn't want to burden Lily with worries about the car, though. She'd leave it in Tamara's driveway and get a ride with someone.

"There's nothing you can do here," the sheriff said in a gentler tone. "Please take care of your daughter, and I'll stop by your house later with any news."

Oliver wasn't looking well himself and reluctantly he nodded. Natalie and Sheriff Meredith watched as the two trudged to the

Lexus and drove slowly away. Then Meredith turned to her, pinning her with a pair of the bluest eyes she'd ever seen. "You don't think Mrs. Hunt was killed by a falling branch."

"No, I don't. I believe this stray dog was around the body last night. It has dried blood all over its neck. Sometimes dogs and wolves will stretch their necks over the neck of one of their kind or a person to protect them. I think that's what this dog did with Tamara, but as I'm sure you can see, there's no way it could have gotten in position to do so with Tam under the limb. The limb fell after Tam was down."

Meredith frowned, looked at her, looked at the dog, looked at the area where Tamara lay, then looked back at Natalie. "I never heard of dogs doing anything like that. Why?"

"Because a predator goes for the throat. The stronger one protects the weaker one's throat from attack."

"How do you know all of this?"

"I'm a veterinarian."

"Are you sure that's what happened?"

"No, I'm not sure. Not all dogs do it. This dog doesn't have blood around its mouth as if it had killed and eaten something, though. The blood is only around the neck, but there is no injury in the neck area. And there's something else." From the pocket in her slacks she withdrew the note Lily had found. "Take a look at this."

" 'Their throat is an open tomb.' " Meredith's blue eyes flashed back at her. "Where did you get this?"

"Lily found it right over there." She nodded to the spot. "There were some leaves lying over most of it or rain would have obliterated the typing. I think that's blood on the edge."

"You think this note was left on her body?"

"Blood on the dog, blood on the note. The wind could have blown the note off the body." Meredith gave her a piercing look. She suddenly felt ridiculous, standing here spouting theories, but she couldn't stop. "The wind probably couldn't have blown the note free if it were trapped under all that foliage, though, so I think the limb fell later, *after* Tam was dead. Or injured," she trailed off, wilting under the intense blue gaze.

A piece of the limb crashed loose and the chain saw stopped. Natalie and Meredith watched as a male deputy dragged away debris and a female deputy moved closer to Tamara's body. In a moment she turned around. "Sheriff, I think you'd better take a look."

Meredith glanced at Jimmy Jenkins, who hovered nearby. "Jimmy, go home." Then he looked at her. "Dr. St. John, you stay here."

"I'll stay with you," Jimmy said staunchly. "You look like you could use a man around."

"Thank you," Natalie said, appreciating his offer. She kneeled by the dog, fondling its ears, talking to it, trying to shut out the horror of the situation. The dog licked her hands as if in gratitude. Gratitude for a few kind words and a gentle touch, Natalie thought, her throat tightening. Poor Tam. Poor dog. God, what a wretched day.

Gravel crunched beside her. She looked up. Meredith stood straight and tall, his strong-boned face grim. "I think you were right, Dr. St. John," he said, his voice without inflection. "Her throat has been slashed."

II

Tamara's throat had been slashed? *Slashed?*

Natalie stood up, her lips slightly parted in shock. She'd known Tamara hadn't been killed by a falling limb. She'd even been fairly sure Tam hadn't been struck by lightning. But *this*?

Meredith watched her intently. "Dr. St. John, do you know anyone who might want to murder Mrs. Hunt?"

"Murder?" Natalie repeated incredulously. "Murder Tamara? My God, no! No one could want to hurt her."

"Someone did. I don't need a medical examiner to tell me her throat wasn't cut in an accident." He seemed to notice Jimmy for the first time. "I told you to get going, boy!" Jimmy hopped on his bike and sped away, although he looked totally unabashed by the sheriff's harsh tone. "Dr. St. John, I asked you about Mrs. Hunt," Meredith said.

Natalie raised her hands helplessly. "I can't tell you anything. I haven't lived in Port Ariel for years. I'm only back for a visit."

"Maybe her father and sister will know something. Or her husband. Is that all the family?"

"Her mother is dead. There are aunts, uncles, cousins, but I don't know where any of them live."

Meredith wasn't taking notes, but Natalie had no doubt he would remember everything she said. She glanced back at the location of Tamara's body. People cleared away the remaining leaves and chunks of wood. Emergency technicians pushed a gurney. Everyone moved slowly and quietly because Tamara was a lifeless, mutilated body headed for a morgue instead of an emergency room. Had there ever been a chance? How long had she lived after someone had ripped open her slender white throat?

"Dr. St. John?" Sheriff Meredith's voice sounded as if it were coming from far away. She looked at him, noticing for the first time a thin two-inch-long scar that slashed above his right eyebrow and the slight bump high on the bridge of his nose as if it had been broken. He also had a strand of silver hair along one temple. Lily had said something about him coming to Port Ariel because of a tragedy in New York City. Had he been injured? "Are you all right?" he asked.

"Not really." She suddenly realized how weak she felt. "Could someone take me home?"

"I thought Miss Peyton left her car keys."

"Her Corvette is a four-speed. I can only drive an automatic. My father tried to teach me to use a manual but I just couldn't seem to learn. He got so frustrated—" She broke off. "I need a ride."

"I've done all I can here for now. I'll take you."

The emergency technicians were carrying the gurney past them. The road was too rough to wheel it. A sheet covered Tamara's body, but Natalie still averted her eyes.

"Did you bag her hands?" Meredith asked.

"Yes," a deputy said. "You told us twice."

"Got a handkerchief?"

The deputy looked at him blankly for a moment, then withdrew a white square from his pocket. The sheriff took it, put the note inside, and handed it back. "Put this in an evidence bag. We've already got three extra sets of prints on it. We don't need any more."

"What is it?" the deputy asked.

"A note that might have been left on Mrs. Hunt's body. Hysell, I'm going to take Dr. St. John home. I'll be back at the office in half an hour."

"Okay, Sheriff." Then: "Natalie?"

She looked up and recognized Ted Hysell. He'd been a couple of years ahead of her in school. "Damned shame, isn't it?" Ted said. "Knew Tamara for years. She was a real sweetheart."

"Yes, she was."

"Pretty as a picture. I used to have a crush on her. Of course that was a long time ago. She never went out with me, but she was always real nice to me. Helped me through French class. I would have failed without her. Anyway, we'll find who did this, Natalie. We won't stop until we've got him and—"

"Thank you, Hysell," Meredith said repressively, clearly annoyed by Ted's chattiness. "Get back to headquarters as soon as possible and *don't* talk to any reporters. I'll prepare a statement for later."

Ted's eyes flickered with resentment before he marched back to the patrol car. The sheriff had been a bit sharp with him, but Ted's nonstop talking would fray anyone's nerves.

"All right, Dr. St. John," Meredith said. "Let's get going. You don't look so good."

Natalie took a couple of steps toward the sheriff's car, then looked back at the dog. It lay on the grass, its amber gaze fastened on her. She hesitated for a moment, then tapped her thigh. "Come on, girl." The dog immediately ran to her.

Meredith stopped. "I thought that wasn't your dog."

"It isn't, but it's hungry and in need of medical attention."

"It's also not too clean."

"Are you saying you won't let it in your car? Because if so, I can call my father." Natalie was afraid he'd tell her to do so. "Dad is at the hospital now—he has a patient in critical condition—but I guess I can wait out here for him."

Meredith sighed, and she thought he half-suspected she was lying. "Okay, both of you get in. I can't just leave you here."

Thank goodness, Natalie thought. Meredith opened the rear car door. The dog hesitated. Natalie slid in and patted the vinyl seat. The dog hopped up beside her.

After Natalie told him her address, they drove in silence for a few minutes. Finally Meredith said, "You going to put an ad in the paper for that dog?"

"Maybe."

"You don't sound too anxious to find its home."

"I have a feeling it was dumped. Lost dogs usually have a collar and tags."

"And you'd like to keep it." Natalie looked in the rearview mirror and saw him smiling. He held his head low, tilted, and looked up at her with those incredibly blue eyes. "You remind me of my daughter."

"How old is she?"

"Eleven. Her name is Paige. She wants to take in every stray she sees."

"So did I. Bunnies, baby robins, you name it. Does Paige have any pets?"

"A male cat. Ripley. Last year an elderly woman's house was burglarized. She was afraid to live alone afterward. Went to stay with her daughter who wouldn't accept the cat."

"So you took him in for your daughter." Natalie thawed toward him a fraction. "That was nice of you."

"The kid was driving me nuts begging for a pet." Even though he referred to his daughter as "the kid," his voice was warm with affection. "So you're a vet. Where do you practice?"

"A big clinic in Columbus called Anicare." To which I might never return because it means working with Kenny, Natalie thought. "There are ten veterinarians on staff and we only take referrals for difficult cases. I've lived in Columbus for twelve years."

"But you grew up in Port Ariel."

"Yes."

"Come back often to visit?"

"Twice a year."

"And you were friends with Tamara Hunt."

"She and Lily are twins. I've known them since I started first grade. We also shared an apartment in Columbus when we attended Ohio State."

"And you've stayed in close touch with Lily and Tamara since then?"

"Yes. They've both visited me in Columbus. I talk on the phone with Lily every couple of weeks. Tamara about once a month."

"So you know Mrs. Hunt's husband. What's your impression of him?"

Natalie hesitated. She thought Warren Hunt was a pompous bag of hot air, but her opinion was largely a matter of instinct. "I attended their wedding and I've been around him maybe five or six times since then. I wouldn't say I know him." She ran a hand over the dog's head. "Is Warren under suspicion, Sheriff Meredith?"

"Nick," he said absently. "And it was just an idle question."

Natalie doubted this. He was making friendly conversation— even telling her to call him Nick—because he wanted to put her off guard. But how could he possibly suspect Warren? He wasn't even here. Still, hadn't she heard on police shows that the spouse was always the prime suspect?

"Turn left here," Natalie directed. "It's the stone house up ahead."

"Nice place. I've admired it ever since I moved here."

"Thank you. My father designed it."

"Architecture a hobby of his?"

"Yes."

"That his Jeep Wagoneer in the driveway?"

"Yes."

"Guess he finished with that critical patient sooner than you expected," he said dryly.

Natalie didn't answer. Even if Andrew had been home earlier, she hadn't wanted to call him from Tamara's. She would have had to answer a dozen questions, then wait for him to arrive when she wanted desperately to get away from the scene of Tamara's murder.

Meredith opened the back door for her. She got out and coaxed the dog to follow. "I may need to talk to you later," he said.

"Fine. Phone number is listed. Thank you for bringing me home."

As she climbed the steps to the front porch, her father swung open the door. "Before you left I specifically asked you not to get in trouble and here you are two hours later delivered home by the sheriff himself." Her father's voice always boomed when he was tense. "Was there a wreck? Are you hurt? You look awful."

"Dad, lower your voice and let the dog and me come in because if I don't sit down and have a cup of coffee—"

"You're going to pass out. There's not an ounce of color in your face." Andrew put his big hand on her arm and drew her inside the coolness of the entrance hall. The dog lingered uncertainly on the porch. "You, too. I didn't mean to scare you. You both look like you need some tender loving care."

While her father poured water and laid out leftover bacon from breakfast for the dog, Natalie sat down at the kitchen table and stared out at the lake. Sunlight flashed over its glassy surface. In one direction she could see no shore—only water. It looked so calm, so soothing.

Andrew set a mug of coffee in front of her. "Take a drink of that and tell me what's going on."

Natalie sipped, then drew a deep breath. "Dad, Tamara is dead."

"Dead! Then there *was* a wreck!" Andrew burst out. "Lily drives too fast. Always did. Are you hurt?"

"There wasn't a wreck." Natalie raised anguished eyes to her father. "Tamara was murdered."

"Mur—wha—*murdered*!" Andrew's face registered profound shock. "Natalie, what are you talking about? How? When? Murdered!"

The dog quit eating and looked at him. "Dad, please stop blustering," Natalie said. "Lily hadn't been able to reach Tam by phone so we went to her house. The windows were open and the draperies damp from the storm last night. The doors were locked. We walked down Hyacinth Lane. Tamara was lying on the road beneath a tree limb. It looked like the falling limb had killed her, but when the police cut it away, they saw that Tam's throat had been—" She drew a deep breath. "*Slashed.*"

"Dear God," Andrew breathed, sitting down heavily. "Who?"

"They have no idea. Mr. Peyton came and took Lily home before the police discovered that her throat had been cut, so they don't even know yet that she was murdered. Neither does Warren. He's at a convention in Cleveland." She shook her head. "Dad, the dog led me to her body. It was horrible. The vultures had been at her eyes."

Andrew reached out and covered her hand with his surprisingly slender one, the hand of a gifted surgeon. "Go ahead and cry, honey."

"I can't. The tears won't come."

"They will in time." He patted her back in a clumsy attempt at comfort. "How's Lily?"

"Alternately sobbing and dry-eyed. Shaking. A wreck."

"Did she see her sister?"

"No, I wouldn't let her."

"Good. That would be a sight she'd take to her grave."

Natalie sighed. "It will be a sight I'll take to mine."

4

SUNDAY AFTERNOON

Charlotte Bishop realized she'd been staring at the same page of her Danielle Steel novel for ten minutes. She started over. Two sentences later her mind drifted again. Normally she devoured the novels, losing herself in the stories. She pictured herself as every impossibly beautiful, virtuous, and brave heroine. But not today.

She tossed down the book and looked around her bedroom. Large. Sumptuous. Adolescent. It hadn't been redecorated since she was fifteen when her favorite color was pink. Blush pink, shell pink, antique pink, strawberry pink. All shades surrounded her in nauseating abundance. And the doll collection! All those rosy-cheeked little creatures staring at her with big, blank eyes were driving her crazy. Abruptly she picked up a delicate crocheted afghan, also done in the ubiquitous shades of pink, and tossed it over the offending dolls. That was better. Slightly.

When Charlotte had returned home six months ago after her very public and humiliating divorce, she'd been too stunned and embarrassed to care what the room looked like. She'd only wanted to hide away in this small town in her old bedroom and lick her wounded ego. But time was doing its work. Her self-confidence was returning. So was her habitual boredom and restlessness. She'd like to do something about this room. After all, she would be staying here until she could marry Warren Hunt, which wouldn't be for a few months.

Warren. A couple of years ago she wouldn't have considered him husband material. Then she had been married to Paul Fiori, a television star. When they had wed five years earlier, her father was furious. She was the only daughter of Max Bishop, owner of Bishop Corporation, one of the country's largest manufacturers of marine electronics such as sonar and radar. Max had raged at the thought of his daughter the heiress marrying a pretty-boy actor who'd had only bit parts and would never amount to anything. The marriage was unacceptable! Unthinkable! But Charlotte had married Paul anyway. Charlotte always did what she wanted. Charlotte always got what she wanted. And she'd wanted Paul.

She had been happy at first, although she was their sole support. The parts just weren't coming in and Paul was frustrated. Charlotte didn't care. This way Paul needed her and she liked being in control. Then he had won the lead in the police drama *Street Life*. The show debuted at number five, and in three months shot to number one in the ratings. Paul was a star and landed a feature movie for his summer hiatus from the show. Charlotte had reveled in the publicity of being Paul Fiori's wife. She hadn't even minded the paparazzi. Not until the second year of the show when they began covering Paul's affair with his co-star Larissa Lyle. In public Charlotte acted calm and charmingly amused by the "ridiculous" rumor of an affair. At home she screamed, cried, threatened, and reminded Paul of every wonderful thing she'd done for him before *Street Life*. Then Larissa became pregnant and Paul walked away from Charlotte without a backward glance.

Charlotte tried to stay in Los Angeles, hoping to milk sympathy while watching the public turn against its newest star. To her surprise, at first, instead of outraged support, all she'd received was embarrassed pity. Then, thanks to Paul's publicity people, the tabloids falsely reported on her bizarre behavior and drug addiction, and the public began to wonder if Paul Fiori had not had good reason to leave his crazy wife. Charlotte was dropped from all Hollywood social functions, while Paul and Larissa became increasingly popular. On the day Larissa delivered their little boy, Charlotte fled for the safety and anonymity of Port Ariel.

To their credit, neither of her parents had said, "I told you so." This was an expected lack of response from her timid, gentle mother but downright miraculous from her bombastic, cocksure father. She attributed it to his recent stroke that had left him partially paralyzed and emotionally stunned. Her parents had left her alone to read, watch television (anything except *Street Life*), and to wander around the six acres of manicured grounds surrounding the white-columned house Max had modeled on Tara in *Gone With the Wind*. After a couple of months, when her depression didn't lift, she'd decided to seek professional help in the form of Dr. Warren Hunt.

Four weeks later their affair had begun and she'd wanted him as badly as she'd once wanted Paul Fiori. True, he wasn't as handsome and charismatic as Paul, but he was much brighter, far more educated, and absolutely adored her. And, oh, how her battered ego wanted his adoration after Paul's devastating rejection. Wanted, needed, *hungered*. The only thing standing between them was Warren's vapid little wife Tamara.

Charlotte wandered over to her vanity table and sat down, gazing into the large mirror. Charlotte knew she wasn't a classic beauty, but she was striking. Sunlight poured through the west window picking up the copper highlights in her short, sleek chestnut hair. When she blinked, long lashes swept over her gold-flecked green eyes and her skin shone like fine porcelain in the strong natural light. She didn't look thirty. She didn't look a day older than Paul's twenty-one-year-old silicone-and-bleach creation Larissa. Well, not much older. And she certainly looked better than Tamara, who didn't even try to be stylish like her twin sister Lily. Of course Lily was no threat. Warren didn't like her. She didn't think he really liked Tamara, either. It was only guilt that held him to her—guilt and fear of the fallout from a divorce.

Warren worried about what scandal would do to his

reputation in a town of twenty thousand people. But as soon as he got his divorce, Charlotte knew she could convince him to move somewhere more cosmopolitan where they both could shine. New York City would be nice. Expensive, yes, but her father was dying and she knew he intended to leave his fortune in her hands, not his wife's. Muriel didn't even like to write checks. She could never handle Bishop Corporation. Charlotte, on the other hand, had a brilliant business mind and could run the company from far away. Yes, New York City would be very nice. An apartment in Manhattan, a second home in the Hamptons . . .

Someone tapped at her door. "Come in," she called absently.

In a moment her mother's small, white face appeared. Muriel Bishop always looked slightly anxious, vaguely worried, but at the moment she appeared positively terrified. "Honey, that nice deputy Ted Hysell from the sheriff's office called," she said tremulously. "He thought your daddy would want to know . . ."

After years of living with the impatient Max, who interrupted constantly, Muriel finished only half of her sentences. The others trailed off into fluttering uncertainty.

"Daddy would want to know what, Mother?" Charlotte asked, picking up a silver-backed brush and fluffing her glossy hair.

"You won't believe this. I can hardly take it in myself. I mean, such a terrible thing . . . It really makes you wonder . . . I want to believe in God, but when something like this happens . . ."

"Mother, what *is* it?"

Muriel's hand touched her throat, then her trembling lips. She looked like she was going to cry. "It's that pretty Tamara Hunt, your doctor's wife . . . She's *dead*."

Charlotte's brush stopped in mid-stroke. She met her own gaze in the mirror and hoped her mother didn't see the satisfaction in the green depths of her eyes.

II

Deputy Ted Hysell waited for a relatively private moment, then called his girlfriend, Dee Fisher. She picked up on the fifth ring.

"What were you doing?" he asked.

"Taking care of Ma, what else? I wish I could afford to put her in a nursing home."

"You're a nurse."

"*Was.* Thanks to Andrew St. John, my illustrious career ended two years ago. Besides, I didn't plan on spending my life taking care of my mother. So much for my troubles. Why are you calling?"

"Got some news I thought you'd like to hear."

Dee shifted from one tired foot to the other, running a hand through her short, curly brown hair. "Well? Do I have to guess?"

"Tamara Hunt was murdered."

"Murdered," Dee said without emotion. "When?"

"It must have happened last evening because she was out on Hyacinth Lane underneath a limb brought down by the storm. Her sister Lily and Natalie St. John found her."

"Natalie St. John?"

"Yeah. I guess she's here on a visit."

"Visiting Daddy Dearest. She hardly ever comes home. Wonder what she's doing here now?"

"She didn't discuss it with me," Ted said.

Dee either ignored or didn't catch his sarcasm. "So how's old Natalie looking these days?"

"Looking?" He'd just told her a woman had been murdered and she was concerned about another woman's appearance. Ted shook his head in amazement. "She looks good. Hair's long. Slim as ever." Silence. Ted realized his mistake and added quickly, "Of course she's not my type."

"I could tell," Dee said coldly. She touched her face. The skin was dry and she'd gained twelve pounds over the past year. She suddenly felt unattractive and depressed. "I guess the animal doctor was freaked out. She liked Tamara, God knows why."

"I liked Tamara, too. She was a good woman, Dee."

"Well, I couldn't stand her," Dee snapped, suddenly angry at the offended tone in Ted's voice. He didn't like her criticizing Tamara and she didn't like his protectiveness. "I worked at her stupid suicide hotline for a year. Volunteered *hours* of my time. And after my trouble at the hospital, she made me quit."

"You told me it was Warren who called you and ordered you not to come back."

"So? He's her husband."

"He's also a jerk and what he did wasn't her fault."

"Pardon me. She was a saint. The whole country will be in mourning over her death." Dee took a breath. "So what about the animal doctor? Did she immediately call for Daddy?"

"No, Natalie didn't."

"I *know* her name is Natalie. I remember her all too well from high school. Part of that stuck-up group that wouldn't wipe their shoes on me."

Ted sighed. "I don't think you really knew any of these people. Natalie's not bad."

"She's a bitch," Dee said acidly. "Not that she had any right to be so snobby. Her mother took off and joined the Manson family."

"Dee, the Manson family was long gone when Natalie's mother left."

"And then there's her father," Dee went on, seething. "He killed poor Eugene Farley on the operating table two years ago."

Ted's face flushed. Dee had once been in love with Eugene Farley. He'd been head accountant at Bishop Corporation, where Viveca Cosgrove was an executive, and he'd dumped Dee for Viveca. Dee remained obsessed with him, though, and she was certain he'd return to her when his affair with Viveca ended. Instead he'd been arrested for embezzlement. During his trial, Dee had taken the night shift at the hospital and come to the courtroom every day.

The jury returned a guilty verdict. As a seemingly limp Farley was led out of the courtroom, he'd suddenly snapped to life.

With amazing speed he grabbed a deputy's gun and shot himself in the head. Everyone screamed and hit the floor, dodging the hail of bullets they thought would follow. But no other shots were fired and when the screaming stopped, someone checked Farley to find him still alive. They'd rushed him to the hospital and St. John operated. Dee was a surgical nurse. She'd hurried back to the hospital, slipped into the operating room and watched Eugene Farley die on the table. For two years she'd never stopped talking about Farley, claiming his death resulted from Andrew St. John botching the operation.

Ted sighed. "Dee, are you going to start this crap about Farley again?"

"It's *not* crap!" Dee snarled. "And just because I told the truth about Eugene dying because of St. John, I was fired."

No, you were fired because Andrew St. John accused you of stealing drugs and an investigation proved him right, Ted thought, although the hospital had not filed charges, fearing bad publicity. But he'd been seeing Dee for six months. She might be short-tempered, she might be loud and bawdy, she was even guilty of stealing a few drugs on the side, but she was still wild and sometimes fun and made him feel important.

Ted needed to feel important now because Nick Meredith obviously thought he was a not-so-smart hick. Big city know-it-all. Important people in county government didn't like him. They'd get rid of him someday. Ted took some satisfaction in this, but he would prefer that Meredith recognize he was a better cop than he seemed. Winning Meredith's respect would mean a hell of a lot.

"Are you still there?" Dee demanded.

"Yeah, sure."

"Well, I wish you wouldn't call if you're just going to daydream and not say anything."

"Sorry. You free tonight?"

"Uh, no, not tonight," she said abruptly. "Ma's not so well. I can't leave her."

"I could come to your house."

"No. She needs to sleep and she can hear a pin drop. We couldn't watch TV or talk above whispers."

"When do I get to see you?"

"I don't *know*." Petulant silence spun out on the other end. She lowered her voice, making it soft and husky. "Just be patient, baby, okay? I'll make it worth the wait."

"Okay," Ted said sulkily. "But it'd better be soon."

Well, hell, Ted thought after he'd hung up. A dull evening alone in front of the television lay ahead. Angrily he filled out another endless, boring report. Then a thought suddenly crossed his mind and he looked up, frowning.

Dee hadn't asked how Tamara Hunt had been murdered.

III

Natalie and her father sat in near silence for the next hour. A second mug of coffee warmed her chilled body, and she was tempted to have a third, but Andrew St. John made strong coffee. Three jolts of caffeine would be too much, Natalie realized as she looked at her hands that already showed signs of chemically induced tremor. "Can't I get you something to eat?" Andrew asked.

Food. Andrew's panacea for all problems. "I don't think I could eat a bite if my life depended on it."

"If your life depended on it, you'd eat that dog standing over there," he answered absently, although the dog's head shot up as if in alarm. They both smiled. "I guess she understands more than I think."

"I believe she's quite intelligent, Dad. Sometimes mixed breeds are smarter than the pure breeds where there's been too much interbreeding among the blue bloods." She sighed. "I think she stayed with Tamara all night."

Her father looked out the window again. "I remember when you were six. Shortly after your mother left, you ran off one December night. It was *so* cold. Harvey and Mary Coombs helped me search for you. We finally found you in an old boathouse half a mile from here. The dog Clytemnestra led us to you. If she hadn't, you might have frozen to death."

"I remember that night," Natalie said softly. "I'd overheard Harvey talking about Kira. He said the responsibility of a child was too much for her. I decided she left because of me. I thought if I took off, she'd come back to you. Running away on a freezing winter night wasn't so easy, though. I made it to the boathouse. I thought I'd spend the night and be on my way the next morning, but I fell asleep."

"And if it weren't for the dog, you would have died." Andrew shook his head. "Harvey thought you were asleep in bed or he wouldn't have said that about your mother. He felt terrible. But Kira didn't leave because of you. She was bored with me and with this town. She wanted to remain a kid having fun."

"I know that now, but I'm *still* mad at her."

"Then why do you always wear the ring she left for you?"

Natalie looked down at the lovely pearl surrounded by small diamonds. "It belonged to Great-grandmother Uehara. I wear it for her."

"You never knew her."

"Kira's mother told me about her. I think I would have liked her." Natalie paused. "Dad, do you wish Kira would come back?"

"I did for a long time but not anymore."

"I wonder if she would come back if I were murdered like Tamara."

"Don't even think about such a thing! My God, if I lost you, Natalie, I'd . . ." Her father stood up abruptly. "More coffee?"

"No thanks, Dad. I think I'll take a shower. I need to feel hot water and soap on my skin."

"Good idea. I'll look after Fido for you."

"Fido?"

"Is there a name on her tag?"

"She has no tags."

"Okay, for now she's Fido. Go take your shower."

Natalie took one last sip of her lukewarm coffee and headed

out of the kitchen toward her bedroom. As she passed through the living room, the phone rang. "I'll get it," she called.

She picked up the handset of the cordless phone and pressed TALK. "Hello."

Nothing.

"*Hello.*"

Finally Natalie heard a long sigh. "Na-ta-lie."

Female voice, soprano, sweet, breathy.

A prank, obviously, but her heart beat a little harder. "This is Natalie. What do you want?"

"Na-ta-lie."

That sweet voice caressing her name. Uneasiness tingled through her. "If you don't tell me what you want, I'm hanging up."

Another sigh. Then the gentle voice. "Their throat is an open tomb."

Natalie drew a sharp breath. "What is *that* supposed to mean?"

"You'll find out soon."

Click. Silence.

Natalie stared at the handset as if it were a snake. A chill passed through her as she realized the voice had sounded exactly like Tamara's.

5

Warren Hunt wiped perspiration from his upper lip and turned the car air conditioner to an even lower temperature. Usually he listened to classical music when he drove, but not today.

He'd returned to his hotel room to pack when he saw the phone light blinking. Voice mail told him to call Oliver Peyton's house. When he did, Oliver's sobbing housekeeper Mrs. Ebert told him Tamara was dead. No, she didn't know any details. No, she didn't know where Mr. Peyton was right now. But Dr. Hunt had to come home. He *had* to come home *immediately*!

What did the sobbing fool think I was going to do? Warren had thought irritably. Hang around here for another night? Why couldn't people maintain a modicum of sense during an emergency? Nevertheless, when he'd hung up on the hysterical woman he'd noticed to his disgust that his hands were shaking.

And why not? he asked himself. He had to go home and face this damned mess—Lily and Oliver, the funeral, keeping his relationship with Charlotte a secret until a suitable period of time passed. And what was a suitable period of time? A year? Impossible. Charlotte would never stand for that. He'd lose her. Six months? He couldn't possibly see anyone publicly for six months, but even that amount of time seemed impossible. Charlotte was demanding. She wasn't the kind of woman you could stall. He didn't *want* to stall her.

Valentine's Day. That was when Charlotte had first walked into his office. He already knew who she was and the story of her divorce. Everyone in town did. Nevertheless, when she arrived he tried to look pleasantly blank as he asked what troubled her. While she narrated the story, he thought about what an amazingly beautiful, sensual creature she was. He'd seen pictures of the woman Paul Fiori had dumped her for. Was the guy crazy? Well, crazy wasn't a word Warren liked to use. Fiori was . . . tasteless.

During their second session Warren realized Charlotte was flirting with him. She wasn't the first patient to do so. Every therapist knew the prevalence, as well as the danger, of this situation. Still, he couldn't help responding, something he had never done before. He felt slightly guilty when he arrived home that evening to Tamara, but the guilt vanished as the night wore on and he realized he found her adoration cloying, her chatter about housework and gardening and the tribe of Jenkins kids excruciatingly tiresome, and her lovemaking totally unexciting.

Two weeks later he told Tamara he had an evening appointment and spent three hours having abandoned sex with Charlotte. He'd never experienced anything like that night and he drove home knowing he wanted the gorgeous, sexually adept, rich Charlotte Bishop in his life forever. She wanted him, too, but Warren knew that in her way Charlotte had adored Paul Fiori. She was rebounding from him, and rebounds didn't last long. He would have to move fast if he didn't want to lose her.

Now he was free. Almost. He still had to pretend great grief, a sense of being lost, regret for the life and children he and Tamara would never have together. No children, thank God. At least he didn't have *that* problem to contend with. Charlotte didn't want a child of her own, much less someone else's.

Port Ariel city limits. Warren found the place rather picturesque when he moved here with Tamara six years ago. His father had told him he was a fool. Warren's hands tightened on the steering wheel at the thought of his father. Richard Hunt was the senior partner in the biggest accounting firm in Cleveland. He'd made a fortune with investments. He had just married his third wife, who was seven years younger than Warren. Richard thought Warren's profession was ridiculous. He thought Warren was ridiculous. His pride and joy was Warren's younger half-brother Bruce, who played football at Ohio State University and planned to go into the firm. Good thing his father had a business for him to enter, Warren thought bitterly. Bruce was a strong, amiable-faced buffoon. Warren knew he possessed the superior intelligence, looks, and culture, but he still hated Bruce for capturing all of Richard Hunt's parental love.

And speaking of parental love, there was Oliver Peyton. The man couldn't get through one day without talking to his precious Tamara and Lily. He was like a mother tigress and he'd always looked at Warren as a predator threatening one of his cubs. The chilly, pretentious, possessive guy was hard enough to take at the best of times. But now? Oh, well, he wouldn't have to worry about Oliver much longer, either.

Warren pulled into the Peyton driveway behind a silver Mercedes. Wonderful, Warren thought. Viveca Cosgrove was here. Oliver had been seeing her for a year. Tamara didn't like her. Even Lily didn't like her. She said Viveca really cared about only one person—her daughter Alison. This was probably the only point on which he and Lily agreed. Oh, Viveca put on a good show of loving Oliver, but the girls saw right through her. So did Warren. Everyone seemed to except infatuated Oliver.

The front door swung open before he reached it. Oh, hell, Warren thought. Alison. Pretty, dainty Alison with her little-girl voice, her predatory gaze, her irreparably fractured psyche. She was his patient. She had a crush on him. She made his skin crawl.

"Warren, I'm so glad you're finally here!" Alison cried. Her blond hair hung straight, nearly touching her waist. She wore no makeup, a blue blouse with a Peter Pan collar, and Mary Jane shoes. Had Viveca known her daughter would look like Alice in Wonderland when she named her? "Lily and Oliver are just devastated," Alison went on dramatically. "Mama and I came right over to help."

I'll bet you're a *big* help, Warren thought with distaste. He forced a stiff smile. "Thank you, Alison."

She did not step aside when he entered the house. He had to crowd past her, forcing their bodies into contact. He knew she'd fixated on her mother's former young lover, Eugene Farley. After Farley's death, she'd transferred her fixation onto him. She was twenty-two and he doubted she'd ever been to bed with anyone. He also doubted she thought about much except sex.

Warren drew a deep breath and was relieved to discover he could. Twenty minutes ago his lungs wouldn't fill. Oliver Peyton walked toward him, his face rigid, his gaze conveying desolation, doubt, and contempt all at once. Even now he couldn't pretend to like his son-in-law, and Warren, to his frustration, could not help being intimidated.

"Here at last."

"Oliver, I'm sorry you had trouble reaching me. I was lunching with colleagues. We got carried away talking and . . ." Oliver's gaze hardened. He didn't want to hear this chatter. "What exactly happened to my Tamara?"

"Come into the living room," Oliver said tonelessly.

Warren followed Oliver. Alison pattered along behind, nearly stepping on his heels. Warren's heightened sense of smell vibrated like an animal's. What was she wearing? Sweet Honesty? Heaven Scent? Some little-girl cologne. Warren could hear her breath coming quick and loud. She was enthralled. This situation was bad enough without her here enjoying the whole thing, a sickening voyeur. Oliver probably felt the same way, but he would suffer Alison's presence because she belonged to his treasured Viveca. Warren didn't like Viveca any better than he liked Alison. At the moment he didn't like anyone except Charlotte Bishop and he didn't dare even call her.

The Peyton living room used to be shockingly Spartan, decorated like the Catholic orphanage where Grace Peyton had spent her childhood. In the last year Viveca had wrought her magic and the place now looked as if it were ready for a photo shoot in *House Beautiful*. Warren did admire Viveca's impeccable taste, although at the time of the redecorating he had resented the sizeable expenditure of money, which would diminish Oliver's estate. He didn't have to worry about Oliver's estate any more. Max Bishop's made it look like a pauper's in comparison.

As soon as Warren entered the living room, Viveca descended upon him. Her hair, its dark golden hue maintained by careful coloring, was swept up in an elegant French twist to show off her magnificent cheekbones. She'd always reminded him of Faye Dunaway.

"Warren," she said simply but with controlled, breathy feeling.

"Viveca," he returned for lack of anything else to say.

"This has been such a shock for you. For all of us."

"Yes." He had the gift of gab. Why had it deserted him? "Yes," he said again and his mind went blank.

Viveca leaned back and looked at him. Her gaze was earnest, searching. What was she looking for? Deep grief? Did she detect its absence? He lowered his gaze. His mouth twitched slightly from nerves. Apparently Viveca mistook the twitch as a close brush with tears because she quickly enfolded him in a Joy-scented embrace. "We're all here for you."

"Oh, yes!" Alison echoed fervently.

Over Charlotte's shoulder Warren saw Lily curled onto a moss-green brocade-covered settee. Her makeup had washed away with tears and without it she looked so much like Tamara he caught his breath. But Tamara had never stared at him so coldly. "Hello, Lily," he said uncertainly.

She nodded curtly. The antagonism between them had always been barely concealed and present circumstances made no difference. But soon he wouldn't have to put up with her anymore, either.

Oliver poured himself a brandy from a cut-glass decanter sitting on a sideboard. He offered Warren nothing. As Viveca detached herself from Warren and drifted gracefully across the room, Oliver swirled his brandy in the snifter, slowly took a sizeable drink, then fixed Warren with pale gray eyes. "Warren, Sheriff Meredith has informed us things are not as they appeared at first."

Blood rushed to Warren's face, then quickly drained. "You mean Tamara's not dead?" he asked in a thin, startled voice.

"Of course she's dead!" Oliver's voice lashed at him. "They're not likely to make a mistake like *that!*"

"Oh, well, then . . ."

"Tamara's death wasn't caused by an accident." Oliver paused. Warren was vaguely aware of everyone intensely watching him. He could almost hear Alison's heart beating rapidly with excitement. "Tamara was murdered," Oliver said in a brittle voice. "Someone cut her throat."

I'm supposed to gasp, Warren thought distantly. I'm supposed to turn pale or sway. I'm at least supposed to look surprised. Instead he stood paralyzed and uttered a weak, "Oh."

"Oh?" Lily repeated in an eerie version of Tamara's voice. "Is that it? *Oh?*"

"I . . . I'm just . . ." His mouth felt full of gauze. Once again he was an inadequate boy reduced to stammering helplessness in front of his disgusted father. "Who?" he managed finally.

Oliver paused, then said, "The police have no idea. Yet."

But he continued to stare at Warren unflinchingly, his steely eyes flickering with suspicion.

II

Since returning home, Natalie had considered calling Lily but decided to wait. Sheriff Meredith had no doubt informed Oliver and Lily that Tamara had been murdered. They needed time to accept this information before friends descended. But she couldn't sit idle and dwell on the image of Tamara's eyeless body, and she certainly couldn't think about the unnerving call she'd received. She hadn't mentioned it to her father. Hopefully he would dismiss it as a prank. More likely he would grow alarmed, and she didn't feel like dealing with his overprotectiveness. Instead she kept quiet about the call and busied herself with the dog.

She led it to the patio and hoped it wouldn't run away at the sight of the garden hose. Thankfully it stood still, patiently enduring being doused with cold water then lathered with Natalie's shampoo. "This is guaranteed to add strength, body, and luster," she told the dog. "Vitamin B5, hydrolyzed wheat protein, glycerin, tocopheryl—that's a form of vitamin E. Thyme and chamomile—sweet-smelling herbs. Expensive stuff, young lady. I don't think it does anything for fleas, though, but we'll worry about them later. Right now our prime concern is dirt and that less-than-delightful aroma you're sporting."

After the bath she patted hydrogen peroxide onto the dog's facial scratch and the shallow cuts on its paws. None of the wounds were serious enough to require stitches and only one looked as if it might be heading toward infection. She would start the dog on antibiotics just to be safe, but now she had a more immediate problem.

"I can't keep calling you 'the dog,' " she said, looking into its amber eyes. "And you're certainly not going to be *Fido*. You need a proper name. Nothing common because I have a feeling you're an uncommon dog." She stared out at the lake, considering and rejecting a dozen names. Then her gaze snapped back to the dog. "I'm reading a murder mystery with a heroine named Blaine." She dabbed a drop of water on the dog's head. "I christen you Blaine." The dog licked her nose and she smiled. "I think you like your new name."

Blaine's head moved sharply. Natalie looked up, following the dog's gaze.

A woman stood in the doorway. She appeared to be in her mid-fifties with short, silver hair and bright aqua eyes. She stared at Natalie intently before she smiled broadly. "So you're the girl I've heard so much about!" She came forward, hand extended. "I'm Ruth Meadows."

Natalie smiled automatically. Ruth Meadows?

"Your father said you'd brought home a dog," the woman went on. "My, he's fine looking."

"It's a she," Natalie said. Free of dirt and oil, Blaine's black hair glistened in the sun.

"She looks like the dog in the photo of you taken when you were about five."

"The framed one in Dad's study? Her name was Clytemnestra."

"Good heavens, that's a mouthful."

"My mother named her. Kira was in her Greek mythology phase then." Natalie looked at the dog. "Someone once cared about her. She's been spayed and I'd say she's only been neglected for a couple of weeks."

"Well, what a shame." Ruth stepped out on the patio. She was about five-seven and trim. She wore ivory linen slacks, a pale pink knit top and small gold hoop earrings. Her lips bore a lovely shade of coral-pink lipstick. Her voice was warm and friendly.

"I love animals," she said, petting Blaine. "I grew up on a farm. I always thought when I reached my age I'd be surrounded by children and animals. Instead I'm childless and I have only one small cat. A calico. I named it Callie because all cats seem female to me."

"All calicos are female."

"They are? How do you know?"

"The calico hair coat color pattern is genetically incompatible with the male Y chromosome."

"Well, my goodness!" Ruth exclaimed. "Did you *ever* hear of such a thing?"

"Calicos are beautiful," Natalie said, her mind working. The woman said she'd heard about her. She had a cat. And she looked quite at ease in this house. Clearly Ruth was Andrew's new romantic interest. Natalie told herself not to stare or ask too many probing questions. She was surprised Andrew was even allowing the two women in his life to meet so soon.

Ruth said gently, "Your father told me about Tamara. I knew her slightly from my work with the suicide hotline she organized. Such a dear girl."

"Yes," Natalie said softly.

"I can't even imagine how awful finding her must have been for you. I'm so sorry."

Natalie swallowed, unable to say anything.

"Don't worry, dear, I'm not going to ask any questions. But I'll be here for a little while if you want to talk and take your mind off things. We can discuss anything. Animals, movies—" She winked. "Your father."

"Oh, no. The last subject is off-limits," Andrew announced as he joined Ruth. "Well, that looks like a completely different dog."

"I knew she was a beauty beneath all the grime." And blood, Natalie thought. She'd soaped the neck area twice. "I named her Blaine."

"Blaine? What kind of name is that?"

"She likes it."

"I don't know how you can tell, but if *you* like it I suppose it's okay." Andrew frowned. "You'll need a leash and collar."

"Which I plan to get immediately along with some antibiotics. I don't have anything with me. Dad, if you'll write a prescription for amoxicillin, I'll run to the drugstore right now." And leave you and Ruth alone *and* try to keep myself busy so I don't replay finding Tam, Natalie thought.

"Prescription coming up," Andrew said, going back inside.

"This dog certainly fell into the right hands," Ruth smiled. "I really don't know much about modern animal care. Maybe you can teach me a few things, Natalie. One of our two vets is retiring next month. The other—Cavanaugh—just doesn't suit me. He's not gentle with the animals and it seems he's more interested in selling medicine than anything else. I've talked to several people who aren't happy with him, either."

"I see." Natalie stood up. "What color collar do you think Blaine should have?"

Ruth came forward and stroked Blaine's head. "With all this beautiful black hair? Red!"

"That's what I thought, too."

Ruth kneeled and took the dog's face in her hands. "Hello, pretty girl. You've found a good home, haven't you?" Blaine licked her hand. "Natalie, are you sure she's perfectly healthy?"

"Yes, except for cuts and scratches and probably a case of tapeworm from fleabites, but tapes are easy to get rid of. Why? Does something look wrong to you?"

"Her tongue, dear. It has black splotches."

Natalie smiled. "That's because she has some Chow blood."

"Chow? They have black on their tongues?"

"Yes indeed."

"My goodness, I'm learning things already. You seem quite capable, Natalie."

"Well, we haven't been discussing any complex animal ailments. I feel I still have a lot to learn."

"As opposed to Dr. Cavanaugh, who's about your age and thinks he knows it all."

"Is she complaining about that young whippersnapper of a vet again?" Andrew asked, coming to stand by Ruth and handing her a mug of coffee.

"I take it he isn't too popular."

"I think his problem is that small animal care is just a sideline with him," Andrew informed her seriously. "He's more interested in cows and horses."

"And his office hours are very limited," Ruth added sadly. "You're just out of luck if there's an emergency. It's awful."

Natalie smothered a grin. Any minute they would burst into doleful tears about the lack of good vets in Port Ariel. Andrew was campaigning for her return and had drawn Ruth in on the scheme, too.

"I'd better be off to the drugstore," she said casually. "I'm sure Blaine will be fine in the house until I come back. Can't leave her out on the lawn unchained. She might wander off." She herded the dog into the living room, picked up the prescription her father had left on an end table, and dashed out the front door before Andrew could object to a new, large housedog.

III
SUNDAY NIGHT 11:30 P.M.

Shadows. Circling. Undulating. She looked up. Vultures. Huge wings. Cold, merciless eyes. Lower. Lower. Down to feast on the delicate face.

Natalie's heart slammed against her ribs. She sucked in air with such a vengeance, pain stabbed her chest. A weight hit the bed and a shard of fear touched her heart. Then a warm, wet tongue licked her nose.

"Oh, Blaine!" she breathed, clutching the dog. "I had such an awful dream. Did I frighten you?"

The dog nuzzled her neck. She smelled of shampoo. She was also heavy but Natalie didn't mind the weight pressing against her body. It felt warm and reassuring, a sign of thriving life.

Life. *She* was alive. Blaine was alive. Tamara was dead. Murdered.

Suddenly Natalie began to hyperventilate. She gently pushed the dog away, trying not to alarm her, and got up. She paced the room, her long nightgown wrapping annoyingly around her legs. Stripping off the nightgown, Natalie noticed how damp it was. Perspiration glistened on her abdomen and dripped from beneath her breasts. She ran her hands through her wet hair.

A panic attack. She'd been having them ever since she was six and her mother left. They'd lessened over the years, but today had been enough of a shock to throw anyone, and this was a bad one. Still, it was only a simple panic attack. She would just ride it out.

Ten minutes later her heart still pounded and sweat still poured. Blaine followed in helpless distress as Natalie paced the room, breathing raggedly. Natalie was touched by how quickly the dog seemed to have bonded to her and her company was a comfort, but Natalie was still unnerved by her condition. Often when she had the attacks, she could calm herself by playing the guitar and singing. That wasn't an option tonight. She would wake her father and he'd make a scene. He'd harangue her about

Kenny. He'd lecture about her diet, tell her to eat meat. He might even take her to the emergency room at the hospital. How embarrassing. Rushed to the hospital for a panic attack. People would think she was as flaky as her mother.

No, she had to handle this on her own. It was bad enough that she'd run home to Daddy after coming face to face with Kenny's infidelity. Now to completely fall apart in front of him would be too much.

She put on her robe and went to the kitchen. A glass of milk? No, it sounded nauseating. Tea? No, tea was a stimulant. Orange juice? Natalie drank a small glass of juice, which hit her stomach like a rock.

A walk. A few times when she'd had panic attacks, walks had been the answer. Walking along the shoreline in front of the house would do the trick. She glanced at the kitchen clock. 11:45. No matter. She needed long strides and deep breaths of fresh air.

She went back to the bedroom and slipped on jeans, a tee shirt, Reeboks, and a windbreaker. Then she glanced at the clock again. 11:52. No matter? Yes, it mattered. Although she planned to stay within sight of the house, just last night Tamara had been murdered not too far away.

Natalie took her suitcase from the closet and unlocked it. Fishing in the side pocket, she withdrew a .38 blue-steel Beretta. Twenty-one-point-eight ounces. Strange she should remember the exact weight. She had not wanted it, but Kenny insisted on buying a gun for her after a string of rapes in Columbus last year. A pocket rocket, he'd called it. She hadn't intentionally brought it along. She'd just always kept it tucked out of sight in the suitcase.

When she'd first begun lessons, her right hand had held the gun stiffly, reluctantly. Then, to her surprise and her instructor's, she'd discovered she had a knack. She was an excellent shot, even though she wasn't actually sure she could shoot someone. "You could in a case of self-defense," Kenny had assured her. "That is, if you'd ever keep the thing handy. What will you do if someone breaks in? Tell them to wait a minute until you unlock your suitcase and get your gun?"

Well, she had it now. She snapped in the eight-shot magazine and stuffed the gun in her pocket. Then she grabbed a flashlight from her nightstand drawer and attached Blaine's leash. "Ready for a night stroll with your new mistress?" she asked. The dog pulled toward the door. "Off we go, then, into the wild blue yonder."

No, the wild black yonder, she thought as she and Blaine strolled down toward the lake. Not a bright night. Not a warm night. A breeze blew off the water. Natalie had brought a large barrette and she pulled back her long hair and caught it in the clip. Cool air touched her warm neck like a caress.

Like when Kenny had dipped his fingers in a cold vodka tonic and stroked her neck as she lay sunbathing on his balcony just two weeks ago. Tears stung her eyes. No, she would not think of that lovely, sensuous afternoon. Or of another afternoon a week later when a big-breasted redhead flailed around in desperate search of a sheet with a naked Kenny beside her.

"Stop it!" she said aloud. Blaine looked up at her. "I wasn't talking to you," she soothed. She stroked the dog's head. "Such a good girl."

Fog rolled in from the lake, coiling around her denim-clad legs. Minute by minute the fog wafted higher, first to her calves, then to her knees. Slowly the outside lights at the house became dimmer as she strolled in one direction, then turned and went in the other, covering only about fifty yards in either direction.

How many times had she walked this stretch of shoreline with Lily in the old days? Hundreds. And what had they talked of on those cool, secret, night-softened jaunts away from the prying eyes and ears of parents? Boyfriends, of course. Lily always had plenty. Natalie had only one, a gawky boy with acne who was president of the chess club and the math club. He was nice in a stuttering, awkward, perpetually embarrassed way, and she felt sorry for him because she was sure he would never amount to anything. Recently she heard he'd become a top executive with Microsoft.

She stopped as she realized that in her reverie, she'd walked farther than she'd intended. She'd completely lost sight of the house. "Time to go home," she said to the dog. But Blaine wasn't listening. The dog tensed, her hackles rising, then suddenly tugged at the leash so hard Natalie lost her grip. "Blaine!" she called as the dog bolted down the beach. "Blaine!" she yelled again, although the dog hadn't had time to learn her new name. She disappeared into the fog, barking.

Natalie stood still for a moment. She should head for home. The dog would return. Or would she? The St. John house wasn't home to her yet. She might get lost in the night, wander around, get hit by a car in the fog . . .

Thoughts of what she *should* do vanished to be replaced by the blind impulse to help the dog before it suffered a worse fate than being dumped in the woods. Natalie took a deep breath and ran in the direction Blaine had disappeared from.

She ran for about a hundred feet, then paused. Lake water, still cold at this time of year, licked the shore. She held her breath for a moment, listening. No sound of paws splashing into the water of Lake Erie. Then barking, fast and furious. Natalie started running again.

Up ahead loomed the remains of The Blue Lady Resort. The son of a railroad entrepreneur had bought two acres of prime lakefront land in 1921 on which to build a lavish hotel and dance pavilion. He'd named it The Blue Lady because of a local legend. Sailors claimed they saw a lady bathed in blue light standing on a rise—the rise where Ariel Saunders's house sat. They swore it was Ariel and the image meant good luck. After all, Ariel had saved two sailors and the captain the night the *Mercy* sank.

Local businessmen had predicted failure for The Blue Lady Resort, but the young entrepreneur laughed with the confidence of youth and money and lifelong privilege. And he was right. Season after season The Blue Lady flourished. Five years after it was built, it had been visited by countless movie stars, six governors, ten state senators, and the notorious dancer Isadora Duncan. After a riotous evening of drinking in the dance pavilion, F. Scott Fitzgerald and his wife Zelda waded into Lake Erie in evening clothes and nearly drowned before hotel staff rescued them. A president's niece married there. Houdini spent a week. Later years saw Lana Turner, Princess Grace of Monaco, and Thomas Wolfe.

By the late sixties, The Blue Lady no longer drew the rich and famous. It had become a tourist hotel of old-fashioned, shabby grandeur. Then in the summer of 1970 three murders took place in and around the resort. "The Blue Lady Murders" enjoyed short-lived notoriety and although police caught the killer, business abruptly ceased. The hotel closed and shortly afterward a fire completely destroyed it. Miraculously the dance pavilion survived. For over twenty years it had sat empty, a crumbling monument to long-dead nights of glamour and good times.

Natalie stopped a few yards from the pavilion, gasping for breath. She looked up at the clouds turned slightly yellow by the crescent moon. The slanted roof of the pavilion bore a film of dark mold. From photos she knew hundreds of tiny white lights had once decorated trees in front of the pavilion. But that had been long before she and Lily, as teenagers, occasionally broke into the pavilion to smoke forbidden cigarettes and collaborate on atrocious musical creations they hoped one day to play for adoring fans.

How blithely they had walked up the steps and in the darkness picked the padlock on the front door. She didn't remember ever worrying about getting caught.

A sharp bark came from the portico in front of the pavilion. Natalie strained her eyes and made out a dark shape. "Blaine!" she called again. Another bark. "Come here!" The dog sat firm. "Oh for heaven's sake," Natalie muttered, stalking toward the portico.

As she neared the dog, Blaine began to make an anxious chuffing sound. Natalie paused. "What is it, girl?" she asked as if the dog could answer. Blaine stood and turned in a circle, then scratched at the pavilion door.

Natalie slowly approached the dog. Blaine looked at her, then at the door. Her leash trailed out to the side and Natalie picked up the loop. Then she glanced at the door. A new padlock hung open.

Natalie stood still and listened. Nothing but the sound of distant wind chimes tinkling in the breeze. With the lock open, silence was not a good sign. Maybe someone was hiding inside, trying to be quiet.

Or maybe someone was hurt. Blaine scratched at the door again and this time it opened slightly. Someone had closed it so lightly the latch hadn't caught. Blaine pulled forward. Then Natalie heard a tiny, high-pitched cry.

Good lord, she thought. Could someone have crept into The Blue Lady just as she and Lily used to do and gotten hurt? After all, the place was a wreck.

Natalie started inside, then hesitated. There had been a murder last night. Maybe she should go home.

But if she simply walked away, deserting someone who might be hurt, she would never forgive herself. And she wasn't defenseless—she had her gun. She had to at least give the pavilion a cursory scan.

Inside, the dance room looked cavernous. "Is anyone here?" Natalie called. Not a sound. She flicked the beam of her flashlight around. Only a few tables sat on a dusty floor. "Do you need help?"

She stood still, barely breathing. Silence. Maybe she'd only heard a bird that had flown in when the door was open and been trapped. Time to go, she told herself, but she couldn't leave just yet. She hadn't seen this place for years.

She and the dog walked across the floor, Blaine's nails clicking on the wood. Beautiful wood, once highly varnished to facilitate the smooth moves of dancing feet. Grandmother St. John had told her all about The Blue Lady where she and Grandfather had spent so many hours of their youth. Natalie closed her eyes and in her mind the room filled with people, the men in formal black, the women in a rainbow of satin with gardenias pinned to their hair. She pictured her grandmother—an elegant woman with dark hair, flashing green eyes, and a taste for fine champagne—dancing to the sounds of big bands.

Natalie opened her eyes and the opulent scene vanished. Once again she stood in a big, empty room filled with dust and ghosts and the sound of dark, cold water lapping against rotting pilings.

A thud of her heart reminded her she was still winded from running. All the exertion after a raging panic attack had left her drained and she suddenly felt woozy. The room spun. She sat down on one of the chairs near a wall and drew a slow, deep breath. Then another. She frowned. What did she smell? Roses? Impossible. She wore no cologne. Imagination, she told herself. She'd been thinking of Grandmother who wore an expensive rose-based perfume. But no rose perfume lingered in the lonely pavilion. Only the memory of a beautiful woman dead over ten years.

A few more slow, deep breaths and she'd be ready to head for home, she thought, glancing around the room. Windows lined the pavilion, providing a panoramic view of the lake. She knew soft blue lanterns once hung around the structure. The slightest breeze sent them dancing, turning the lake water into a rippling sapphire fairyland. Now only a yellowish glow from the sodium vapor lamps in the parking lot of a nearby convenience store struggled through the filmy, flyblown windows.

She darted the flashlight beam around again. Overhead soared a high cathedral ceiling. In the center hung a huge, mirrored ball.

Natalie started. She'd never seen it except in pictures. In all the years she'd come here, it had been covered in burlap. Now the ball glittered, reflecting the room in a hundred prisms of polished glass. *Freshly* polished.

"Is anyone here?" she called again, this time her voice not so strong.

"Na-ta-lic?"

Natalie stiffened. Blaine's ears lifted and she turned her head to the right.

No one.

But it had been a woman's voice—young, clear, delicate. A familiar voice. The voice on the phone this afternoon.

No, no that couldn't be, Natalie told herself sternly. She was deeply shaken by the murder, by her dream, by the phone call, by the eerie atmosphere of this place. The voice existed only in her mind.

But Blaine's head had turned.

I must have made a sharp movement, Natalie thought. I startled her and she instinctively lifted her ears and turned her head.

"Na-ta-lie. I know you *hear* me. Can't you *see* me?"

Natalie jumped. Blaine lunged, but Natalie clutched the leash. If the dog found the voice, the dog would die. She didn't know how she knew, but she did.

"Who's there?" Natalie could not get an exact fix on the voice although Blaine pulled toward the end of the room with the dais where the bands had once played "String of Pearls" and "Take the A Train."

"Aren't you going to answer, Na-ta-lie?"

Blaine pulled harder. Natalie shot the flashlight beam around the room. Cobwebs. Dust. Mildew.

The highly polished mirrored ball.

"Who *are* you?" Natalie asked, trying to steady her voice. She wouldn't run. She sat against a wall. Someone might be trying to lure her into the open.

"I'm Tamara."

Natalie's breath came hard and fast. "Stop it!"

"Their throat is an open tomb."

"You said that earlier on the phone. What are you talking about?"

"Romans, chapter three. It's about bad people. So many bad people in the Bible!"

Freezing water seemed to run down Natalie's back. That voice. *So* like Tamara's, so lost, so sad. And so frightening. She felt as if she were spiraling down into another world—a world of shadows and voices and bone-chilling cold.

The voice rose. "I want you to be with me, Natalie. And you *will*. Even if I have to kill you."

As Natalie's fear intensified, so did her instinct for self-protection. In one smooth movement she lay the flashlight on her thigh, reached into her windbreaker pocket, and withdrew the gun.

"I'm armed," she said loudly, although her voice cracked. "Do you hear me? I have a gun and I *will* use it."

"You can't kill someone who's already dead."

A whisper of movement. Blaine growled, then barked ferociously. Natalie held tight to the leash as the flashlight dropped to the floor. She couldn't see, but she could hear something coming closer . . .

She aimed and fired.

6

1

Blaine hit the floor as the noise of the shot reverberated around the pavilion. For an instant Natalie feared her grip had wavered and she'd shot the dog. Then she looked at her hand. Level and steady. How many operations had she performed on animals? Steady hands were a necessity. Slowly Blaine stood up.

No answering cry of pain followed the gunshot. Somewhere a fog horn bellowed. Other than that there was only silence except for the loud breathing of Natalie and the dog.

"Are you still there?" Natalie asked with a quaver. "Are you hurt?"

Nothing. Blaine looked around, trembling. Natalie trembled, too, but she tried hard to control herself. "Are you *hurt*?"

Still no answer. Oh, God, what if there hadn't really been any danger? What if someone, maybe just a kid, had been playing a joke and she'd killed them? She should never have come in here.

She could not move. She was too frightened, too horrified at actually firing her gun at anything except a paper target. She sat motionless, the gun frozen in her hand as the seconds ticked by, trying to decide what to do. Then—

"Police!"

Her throat tightened, strangling a shriek. An urge to run madly from the pavilion took hold of her, but immediately she quelled it. She wasn't a criminal. She hadn't done anything wrong.

Except maybe kill someone.

"Drop your weapon! We're coming in!"

Natalie placed her gun on the table, pushed it an arm's length away, and sat rigidly in her chair as the front door opened. A man walked in, gun drawn. He shone his large flashlight around the room, then directly into her face. She squinted but didn't dare raise a hand to shield her eyes. "I put down my gun and I'm holding onto the dog," she called. "Please don't shoot."

A pause. Then: "Dr. St. John?"

She recognized his voice. "Sheriff Meredith."

"Who was shooting?"

"I was. Only once."

"*You!* What's going on?"

"Please take the light out of my eyes, but don't lower your gun. Someone is in here. Someone threatened to kill me.

The light shifted slightly. Blaine remained tensed and growled steadily. Natalie put a hand on her head to calm her. "Who is trying to kill you?" the sheriff asked.

"I don't know. There was a woman's voice. It seemed to be coming from the band area. I couldn't see anyone, though." She hesitated. "She said she was Tamara."

"Tamara? Tamara Hunt?"

That's it, Natalie said to herself. He thinks I'm drunk or crazy. "She *said* she was Tamara. Then I heard someone coming toward me and I fired."

"I see." The sheriff played the flashlight around the room, but whoever it had been was gone. Natalie knew that even before he searched the band area and backstage. "Back door is open," he said when he finally returned to her. "You didn't come in that way, did you?"

"No. I came in the front door. The padlock was open."

"So you just strolled in."

"I thought someone might be hurt."

"Come out to the car with me."

Natalie followed meekly. He'd yelled, "*We're* coming in," but he was alone. Clearly he didn't want whoever was inside to know he had no backup. In the patrol car she told him everything that had happened. When she finished, he was silent for a moment, staring straight ahead at The Blue Lady. Finally he said, "Do you know how dangerous it was for you to come here in the middle of the night?"

"I do now."

"But not before?"

"I had my dog. And my gun."

"I assume you have a permit for the gun."

"Absolutely," she said virtuously.

"But not a permit to carry."

"Well . . . uh . . . no. But I *have* completed a course in marksmanship and gun safety and I finished with flying colors."

"I'm thrilled for you," he said dryly. "You still broke the law."

"Are you going to arrest me?"

"I'm thinking about it."

Natalie's confidence fell further. Was carrying a weapon without a permit a felony or a misdemeanor? What was the sentence? Was she going to end up in jail because of her stupid night stroll?

"Look, Sheriff, I told you I wanted to walk but only in front of my house. Then the dog started barking and ran away. I followed her. She came to the dance pavilion."

"Why the pavilion?"

"I don't know. Maybe she was chasing whoever was inside. Maybe that person had been close to me—I couldn't see in the fog—then ran to the pavilion when the dog started barking."

"The doors were unlocked. Someone didn't decide to hide in there on the spur of the moment," the sheriff said slowly. "The whole thing could have been a set-up to lead you there."

"I guess you're right," Natalie said weakly, horrified by her close call.

"So the dog ran off, you went in hot pursuit, and then you charged into a deserted building. And then Tamara spoke to you."

"I did not *charge* into the building. I went in cautiously thinking maybe someone was inside and injured," she repeated. "And I told you the person *said* she was Tamara. I didn't say it *was*

Tamara. I'm not a lunatic." He gave her a doubtful look that said he wasn't too sure. "Actually, the voice was slightly different than Tam's. It was more breathy. A little more dramatic." She hesitated. "I got a call this afternoon, supposedly from Tamara. I'm sure it was the same person."

"A call?"

"Yes. She talked about their mouth being an open tomb."

"What the hell does that mean?"

"I don't know. It's something from the Bible. Romans, Chapter Three. She just told me that inside."

"I thought she said it on the phone."

"She said it *again* inside."

"Do you have any idea who made that call?"

"No. We don't have caller I.D. After she hung up I tried star-six-nine but was told that number was not receiving calls."

"Whoever called you has call block."

"Probably. Anyway, tonight she talked about wanting me to be with her even if she had to kill me to do it. It was dark. I couldn't really see, but I could hear someone coming toward me. I was frightened, so I fired the gun."

"You could have *killed* someone!"

"I didn't aim directly at the voice. I wasn't *trying* to kill anyone. Someone was threatening to kill *me*. I was only trying to scare them away, and I guess I did."

"I was driving by when the guy who owns the convenience store flagged me down and said he'd heard gunfire. As I pulled up, I saw something coming from around the back. It was gone by the time I got out of the car." He gave her a hard look. "You were incredibly careless entering a place like the pavilion the night after a murder. And you were equally reckless with your gun."

"I know," Natalie said humbly. "I won't do it again."

"You sound like you're apologizing for a traffic violation."

"Well, how am I supposed to sound?" Natalie flared. "Do you want me to fly into hysterics? Beg? Throw my gun into Lake Erie?"

"Hysterics and begging would be okay, but there's no sense in wasting a perfectly good gun," he said equably.

He's softening, Natalie thought in relief. "Are you going to arrest me?" she asked again.

He thought for a few moments. "No. A night in jail might do you some good, take some of that recklessness out of you, but I'm going to do something foolish. I'm just going to drive you home."

Relief rushed through her. "Are you going to take the gun?"

His eyes narrowed slightly and she almost squirmed under his gaze. "I'll probably regret this, but I'll let you keep it if you promise to act more responsibly in the future. I want you to unload it, put it away, and *don't* carry it around with you."

"I will and I won't." He looked at her. "I will unload it and put it away and I won't carry it around. Thank you."

"Don't thank me," he said, turning on the ignition. "If you *were* lured into the building, I have a bad feeling you might need that gun in the future."

II
MONDAY MORNING

"You know I'm gonna get killed, don't you? It's almost one-thirty. In the *morning*!"

"So?"

"So my dad's the *sheriff*, for Pete's sake. If he finds out I'm sneaking around at night with a boy . . ."

Jimmy Jenkins turned indignantly. "So what? I'm not your *boyfriend*. You're only eleven, Paige."

"Yeah, I'm eleven and it's late. I didn't know it was so far to this place."

"What do you mean you didn't know? You've been to my house and I told you Tamara Hunt got murdered almost right across the street."

"And down a dirt road. You didn't talk about the dirt road."

Actually Paige Meredith was frightened but she didn't want

Jimmy to know it. She wanted him to be her boyfriend, even if he was a year older than she, and that was a lot to hope for. Still, there was always a chance. Unless he thought she was just a scared little kid.

He'd bicycled at top speed to her house this afternoon to inform her of the murder, which was sad and awful and absolutely thrilling to Paige, who was bored silly this summer stuck home with Mrs. Collins. Mrs. Collins was nice and meant well, but she was old—at least fifty—and she talked constantly about her baby grandchildren and recipes. Paige thought the woman was duller than dull, although she always tried to act interested in her stories. Her mother had taught her to be polite.

Her mother wouldn't like what she was doing right now, Paige thought as she and Jimmy crept down the dirt road, walking their bikes because of all the ruts and holes. Daddy had come home very late and Mrs. Collins had been all snippy. After she left, Daddy went straight to bed.

Jimmy had suggested earlier today that they sneak out tonight to see where Mrs. Hunt got murdered. It wouldn't be the first time they'd sneaked out, but never for anything so *important* as visiting a murder site. When Jimmy came back long after Daddy had gone to sleep and conditions were perfect, she couldn't refuse him without looking like a wimp. She had put her big doll in her bed, pulled up the quilt until only the doll's auburn hair— the same color as her own—showed on the pillow, and crawled out the window onto a limb of an oak tree and skimmed down slick as a cat. Jimmy looked proud of her and her heart had beaten a little faster. His approval was worth the minor risk that she might get caught. It was even worth knowing her mother was frowning in disapproval somewhere in Heaven.

Now she was beginning to have doubts. The night was darker than the last time she and Jimmy had ventured out. Of course then there had been a full moon and now there was only a crescent slice that looked really pretty as it glowed through a fog coming in off the lake, but it didn't put out a lot of light. There were only a few stars, too. And somewhere an owl was hooting.

"The Egyptians believed the owl meant death," Paige said. Jimmy stopped in his tracks. "*What?*"

Paige felt silly. She hated it when things like that popped out of her mouth. "I read it."

"You read too much," Jimmy declared.

"But it makes sense. About the owl, I mean," Paige said defensively. "Somebody died here and now an owl is hooting."

"Owls always hoot. It's all they know how to do."

"I still think it's neat."

Jimmy snorted. "I think it's dumb."

Paige was crushed until the next time the owl hooted and Jimmy looked around uneasily. She smiled in satisfaction. He took her more seriously than he pretended.

"Okay, here we are," Jimmy said. They both halted, staring wide-eyed at the mangled branch that had lain on Tamara Hunt's body. Yellow tape surrounded the area.

"That's crime-scene tape," Jimmy informed her.

"I know."

"We can't go past it. We might mess up important evidence."

"I *know*. Gee, Jimmy, my dad is a cop." Which was, Paige also knew, why Jimmy had befriended her even though she was younger and a girl. His dream was to become a detective like that guy on his favorite show, *Street Life*, Eddie Salvatore. Jimmy told Paige that Eddie was played by an actor named Paul Fiori who used to be married to some woman who lived right here in *this very town*! Jimmy was obsessed with Eddie Salvatore. Paige told him her dad said if any detective acted like Salvatore—always bossing around the other detectives, going off on hunches when his lieutenant ordered him not to—he'd get fired. "No way," Jimmy argued staunchly. "Eddie Salvatore is *always* right." Paige would roll her eyes, but she still thought Jimmy was basically wonderful.

Jimmy had brought a flashlight and bounced the beam around the area. "I see blood."

"Maybe it's blood. I'm not sure. Anything else?"

"Well . . . no actual clues. But I've got a theory."

Jimmy almost always had a theory. "What is it?"

"I think the murderer is hiding in Ariel Saunders's house."

"That big spooky house you're always talking about?"

"Yeah. The one at the end of this road. Let's go check it out."

"Wait a minute," Paige stalled. "What makes you think the murderer is hiding in that house?"

"I've got a *hunch*."

Oh, no. Jimmy was being Eddie Salvatore again. "How did you get your hunch?"

"Hunches can't be explained," Jimmy said loftily. "They just *are*." Which meant he had no idea what he was talking about, Paige thought. "You coming?"

"We've been gone an awful long time."

"You're right. I guess little girls should be home in bed."

"I am *not* a little girl," Paige answered hotly. "Everyone says I'm mature for my age."

"Whatever. You play it safe and run home. *I'm* gonna investigate."

He began guiding his bicycle around the crime-scene tape. Paige hesitated. It was *late*. It was *dark*. There was a *murderer* on the loose.

And there was Jimmy who looked kind of like Angel on *Buffy the Vampire Slayer*. Gosh, life was hard when you were eleven and had a strict father and a better-than-cute potential boyfriend who thought he was tough and grown-up.

"Okay, I'll come."

"Let's leave our bikes here. We can move faster without them."

They hid their bicycles in tall grass beside the road. Now that they were out of sight of other houses, Jimmy left the flashlight on. They walked in silence for a few moments. Somewhere close by frogs croaked and a dog barked.

"Is that the dog you said was hanging around out here with the body?" Paige asked.

"No, it's Old Man Harker's basset hound Malcolm. I think that woman took the other dog. The one I told you was with Tamara's sister. Your dad called her Dr. St. John."

"Was she pretty?" Paige asked, wondering if her dad had been talking to the woman because she was pretty. She wasn't sure how she'd feel about that.

"I don't know if she was pretty. She was older, but not as old as my mom. Maybe the same age as Tamara."

Paige heard the little catch in his voice when he said *Tamara*. She also thought he looked like he'd been crying when he came to her house earlier to tell her about the murdered woman. She considered being jealous, but Jimmy couldn't possibly have thought of Mrs. Hunt as a girlfriend. He'd just liked her and he was sad that she was dead.

"Hey, there's the house!" Jimmy said.

Paige frowned. She couldn't see much except for a hulking shape in the dull moonlight. "What's so great about this place?"

"It's over two hundred years old for one thing. And there was a shipwreck right down the beach and Ariel saved three guys including Zebediah Winthrop, the captain. He was her *lover*. Anyway, the place is really big and there's this really cool little walkway that goes all around the roof—"

"A widow's walk!"

"Yeah. Ariel was up there watching for Zebediah when she saw the shipwreck. It's an awesome house, but the woman who owns it now is letting it fall apart and Ariel's mad so she's coming back to haunt it."

Paige grinned. "You believe this place is haunted by a *ghost*?"

"No, not me!" Jimmy answered quickly. "But people are scared of it so they stay away. That makes it the perfect place for a murderer to hide out. And just look how close it is to the Hunt house. Tamara must have come out for a walk and—" He drew a finger across his throat, made a slashing sound and a horrible face.

Paige cringed. "Why would somebody kill her?"

"Murderers don't need reasons," Jimmy explained in a worldly-wise tone. "They just enjoy murdering people. Take your serial killers like . . . um . . . Ted Bundy who killed *hundreds* of girls and Jeffrey something who cut off people's heads and kept them in jars so they'd never leave him!"

Paige's eyes flew wide. "And you think somebody like that is in Ariel's house?"

"Maybe. And I'm gonna catch him."

"*You* are?" Paige asked incredulously. "Jimmy, you're twelve!"

"I can still find a killer. I'd probably be even better at it than the police because nobody would ever suspect me. They'd think I was just a dumb kid." Paige frowned. This *was* pretty good reasoning. "Now are you gonna help or are you gonna stand here and act like a baby?"

"I'll help," Paige said resignedly, fearing that if she didn't add her own common sense to this project, disaster could result. Jimmy might get murdered, too. She shuddered at the thought. Losing Jimmy would be like seeing a shining star blink out of the sky forever. "What do we do now?"

"Stakeout."

"But that could take *hours*. I can only stay for a little while."

"Fair enough. Let's get closer. We'll hide behind those bushes in front of the house."

Jimmy darted across the ragged lawn of the Saunders house, Paige hot on his heels. They dived behind the bushes, both panting. "Jimmy," she hissed, "what if the killer comes out? We don't have a gun or knife or *anything*."

Jimmy blinked at her for a moment. Apparently he hadn't considered this wrinkle in his plan. "Well ... uh ... we'll just have to make sure he doesn't see us. For now."

"What do you mean *for now*?"

"Shhh!"

Paige subsided unhappily. She had a bad feeling about this. A very bad feeling.

She peered between the bushes, trying to see the house more clearly. She couldn't. Even the crescent moon had vanished behind a drifting cloud. Shadows pooled around Ariel Saunders's long-deserted home. Jimmy said she haunted it. *If* Paige believed in ghosts, this would certainly be the place for one. The big, old, musty house loomed over them, and Paige had the persistent feeling of being watched.

Something screeched not far away. She nearly leaped from behind the bushes. Jimmy restrained her. "That owl got a mouse," he whispered.

"I told you owls mean death."

They sat quietly on the ground for what seemed like an hour. When Paige looked at the luminous hands of her watch, though, she saw that it had only been fifteen minutes. Time seemed suspended. She smacked at a mosquito. Another bite to add to the five others that itched maddeningly. And she needed the bathroom. Bad.

Horror shot through her. What if her bladder gave way and she wet her pants in front of Jimmy? She'd *die*. Right on the spot her heart would stop from pure mortification and she'd keel over. Paige pictured herself lying pale and motionless on the dew-laden grass, her hair spread in a halo around her head, her white eyelids tragically shut forever . . . and a big wet circle on her jeans.

"Jimmy, I have to go home."

"*Now?*"

"Yes, now." She couldn't tell him the truth. "If I get caught, I'll never be able to sneak out again—"

The sound of electric guitars tore through the black tunnel of night. Jimmy and Paige both jumped. Drumbeats seemed to shake the ground. Their gazes met. Music! *Rock* music crashed inside Ariel Saunders's dark, deserted wreck of a house.

Paige clutched Jimmy's arm as a young male voice sang with rock's intensity:

> *When night falls*
> *And the shadows call*
> *He hovers in the dark*
> *Hungering for your heart.*
> *Don't close your eyes*
> *He's watching for you.*

Paige's grip on Jimmy's arm tightened. "Let's go," she quavered as the air vibrated around them.

> *He longs to take your soul*
> *And put it in the hole*
> *Deep down inside*
> *Where now the devil hides.*
> *Don't close your eyes . . .*

Don't close your eyes? All Paige wanted to do was close her eyes. But she didn't. She stared, mesmerized, as light suddenly flared from a window beside the door. It glowed and flickered. Candlelight.

She began to shiver. She didn't need the bathroom anymore. She just wanted to be someplace else, anyplace else. She looked at Jimmy, who stared intensely at the light, his lips pressed together in a tight line of fear and excitement.

Piercing electric guitar chords raced frantically up and down the scale, pulsating through the warm summer night, striking deep within Paige's stomach. The young man sang feelingly, menacingly, seeming to be right next to her, singing only to Paige:

> *And you try to escape*
> *From the one who wears the cape*
> *But he's stealthy as a cat*
> *And silent as a bat.*

Silent as a bat? Paige looked nervously over her shoulder. Nothing she could see, but she *felt* something. "Jimmy, what'll we do?" she almost sobbed.

Jimmy seemed frozen in place. His face was rigid as the song started again.

The light grew brighter, flickering from the windows. Paige knew another candle had been lit. *More* light. Another candle. What was this? Some kind of ceremony? Maybe a *pagan* ceremony? A Satanic ritual? The music grew even louder. Couldn't the whole world hear it? Paige wondered as it shook and shuddered its way up to the black sky. Would that loving but also fearsome God everyone talked about now retaliate, sending down a lightning bolt, destroying the house and everything around it, including her and Jimmy?

> *Don't close your eyes,*
> *He's reaching for you . . .*

The night. The mist. The music. The dancing candlelight. Paige's chest tightened. Each breath was an effort. She'd been worried about what her mother would think of her sneaking around at night. Her mother was a spirit now. They said this place was haunted but it couldn't be her mother's spirit inside. Meagan Meredith wouldn't scare her little girl this much, even if she were angry with Paige for sneaking out. Could it be Ariel? Could a furious Ariel Saunders be laying claim to her house invaded by two kids? The scene began to swirl and Paige shut her eyes tight, trying to stop the spinning. If she fainted she couldn't get away from this awful place.

"I'm gonna look in the window."

Paige's eyes snapped open. "No!" she rasped.

"I *have* to, Paige. The killer's inside."

"Don't be crazy!" Paige said frantically, but Jimmy looked determined. She forced down her fear. This was getting serious and even if her adored Jimmy wanted to live in a fantasy world, she didn't and she wouldn't let him, either.

"Jimmy, *no!*" she said firmly. "You could get killed—"

The music shot a notch higher. The shadows around the house shifted and ebbed in the candle flames, seeming to dance along with the heart-thumping music. The night was chilly but sweat trickled down Paige's sides and dampened the nape of her neck. "Jimmy, I'm *going*. You're going too if I have to drag you—"

The front door flew open, slamming into the side of the house so hard Paige thought she heard wood splintering. The music soared. A hulking shape appeared in silhouette against the candlelight. Paige stopped breathing as a scream rose in her throat. The shape dipped and drifted toward them, snickering, muttering, "Don't close your eyes . . . He's reaching for you . . ."

Closer.

Closer .

A shadow fell over them. Paige and Jimmy screamed simultaneously. Paige's bladder let go as they leaped from behind the bushes and ran blindly from the terrible throbbing house, ran heedless of grasping vines and wet grass and animal holes, ran until they felt as if their hearts would burst.

And somewhere in the distance an owl hooted . . .

7

I

MONDAY MORNING

Music. Mist. A hulking, dancing figure swooping down on them!

Paige screamed and jerked upward. Her father caught her in his big, hard arms. "Just a nightmare, honey."

Paige took a deep breath and blinked several times. Yes, here she was in her twin bed with the pretty peach-and-green puffy quilt, her lacy curtains, her stuffed animal collection, her black-and-white cat Ripley lying by her side studying her with calm, green eyes.

"I came in because you were whimpering in your sleep. What were you dreaming?" Nick Meredith asked.

"It was all mixed up," Paige lied. "But it was scary. Something about Mrs. Hunt's murder." Paige hated lying to her father. "I dreamed about the person who killed that poor woman. So *awful!*" she added, imitating Mrs. Collins's voice when she'd spent the afternoon calling her friends to tell them about the murder.

"I see," Nick said slowly. "In your dream did you see that person?"

"No. Just somebody big and mean." Who likes candlelight and loud rock music, she thought with a shudder. "Did you catch him yet, Daddy?"

"No, but I will." Nick smiled and kissed Paige on the forehead. "You get ready for school, kid."

"Daddy, it's *summer.*" Boy, he *was* tired, Paige thought. "Jimmy and I might hang out."

"Doesn't he know any guys?" Nick asked querulously.

"Yeah, but they swim all day. Or play baseball. Jimmy is more intellectual."

Her father's lips twitched. "Intellectual, huh? I never thought of Jimmy Jenkins as intellectual."

"Oh, but he is, Daddy. He's *really* smart."

"I'd still like to see you play with Barbie dolls for a change."

"I *hate* Barbie dolls!"

"Don't the other girls play with them?"

"I guess, but I don't have any friends that are girls."

"Make some."

Mrs. Collins hovered in the doorway. "I know some lovely young girls I could introduce her to."

Wonderful, Paige thought. If Mrs. Collins liked them, they'd probably be a dull as she was. They'd want to have tea parties rather than solve murders.

"Hey, Dad," Paige said quickly to change the subject, "Jimmy said out where Mrs. Hunt got killed yesterday there was a woman with black hair."

"Yes." Nick stood up, straightening his tie. "Natalie St. John. Her father is Andrew St. John who took out your tonsils in February."

"Pretty?"

"Andrew St. John? Not especially."

"Daddy! I mean his daughter. Is she pretty?"

"I guess. I really didn't notice."

Too casual, Paige observed. He'd noticed *and* he thought she was pretty. She didn't like thinking of him with any woman except her mother, but she didn't want him to be lonely, either. And she could tell he was really lonely in spite of her efforts to entertain him. "Jimmy said she probably took that lost dog home with her."

"She did. She's a veterinarian."

Paige's interest soared. "She likes animals!"

"Just like another young lady I know." He looked at the shining black-and-white cat. "I think Ripley is getting fat."

"Daddy, you'll hurt his feelings!"

"He looks devastated."

"If you think he's too fat, maybe he should go see Natalie St. John."

"She's not in practice here. Besides, there is nothing wrong with the cat except a few extra pounds."

"And he does have that annoying habit of jumping off the newel post on the stairs," Mrs. Collins put in. "He startles the life out of me when he comes springing out of nowhere."

"See, Daddy, that proves he's not too fat or he couldn't jump so well. But he does scratch his ears a lot." Paige assumed a distressed look. "I'm worried."

"You're *curious*, Paige Meredith," Nick laughed. "For some reason you want to get a look at Natalie St. John." He shrugged. "If I see her, I'll ask her about checking out Ripley. She'll probably say no."

"Not if she's nice she won't," Paige muttered to Ripley when her father left the room. She lovingly touched the small black spot on the end of his pink nose. "That's how we'll know if she might be the right girl for Daddy."

After Nick went to headquarters and Mrs. Collins drifted back downstairs to her knitting and her morning talk shows, the phone rang. Paige grabbed up her extension before Mrs. Collins could rouse herself from the couch. It was Jimmy. "Get in trouble?" he asked abruptly.

"No."

"Told you. Did you tell your dad what we saw at the Saunders house?"

"Are you kidding? First I'd get grounded for life because of sneaking out and going to that place. Then he'd lock me up for being crazy. He'd never believe what we saw last night. No grownup would."

"That's why I've got another plan."

Paige groaned inwardly. Jimmy and his plans. "What *now*?"

"We go back—"

"Go *back*! Are you completely nuts?"

"Let me finish. We go back with a camera! A Polaroid so we don't have to wait for the film to be developed. We take a picture of that thing in the house. Then we show your dad."

"A picture?"

"It's the only way to get proof."

Paige thought, gnawing her lower lip. "Well, it would be proof, but I don't know about going *back* there . . ."

"Look, I know you're scared because you're a girl—"

"I'm *not* scared because I'm a girl! I'm not scared at all!"

"Okay, okay, don't wet your pants." Paige caught her breath. Had he seen her wet jeans last night after all? No. It was just an expression. "So you're not scared," Jimmy went on. "Fine. You just don't want to get caught, so I'll take my dad's camera and say I was there all by myself. I won't even *mention* you. That way you can be in on the action without getting in trouble."

"You'd do that for me?" Paige asked.

"Yeah. We're partners. Partners cover for each other."

Paige was thrilled. Jimmy thought of her as his *partner*? She was frightened to go back out to Ariel Saunders's house, terrified of seeing that awful creature again, but if she didn't, Jimmy might no longer think of her as his partner. That was even worse than being scared silly.

"So are you coming with me?" Jimmy asked.

"Of course," she answered with cool assurance she didn't feel.

"Good, because we have to do *something*," he said dramatically. "There's a killer in that house, a *madman*, and we're the only ones who know about it."

II

Seven o'clock the previous evening Natalie finally had called Lily at Oliver's house. "Natalie, my sister was *murdered*," Lily had wailed. "Her throat was cut. And that note—the one about the throats and an open tomb—the sheriff thinks that was left on her body by the killer. But you knew that, didn't you? That's why you took the note from me. You *knew* my sister had been murdered. How?"

"I didn't know, I just suspected. How are things at home?"

"It's so strange around here," Lily had said. "Dad is alternately raging or morose. And of course we've been graced with the presence of Viveca and Alison. I should be grateful. Viveca has a calming effect on Dad, but her syrupy concern drives *me* up the wall. And Alison! I don't know how someone manages to be so creepy by doing so little. If Dad marries Viveca and Alison Cosgrove becomes my *stepsister*—"

"Don't worry about that now."

"I can't help it." Lily's voice raced and shook. "She is just madly in love with Warren. Or whatever she thinks love is. She looks like she wants to tear off his clothes every time she glances at him. It's sickening. I used to tell Tam that Alison was fixated on Warren, but Tam didn't believe me. At least she pretended not to believe me. Even her innocent eyes couldn't have missed Alison nearly drooling over Warren now, though. And don't tell me I'm imagining things!"

"I wasn't going to say anything. Good heavens, Lily, don't get mad at *me* because you don't like Viveca and Alison."

"I'm not. I just wish they'd go home. For good."

"How's Warren doing?"

Lily had drawn a fresh breath and swept on at breakneck speed. "He seems lost but not out of shock or grief. It's like he's feeling his way along, deciding how he should act based on *our* reactions. It isn't normal, Nat! Something is wrong where he's concerned. His wife has been murdered, for God's sake, and he just watches my father like a little boy waiting to get yelled at!" She had paused. "If you ask me, it's guilt."

"Guilt for what?"

"That's the question. Guilt for not loving my sister? Or guilt for something worse? Nat, maybe *he* murdered her!"

Lily had gotten on a dangerous track. Natalie changed directions. "Do you need any help tomorrow? I know Warren will handle the funeral arrangements—"

"No, he won't!" Lily had burst out. "He said he'd leave everything up to Dad and me because we'd do a better job. Better job my ass! The creep just doesn't want to be bothered!"

"Lily, you're really wired," Natalie had said gently. "I'm having my father phone in a prescription for tranquilizers. They'll be delivered and you *will* take one."

"I don't want—"

"I don't care what you want. You sound like you're going to start screaming."

"My *sister* has been *murdered*!"

"I know. I'm not criticizing you. I'm just saying you're falling apart. I want you to take a tranquilizer and try to get some sleep," Natalie had said firmly. "I'll do anything I can to help you with the funeral arrangements tomorrow. Deal?"

"Okay, deal," Lily had said resignedly. "Thank you, Natalie."

After she hung up, Natalie had thought of how strong, how assured she'd sounded. But she didn't feel strong and assured. She was shaken and afraid she wouldn't be the help Lily needed so desperately.

After the call had come her dream, her panic attack, and her frightening trip to The Blue Lady pavilion. After Nick Meredith rescued her, then lectured her, he had dropped her off at her house, and she'd hoped her father would not be awake. As she tiptoed down the hall, she'd heard him snoring. Thank God. She could never explain this exploit to him. She had immediately unloaded her gun and locked it back in the suitcase. Then she spent the rest of the night awake, coldly shaken by her encounter with someone claiming to be Tam, someone saying they wanted to kill her. What in the world was going on? Who would impersonate Tamara? Who would continue taunting her knowing she was armed?

The next morning Lily called at nine. Natalie had not gotten a moment's sleep. "Still want to help me today?" Lily asked.

"Certainly." Natalie tried to sound alert and as chipper as possible although her eyelids felt heavy. "What do you need for me to do?"

"Well, there's the matter of Tam's clothes. Will you go with me to her house and help me pick out an outfit for burial? And I need to go to the florist to select a blanket for the coffin—" Her voice broke.

"Lily—"

"I'm okay. I stayed at Dad's last night. The tranquilizer helped. I got a little sleep." She took a deep breath. "I left my car with you so would you mind picking me up?"

"Actually, I can't drive a four-speed. I left your car at Tamara's and Sheriff Meredith drove me home. I'll pick you up, then you can get your car at Tam's."

Lily emerged from the Peyton home before Natalie could even honk the horn. When she got in the car, she didn't look like the same lovely, jaunty woman who had picked up Natalie for lunch less than twenty-four hours earlier. Her blond hair hung sleep-flat, her skin was pale, and her eyelids were puffy from crying. She wore jeans and a light shell-pink sweater but no makeup and no jewelry.

Lily didn't need any more worries. "You told me you slept, but you don't look like it," Natalie said gently.

"I slept a couple of hours near morning. I remember it was just starting to get light. Dad stayed up all night listening to music. 'Clair de Lune' again and again. It was Tam's favorite song. She used to ice skate to it when we were kids." She scrutinized Natalie. "You're not looking so well yourself."

Natalie longed to tell Lily about what happened at The Blue Lady. Even during the years when they'd lived in different towns, she'd always called Lily to discuss anything exciting or upsetting. But what could she possibly say? "I went to the pavilion last night and your dead sister talked to me. Actually, she quoted the Bible and told me she wanted me to be *with* her"?

"God, Nat, what's going through your mind?" Lily asked sharply. "The look on your face . . . What's happened?"

"Nothing. I'm just tired."

"You're more than tired. You look scared to death."

She'd been terrified last night and she was still frightened

today, but she couldn't tell Lily the truth. Sharing would be a
relief for her, but knowing someone was pretending to be her
murdered sister would be horrifying to Lily. Natalie wouldn't
put her through more suffering. "Yesterday was a big shock for
me, too, and I couldn't sleep so I tried to calm myself down with
alcohol. I drank too much," she lied. "I felt sick for a moment,
but I'm okay now." Lily continued to stare at her skeptically and
she changed the subject. "Are you sure Warren won't mind us
taking over the funeral arrangements?"

"I *told* you—"

"I know. You think he doesn't give a damn."

"When you see him, you'll know what I mean."

But Lily looked surprised when they reached the house.
Warren opened the door, a hollow-eyed figure wearing an old
sweatshirt and a day's growth of beard. He held a coffee mug.
The coffee smelled like espresso. Warren smelled like gin.
Clearly he'd put in a hard night.

"Lily, Natalie," he said expressionlessly, his shadowed eyes
bloodshot. "Thank you for coming to help with Tamara's
clothes. I wouldn't have the faintest idea what she should wear.
Would you two like some coffee?"

"I would." Natalie didn't really want coffee but preparing a
cup for her would send Warren out of the room. When he disappeared into the kitchen, she turned to Lily. "He looks fairly bad
to me, Lily."

"Obviously he didn't sleep. And he drank too much, also. But
I still don't believe he's feeling real grief."

"Lily the mind reader."

"Well, can't you see that he doesn't care?"

"No."

"You don't know him as well as I do."

Natalie sighed. "Lily, please, just don't give him a hard time
today. Tamara wouldn't want you to."

"I'd intended to say as little as possible to the jerk."

Warren reappeared with the coffee and Lily and Natalie went
directly upstairs to the master bedroom. A few delicate floral

watercolors hung on the creamy white walls and a quilt with a wildflower pattern in pink, peach, yellow, and green covered the king-sized bed. "Beautiful quilt, isn't it?" Lily said almost to herself. "Tam made it, of course. She was so much more artistic than I am."

"You got the business sense." Natalie opened the closet door. "And the fashion sense. Help me pick out an outfit."

Tamara's wardrobe bore little resemblance to Lily's. All her summer clothes were muted tones, her winter in gray, black, or navy blue. "My sister didn't own one piece of red clothing," Lily said, shaking her head slowly. "Mom's influence. She wanted Tam and me to look like little nuns. Tam, as always, wanted to please. I, as always, rebelled."

"You each wore what was right for your personality."

Lily thumped down on the bed. "Damn it, Natalie, will you stop sounding so reasonable and placid? I'm not going to fly into a million pieces if you show a little emotion. I *am* going to jump up and down and scream if you don't."

Natalie turned away from the closet. "I'm sorry if I'm annoying you. I don't know how to act. I don't want to do anything to make things worse for you."

"You couldn't possibly make things worse except by acting like some impassive woman I don't know. I need my good old emotional, expressive Natalie right now."

"Okay. I'll be emotional and expressive. I won't be old."

Lily grinned. "That's more like it." She screwed up her face. "How about that powder-blue suit by your right hand? I know it doesn't really matter because the casket will be closed given the state of her face, but she liked that suit. We'll put Mom's pearls with it."

Natalie hesitated. "The suit is perfect, but the pearls? They were a birthday present from your father and they're worth a fortune."

"I took Mom's diamond earrings. The pearls are Tam's."

"Your mother wanted one of you to *wear* the pearls. She wouldn't have liked for them to be buried forever."

"Do you have a direct line to the afterlife?" Lily asked half humorously. "First you know Tam wants me to be kind to Warren. Now you know Mom wants me to have Tam's pearls. Did you stay up all night communing with the dead?"

"Lily!" Warren said severely from the doorway. "Have a little respect for your sister. This is no time for jokes."

"It's exactly the time for jokes," Lily snapped. "If we don't laugh, we'll cry." She paused. "At least some of us will."

Warren's eyes narrowed. "And what does that mean?"

"Nothing," Natalie intervened. "Could you call the florist and tell her we'll be there soon? I don't suppose you want to go with us, do you?"

"No. I don't know anything about flowers. I don't even like them. I think we should ask for donations to the suicide hotline in lieu of flowers."

"Tam *loved* flowers and she didn't give a damn about the suicide hotline," Lily fired back.

Warren looked incensed. "There you go, giving all the orders as usual. You see, Natalie, this is why I'm not getting involved in the funeral arrangements." He turned and stalked downstairs.

"Lily, Tamara *organized* the suicide hotline," Natalie said.

"She only organized it to please Warren. Writing grant applications, making public pleas for donations, was pure misery for her. Besides, *I* want her to have flowers," Lily fumed. "Warren just wants to stick her in the ground as quickly and cheaply as possible." Good Lord, Natalie thought. Were all funerals so fraught with familial antagonism?

"Okay, you can fill the funeral home to the roof with flowers, but please *try* to get along with Warren for the next few days."

"No. I hate him."

"Lily, you sound like a petulant five-year-old."

Lily ignored her and Natalie could have been angry with her if she hadn't known the petulance was simply a manifestation of unbearable grief. While Lily seethed on the bed, Natalie finished assembling clothing for Tamara, insisting that the pearls be excluded. She placed everything in a shopping bag.

Lily took one last look around the room. Her gaze lingered on a silver-framed wedding picture of Tamara and Warren. In the photo Tamara looked young, lovely, and unsure of herself. Warren smirked—impeccably handsome and self-satisfied. "It was a beautiful wedding," she said softly. "Tam thought Warren was so wonderful then."

"She thought Warren was wonderful until the day she died," Natalie said softly. "She was happy, Lily. Warren did *not* make her miserable."

"I guess you're right. I don't like him and I don't trust him, but Tam loved him. I just hope he was worth her love."

The phone rang once. Warren must have picked it up. "We're ready to go," Natalie said. "They'll be expecting us at the florist's."

She descended the stairs first. The lush carpet muffled her footsteps. When she reached the bottom, she saw Warren sitting in an armchair with the phone receiver in his hand. His head was slightly lowered, his face turned away from the stairs. "I *can't*. Not today. Not for several days," he said. Something in his tone made Natalie freeze. After a brief pause he went on. "I don't want you to come to the funeral. You weren't friends with Tamara. It might look suspicious." Silence. "I need to see you, too, but—" Silence again, then a sigh. "All right. Tonight." He glanced up and saw Natalie. A burgundy stain bloomed across his face. "I must go now," he said formally. "Thank you for your condolences."

After he hung up, Natalie glanced behind her. Lily stood there, rigid, her hazel eyes simmering with hatred.

III

Nick Meredith swiveled his desk chair around and looked out the office window. Another beautiful, crystal-clear day in Port Ariel, where the air was pure, the scenery spectacular, the crime rate low. He'd spent his childhood in a tough Bronx neighborhood where learning how to fight was essential for survival.

When he was twenty, his younger brother had been stabbed to death on a street corner. Fifteen years later his wife Meagan had been shot to death in a liquor store. So he'd left New York City and brought his little girl to a place that was safe, a place where murder was nearly unheard of . . .

Until now.

Not all the toxicology reports on Tamara Hunt had come back yet, but Nick didn't really consider them important. Someone dragging a razor-sharp, smooth-bladed knife across her slender neck had killed Tamara Peyton Hunt. According to the preliminary M.E. report, she bore a three-inch single incised wound at the base of her neck, directed backward, medially and downward. The carotid artery and external and internal jugular veins had been severed. Bruising appeared around the throat, indicating that the victim had been grabbed from behind and held while the fatal wound was administered. The state of rigor placed the time of death between eight and ten P.M. the previous evening. The pattern of lividity showed that the body had not been moved. There were no signs of sexual assault and no skin had been retrieved from beneath the victim's fingernails. Human hair not belonging to the victim had not been recovered, although canine hair was found on the hands and around the neck.

And, finally, Tamara Peyton Hunt had been eight weeks pregnant.

Nick remembered when his wife Meagan had told him she was expecting. She'd been finishing her master's degree in English. He'd just made detective second grade. He'd been at work when she called and said abruptly, "Nick, you're going to be a father," then hung up. He'd immediately called home, but there had been no answer. When he arrived back at the apartment for dinner, Meagan was furiously stirring a pot of spaghetti sauce. She'd looked at him almost fearfully with her big brown eyes. Then she saw the yellow roses and the bottle of sparkling cider topped by a bow he carried, and she'd burst into happy tears.

He hadn't told her how much he wanted a child because he knew becoming a college professor was so important to her. He didn't want her to feel pressured to interrupt her education. He later learned she hadn't talked about how much she wanted a child because he was the eldest of seven children. She thought he was sick of kids and she didn't want *him* to feel pressured. But the day Paige was born was the happiest of their marriage.

Had Tamara Hunt wanted this baby as much as Meagan had wanted Paige? From everything Nick had heard about her, she had. Desperately. How about her husband? Warren Hunt seemed more of a mystery than his wife was. Everyone they'd questioned had wonderful things to say about Tamara. They talked about her sweetness, her generosity, her devotion to her husband. No one seemed willing to volunteer much about Dr. Hunt except that he seemed to have a fairly successful practice and he dressed well. Glowing comments, Nick thought wryly.

"We going to question Warren Hunt today?" Ted Hysell asked.

Nick swiveled back in his chair, looking at Hysell's eager face gazing at him from the doorway. The guy tried to hide his excitement over the case beneath a stern veneer, but it wasn't working. Even though he'd known Tamara Hunt and supposedly liked her tremendously, he was delighted to be working on a murder case. Maybe if Nick had spent ten years on the police force and never encountered a serious case, he'd feel different, too. But Tamara was only slightly younger than Meagan had been, and so much he'd heard about her reminded him of Meagan— Meagan, too, kind and loving and murdered with the world ahead of her.

Hysell's enthusiasm rankled and Nick stared at the man for a moment. He would like to take someone else with him, but Hysell had seniority among the deputies. Nick forced away emotion. "Give Hunt a call and make sure he's home. Don't let him put you off, but don't scare him, either."

"Give him the 'it's just routine' routine, right?"

Hysell beamed at his own clever turn of phrase. Nick nodded, sighing within. Hysell annoyed the hell out of him.

Twenty minutes later they pulled into the Hunt driveway. Nick saw Jimmy Jenkins standing in his own driveway watching avidly while from somewhere outside, his mother bawled reprimands to one of the other children. He waved briefly at Jimmy, who returned something like a salute. Jimmy was a pistol, Nick thought. Bright, funny, obsessed with that smartass TV cop, and seemingly with Paige. Nick didn't mind them being friends. He just didn't want them to be *best* friends. He wasn't sure Jimmy's influence was all that healthy on an impressionable eleven-year-old girl.

Warren Hunt opened the door promptly. He wore neatly pressed khaki pants, a pale blue oxford shirt, expensive loafers, and CK cologne. He was clean-shaven and his dark brown hair was still damp from the shower, but the whites of his eyes bore a network of red lines and his well-kept hands shook slightly. "Good morning, Sheriff," he said affably, smiling broadly. Then doubt flashed in his eyes and he turned down the smile a notch. "Come in."

"Thanks," Nick said. "This is Deputy Hysell—"

"I knew Tamara," Hysell interrupted. "Lovely girl. I'm a few years older. We met skating. She was better than I was. And pretty as a picture. Sweet, too." Is it *possible* for this guy to shut his mouth? Nick stormed mentally. "This is a real tragedy, Warren."

Warren Hunt looked blankly at Hysell, clearly having no idea who this chatterbox was. Nick ignored his deputy. "Do I smell coffee?"

Relief shone on Hunt's face. "Yes. Would you like some?"

"Sure would. Black."

"Deputy . . ."

"Hysell. I'd like some, too. Cream. Or milk, but not too much. No sugar."

When Warren went into the kitchen, Nick forced himself to sound mild. "Hysell, let me do the talking for now." Hysell immediately looked sullen. "I'll give you a signal if I want you to spring something on him."

Some of the deputy's irritation dissipated, although Nick hadn't specified what Hysell was to "spring" on Hunt. It didn't matter. Hysell walked to the fireplace and fell into a deep study of an oil painting hanging above the mantel, an act clearly meant to communicate nonchalance to Hunt.

Warren entered the room carrying two mugs of coffee. Hysell took his with merely a nod. Nick sipped and smiled. "Good." Hunt looked relieved again. Nick sat down on the couch. "Sorry to inconvenience you this morning, Dr. Hunt. I know you're probably busy with funeral arrangements."

Warren took a seat on a wing-backed chair. "Actually Tamara's father and sister are handling all that. They wanted to and I thought it might be therapeutic."

"I see. Well, I just have a few questions for you, things you told me yesterday but I need to confirm." Nick gave him an offhand look. "Everyone was pretty upset after just getting the news. I want to make sure I have everything straight."

"Certainly. I understand." Warren seemed to relax and crossed an ankle over a knee. "How can I help you?"

"I understand that you were attending a three-day convention in Cleveland."

"Yes. It began Thursday morning at nine. I left Wednesday evening and stayed at the Hyatt where the convention was being held. Saturday night we had a banquet. I planned to wrap up a few things Sunday and be back here by five or six o'clock. Then I got the call about Tamara . . ." He took a deep, shuddery breath.

"Why didn't your wife go with you?"

Warren blinked at him. "What?"

"Why didn't your wife go with you to Cleveland? Wouldn't she have enjoyed shopping, dining out, that kind of thing?"

"No." Warren's fingers began to tap lightly on the arm of the chair. "Tamara was shy, almost reclusive. Oh, if the trip had just been a little weekend excursion for the two of us, she would have loved it. But she didn't want to be thrown in the midst of all those people. There was a cocktail party Wednesday night and the banquet Saturday. She hated that kind of thing."

"I see." Nick withdrew a notebook from his pocket and pretended to check it, although he knew its contents by heart. "The banquet was held the night of your wife's murder."

"That's right."

"You sat between Dr. Forbes Evans and Dr. Charles Feldman."

"Yes."

"You arrived at seven and left around ten."

"Yes."

"Hmmm. Well, here I have a problem because Dr. Evans says he returned to his room around eight-ten and you were getting ready to leave."

"Forbes is elderly. He was exhausted and embarrassed about darting away from the banquet so early, so I said I was leaving, too. But I didn't."

"That was considerate of you. But Dr. Feldman says he actually went back upstairs with you at eight-twenty."

Warren's tapping fingers went still. "He's mistaken."

"His wife says he called her around eight-thirty from his room."

"I don't know when he called his wife, but we did *not* leave the banquet that early. Anyway, what difference does it make?"

"Time of death, Dr. Hunt. The M.E. places your wife's time of death between eight and ten."

"That's fairly vague."

"Unfortunately in real life they can't be as accurate as on television where the M.E. can place time of death within fifteen minutes." Nick gave him a casual smile. "Impossible."

Warren smiled back woodenly. "Of course."

"Nice ship model you got here," Hysell intervened. Nick had an urge to bash him over the head with something heavy.

Warren Hunt looked completely confused. "Ship model?"

"Here on your mantel. It's the *Mercy*, isn't it?"

"The *Mercy*? Why, yes, I believe it is. Had it so long I forgot."

"Did you build it?"

"Build it? No. I have no interest in ships. Tamara picked it up somewhere." He looked at Nick. "Now what's all this about Tamara's time of death?"

Nick took a deep breath, trying to maintain his cool. He'd have a few choice words for Hysell when they got outside. He was also furious with Warren Hunt for playing dumb with him. Did he actually think that would work? "The time of death is very important, Dr. Hunt. You see it's fifty-five miles from here to Cleveland. You could drive that in less than an hour, which means if you and Dr. Feldman left the banquet at eight-twenty, you could have been back in Port Ariel by nine-twenty."

"By nine-twenty? Yes, I suppose I could. But why?" Warren's eyes widened. "So I could slash my wife's throat?"

"It's a possibility we have to consider," Nick answered calmly.

"But that's preposterous! I was at the hotel all evening."

"Did anyone see you after you left the dining room?"

"I don't know. Surely *someone* did. A colleague. A maid. I believe I ordered a brandy from room service around eleven. No, that was the night before. Anyway, I called my wife at ten. My message is on our answering machine."

"But you didn't call from your room at the Hyatt. We checked the phone records."

"You did? Why would you do that? Oh, this ridiculous suspicion of me." Warren shook his head as if baffled and slightly amused by Nick's stupidity. "I called from my car phone, Sheriff Meredith."

"That would explain it," Nick said agreeably.

Warren managed another shaky smile. "Yes, you check my *car* phone records and you'll find a record of the call."

"Good." Nick paused. "Except you said you were in your room all evening."

Warren's smile disappeared. "Well, I *was*. But I went out. Briefly." Nick looked at him questioningly. "To see a friend."

"And what would that friend's name be?"

"Is this really important, Sheriff?"

Nick finally gave him a hard stare. "I thought I'd already

conveyed its importance, Dr. Hunt. Your wife was murdered last night. We're talking about your alibi."

Warren Hunt's carefully shaved upper lip now sported beads of sweat. "All right. But I'd appreciate your keeping this information confidential." Nick remained silent. "A female colleague of mine was at the conference. Dr. Lorraine Glover. We decided to meet for a drink at a little bar away from the hotel."

"Why not the hotel bar?"

"We wanted some place more private."

"More *private*?"

Warren's face had turned bright red. "Well, you see . . ." He took a deep breath. "Oh, hell. Now isn't the time for lies. Lorraine and I had an affair two years ago. It's not something I'm proud of. It's the only time I've ever been unfaithful to my wife, but Lorraine and I just . . . well, we just did something stupid."

"And you were going to do something stupid again?"

"No! It was just a drink for old times' sake. But back when we were having the affair, another psychologist named Henry Simon found out about it. The man is a toad. A disgrace to the profession. Anyway, he'd been after Lorraine for years and he didn't take rejection well. When he found out about the two of us, he told everyone. Lorraine's husband almost left her."

"And Tamara?"

"She never heard about us."

"Another advantage to her being such a homebody. And a good reason for you not to encourage her to attend the convention."

Warren gave Nick a sickly smile. "Yes. I *am* guilty of discouraging her from attending these functions. But as I said, all Lorraine and I intended to do was have a drink. We just didn't want to be seen and start the gossip mill again. I was on my way to the bar to meet her when I remembered my ten o'clock call to Tamara, so I called from the car. Our answering machine here at the house recorded the call at 9:57. I returned to the hotel around eleven."

Nick wrote in his notebook mostly to make Warren nervous. "I understand why you didn't want to volunteer that information, but I'll have to ask for more. I need Dr. Glover's address and phone number."

"I can't give you that. It would be a violation of privacy."

Nick looked up. "Dr. Hunt, you *still* don't seem to comprehend the importance of establishing your whereabouts at the time of your wife's death. Now I understand you wanting to protect this woman's privacy, but given the circumstances, if you refuse to tell me how to contact her so I can verify your story, I'm going to assume you're lying."

"I am *not* lying."

"Then prove it."

Warren glared at him. A muscle in his jaw flexed. Finally he said, "Okay. But you *cannot* call her at home. Call her office. I don't know the number, but it's on High Street in Columbus."

Nick jotted down the information then snapped shut his notebook. "Sorry that had to be so difficult."

"So am I," Warren said stiffly. "Is that all?"

"For now." Nick stood. "I know you'll be around if I have any more questions. Hysell, let's be on our way. Dr. Hunt looks tired."

"Sure, Sheriff."

They paused at the door. "Once again, Dr. Hunt," Meredith said, "I'm sorry I had to put you through this. Such an awful thing, particularly with Tamara being pregnant."

Warren Hunt's face went slack. "Pregnant?" he repeated vacantly.

"Why, yes. Eight weeks. Didn't you know?"

Warren opened and shut his mouth twice. On the third try something emerged. "We hoped." Flat. "After all these years."

Hysell took Warren's hand and shook it vigorously. "A tragedy, Warren. No Tamara, no pitter-patter of little feet."

Color drained from Warren Hunt's face and his eyes seemed to lose their focus for a moment. Nick thought he was going to pass out. Then he stiffened, muttered a curt good-bye, and slammed the door behind them.

"Well, at least we know he didn't know anything about a baby," Hysell said as they walked away from the house. "He didn't strike me as a guy who *wanted* a baby, either."

After they got in the patrol car and crept away from the curb, Nick opened his mouth to blast Hysell for interrupting his interrogation with that nonsense about the ship model, but Hysell began before Nick could get out a word. "That phone call he made to the house doesn't prove anything—"

"Except that he called his home from his car at 9:57. But, Hysell—"

"Oh, and did you hear him? 'It's the only time I've ever been unfaithful to my wife.' " Hysell imitated Warren's perfect enunciation. "Bullshit!"

Nick glanced at him. "You know something I don't?"

"I've been hearing rumors about our Dr. Hunt's sex life for years. They're part of the reason Oliver Peyton can't stand him."

"Are they just rumors?"

"No. I've had my own suspicions and they just got verified."

"Now we know he'd had an affair with Lorraine Glover. I'll have to check her out. But, Hysell, I want to talk to you about—"

"Not just that Glover woman! Someone right here in Port Ariel." Nick raised an eyebrow. "You ever heard of Charlotte Bishop? Max Bishop's daughter? Max owns Bishop Corporation. They make parts for boats. He's had a couple of bad strokes, but he still controls the business."

"I know who Max Bishop is, Hysell. Everyone in town knows who Max Bishop is. And Charlotte was married to that actor—"

"Paul Fiori. He plays Eddie Salvatore on *Street Life*."

Eddie Salvatore. Wasn't that Jimmy Jenkins's hero? He'd have to ask Paige. "What about Charlotte?"

"Fiori dumped Charlotte when he made it big, so she came slinking home a few months ago," Hysell went on confidentially. "Well, one day I saw her coming out of Hunt's office!"

Hysell fell silent after dropping that bombshell. Nick glanced at him. "That's it?"

Hysell looked insulted. "*No.* About a week later I was at The

Hearth with Dee having dinner. Dee Fisher, that's who I've been going out with the last few months. She's a nurse. Got fired from the hospital, but it was all a mistake. She's a lot of fun. We like The Hearth—"

"*Hysell!*"

"Okay. I went to the rest room. You know the restrooms at The Hearth are back through this long hall. So I'm going back and I see Charlotte and Hunt talking. I wouldn't have thought too much about it, but Hunt lowered his head and took off fast and Charlotte nearly pounced on me. Acted like she was thrilled to see me."

"You know her?"

"Sure. Didn't I say so? Well, actually I was a friend of her brother Bill. Maxwell William Bishop II. Not junior, the *second*. He was okay, though. I met him in Boy Scouts. He was nothing like Charlotte. She was gorgeous and she knew it. She never forgot she was Max Bishop's daughter, either. Uppity as all get out. Anyway, her brother Bill got killed in a car wreck a few years ago. A damned shame."

Nick waited. Finally he asked, "What does any of this have to do with Charlotte and Hunt?"

"Yeah, well, when I was a kid, I spent some time at the Bishop house. Charlotte wouldn't wipe her feet on me then. Acted like I was invisible or something. But that night at The Hearth we were just long-lost pals. *And* she kept going on about how she'd just run into Dr. Hunt. On and *on*. What do they call that? Protesting too much? That's when I got suspicious. Today the ship model clinched it."

"The ship model?" Nick asked, bewildered.

"The one on Hunt's mantel. That's why I called attention to it. I know you got pissed, me interrupting that way and all, but when I realized what it was, I got all excited and I wanted to hear what Hunt had to say about it when he got taken by surprise. You told me to spring something on him and I did."

"He said the model was something Tamara picked up a long time ago."

"Yeah, sure it was. Listen, that was a model of the *Mercy*. That's the ship that wrecked off the coast here. Ariel Saunders was this beautiful young gal who saw the shipwreck and saved the captain, Zebediah Winthrop—"

"I've heard the story about a hundred times since I've been here."

"Okay. Well, Bill Bishop built a model of the *Mercy*. *That* model."

"The one on the mantel?"

"Yeah."

"Hysell, there must be dozens of models of the *Mercy* around here."

"Sheriff, I helped Bill build that model. We spent weeks on it. Besides, our initials were on it—M. W. B. and T. Z. H. Charlotte must have given the model to Hunt."

"Are you sure she didn't give it to Mrs. Hunt?"

"Charlotte wouldn't give anything to any woman, much less her dead brother's model ship. I bet if old Max knew it was gone, he'd have one final stroke. He worshipped Bill, and Charlotte was jealous as hell. That's probably why she gave the model away. She could strike back at Daddy and at the same time give Hunt something she thought would mean something to him, something he thought meant something to *her*."

Nick's opinion of Hysell's powers of observation, deduction, and psychoanalysis were escalating by the minute. Maybe he had a more valuable deputy here than he'd thought. "Wouldn't Mrs. Hunt notice the initials?"

"They were tiny and sort of hidden. A little faded after all this time. You'd have to really be looking for them. Besides, I can't believe she'd put it all together. Bill has been dead for years, and I'm sure Tamara didn't know my middle name. She wouldn't know who T. Z. H. was."

"Hysell?"

"Yes, Sheriff?"

"What does the Z stand for?"

Hysell hesitated. He hated answering this one. "Zebediah."

He grinned and added sheepishly, "I think everyone in this town is crazy for that Ariel and Zebediah story."

"I got that impression when I heard it twice the first day I was in town." He frowned. "Do you believe Hunt would have asked Tamara for a divorce?"

"He *could* have, but it probably wouldn't have done him much good. Tamara was a devout Catholic. *And* she was pregnant. She wouldn't have given in without a fight. Hunt could have gotten a divorce eventually, but not without a lot of time and struggle. And scandal. Charlotte's already been through all that and it's my guess she wouldn't consider Warren Hunt enough of a prize to go through it again."

"So you think Warren Hunt murdered his wife so he could have Charlotte Bishop?"

Hysell looked surprised. "Maybe, but this situation called for immediate, decisive action."

"And you're saying Warren Hunt isn't capable of that?"

"Let's just say I think Charlotte Bishop *is* . . ." Hysell paused. "You know, I think Charlotte Bishop is capable of just about anything."

8

Alison sat at the piano. She began Debussy's "The Girl with the Flaxen Hair." Viveca walked through the room and paused at the piano, smiling. Alison immediately stopped playing. "What's wrong?"

"Nothing, dear," Viveca said carefully. "That's *your* song, isn't it?"

"What's *wrong*?"

Viveca's smile locked into place. "Well, you've played it five times in a row. How about something else?"

"All right," Alison said pleasantly and immediately launched into "The Merry Widow Waltz." Viveca's face slackened. Alison paused. "Don't you like that song?"

"Not particularly."

The ghost of a malicious smile capered around Alison's rosebud mouth. "Oh. I forgot. That's what people called you after Papa died. 'The Merry Widow.' "

"They did not, but please play something else."

Alison dropped her hands in her lap. "I'm not in the mood to play anymore. I would like to see Warren."

"I'm sure he's very busy today making arrangements for Tamara."

"I need to see him. He's my doctor."

"You don't have an appointment with him today. Besides, you just saw him yesterday." Viveca nervously touched the topaz pendant hanging from a gold chain at her neck. It had been a gift from Oliver Peyton. "Dear, please play something nice."

Alison raised her long, strong fingers to the piano keys. They hovered for a moment. Then they crashed down, sending loud, discordant notes jangling around the serenely beautiful room until at last Alison settled into the piano section of Eric Clapton's "Layla." She'd only played for a minute before Viveca shouted, "Stop!"

Alison stopped immediately and Viveca looked contrite. "Darling, I'm sorry, but you know I hate rock music. With your talent it's almost sacrilegious to hear you playing it."

"I like it. Why can't I play what I like?" Alison looked up at her mother with her wide Dresden blue eyes and shouted, "Why can't I *ever* play what *I* like?"

Viveca recoiled. Her face paled. She drew a deep breath. "Forgive me. Of course you may play what you like." She took a step closer and hesitantly, almost fearfully, touched her daughter's cheek. "I only want you to be happy, Alison. It's all I've ever wanted."

But Alison had retreated to her own world. It was seventeen years ago. Alison was five. Mama was going away again. Just for a couple of days. She was what they called an "executive" at a big company called Bishop and she had to go on business trips. "I'm sorry I have to leave, darling," she'd said, clutching Alison to her for a final embrace.

Alison thought her mother was the most beautiful woman in the world. She had long golden hair. She had huge blue eyes. She always wore pretty clothes. She always smelled good. Alison admired Mama. She tried to please Mama. But it was Papa she loved, Papa who didn't care that she was scared of so many things, that she liked to spend lots of time alone talking to herself but couldn't find her tongue in front of strangers, or that she had persistent nightmares, or that doctors said she was something called *neurotic*. Papa didn't give lectures about how she should act like Mama did. Papa liked her just the way she was.

She'd stood on the porch, her little hand in Papa's, and waved as Mama drove away. Papa had turned to her. "Your mother left us some very healthy food to heat up for dinner. She says you are to eat, practice the piano for an hour, watch one hour of educational television, and be tucked into bed and sound asleep by eight."

"Yes, Papa."

"I, however, am the man of the house in your mother's absence," he had said with a dryness Alison didn't quite catch. "It is Friday night. Therefore, we will order a great big greasy pizza for dinner, play Candy Land, and watch a Disney movie on video." Alison's solemn little face broke into a picture of pure bliss. "We'll have a regular debauch, kiddo. Port Ariel has never seen the like. They'll be talking about this night a hundred years from now!"

Papa let her choose the pizza toppings and it had been the best she ever had. They'd eaten with their fingers! They'd played two games of Candy Land, watched *One Hundred and One Dalmatians* and part of *Lady and the Tramp* before she fell asleep. When her father had placed her gently in her bed, her eyes had snapped open. "What time is it?" Her father had grinned. "Magic Midnight, bunny ears." She still called it Magic Midnight.

The next day they'd eaten lunch in an open-air restaurant by the lake. They'd walked along the shore, holding hands and talking about everything that interested her. Then Papa had driven her to a giant old house. She'd been afraid of it at first, but Papa said the house had belonged to a brave and beautiful lady who would protect her when she was inside.

That was when she had first heard the saga of Ariel Saunders. Papa talked about how Ariel had run down to the beach and pulled Captain Winthrop from the freezing water and how later they had married and Zebediah changed the name of the town to Port Ariel in honor of his beloved bride. And best of all, Ariel was Alison's very own great-great-grandmother!

Even then Ariel's house was not in good shape, but Papa had carried her through every one of its damaged rooms, talking in his sonorous voice, conjuring up the splendor that had been Saunders House. Mama said he had a way with words because he used to be a novelist. A strange look always came over Papa's face whenever she said "used to be." Lots of times he got out legal pads and pens and called for quiet in the house, but he usually ended up only with pages of crossed-out words. Then he would listen to sad music and drink brandy and Mama would look disgusted and not speak to him, which made everything worse. But today Papa was happy and Alison was ecstatic. She loved Papa and she loved Ariel Saunders's house, the house overlooking the lake, the house of romance and legend.

By late afternoon Alison was still in a joyful daze, lost in the world of Ariel and Zebediah, posing and preening in front of Mama's full-length mirror, pretending to be Ariel. Papa had passed the doorway, smiling. He carried a laundry basket. "Want to help me do the washing?"

Alison looked at him in surprise. "But Mrs. Krebbs comes and does it every week."

"I'm in the mood. I used to help my mama with the laundry when I was a little boy. Come on, bunny ears, it'll be fun."

So Alison had gone with him to the basement where the washer and dryer sat. Alison rarely visited the basement. She didn't like places full of shadows and she worried about spiders and mice and all kinds of terrors that might be lurking. But she was with Papa and he wouldn't let anything bad happen.

There were windows high in the walls that let in some daylight, but Papa still flipped a switch and a fluorescent bulb hummed to life. Then they descended the steps and he groaned, looking at water flowing across the floor. "Dammit, we just had the washer fixed two weeks ago. I knew that repairman didn't know what he was doing." He sighed. "I'm going to fix this myself."

"Do you know how?" Alison had asked, wanting to run away from the water that looked dark and scary like snakes or alligators might lie in its depths.

"It's probably just a hose on the washer that fool didn't

tighten," Papa said. "I think I can fix something that simple. Sit on the stairs, honey."

So Alison had sat down and Papa had placed the laundry basket beside her. Then he had waded into the water. His shoes made squishy sounds and he muttered and fussed and uttered words Alison knew he wasn't supposed to say in front of her. She twisted a lock of her silky white-blond hair around her finger the way that always annoyed Mama.

"Okay, you infernal beast," he said dramatically to the washer, making Alison giggle, "let's see who's boss."

Papa stepped behind the washer, facing her, and leaned on the machine. Abruptly blue-red light flared around him. The fluorescent light dimmed. Papa went rigid. A small, agonized sound escaped the rictus in his face, his body shook, and his eyes looked as if they were going to explode from his head. Alison heard a clicking sound nearby. The fluorescent bulb shut off. Papa fell on the concrete floor, his head making a sickening thud as his skull fractured and skin split. Blood rushed out and mixed with water swirling around his motionless body.

Slowly the world went fuzzy for Alison. She felt as if a heavy, swirling fog enveloped her. She loved the fog because it shut out the awful sight of Papa.

A day later, when Viveca returned from her trip, she found her husband in full rigor mortis, a stiffened corpse collapsed beside the washing machine. Her little girl sat on the basement stairs, rocking back and forth, twisting her hair around her finger. She'd soiled her clothes and her lips were chapped from dehydration. But the worst, what had choked off Viveca's horrified scream, was the child's eyes—wide, vacant, unblinking. Viveca had rushed her to the hospital. Alison remained unresponsive for nearly a week. Afterward came years of psychiatric care—clinics, medication, endless analysis, even hypnotherapy. But Alison had never been the same since that day in the basement when Papa had tried to fix the washer.

"Are you going to wear black to Tamara's funeral?"

Viveca looked up from the magazine she'd been staring at

blindly. Whenever Alison mentally left this world, Viveca sat patiently waiting for her to return. Sometimes it took a few seconds. Sometimes it took hours. Today it had been fifteen minutes.

"I think I'll wear navy blue."

"I'm wearing black. Even black jewelry. My marcasite and onyx brooch that belonged to Ariel."

The brooch had not belonged to Ariel, but Alison could not be convinced of this. It didn't matter. It made her happy to think she owned a piece of Ariel's jewelry. But Alison's train of thought was disturbing.

"Dear, I've been thinking," Viveca said carefully. "Tamara's funeral might be too depressing for you. Perhaps you should stay home."

Alison looked outraged. "Stay home! I *can't*. Warren will need me."

Viveca had been increasingly aware of Alison's interest in Warren. At first she'd been pleased. Alison had hated all of her doctors. Then through Oliver's daughter Tamara she'd met Warren Hunt and wanted to be treated by him. Viveca didn't like Warren, but Alison violently refused to continue with her present psychiatrist or any other. Viveca realized she would either have to relent about Warren or send Alison off to a clinic once more.

Alison seemed to improve for a while. Then Alison began talking about Ariel again. After her father's death, she talked incessantly of Ariel and even believed she *was* Ariel. Time and drugs seemed to alleviate the delusion and finally she had completely stopped talking about Ariel. Until lately. First Alison had found a brooch in Lily Peyton's antique shop she was certain belonged to Ariel Saunders and insisted her mother buy it. Last week Viveca had found a book on reincarnation in Alison's room.

Now there was her preoccupation with Warren Hunt. There was something in the way she said his name, an almost caressing quality, that tripped alarm bells in Viveca's mind. And in the last few months Alison had grown cooler toward Tamara. In fact, cool was too mild a word. Almost hostile was more like it. Hostile and—Viveca cringed at the word—*competitive.*

"Dear, Warren will have plenty of moral support," Viveca said soothingly. "He wouldn't want you to go. Funerals are so sad."

"You mean like Papa's?"

"Yes."

"And Eugene's?"

Viveca's face tightened. "You were not supposed to attend Eugene Farley's funeral. You did that against my strict orders."

"I think it's terrible that *you* didn't go. After all, he was one of your boyfriends."

"Alison!"

"Why do you keep squawking 'Alison!' at me? He *was* your boyfriend. What are you so embarrassed about? That he was young enough to be your son or that he got convicted of embezzlement and killed himself?"

"He was not young enough to be my son," Viveca said tiredly. "And his death was tragic, but we were no longer together. I really don't want to talk about that sad time."

"No wonder. You deserted him. *I* didn't. I loved him."

"I know. He was like a brother to you."

Alison let out a peal of laughter with a note of hysteria beneath it. "I did *not* think of him as a brother, Mama."

Viveca had trouble conceiving of Alison as anything except a child. The idea of her having a sexual interest in anyone was repugnant, like picturing a five-year-old girl lusting after an adult man. But as much as she hated to admit it, Alison had a libido. Maybe an overactive libido.

She had first noticed it when Alison was around Eugene Farley. Eugene had been the head accountant at the Bishop Corporation. Handsome, intelligent, funny, he had been sought after by all the single females at Bishop and some of the married ones, too. Before long and against her better judgment, Viveca found she couldn't resist him, either.

He'd come to her home several times and treated Alison like any normal young woman. He'd talked about literature and music with her, trading books and CD's. They laughed and the girl seemed to blossom. Viveca *had* thought they acted like brother and sister and she was delighted. She didn't even care that Eugene indulged Alison's taste for rock music.

Then Viveca saw the way Alison looked at Eugene. A crush she told herself, but self-deception had never been her forte. She couldn't hide from the truth. Her perpetually, innocent child looked at Viveca's lover with a naked carnality that made her sick.

Eugene was gone now. First she'd banished him from her life and then he had taken his own. As bad as Viveca felt about Eugene's death, she had been relieved to see the hunger vanish from Alison's eyes. But now it was back, flaring uncontrollably whenever Warren Hunt's name was mentioned.

"Mama, you *will* let me go to Tamara's funeral, won't you?"

It wasn't really the question it seemed. It was a threat. When Alison did not get her way, she would inflict the punishment of her illness on her mother, and it always worked. Viveca's guilt over Alison's emotional state was crushing because she had not been attending a meeting when her husband died. She had gone off for a weekend with another man and in the throes of her passion, she had not bothered to call home during the twenty-eight hours when Alison sat on the basement steps staring at her father's body as she slowly descended into the mental hell from which she would never rise.

"Of course you may go, Alison."

"Good. Warren needs me now." Her lips twitched. "Especially now that *she's* gone." Viveca stiffened but before she could reply, Alison announced, "I'm going to my room."

To do what? Viveca wondered. The girl was getting agitated. "Alison, why don't I make tea and heat up some croissants and we can have a girl talk?" she tried feebly.

"I don't know how to make girl talk. You never let me have friends. You've always kept me a prisoner." Alison rose from the piano bench and stomped up the stairs to her room. She was prone to sudden rages and the look in her eyes was dangerous. Vivcca stood, anxiously fingering her topaz pendant until she heard Alison's door slam.

What would happen tonight was anyone's guess.

II
MONDAY NIGHT

Warren didn't like the marina at night. He didn't like it in the day, either. Frankly, he hated the water and boats, but you just didn't admit that around here where everyone was mad for Lake Erie. He certainly wouldn't admit it to Charlotte, whose father owned the biggest craft in the marina and of course named it the *Charlotte*. They always met on the *Charlotte*. Warren would rather they went to a secluded motel, but being with Charlotte was worth an evening on a boat.

Slip Thirty-four was the home of the *Charlotte*. Custom-built, it sat smugly majestic in the moonlight, eighty-five feet of white aluminum, housing four staterooms, a formal dining room, a sky lounge with an entertainment center, a flying bridge with sunning and seating areas, a wet bar, and a saloon with a home theater system and projection unit that dropped from the ceiling. Charlotte said Max had wanted something big and elaborate for corporate cruises. Warren thought Max Bishop just wanted something ostentatious to show how rich he was and that his corporation dominated Port Ariel just as his yacht dominated the marina. The *Charlotte* was certainly a tribute to conspicuous consumption, Warren thought, and Charlotte loved it.

Warren threw another furtive look over his shoulder. He always imagined people were looking out the windows of dark-ened boat cabins, identifying him, noting his destination. The marina was too public, even around midnight. And what if he was spotted tonight, forty-eight hours after his wife's murder? His reputation would be ruined. Worse yet, that damned

Meredith would be all over him. The guy was itching to nail him for Tamara's murder. Today he had looked at Warren as if he were a stuck bug. He only prayed Lorraine Glover would back up his alibi. She hadn't sounded too willing over the phone when he'd called right after Meredith left, but Lorraine was scared. He'd lied to Meredith. Lorraine's wealthy husband *didn't* know she'd been having an affair, but Warren could see to it that Alfred Glover found out. Even if Lorraine corroborated his alibi, though, discovering he was having an affair with Charlotte Bishop would give Meredith a motive to pin on him.

Then there was that annoying deputy who kept looking at the ship model Charlotte had given him. Warren didn't care a thing about Port Ariel history, but he didn't tell her. He'd kept the model at his office. One day Tamara had dropped by unexpectedly, seen it, and insisted on taking it home. When she spotted the initials, he'd truthfully claimed ignorance and she didn't seem bothered. He'd been uncomfortable every time he looked at it sitting on the mantel, though. And today that deputy had spotted something.

I shouldn't have come, Warren thought abruptly. What had he been thinking? Yes, he wanted to be with Charlotte. Yes, he knew she needed his reassurance, but this meeting was not a smart move. *Why* had he let her talk him into it?

He stopped as panic grew. He would go home immediately. Charlotte would be furious, but he could smooth it over somehow, make her see reason, convince her not to call the house again. But right now he *had* to leave—

"Warren!"

Charlotte was leaning over the side of the yacht. Her soprano voice seemed to shrill through the night. Warren flinched and quelled an impulse to loudly shush her. Instead he darted forward.

"Hi, sweetheart," he said softly. "You know, I'm not sure this is—"

"You're *late*! I thought you weren't *coming*!"

Her volume hadn't lowered. Warren looked at her closely.

Even in the bleaching light of the moon he could see her flushed cheeks. She'd been drinking. He'd never seen her take more than one glass of wine. "I'm only ten minutes late, darling," he said just above a whisper. "As I was saying, this isn't a good idea tonight. I had a grueling session with Sheriff Meredith today and—"

"Meredith is an *ass!*"

Warren winced. "Charlotte, the whole marina will hear you."

"Get on board." She extended her hand invitingly, but there was steel in her voice. "*Please.*"

His heart raced. He could stand here and argue, with Charlotte getting angrier and louder by the minute, or he could board the yacht and disappear inside. He wanted to be with her. Besides, it was a little late to worry about being seen.

Five minutes later Charlotte poured him a glass of champagne. She'd already finished half the bottle. She insisted they toast to "new beginnings." Warren's stomach tightened. His wife of six years was dead. How could he be here with his lover toasting to the future? Because until a few weeks ago the future had stretched before him like an endless desert? Because the thought of enduring Tamara for even one more year had become unbearable?

"You're not drinking," Charlotte said, her beautiful gold-flecked eyes glittering up at him. She wore tight white slacks and a filmy blouse with no bra underneath. "This is *very* good champagne. Don't let it go to waste." He took a sip and she smiled. "All right, tell me about the great Nicholas Meredith's visit."

"He's very suspicious."

Charlotte's pupils seemed to dilate. "Does he know about us?" she asked sharply.

"No."

"You're sure?"

"Yes. He would have hit me with it if he did. But he had some questions about my alibi."

"Which you answered to his satisfaction."

"Yes. I think so."

"What do you mean, you *think* so?"

"I meant yes. Period." He could not tell her about Lorraine Glover. He'd sworn to her that he'd never had an affair before she came along. Nor could he let Charlotte find out about Tamara's pregnancy. He'd also sworn to her he hadn't slept with Tamara for a year. "Meredith had a deputy who was looking at the model of the *Mercy* with a lot of interest. Hysell."

"Ted Hysell? The guy we saw at The Hearth?"

Warren was stricken. "I didn't recognize him."

"Don't worry. He's an idiot."

"But he's seen us together."

"Forget him. Listen, Warren, now is *not* the time to get rattled," she said calmly, "although I wish Sheriff Purdue were still in office. He was a great friend of Daddy's. He was also too lazy to do much investigating."

"He'd have to do something in a murder case."

"Nothing productive, I assure you." She smiled brightly. "You look so unhappy. Drink up, darling. You'll feel better."

Two glasses of champagne later he *did* feel better. Charlotte opened a second bottle of champagne. When he protested, she insisted they both needed it to relax. The champagne did not seem to relax her—just the opposite. With each glass she grew more animated. This was an unfamiliar Charlotte. Warren decided nerves were responsible for the drinking. She didn't want to admit Tamara's murder worried her, so she hid the anxiety beneath alcohol. Drunk or not, she was still charming. Charming, delightful, completely irresistible.

Warren took her oval face in his hands. He kissed her forehead, her eyelids, her nose, each flushed cheek. "I love you, Charlotte," he said urgently. "God, I love you."

She made a sound like a contented cat purring, then pulled down his head, pressing their lips together briefly. Then she pushed him farther down until his lips touched the cleft between her small, firm breasts. "You're a free man now," she breathed. "Make love to me as a free man."

They always made love in the master stateroom on the bed

Warren was sure Max Bishop meant only for his personal pleasure. Charlotte said that before his strokes, her father frequently "entertained" women in the stateroom. Now that Max's right side was seventy-five percent immobilized, Charlotte had appropriated the room. Max was stuck at home with poor faithful Muriel who'd overlooked his many affairs. The lavish stateroom belonged to Charlotte. And him.

Mine, Warren thought in the midst of their abandoned lovemaking. This beautiful, exciting woman, this excessive but impressive yacht, this privileged life Charlotte's money could buy. All his. That would make his father sit up and take notice. The future no longer looked endless and bleak to Warren. The future looked like a city shimmering on the horizon. The Emerald City, he thought, although he'd always hated *The Wizard of Oz.* Snagging Charlotte was like Dorothy reaching the Emerald City.

They made love twice, then lay spent, Warren on his back, Charlotte on her abdomen with an arm thrown across his chest. Water lapped at the sides of the *Charlotte.* Warren smiled, realizing that for the first time in his life he didn't mind being on a boat. The funeral and everything else that must be done for Tamara in the next few weeks didn't seem insurmountable now. He would get through it because he had something wonderful waiting for him . . . over the rainbow.

Warren burst out snickering. What was wrong with him tonight? *Wizard of Oz* on the brain. He must be drunk. He felt young and floating and a trifle silly. And sleepy. How tempting it was to just relax into the thick down pillows and drift off. But that would be a disaster. Imagine waking up at eight in the morning when the marina was coming to life. He *couldn't* stay on board for the rest of the night. He must wake up in his own bed and carry through with the day as people expected. He had to leave.

"Charlotte," he said softly. No response. "*Charlotte.*"

She breathed heavily beside him. She had dozed with him before, but this was deep sleep. Too much champagne. He jiggled her. Nothing. She was all right but certainly not able to rise, dress, and go home. Oh, well, he needn't worry about Charlotte. She often spent the night on the yacht, so her family wouldn't be concerned if she wasn't home in the morning. He wasn't so lucky.

Warren gently moved her arm. She didn't stir. He smiled. Sleep, my beautiful prize.

He dressed by the one dim light they'd left on. Glancing in the mirror he decided he looked like hell—bloodshot eyes, dark circles, deepened lines in his forehead. Warren was usually vain about his appearance, but now he was glad he looked ragged. After all, he was supposed to be the grieving widower.

He glanced at Charlotte one last time. She hadn't moved. Colossal headache tomorrow, he thought. Maybe that would keep her too occupied to make any more unwise phone calls to his house.

He left the bedroom and went up to the beautifully appointed saloon. Saloon. The word had always seemed foolish to him, conjuring up images from *Gunsmoke*. Miss Kitty should be lurking somewhere ready to flirt with Marshal Dillon. Nevertheless, people were insistent on using the correct terms, like saloon for what would be called the living room, galley for kitchen, port and starboard for left and right. Nonsense.

He paused. Was that a shadow passing by one of the windows looking out onto the walk-around deck? He rushed to the glass and looked out. The deck was empty. The boat beside the *Charlotte* was lighter and rocked while the *Charlotte* remained nearly motionless. Moonlight played over the water. That's all he'd seen—a cloud passing across the moon. He took a deep breath. He was being paranoid, thinking that Meredith had people everywhere. He had to stop jumping at shadows, literal or otherwise. The appearance of innocence was essential.

Warren crept forward. Twenty minutes and he'd be home. He had rarely looked forward to being at home in the past. How many nights had he lain beneath one of Tamara's quilts with her rolled into a tight ball, just like her inhibited little psyche, and felt himself breaking into a sweat, the sweat of panic at the thought that *this* was the rest of his life? Hundreds of times. But now that bed seemed like the safest place in the world. That was where he should be, where he *wanted* to be if Sheriff Meredith should come looking.

Warren passed through the formal dining room and went up on deck. Cool air wafted over him. Some of the fuzziness left his head. Even his vision seemed clearer. In the distance a small bell clanged into the night. Nearby a board creaked.

He whirled around with the sharp, blinding awareness that something horrible waited for him in the chill darkness. His hands shot out blindly and he felt as if he were losing control of his bowels.

He barely made a sound as the long razor plunged into his neck, stabbing through flesh, puncturing the trachea. Warren's heartbeat soared. Blood frothed from the wound and pain seared like lightning through his gut. As he reflexively bent double, the razor ripped a quarter of the way around his neck, destroying muscles and veins. His hand flew to the wound and he futilely tried to stanch the relentless flow of his life fluid. He could see, but all he could make out was a dark shape wavering in front of him.

Warren stumbled forward. The figure sidestepped and he crashed onto the wooden deck, rolling onto his back. Still grasping his throat, opening his mouth only to emit noisy gurgles, he blinked. Someone hovered above him, but he couldn't make out the face. His attacker was only a dark shape against darkness mumbling words he could not understand.

Warren felt his consciousness slipping away. The figure moved, almost faded, backward down into the yacht . . .

To Charlotte.

And in the distance the boat bell went on ringing calmly in the breeze of an oblivious night.

9

I

TUESDAY MORNING

The sun seemed unusually bright, maybe because she hadn't gotten much sleep last night. Natalie put on her sunglasses as she drove into downtown Port Ariel. Destination: Curious Things.

Natalie had not visited Lily's shop for three years. Last summer Lily had renovated, turning the nondescript brick building into a striking establishment that looked like something from the pages of Dickens. A huge bay window jutted over the sidewalk displaying an antique cradle, music boxes, crystal decanters, two of Tamara's lovely quilts, and pieces of jewelry. When she opened the dark green door with its paned window, a bell jingled merrily, announcing the arrival of a customer.

Lily stood behind the counter talking to a young man. She looked past him and smiled at Natalie.

"When I called your place this morning, your answering machine message said you'd be at the store," Natalie said. "I didn't expect you to be working today."

"I'm only here because of a shipping snafu I had to straighten out." Lily still had mauve shadows beneath her eyes and Natalie didn't like her pallor, but she looked slightly more animated than the day before. "Natalie, I'd like for you to meet Jeff . . ."

"Lindstrom," he supplied. "I'm vacationing here. Ms. Peyton told me about some of the places I should visit."

Natalie took his extended hand. "Natalie St. John. I grew up here. I'm back for a visit."

Jeff smiled broadly. His dark blond hair touched the collar of his denim shirt and his slightly prominent teeth were astonishingly white. Natalie guessed him to be no more than thirty.

The bell above the door jingled. Everyone glanced up as Nick Meredith entered. Natalie felt color creeping to her cheeks. The very thought of their last meeting at The Blue Lady made her feel like running from the store in embarrassment. Please don't let him say anything about it, Natalie thought fervently. But he barely glanced at her. His solemn attention was for Lily. "Hello, Miss Peyton. Your father told me I would find you here."

"What's wrong?" she demanded tensely.

"Do you know where your brother-in-law is?"

"Warren?" Lily looked blank. "No. Why?"

"Because I need to talk with him as soon as possible and I haven't been able to reach him."

"Well, I'm sure he's around somewhere. Even *he* wouldn't have the nerve to leave town with the funeral tomorrow." Lily's eyes narrowed. "Why is it so important that you talk to him?"

"I just have a couple of questions." Meredith's casual tone did not ring true. "I'll try him again in an hour or so. Thanks, Miss Peyton."

The bell jingled again and a high, childish voice cried, "Daddy!"

Heads swiveled. A little girl with long auburn hair and a sprinkling of freckles beamed at Sheriff Meredith. Behind her stood a heavyset woman with short salt-and-pepper hair and dark eyes behind black-framed glasses.

"Paige," Sheriff Meredith said. "I didn't know you and Mrs. Collins were going shopping today."

"I clean forgot that today is my sister's birthday," the woman explained. "Of course I wouldn't leave Paige home alone and I absolutely had to get a gift. I hope you don't mind me bringing her. I called your office to ask, but you weren't in and it's something of an emergency or I wouldn't have thought of taking her out without your permission."

She sounded as if she'd dragged the child along on a

dangerous expedition, Natalie thought. Sheriff Meredith looked faintly amused. "You don't have to get clearance for a trip to downtown Port Ariel, Mrs. Collins, unless you plan to stop in at the local bar for a sandwich and a beer at lunch."

"Oh, no!" Mrs. Collins earnestly assured him. "We're going to McDonald's."

Natalie realized the child was staring at her and smiled. "Hi."

"Hi. I'm Paige Meredith. Are you Natalie St. John?"

"I am indeed," Natalie laughed. "How did you know?"

"My best friend is Jimmy Jenkins." Natalie raised her eyebrows questioningly. "He's twelve and has black hair like yours. He met you the day Mrs. Hunt got murdered."

"Paige!" Meredith said sharply. He motioned toward Lily. "This is Mrs. Hunt's sister."

Paige's sunny smile vanished. "Oh, gosh, I'm sorry."

"It's all right," Lily murmured. "Did Jimmy describe Natalie to you?"

"Yeah." Paige looked relieved that Lily was changing the subject. Her gaze shifted back to Natalie. "Daddy says you're a vet. Do you make house calls?"

"House calls? Not usually. I don't even practice around here."

"Oh." Exaggerated disappointment throbbed in Paige's voice. "I'm *so* worried about my cat Ripley."

Natalie saw Nick Meredith roll his eyes. What was this all about? she wondered. "What's wrong with Ripley?"

"He's fat," Meredith said flatly.

"No he's not," Paige retorted. "But he scratches his ears a lot."

"Mites," Natalie said. "Maybe an infection."

"In*fec*tion!" Paige made it sound like plague. "Also . . . he limps."

"Since when?" Meredith demanded.

"Since . . . this morning."

"Have you checked to see if there's something between his pads?" Natalie asked. "Maybe a pebble?"

"I didn't see anything. Dr. St. John, Ripley doesn't like his usual vet, Dr. Cavanaugh. He gets all nervous and upset when he has to go see him. The last time, he scratched Dr. Cavanaugh and he *yelled* at Ripley. A lot. Ripley didn't eat for two days."

"That's too bad, but surely there's more than one vet in Port Ariel."

"There is," Meredith said firmly. "Dr. Landers."

"Daddy, he's *ancient*," Paige wailed. "He bumbles around and talks to himself and last time we were there he called *me* Ripley. He might give Ripley the wrong medicine and *kill* him. He also says every pet has the same thing—worms!"

"Worms *are* fairly common, Paige." Natalie tried not to grin. The child was certainly laying it on thick—thick enough to win her admiration for dramatic tenacity. "However, if you're so worried about Ripley, I'd be happy to take a look at him."

Paige beamed. Meredith scowled. "Dr. St. John, this isn't necessary," he said. "The cat is *fine*—"

"Is not," Paige asserted.

"—and I know you're here on a visit," Meredith continued. "We're not going to press you into service."

"I don't mind, really."

Paige didn't look at her father. "We live at 312 Elmhurst—"

"*Paige.*" Meredith drew a deep breath. "Dr. St. John is obliging you by seeing Ripley. You aren't going to insist she drive to our house, too."

"Actually, it would be better if I come to your house than if you bring the cat to mine," Natalie said. "I have a new dog and I don't know how she feels about cats."

"The dog that found Mrs. Hunt's body?" Paige's eyes—the same intense blue as her father's—flew wide and she gasped in Lily's direction. "I'm so *sorry*! I didn't mean—"

"It's all right, honey," Lily said kindly. "My sister is dead. That's just a fact, so you don't have to worry about everything you say to me."

Natalie could feel some of the tension leaving the room. Even Sheriff Meredith's stiffness dropped a few notches. "I have work to do." He looked at Lily. "If you hear from your brother-in-law, will you let me know?"

Lily nodded. "Of course, but I think I'd be the last person he'd call."

Meredith turned his dark blue gaze on Natalie. "Thank you for agreeing to check on Ripley. I really don't think it's necessary."

"I'd like to ease Paige's mind."

"Yes, I'm sure she's tied in knots over Ripley's dire condition." He shot a meaningful look at his daughter who assumed a guileless expression. "I will see *you* at home tonight."

"Yes, Daddy," she said meekly. "I love you."

Meredith left the store shaking his head. Lily smiled at Jeff Lindstrom, who was watching Meredith closely. "And that is our sheriff, Nicolas Meredith," she said.

"Pretty imposing guy."

"Who apparently doesn't have time for introductions."

"That's all right. No reason for him to be interested in me. I'm just a harmless tourist." He gave Lily an earnest look. "Ms. Peyton, I'm very sorry about your sister. I had no idea."

"How could you?"

"I did read about the murder in the newspaper but I didn't realize the poor woman was your sister."

"My identical twin."

"God, that's awful." He hesitated. "I guess they have no idea who . . ."

"Slashed her throat?" Natalie winced at Lily's bald language. "No, although I wonder if Sheriff Meredith isn't suspecting Tamara's husband Warren. That must be why he's in such a fizz to talk to him this morning."

Paige lingered around the counter, looking in the glass case at several pieces of antique jewelry. And taking in every word, Natalie thought. She caught Lily's eye and nodded at the child. "Where are you off to first?" Lily asked Jeff.

"I might visit the nautical museum." His stomach growled loudly. "Or I might eat," he laughed. "Can you recommend a restaurant that serves a hearty breakfast?"

"Trudy's Diner, right down the street. They make the best

cinnamon rolls in the world and they load your plate as if you're headed into the Yukon for the day."

"Sounds like just the ticket. Well, thank you for all the information. And once again, I'm sorry about your sister, Ms. Peyton."

"Lily."

"Lily it is." He looked at Natalie. "Nice meeting you, Dr. St. John."

"And I'm Natalie. Nice meeting you too, Jeff. Enjoy your day."

As he walked out the door, Paige moved away from the jewelry counter and joined Mrs. Collins, who was looking at a brass bedwarmer. "I wonder if Nell would like this?" she asked no one in particular. "Oh, no she wouldn't. Her husband left her a month ago. She'd think I was rubbing it in. Maybe a pretty ceramic thimble. No, she'd think I was being cheap. Oh, this art glass is pretty . . . Good gracious, look at the price!"

"Decisions, decisions," Lily murmured to Natalie.

"He was nice-looking," Natalie said.

"Jeff? Yes. Under different circumstances I might even have flirted, but I don't have any coquetry in me this morning."

"It will return, maybe even before he leaves town."

"If you don't get to him first."

Natalie smiled. "We sound desperate."

"We are," Lily said wryly. "So, Natalie St. John, why did you need to talk to me this morning?"

"We didn't discuss the post-funeral arrangements. I assume everyone will be coming back to your father's house."

Lily sighed. "Yes, and how I dread it. Maybe some people take comfort in having a bunch of people stand around stuffing themselves with food after the burial of a loved one, but I find the custom repugnant."

"I'm not crazy about it myself," Natalie said. "Need my help?"

"Surely you jest. With Viveca Cosgrove in the picture? She started making plans an hour after she heard Tam was dead."

"Viveca? What about Mrs. Ebert?"

"Oh, forget that she's been the housekeeper forever and has impeccable taste. Viveca pushed her aside and Dad let her. She's having the damned affair catered. I've heard her on the phone making arrangements. They sound like they're for a party. I'm surprised we're not having a reception with a band at the country club. Maybe even a door prize. I told Dad I thought the whole shebang was in terrible taste. He said I should appreciate Viveca's efforts. I can just imagine what my poor mother would think."

"She'd be appalled. Is Alison coming?"

"With bells on. Even Dad isn't too happy about that, but last night on the phone Viveca told him it was important to Alison." She glanced around like a guilty child and lowered her voice.

"While they were talking on the phone, I happened to pick up the extension and I didn't hang up."

"Lily!"

"Yes, I'm thoroughly ashamed of myself," Lily said, not looking at all ashamed. "Viveca was upset. She said Alison got quite *distressed* when she told her she didn't want her to attend the funeral and that she'd flung off to her bedroom in a fury. At around one-thirty in the morning she thought she heard the front door closing softly and someone coming up the stairs. Viveca got up and peeked in Alison's room. She was in bed, but she was dressed. Viveca said she didn't want to upset Alison by asking if she'd left the house, but it's pretty obvious she did." Lily raised an eyebrow. "Now where do you think someone like Alison Cosgrove would go in the middle of the night?"

II

Mrs. Collins had looked at every item in Curious Things. She picked up one thing after another, rejecting each after careful inspection. Finally she'd dithered over a pair of brass candlesticks until Paige thought she would scream. At last she bought them, paying the whole amount in five- and one-dollar bills.

Purchase in hand, she'd marched from the store to window-shop, although how anyone could enjoy window-shopping at the hardware store and the office supply outlet Paige could not imagine. At last they'd made it to McDonald's where Mrs. Collins complained steadily about the terrible food although she ate every bite of her Big Mac, large order of fries, and apple pie.

When they reached home, Paige tore up the stairs to her bedroom and the precious phone. She stroked Ripley as she endured Mrs. Jenkins's inquiries about Paige's health, her father's health, and Mrs. Collins's health while a child whined maddeningly in the background. At last she put Jimmy on the line.

"Can you talk in private?" Paige asked.

"Yeah. Mom took my sister to her room. What's up?"

"This morning I was in a store owned by Mrs. Hunt's sister. Her name is Lily Peyton."

"I know who she is. She looks just like Tamara. She told me to call her Tamara, you know, not Mrs. Hunt. I liked her a lot. She always made me chocolate chip cookies."

Chocolate chip cookies, Paige thought. She would immediately learn to make them. "I met Natalie St. John."

"Who?"

"The lady vet who took home the dog that found Tamara's body. I think she's pretty. *Real* pretty."

Jimmy sighed. "Did you call just to talk about her?"

"No I did not," Paige snapped. "When we were in the store, my dad came in and asked Lily Peyton where her brother-in-law was. That would be Tamara's husband."

"Sure. His name is Warren but I always had to call him Dr. Hunt. Dad says he's a stuffed shirt."

"My dad seemed like he really wanted to talk to Dr. Hunt. You live right across the street. Isn't he home?"

"No. He's been gone all morning."

"How do you know?"

"The garage door is up. No car. And his morning paper is on the porch. He always gets it real early." There was a moment of silence. "Hey, I just remembered something! When we couldn't go to Ariel's last night because my sister Ivy got sick and every-one was up and I couldn't sneak out, I stayed awake and watched television. Ivy went to the emergency room."

"What's wrong with her?"

"Chest cold. She'll live. Anyway, I was looking out the window and I saw Dr. Hunt leave in his car. It was before midnight."

"When did he get back?"

"Mom and Dad brought Ivy home about one o'clock. I was watching *Lethal Weapon 4* on HBO. Mom got mad. She thinks it's too violent. She made me go to bed, but I looked at the Hunts' house first. He hadn't come back."

Paige sat silent for a few seconds, thinking. Finally she said, "I think Dr. Hunt was gone all night. You have to tell my dad."

"He wouldn't believe me," Jimmy said glumly.

"He might not believe you about that creature at Ariel's house, but he'd believe you about this."

"Gosh, Paige, I don't know. My mom already gripes at me for spying. She calls me a little Peeping Tom. She'll be mad."

"You weren't spying. You just noticed. For Pete's sake, the guy lives right across the street."

"She's all upset over Ivy today and she'd blow up and call it spying and maybe ground me."

"Jimmy?"

"Yeah?"

"Eddie Salvatore would do it."

Silence. Then a voice full of determination. "You're right. I can't worry about getting grounded. I have a civic duty. I'll call your dad right now."

III

"Why aren't you at work today, Mama?"

Alison sat at the kitchen table tearing her wheat toast into tiny pieces.

Viveca poured a cup of tea and sat down. Her honey-blond hair fell in soft waves to her shoulders and without makeup her skin was pale but unlined. "I'm taking a week off so I can arrange the funeral."

Alison began stacking the pieces of toast. "I don't like Lily."

"Really?" Viveca asked casually. "I thought you did after she sold us that brooch."

"It was Ariel's brooch. It belonged to us anyway and she should have just given it to me. But that's not why I don't like her. She looks at me like I'm crazy."

Viveca sipped her tea. "I'm sure that's just your imagination."

"Now you sound like *you* think I'm crazy," Alison huffed.

"Of course I don't. You're being too sensitive. Now eat your breakfast."

Alison threw her a mutinous look. "I *hate* wheat bread and I *hate* tea. Mrs. Krebbs, my keeper, knows that. Where is she?"

"Taking a few days for herself. Since I'm off this week, I thought we could spend some time together."

"Doing what?"

"Whatever you want. We could just relax and talk—"

"Warren had a girlfriend," Alison burst out.

Viveca's cup stopped halfway to her mouth. "What are you talking about?"

"He was having an *affair*. You know what an *affair* is."

Viveca set down her cup. "How do you know he was having an affair?"

"I have my ways."

"With whom?"

"I'm not going to tell you. You'll know soon enough. And you'll be surprised." Her malicious smile faded. "I was. I thought he was better than that. I thought he cared about me.

Viveca suddenly wanted nothing else to eat or drink. Her stomach had immediately twisted into a knot. "Dear, you've been listening to gossip."

"It is *not* gossip. I *know*."

Viveca's tongue touched her dry upper lip. "Do me a favor and don't repeat this. It's vicious."

Alison shrugged. "All right. Whatever you say. Your wish is

my command. I live to please you. But everyone will know soon."

Alison pushed her plate away and glared out the window, twisting a lock of hair around an index finger.

Viveca made an effort to sound composed and offhand. "Dear, did you go out last night?"

"No."

"Are you sure?"

"No. I'm crazy. I'm not sure of anything."

"Darling, you are not crazy. Don't say such a thing. But you know it isn't safe for you to be out at night. After all, Tamara Hunt was *murdered*."

"So you think I might be murdered by the same person who killed *her*?"

"Yes."

Alison stared at her mother. Then she burst into shrill laughter.

IV

"I need to talk to the sheriff."

Ted Hysell idly sketched a twelve-point buck. At least it was supposed to be a buck. It looked more like a Great Dane with antlers. "Look, son—"

"Jimmy. My name is Jimmy Jenkins. I already told you that."

Ted sighed. He'd have something to say to the new receptionist for putting this call through to him. She probably thought it was funny. She was a smart-alec and he didn't like her. She wouldn't have dared to show Meredith such a lack of respect.

"Okay, *Jimmy*. Sheriff Meredith is very busy. He only takes important calls, not calls from kids."

He could feel Jimmy bristling on the other end of the phone. "Just because I'm a kid doesn't mean I don't have anything important to say."

"I'm sure."

"Quit making fun of me. Look, I'm friends with Paige Meredith."

"Is this about Paige?"

"Is what about Paige?" Hysell looked up to see Meredith looming over his desk. "Who is it?"

"Some kid named Jimmy Jenkins. Says he has something important to say but he won't tell me. Insists on talking to you."

"Switch the call to my office," Meredith said.

He's going to bother with this kid, Hysell thought in annoyance. Maybe he thought the boy had information about Paige. Or maybe the kid was just using Paige's name as an excuse to talk to the sheriff. Oh, well, *he* hadn't put through the call. Meredith couldn't get mad at *him* for wasting his time.

As soon as he hung up, the phone rang again. Great. His head hurt and he'd abandoned his lunch to take care of old Harvey Coombs, who this morning had sat out in his rowboat shouting that he had a bomb. Harvey got really ripped on bourbon and pulled this stunt at least three times every summer. He claimed the tourists got a big kick out of it. The Sheriff's Department didn't, even though former Sheriff Purdue had always let it slide. Not so Meredith, who had ordered Hysell to arrest Coombs. Harvey's wife said a night in jail might do him some good and refused to bail him out until tomorrow, leaving the drunken old coot to sit weeping in a cell like a lost child.

Now it was three o'clock, Hysell's head pounded, his stomach rumbled, and he felt half bad for Harvey even though the guy was a pain in the ass. What a terrific day so far.

The phone rang again and he picked up the receiver. After hearing his name, the woman caller nearly burst into tears. "Oh, Ted, I'm so glad it's you. I don't know what . . . This kind of thing has never happened before . . . Max doesn't know yet . . ."

Hysell would recognize the tentative voice and unfinished sentences anywhere. "Mrs. Bishop, why don't you take a couple of deep breaths and tell me what's wrong?"

"It's Charlotte of course!" She sounded as if she thought Hysell was being dense. "She didn't come home last night!"

Wow, Charlotte Bishop had a one-night stand, Ted thought. Alert the media. "Mrs. Bishop, when did you last see her?"

"About ten-thirty last night. At dinner she was wearing her gray slacks with that cute little silk tunic I gave her last Christmas. Then I looked out the window and saw her in the driveway. Saw her clear as day . . . all those lights, you know. She had on tight white pants and a filmy blouse unbuttoned *far* too low. I rapped sharply on the window. She ignored me. She got in that sports car of hers . . . Oh, something happened first. She was approached by a *man*."

"Not someone you know?"

"No."

"Someone she knew?"

"Well, I'm not sure. Charlotte has many friends. She's always been so popular . . ."

Oh, sure, Hysell thought sourly. Port Ariel's Miss Congeniality. "What did this guy look like?"

"Youngish. About your age. Dark blond hair a bit long for my taste. Dungarees. I don't understand why people wear those things. Paul Fiori wore them. It always seemed to me that if he wanted to get movie parts he should *look* like a movie star. Rock Hudson didn't wear dungarees. Of course, he was *funny*, if you know what I mean . . . Died a terrible death. Max said he got what he deserved, but I felt sorry for him, so handsome and all—"

"Mrs. Bishop," Hysell said firmly to one of the few people in town who could out-talk him, "this guy had dark blond hair and wore jeans. Can you remember anything else about him?"

"No. Except that he was tall and slender like my Billy used to be. You remember Billy. Such a wonderful boy . . ."

"Did the guy last night act like he was threatening Charlotte?"

"Well, not exactly. But I could tell she didn't want to talk to him. She kept shaking her head . . . She looked cross. Charlotte can be quite irritable sometimes. She gets that from her daddy. After she left, the man in dungarees went out to the street and got into a white car. I don't know car models. It was ordinary, not sporty or luxurious . . . just, well, you know . . . ordinary." Her voice rose. "Ted, I'm afraid he followed Charlotte and maybe hurt her!"

"Don't worry, Mrs. Bishop. We'll locate her. I promise."

Muriel Bishop sounded teary. "Thank you, Ted. You've always been a sweet boy. Please call when you know something. I haven't told Max yet," she repeated. "He gets so upset because he's helpless. But if he finds out and I *didn't* tell him, he'll be furious with me. I don't know what I should do. Life is so confusing . . ."

She hung up.

Charlotte hadn't been gone for even twenty-four hours. Officially there was nothing Hysell *could* do. Unofficially there was nothing he *wanted* to do. Charlotte was probably shacked up with someone. With Warren Hunt? Now that would be pushing it, even for Charlotte. The guy's wife had just been murdered. He was under suspicion, although Hysell wasn't sure Hunt quite realized the seriousness of his situation. He seemed to think he was far too classy to ever be considered capable of murder.

Meredith strode from his office. "Hysell, the Jenkins kid lives across the street from Warren Hunt. He says Hunt left around midnight last night and never came back."

Hysell tensed. "I just got a call from Muriel Bishop, Charlotte's mother. She says Charlotte left about ten-thirty and *she* hasn't come home, either."

"Well, well, what a coincidence."

"Do you think they ran off together?"

Meredith shook his head. "They can't be *that* stupid. No, something's wrong. Did Mrs. Bishop have any idea where Charlotte went last night?"

"I don't think so. She left in some sort of outfit Mrs. Bishop didn't like. Something about a filmy blouse unbuttoned too low. And there was a guy outside the house. Tall, slim, dark blond hair, maybe early thirties. Mrs. Bishop said they seemed to be arguing. Then Charlotte drove off and the guy left in his own car."

"What kind of car?"

"Don't know. White. *Ordinary*, Mrs. Bishop said."

"Call her back. Ask where Charlotte went at night for fun.

Also ask if Charlotte has ever stayed out all night before. Don't sound like you're implying any misconduct on Charlotte's part. That might make Mrs. Bishop clam up."

"It sure would. I know how to handle it."

"Make it quick. I have a feeling time is important."

Half an hour later they were headed toward the marina. Muriel Bishop said sometimes her daughter spent the night aboard the yacht, but she was always home by noon. She *couldn't* still be there, Muriel insisted. Besides, she'd called the yacht and there was no answer. Hysell had assured her they weren't alarmed—only curious. "If you want to know the truth, I think Sheriff Meredith just wants an excuse to look at the *Charlotte*" he'd laughed. "She's really something."

"I suppose," Muriel had answered unenthusiastically. "Max and Charlotte certainly think so. I haven't been aboard many times . . ."

Meredith let out a low whistle as they neared the *Charlotte*. "Now that's what I call a nice toy."

Hysell cleared his throat and offered uncertainly, "Uh . . . people around here take boating pretty seriously, Sheriff."

"So I shouldn't refer to a boat as a toy?"

"Well, maybe not," Hysell said, certain he'd offended Meredith.

Miraculously, the sheriff grinned. "Thanks for the tip. I don't want to make enemies without even knowing what I've done. Or said."

Was Mr. Hot Shot New York City listening to him? Hysell wondered. Hard to believe. But Meredith had seemed to treat him differently after they were at Hunt's yesterday. Maybe there was hope yet.

"No sign of activity." Meredith looked up at the yacht. "Let's see what's inside."

As soon as they stepped on deck, a cloud of flies rose from a circle of dried blood at least two feet in diameter. A trail of black blood led down the steps to the saloon. Warren Hunt sat propped on a beige couch, his eyes wide and glazed above a gaping slash in his throat. His head lolled to one side and flies crawled all over his face, gorging. For an awful instant, Ted thought he might vomit. In the master stateroom, Charlotte Bishop lay in a tangle of blood-soaked satin sheets, her lovely head nearly severed from her naked body. Flies hovered everywhere, even around the words written on the wall in blood, OPEN TOMB.

Ted ran from the bedroom, through the saloon and up to fresh air before heaving his stomach contents over the side of the magnificent *Charlotte*.

10

Nick Meredith felt a hundred years old—shocked, disgusted, hopeless, emotionally and physically drained. He'd come to Port Ariel because he wanted to rear his daughter in a safe, wholesome environment. Safe? Someone had committed three homicides in forty-eight hours. Wholesome? Someone had nearly decapitated three people. What would Meagan think of this new life he'd created for Paige? Meagan would say nothing in life is certain except that nothing in life is certain. She would be understanding and philosophical. He was angry and resentful. Hadn't Paige been through enough? Hadn't he?

He had more work to do, but at six he felt an overpowering need to see his daughter, to hear her laugh, to feel her slender arms around his neck. At times like this only she could restore him. He also wanted to make absolutely certain she was safe. He had niggling doubts about Mrs. Collins's diligence in the childcare department.

When he arrived home he was surprised to see a gold Cougar sitting in the driveway. He knew no one with a Cougar. Had something happened?

Nick nearly bolted in the front door and was greeted by the sound of laughter. In the living room Paige sat on the floor with a dark-haired woman. Natalie St. John. They were bent over Ripley, who lay on his back bouncing a toy mouse between his paws. Nick realized he'd been holding his breath when it came out as a loud *whish*.

"That certainly looks like a sick cat to me," he said, grinning.

Paige jumped up and ran to him. "Hi, Daddy. Natalie says—"

"Dr. St. John," Nick corrected.

"I asked her to call me Natalie." He hadn't noticed before that her voice was slightly husky. "It gives me the illusion of youth."

"Anyway, *Natalie* says that Ripley does have mites. I told you he'd been scratching his ears."

"What about that terrible limp I've never noticed?"

"Maybe just a muscle spasm," Natalie said. "Nothing life-threatening."

"And his weight?" Nick asked.

Natalie smiled. "Ripley could stand to lose three or four pounds."

"He eats from nerves," Paige explained.

"And what does Ripley have to be nervous about?" Nick asked, smiling.

"These murders. I heard there were two more."

Nick's smile faded. "How did you hear about them?"

"Somebody called Mrs. Collins and they talked about them for a long time. Two people got their throats cut on a big boat! One was Tamara Hunt's husband. He was having an *affair!*"

Nick's jaw tightened. He was furious that the child was privy to all this information. He looked at Natalie, who shook her head regretfully. Apparently she felt the same way. "Did you catch the murderer?" Paige asked anxiously.

"Not yet, but we will soon. I don't want you to be afraid."

"I'm not afraid," Paige said staunchly. Nick did not believe her. "Do you think this crazy person is killing special people or just anyone?" she asked.

"We don't know that yet, but probably special people, *partic-ular* people," Nick said uncomfortably. "I don't think you have to worry. They were all grownups."

"Yeah, but he could decide to kill kids. Especially if they know something important."

Nick looked at her closely. "Do you know something important?"

"What would I know?" Except maybe where the killer is hiding, Paige thought miserably, but she could *not* tell Daddy about the Saunders house. She would be in so much trouble she'd never be allowed outside again. She'd never get to see Jimmy again, either, and that would be too awful to bear. "I just like mysteries," she ended lamely.

"I'd prefer it if you kept your mind off this particular mystery," Nick said firmly.

"Paige, Ripley is scratching his ears again," Natalie interrupted with false urgency. "Blaine had fleas *and* ear mites so yesterday I had the clinic where I work send me some prescription-strength flea medicine and drops for mites. The mite drops are right here in my purse. I'll show you how to put them in Ripley's ears and then you can do it until he's well."

"Do you think I can put them in right?"

"I'm sure you can. Come give it a try."

Nick cast her a grateful look for changing the subject. Mrs. Collins was another matter. While Natalie and Paige worked on a less-than-cooperative Ripley, he walked into the kitchen. The woman sat at the kitchen table drinking coffee. She gave him a bright smile. "Sheriff, I wasn't expecting you home so early. I just put some pot roast and potatoes and green beans in the refrigerator. I'll fix a plate and heat it in the microwave."

"Before you do, I'd like to talk to you." The woman immediately looked wary. "Did you tell Paige about the murders this afternoon?"

She flushed guiltily. "I'm so sorry. A friend called to tell me— her nephew works at the marina—and Paige overheard me on the phone. But I think she got a call from that Jenkins boy. I'm sure he knew all about it and told her more than she should hear. He's a regular town crier. His mother should keep a tighter rein on him. I don't think he's a good influence on Paige."

The woman was valiantly trying to shift attention from

herself to Jimmy. It wasn't going to work. "Mrs. Collins, I wish you had waited until you got home to discuss the murders with your friend."

"She called *me!*"

"You should have told her you couldn't talk at the moment."

"We hardly said *anything.*"

"My daughter knows quite a few details and she said she heard them from you." Nick looked at her sternly. "Mrs. Collins, Paige is eleven—"

"She would have heard about the murders sooner or later!" the woman burst out indignantly.

"Later would have been better. Later when I got home and could tell her in my own way."

Mrs. Collins stiffened. "I suppose I'm fired."

"No. I just want you to be more careful about what you discuss in front of Paige."

"I raised a girl of my own," she said in vindication. "I know what I'm doing!"

"I'm sure you do." Nick fought to keep his voice even. "We simply need to be clear on this point."

"We *are.*" Mrs. Collins stood. "I will be going, now that you're home."

"I have to go back to work. I need for you to stay."

"Stay! Tonight?" She shook her head violently. "I stayed late two nights ago. I can't *always* stay late without notice."

"I'm sorry. The next time someone is going to be murdered, I'll ask them to let me know several hours ahead of time so I can clear it with you."

Mrs. Collins gave him a long, icy stare. "You don't need to be obnoxious, Sheriff. I'm doing the best I can. When I took this job you didn't say a word about night work. If you're so unhappy with me, I won't be back tomorrow."

What will I do then? Nick thought. He couldn't lose the woman on such short notice. Feathers definitely needed smoothing.

"You're right, Mrs. Collins. I've had a tough day, but that

doesn't give me the right to take it out on you. Will you accept my apology?"

She hesitated and Nick felt she was deliberately trying to make him squirm. "Well, okay," she said in a tiny, injured voice. "But I really can't stay any longer tonight. I'm having a birthday party for my sister. I can't cancel."

"I understand." I understand you've just manipulated me into feeling like a creep when *you* were in the wrong, Nick thought. But what the hell. "I'll figure out something else for Paige tonight. We'll see you in the morning."

Mrs. Collins marched past him cloaked in martyrdom. In the living room he heard her say, "Good night, Paige dear. Have very sweet dreams. We'll have a wonderful day tomorrow."

Nick sauntered back into the room after the front door closed. Paige looked up at him. "How come she's being so *mushy*?"

"Beats me. She's just in a mushy mood."

"A weird mood. Daddy, I put the drops in Ripley's ears."

"She did a fine job in spite of Ripley's protests," Natalie said. "We might have a future vet here."

"I'd like to be a vet!" Paige exclaimed. "Either that or a police detective."

"I vote for veterinarian," Nick said. "Safer."

Natalie raised an eyebrow. "Have *you* ever treated a bad-tempered pit bull in pain?"

"I stand corrected." Nick sighed. "Paige, I'm going to have a cup of coffee. Then I have to go back to the office for a while. I'm afraid that because Mrs. Collins went home, you have to go with me." Paige made a face. "I thought you liked police headquarters."

"I do. It's just that you only have a little-bitty TV and *Jane Eyre* is on PBS at eight. I love *Jane Eyre*."

"Me, too," Natalie said.

Paige's eyes widened. "Isn't it creepy when Mr. Rochester's crazy wife comes down from the attic and looks at Jane asleep?"

Natalie shivered dramatically. "And when Jane comes back and Mrs. Rochester has burned down the mansion?"

"Oh, yeah! And poor Mr. Rochester is *blind*!"

"I see the Port Ariel *Jane Eyre* fan club is alive and well," Nick laughed. "I'm sorry, honey, but you'll have to watch it on the little-bitty TV set."

"Sheriff Meredith, I could stay with Paige until you get back," Natalie said.

"It's *Nick* and we couldn't impose. I'm sure you have things to do."

"Actually, I don't. I'd like to stay and watch *Jane Eyre* with Paige." And he remembers you as the woman who shot up the local dance hall with a gun you were carrying illegally, Natalie thought. Very reassuring. She felt ridiculous for suggesting he entrust his daughter to her when there was a murderer on the loose. "Of course, I understand your wanting her to be with you, though," she stumbled. "I didn't mean to interfere—"

"I love Paige's company, but I'm going to be busy," Nick said suddenly. "If you're sure you don't mind staying, I would appreciate it and I know Paige would, too. I don't want to spoil the movie for her."

"Great!" Paige burst out.

Amazing, Natalie thought. Maybe he didn't think she was a nut after all.

"I'll be home by ten," Nick promised. "Keep the doors locked."

"Oh, Daddy, I always do," Paige said. "I'm going to fix popcorn. And Cokes. Or 7Up. Or whatever you like, Natalie."

"Sounds terrific." Natalie looked at Nick. "I'll take good care of her. You go do your duty. We'll be here suffering through the trials and tribulations of a nineteenth-century heroine and loving every minute of it."

II

It was 10:45. He'd told Natalie he'd be back by ten. Would she be mad?

"Nick Meredith, you act like you're married," he said aloud.

"Natalie is *not* your wife. She's some woman you barely know. Probably shouldn't even have trusted after that dumb stunt she pulled at The Blue Lady. If she's mad, you never have to see her again."

He hoped she wasn't mad.

When he unlocked the front door and walked in, he saw her curled into a corner of the couch hugging an oversized pillow and watching *Street Life*. Her sandals lay on the floor and her long hair hung in a sloppy braid somewhere near her right ear.

"Natalie?"

She jumped, then smiled sheepishly. "I'm afraid I was somewhere between waking and sleeping. The movie ended at ten and Paige was worn out. She and Ripley are in hypersleep."

Nick laughed. "I take it you two had quite an evening."

"We did indeed. Before the movie we played the piano."

"You actually got her to play?" Nick asked.

"Yes. She said she hated her lessons, but I taught her a few songs. She has talent."

Nick smiled. "Both the piano and the talent come from her mother."

"I think she doesn't like her lessons because the teacher concentrates on classical music. It isn't her favorite. Afterward she got out her boombox and we danced and sang to some songs she does love. Did you know she's a closet rock star?"

"I've had hints."

"So was I at her age. I've promised to give her a few guitar lessons, if you don't mind."

"You play the guitar?"

"Yes, since I was younger than Paige."

"Guitar lessons," Nick said thoughtfully. "Maybe they would spur her musical interest the way the piano doesn't. I don't have an ounce of talent myself, but I'd hate to see hers go to waste just because she's playing the wrong instrument."

"It's not the instrument—it's the type of music. 'Für Elise' doesn't inspire her," Natalie told him. "She'd prefer something more modern. Anyway, after our concert we played beauty shop. She's practicing her French braid."

Nick grinned. "Judging by the looks of your hair she needs more practice."

"Don't tell her that. She said this was her best braid yet."

"Good Lord."

"She'll improve." Natalie reached up and began untwining the long, shining strands of her hair. "During the movie we ate approximately five pounds of popcorn. After the movie she was determined to stay up until you came home but her eyelids were drooping. She'll sleep late tomorrow."

Nick looked troubled. "Was she still frightened about the murders?"

"She stopped talking about them. I'm sure she's still afraid, though."

"She and the rest of the town. It's been one hell of a day."

Natalie stood. She wore faded jeans and a pale green tee shirt. "You look tired," she said, slipping her slender feet into the sandals.

"So tired I'll never get to sleep."

"I'd suggest a drink but alcohol makes you sleepy, then wakes you up in the middle of the night. May I fix you some warm milk?"

"I would love some warm milk, but after the evening you've put in with my daughter, I certainly can't ask—"

"You certainly can," she said briskly. "Warm milk coming up, on one condition."

"And that would be?"

"You get milk, I get information."

"About the murders?"

"Yes." Sensing his reluctance, Natalie said, "Sheriff Meredith—Nick—I *knew* these people. Tamara was one of my closest friends. Warren was her husband. This is all striking pretty close to home."

He sighed. "Okay. You deserve information. Just give me a few minutes to unwind."

Nick followed Natalie into the kitchen and took mugs from the cabinet while she got the milk. "Sit down before you fall down," she directed, putting the full mugs into the microwave. "Do you like cinnamon in your milk?"

"I never tried it, but it sounds good. I feel like living dangerously tonight."

She smiled. "I guessed you were a risk-taker."

When he took a sip of warm cinnamon-flavored milk he said, "That's great. I didn't know what I'd been missing for thirty-six years."

"My mother used to fix milk this way." Suddenly she laughed. "Once she read some silly article that said nutmeg had the same effect as LSD, so she rushed out and bought some for herself, sprinkled it in milk, and gulped it down. She looked *so* disappointed when nothing happened."

Nick stared at her.

"Let me explain Kira to you," Natalie went on. "I was never allowed to call her Mommy—only Kira. Her parents lived in San Francisco. They were artists, very successful and very bohemian. Their son Peter was straight as an arrow. He and my father met in medical school. Unlike Peter, Kira was even more unconventional than her parents. She and my father were a total mismatch. I still don't understand why she married him and had me. Maybe Dad and I were an experiment for her. Anyway, when I was six she took off. She was supposed to pick me up at school. She didn't show. Lily's mother took me home. The house was empty except for the dog. Three hours later when Dad got back from the hospital, he found a brief note in the bedroom saying she was sorry but she had to explore her inner self or some such nonsense. She said she'd be fine and in touch with us soon. *Soon* turned out to be six months. She was in California. She'd joined a commune, she called it. I think it was really a cult."

Natalie tossed Nick a lighthearted smile, but he saw the pain behind it. "She's still floating around from group to group, man to man. I hear from her a couple of times a year. I haven't seen her since I was twenty-one. She actually came to Columbus to talk me out of going into veterinary medicine. She said it was plebeian and that I should pursue my music. I ignored her."

"That's sad," Nick said, and immediately felt foolish. The woman had poured out her heart and all he responded with was "That's sad." He tried again. "Back in New York I ran into cases of neglect and desertion by parents all the time. I got almost used to it, but then I never knew the people involved. It seems almost unbelievable to me when I think of my own mother, though. She had seven kids. Didn't believe in birth control. My dad worked two jobs and Mom was a waitress, but things were still tough. She didn't have a lot of free time, but what she had she devoted to us. And my own wife Meagan . . . well, she was a great mother. A wonderful, loving mother. I wish she could have seen Paige grow up," he ended, feeling his throat muscles tighten. He took a sip of milk and sat rigid-faced when it wouldn't go down.

"Paige was lucky," Natalie said softly.

Nick nodded and managed to swallow. "Meagan died two years ago. That's why we left New York."

Natalie looked at him, clearly expecting him to go on with more details. But he hadn't discussed Meagan's death since it happened. A few people in Port Ariel knew that he was a widower. He'd never told anyone here how he had become one.

Natalie lowered her gaze and said casually, "It's tough on a little girl to be without a mother—"

"Meagan was murdered." The abruptness of the statement startled Nick. Natalie raised her eyes and the words began spilling from him. "She was working on a doctorate in English at N.Y.U. and had almost finished. One evening I came home and she was ecstatic. She'd done great on a general exam and wanted to celebrate with champagne. I offered to go to the liquor store, but she said I looked beat. The store was only a block away."

He looked down, lines digging into his forehead. "Just as she was paying for the champagne, in came a couple of punks with guns. The clerk had to play hero and go for the owner's gun under the counter." He drew a deep breath. "The punks started shooting. Two people were injured slightly. The clerk took a bullet in the head and died instantly. They got Meagan in the abdomen and the neck—the carotid artery. She lived four hours."

"Nick, I'm *so* sorry."

"If only *I'd* gone for the champagne. Instead I was sitting at home with my shoes off watching television while my wife—"

"You couldn't possibly have known what would happen," Natalie interrupted firmly. "Certainly she'd gone to that store before and there weren't any robberies. It was a random event. You can't control the world."

"More's the pity."

"It's a pity, but it's also a fact." Natalie added hesitantly, "Paige never said a word about what happened to her mother."

"She never does and it really worries me. I don't want her to dwell on her mother's death, but she won't discuss it at all. I know she thinks about it constantly, though. They were *so* close. She adored her mother," Nick said raggedly. "For five months after Meagan's death I went around in a haze, furious one minute, lost in grief the next. I even got this weird silver streak in my hair."

He paused and drew a deep breath. "Then Meagan's sister Jan started making noises about getting custody of Paige. That scared the hell out of me. There I was single and with a high-risk job. Not an ideal father, and Jan's husband has powerful contacts in the New York judicial system. So I pulled myself together and decided I had to get Paige out of New York, away from the memories, away from the threat of Jan, away from the *danger* of the city because if I lost her, too . . ."

Nick laughed mirthlessly. "I started looking frantically for jobs in small places. Someone I knew who vacationed here every summer told me about Port Ariel. I came and looked it over and discovered I could get on the police force. It seemed like a miracle, even if I had to work for Sheriff Purdue. Then came the election. I ran and to my amazement, I won. I thought I had it made. I was the sheriff of a beautiful little town. I'd made a home for my child in a safe haven, or so I thought."

"Port Ariel usually *is* a safe haven."

"I guess I was just lucky enough to move here and become sheriff when all hell is breaking loose. People are looking to me for answers."

"And you'll find them."

His dark blue eyes were anguished and the scar on his forehead turned dead white against the tanned skin. "Do you really believe that?"

"Yes," Natalie said sincerely. "Don't start doubting yourself now."

Nick studied her oval face, the fine skin, the intensely dark eyes with that beautiful slight slant. She not only looked lovely, she looked calm and intelligent and full of good sense. He suddenly felt astounded that he'd told her not only about Meagan's murder, but also his anxiety over his daughter's safety and her refusal to discuss her lost mother. Natalie had sat there with her warm milk and cinnamon, her soft husky voice, her tranquil manner, and elicited his darkest memory and his deepest fears. "Well, I'm a laugh a minute, aren't I?" he asked dryly.

"You're tired and worried." She smiled. "You're human."

"I don't think the citizens of Port Ariel want a human for a sheriff right now. They want a superhero."

"Can you blame them? They're scared."

"You don't seem scared, even after your visit to The Blue Lady."

Natalie flushed. "Can we please forget that appalling lapse of good sense? I'm not usually such a fool. And for the record, I'm just as scared as everyone else."

"And you're also full of questions about the murders."

"Maybe now isn't the time for me to be asking questions."

"Because I sound like I might blow into a million pieces? I won't. I never do. And it might help me to talk about all of this. Actually I have a few questions of my own."

Natalie raised an eyebrow. "*Quid pro quo?* You trust my assessments even after our meeting at The Blue Lady?"

"No one shows perfect judgment all the time." Nick smiled. "Not even me."

"I'm glad you can be forgiving. Okay. What can I tell you?"

He leaned forward. "Did you know Warren Hunt was involved with Charlotte Bishop?"

She shook her head. "Lily can't—couldn't—stand him and I think she suspected affairs, but she never mentioned anyone in particular. Frankly I'm shocked to hear about him and Charlotte."

"Why?"

"Warren was a nice-looking man, a professional, but Charlotte was beautiful and rich and fresh out of a marriage to a gorgeous television star. Warren Hunt seems a bit mundane for her."

"I thought the same thing. About Warren being boring after what she's used to, not about Paul Fiori being *gorgeous*." She made a face at him. "So you have no idea how long they've been seeing each other?"

"Certainly not when Charlotte was in California. The affair must have started after she came back to Port Ariel just a few months ago."

"Do you think Lily knew about it?"

"No. If she had, she would have told me."

"You're absolutely sure? Maybe she was being discreet."

"Lily is *not* discreet, particularly around me," Natalie said wryly. "Now it's my turn. Were Warren and Charlotte murdered like Tamara?"

"Yes. Throats slashed. As of now it looks like the same or a similar weapon was used. A long-bladed razor. We found Warren in the living room or whatever they call it on a boat. He'd been murdered on deck, though. Charlotte was in the bedroom." He paused. "On the wall was written in blood, 'open tomb.' "

Natalie drew a sharp breath. " 'Their throat is an open tomb.' The Biblical quotation the woman said on the phone and in the dance pavilion."

"Do you know where in the Bible the quotation is from?"

"I'm not a Bible scholar, but she told me it was Romans. She even said the chapter, but I don't remember. I was going to look it up at home, but I couldn't find Dad's Bible. I don't know if he even has one. He's never been particularly religious. Do you happen to have one?"

Nick rose from the table. In a moment he returned with a large, battered Bible. He handed it to Natalie. When she flipped it open, she saw a list of births and deaths recorded in various shades of faded ink. The last was for Meagan Marie Lincoln Meredith. She quickly riffled pages until she came to Romans. She began scanning pages and after only a couple of minutes she said, "Here it is!"

"That was quick."

"It's in chapter three, in italics, no less! Must be bad."

"Read it to me. I'm so tired my eyes are blurry."

Natalie read slowly and clearly:

" 'There is none righteous, no, not one;
There is none who understands;
There is none who seeks after God.
They have all gone out of the way;
They have together become unprofitable;
There is none who does good, no, not one.
Their throat is an open tomb;
With their tongues they have practiced deceit;
The poison of asps is under their lips;
Whose mouth is full of cursing and bitterness.
Their feet are swift to shed blood;
Destruction and misery are in their ways;
And the way of peace they have not known.
There is no fear of God before their eyes.' "

Nick sighed. "Well, that was cheerful."

Natalie frowned. "The reference to their throats being open tombs is obvious because all the victims had their throats slashed. But what about 'they have practiced deceit'? Warren and Charlotte were deceitful, but Tamara? She was probably the most honest person I've ever known."

"It says none seek after God. That could mean none of the victims was religious."

"I don't know about Warren and Charlotte, but Tamara was a devout Catholic. 'Destruction and misery are in their ways.' 'There is none who does good.' You could apply those lines to Warren and Charlotte, but not Tamara. Nick, *nothing* in this quotation fits Tam."

"I guess finding the motive for these killings so easily was too much to hope for."

"Maybe these are motiveless murders."

"I've always thought the phrase 'motiveless murder' was stupid," Nick said. "No murder is without motive, not even the murders committed by serial killers. They have motives, although often those motives don't make sense to the average person."

Natalie was quiet for a moment. "But you don't believe this is the work of a serial killer."

"No, I don't," Nick said slowly. "I'm not even convinced the three murders were committed by the same person."

"But you said they were all killed the same way."

"Yes, but Charlotte and Warren were killed with more savagery. They each have multiple stab wounds besides those to the throat. Tamara didn't."

"So you think there might be *two* killers?"

"Maybe." He paused. "I have another question for you to answer. Lily and her father didn't like Warren."

"That's not a question."

"No." He paused. "I probably shouldn't tell you this, but Warren's alibi for the night of Tamara's death didn't check out. He claimed to be at a bar having a drink with a woman. She corroborated his story, but I thought she seemed nervous. She sounded as if she'd practiced her story. She also made the mistake of volunteering too much information. One detail she mentioned was the name of the bar. I checked. The owner had died and they were closed the night Warren was supposed to have been there. That's why I was trying to find him this morning."

Natalie's face froze. "You think he might have killed Tamara?"

"Considering his affair with Charlotte and the lack of an alibi, yes."

"But how does that explain *his* murder?" Natalie's lips parted as realization dawned. "You think Warren might have murdered Tamara, Lily and Oliver suspected, so one of them murdered *him*?" She shook her head. "No. Absolutely not. I've known Lily most of my life. She's not as gentle as Tamara was, but she could never deliberately hurt anyone."

"And Oliver?"

"No. I mean, he wouldn't *murder* someone. He just couldn't . . ."

Nick's eyes narrowed. "You don't sound as sure of yourself as you did about Lily."

"I don't know him as well. Well, I really don't know him at all. He's rather cold and formal. I don't believe I've ever had a real conversation with him even though I was a friend of his daughters."

"And those daughters probably sounded a lot alike. Especially on the phone."

"You're back to the anonymous call I got after finding Tamara's body. Nick, Lily was at her father's when I got that call. I told you I tried to reach the number of the caller but I was blocked. I've called Lily at Oliver's, though. My father's number is not blocked from Oliver's phone."

"He might have more than one phone line, Natalie. Many people do now with fax machines and the Internet."

"Lily would *not* make a call like that or hang around The Blue Lady dance pavilion trying to scare me. What would be the purpose?"

"Maybe as soon as her sister was murdered, she knew who did it and she planned revenge. She thinks you know her so well she might give something away, so she's trying to frighten you into going back to Columbus."

"That's really stretching things. Besides, what about the person on the phone saying 'their throat is an open tomb' and 'open tomb' being written on the wall of the *Charlotte* just like in the note that was left with Tam's body? It's the same person using the same phrase."

"Is it? Lily saw that note and she knows *you* saw it. By the time you got the anonymous call, I'd had time to tell her and Oliver I thought it had been left by the murderer. By repeating the phrase, she could be covering her tracks by making you come to the conclusion you just did—that the same person who left the note on Tamara also called you, hid in The Blue Lady, and killed Warren and Charlotte."

Natalie stared at him as she absorbed his speculation and realized it did make a kind of sense. But she wouldn't accept it. "Nick, this all must seem perfectly plausible to you, but it's just absurd if you know Lily. She isn't capable of murder."

"Profound grief and shock can make you capable of things you never imagined."

"Not murder. Not Lily."

"If you *did* think Lily might have murdered Warren and Charlotte, would you tell me?"

Natalie glanced down at her hands. They were slim with long fingers and short, unpainted nails. The creamy pearl in her ring seemed to glow. Tamara had always loved the ring.

Natalie lifted her gaze to Nick's. "If I thought someone had committed cold-blooded, premeditated murder—even Lily in revenge for Tamara—I would tell you. I'd have to. I couldn't let someone so dangerous walk around free."

Nick nodded. "Good. You know the people involved in this case. I'd like to believe I can count on you for information."

"That makes me uncomfortable. These people are my friends."

"One of them could be a murderer. Maybe not Lily. Maybe it's Oliver, and Lily is just lending her voice to the project."

"That's almost as bad." Natalie's face set stubbornly. "No, stumbling on information is one thing, but I won't be a spy."

"I don't want you to be a spy," Nick said earnestly. "I don't want you to divulge anything about these people's private lives that doesn't directly pertain to the murders. I wouldn't ask for *any* information of you, but I need help."

"You? The big-city detective?"

"Please don't plaster that local stereotype on me. The people in this town *elected* me sheriff, then they seemed to resent me because I come from New York City. I don't understand it."

"They elected you because they thought you had more knowledge and experience than anyone else running for the position. At the same time, a lot of them are intimidated by that expertise. And some, like Max Bishop, are simply used to calling the shots with guys like Purdue. I don't think that man made a move without first clearing it with Bishop."

"I know all about Purdue. I also know that some people think I run too tight a ship. And I admit to being a hard-ass lately. But Natalie, this department was a mess. I had to pull things back in line, institute some order." He sighed. "However, just because I was on the N.Y.P.D. doesn't mean I'm omniscient. I know investigative techniques, and I'm good at my job if I do say so myself, but I'm not a damned psychic." He leaned forward. "We have had *three* brutal, bizarre murders in less than three days. I'm afraid we'll have more. That's why I need all the information I can get. Can't you see that without getting up your hackles because you think I'm persecuting your friends?"

She twisted her ring, catching her lower lip between her teeth as she studied the salt and pepper shakers on the table. "You're right," she said reluctantly. "I know these people better than you do and I can't deny there's a connection among the killings. In that case maybe I can help in some small way." She raised her dark gaze. "So I'll keep my eyes and ears open but only for the sake of justice." She grinned. "God I sound sanctimonious!"

"Only to you."

"I doubt that." She frowned. "I'm having some trouble with

guilt, but as long as I've agreed to offer information, I guess there is one other person I should mention. Alison Cosgrove. She's Viveca Cosgrove's daughter. Viveca has been seeing Oliver Peyton for a couple of years. Alison is twenty-one or -two and she's deeply disturbed. She's been under psychiatric care for years. Lately she'd been seeing Warren professionally, but Lily thought Alison had a fixation on him."

"Do you believe she's right?"

"Lily is pretty perceptive and I trust her judgment. If she thinks Alison had a thing for Warren, I'm sure she did. Anyway, earlier this evening I was speculating about all of this and . . ."

She looked troubled. "Go on," Nick urged.

"Well, you're the professional. I don't want to sound silly. But I wondered if Alison could have killed Tamara because she thought Tamara stood between her and Warren. Then she could have found out that Warren wasn't interested in *her* but in Charlotte. Maybe she followed him and saw them meet on the boat." Nick stared at her and she felt color coming to her cheeks. "It sounds outlandish—"

"It sounds perfectly reasonable, particularly if this Alison is as disturbed as you say. Why isn't she in a hospital?"

"She's been in and out of them ever since she was five. She's also been heavily medicated until recently."

"Why not now?"

"Because Warren was a psychologist, not an M.D. He can't write prescriptions."

"Then why was Alison seeing him?"

"Lily said Alison insisted on being treated by Warren."

Nick leaned back in his chair and looked at the ceiling. "Well, I'll be damned. You just put a whole new spin on this case."

"I feel like I just committed slander."

"You merely presented a theory in a confidential context. You stated nothing as fact and I'm certainly not going to descend on Alison Cosgrove, although I'll be watching her. Do you think she's capable of imitating Tamara's voice?"

"I'm not sure. Alison's voice is higher and more childish than

Tam's, but that doesn't mean she couldn't alter it. She'd certainly heard Tam's voice enough. Lily's, too. They weren't that different." She sighed. "Now I've just implicated two people."

"You didn't implicate anyone." Nick gave Natalie a long, direct look. "I know you're not a gossip. You only told me anything because you thought you should. That makes you invaluable to me."

That's not all you are to me, Nick almost said, but of course he couldn't. He wasn't even sure he meant it. He was exhausted and in need of some reassurance. She was beautiful and kind and smart. But he hardly knew her. Use your head, Nick, he reminded himself. Keep it light.

"One other thing," he said quickly. "Mrs. Bishop said that before Charlotte left the house last night, she was waylaid by a young slender man with dark blond hair. Does that sound like anyone you know?"

Natalie shrugged. "It could be a lot of people. No one immediately springs to mind."

"How about the guy that was in Lily Peyton's shop yesterday morning?"

"Now that you mention it. He said his name is Jeff Lindstrom."

"What does he do?"

"I have no idea. He said he's here on vacation."

"Staying where?"

"I don't know. He was headed for Trudy's Diner for breakfast, though. Maybe he struck up a conversation with someone there."

Nick smiled. "Dr. St. John, you are a gold mine of information."

"Only one of my many fine qualities." Natalie stood abruptly. "I should be going now. My father is under the impression that I'm fifteen and he'll probably be calling to check on me, which would be too embarrassing to endure."

"A concerned father is always a concerned father."

"So he keeps telling me. But I hope when Paige is an adult, you give her a little more leeway than my father does me."

"I'll try, but I'll probably be a complete pain."

She laughed. "Tell Paige I had a wonderful time with her."

"I will and thanks for staying."

"I suppose I'll see you at the funeral. I've read that police come to funerals of murder victims to see if the killer might turn up to get a big thrill out of the whole thing."

"The only problem is that if they're getting a thrill, they usually don't look like it. Natalie, I'd rather Lily didn't know the real reason why I'm coming to the funeral."

"I won't have to tell her—she'll already know. She won't come up to talk to you about the case, either. She'll stay out of the way." She frowned. "Alison is another matter."

"She's attending?"

"Viveca says she wants to and Alison gets what she wants. She might sit like a stone and behave herself. Or she might make a scene and have to be taken away. Or she might play Lois Lane and come up to interview you."

"Oh, God," Nick moaned. "I vote for the stone."

"Don't count on it."

He trailed behind her to the front door. He wanted to say something clever, but the only thing he managed was, "Sure you can make it home after all that milk?"

"I think so. It didn't have nutmeg in it, remember?"

"Nutmeg. I'll have to try it." Well, you've certainly impressed her with your witty repartee, he thought gloomily. As she strode to her car, though, one more comment burst from his mouth. "Do you really think Paul Fiori is gorgeous?"

She turned, her silky hair swinging over one shoulder, and winked at him. "Absolutely irresistible."

He shook his head. "I knew it. Too much milk."

III

"Tell me again what they looked like. Warren and Charlotte, I mean. No, wait a minute. I wanna see this."

Ted Hysell sighed and glanced back at the television. Eddie

Salvatore leaned across the table, his brown eyes smoldering in his chiseled face. "So you don't know *nothin'* about this murder that went down today, I got that right, Ice Pick?"

A sweating hulk with acne scars and bulging arms sprouting from a sleeveless sweatshirt dropped his sneaky gaze. "Yeah, man."

"I *love* this show!" Dee gushed "Paul Fiori is a walking, breathing piece of *perfection*!"

"He's good as Salvatore," Ted agreed without her panting enthusiasm.

"Yeah?" Salvatore demanded. "*Yeah?* Is that what you're tellin' *me*, Ice Pick?" More shifting of eyes and sweating from Ice Pick. " 'Cause I'm gonna tell *you* somethin'." Salvatore sprang from his seat and grabbed the giant around the throat, rushing him across the room and slamming him against a wall. "I'm gonna tell you about how a little girl got found in the street, a little girl in a sweet blue dress pulled up around her waist from where some animal *raped* her over and over before he wrung her sweet little neck until her face turned as blue as her dress and her mother had to see that little girl, had to look in that little girl's face and say, 'Yes, that's *my* baby,' and for the rest of her life every time that mother tries to sleep she'll see that little girl's sweet face all blue and the eyes bulgin' out—"

Salavatore's well-meaning but vastly inferior partner stood back reverently, gazing at the law enforcement god that was Eddie Salvatore. "You gonna tell *me* that, Ice Pick?" He pounded the man's huge head against the wall. " 'Cause I got a *hunch*, Ice Pick. I got a hunch you didn't have nothin' to do with hurtin', rapin', *stranglin'* that little girl, but you gotta give up the truth, you hear what I'm sayin'? 'Cause you don't give up the truth I'm gonna beat you till I turn that head of yours into a big, soft *melon* with brains drippin' outta your ears—"

"It was Snipe, man!" Ice Pick screamed, spraying saliva, overwhelmed by the blazing rage of Salvatore. "It was Snipe, I swear!"

"Hot damn, that was great!" Dee took a slug of beer from a

can, now willing to talk because the scene had swung away from Salvatore. "You get confessions that way, Ted?"

Terror of the interrogation room, that's me, Ted thought dismally. "Sometimes it gets pretty rough."

"Like when?"

"It's hard to remember *all* the times." Ted gulped beer, thinking furiously. "You remember that old man found floating in the lake a couple of years ago, bullet in his heart? We got the guy what was seen with him last . . ."

"Yeah?" Dee asked eagerly.

And Sheriff Purdue had conducted the interrogation, half-drunk and belligerently ignoring the guy's plea for a lawyer, bullying him into a confession that a judge rightly labeled fruit of the poisonous tree. The guy had walked away a free man with a smirk at Ted he'd never forget. "It was pretty bad," he said lamely. "I'm not supposed to go into details, though."

"Oh, hell." Dee sounded as if she knew he was trying to snow her. "Tell me about Warren Hunt and Charlotte Bishop."

He had to make up for her disappointment in his previous murder tale. "Got their throats slashed." He paused for effect. "Somebody nearly took off Charlotte's head."

"Wish I'd have seen them! Given me a *real* thrill to see those two mutilated like a couple of pigs."

Ted blinked at her. "Jeez, Dee."

She threw back her head and laughed. "I was joking. You should see the look on your face!"

"Shut up down there!" The voice of Dee's mother shrilled down the dingy stairway and bounced around the living room. "And turn off that damned TV. You're runnin' up the electric bill."

"Why don't you turn off your heating pad and your dehumidifier and your air conditioner, too?" Dee muttered savagely.

"Is she cranky tonight?"

"*Cranky?* That one of your mother's words? She's a bitch all the time now, not that she was ever a bed of roses to live with. Being deserted by two husbands didn't improve her disposition, but my brothers and I couldn't help it."

"They don't come around much anymore, do they?"

Dee flushed. "Not anymore."

Not now that she'd been fired from the hospital where she occasionally lifted drugs for her brothers to sell, Ted thought. He always told other people the charges against her were false. They weren't and he had mixed feelings about the drug theft. What she'd done was against the law, but the brothers were losers with kids who were going hungry. She'd denied the allegations Andrew St. John had brought against her, even to Ted. She had only told him the truth one night when she was particularly drunk after a call from one of her nieces who'd run away from home. The girl was sixteen and Dee was afraid she would become a prostitute. There was no mistaking the sincerity of her love for the kids, but she'd done what she'd done and she was just lucky the hospital was more concerned about bad public relations than pressing charges or she would have landed in jail.

After losing her job, Dee would have left town if her mother hadn't been diagnosed with lung cancer. She now lived in her mother's house rent-free in return for nursing care. She earned enough to exist by typing. She also did other people's laundry, although Ted wasn't supposed to know this. He did know, though, and often anonymously threw business her way.

Dee hoped he would marry her. She'd never said so, but her desire was obvious. She was attractive in a strong-boned, earthy way. She lived life with a vengeance, though, and when she was forty, she'd probably look hard. That's what his mother kept telling him. Of course at fifty-seven Rhonda Hysell looked twenty years older with her long, shapeless, dark clothes and equally long shapeless hair that had never been touched by a beautician. Then there was her constant church work, her obsessive collection of Hummel figurines she couldn't afford, her fervent attacks on dust and mildew, her unending war on grubs and mealy bugs and other garden pests. And for him she wanted a woman just like herself. Instead her son seemed to prefer Dee Fisher, a hard-drinking, raucous atheist. However, in Rhonda Hysell's mind Dee's worst sin seemed to be the blatant sporting of a tattoo.

Ted snickered at the thought. "What?" Dee demanded.

"Show me your tattoo."

"What? *Why?*"

"I just want to see it."

"You're in a weird mood," she said good-naturedly and pulled up her sleeve. A red rose in full bloom sprawled three inches up her bicep. "You hate it, don't you?"

"No. I've decided I like it."

"You *do?*" Dee looked surprised and pleased. "Maybe I'll get another one."

"Let me guess. A big heart with 'Mom' written inside."

"Not in this lifetime. I was thinking of a butterfly." She paused. "On my right cheek."

"Your right *cheek!*" Ted shook his head violently. "Oh, no, Dee. That would look awful. Why would you want to spoil your face that way?"

She whooped with laughter. "My right buttock. My *ass*, you big dope!"

Ted stared at her a moment. Then his laughter joined hers. Mrs. Fisher thundered for quiet, displaying astonishing volume and shocking vocabulary, which set off Dee and Ted in a fresh fit of hilarity. They collapsed against each other, tears streaming from their eyes.

"Damn, I have a good time with you," Dee gasped.

"As good a time as you had with Eugene?" Ted asked and immediately regretted the question. The ghostly hand of Eugene Farley seemed to pass over her face, wiping away all happiness. "Eugene was different." Her voice always became eerie and flat when she spoke of her former lover.

At times like these, when Ted felt jealousy rising in him, he was tempted to tell Dee the truth about Farley. But he couldn't hurt her that way. He couldn't tell her about one day during the trial when he'd found himself sitting next to the elegant young Farley during a recess. He'd never spoken a word to Farley and was surprised when he'd suddenly asked, "Have you seen that young brunette who sits in the courtroom every day? The one who always wears the navy blue suit?"

"Yeah," Ted had answered. He'd noticed her great legs the first day.

"I used to date her. She has a good heart."

Ted didn't know what to say. He didn't know about her heart. He only knew about her legs.

"She was the first single woman I met when I came to Port Ariel," Farley went on. "She was in love with me. I enjoyed her company for a while, but she was too rough around the edges. I'm afraid I treated her shamefully, but there she is, every day, with her heart in her eyes when she looks at me."

"If it bothers you, maybe she meant more to you than you thought," Ted speculated uncomfortably.

Eugene Farley's perfect profile had remained calm as he considered this. Then he shook his head. "No. She meant nearly nothing to me. I'm just sorry I wasn't kinder to her." He'd looked at Ted. "There is a balance in the great scheme of things, you know. Maybe I'm in so much trouble because I'm being paid back for my indifference to that young woman."

No, you're being paid back for embezzlement, you dumb shit, Ted had thought in disdain.

He had absolutely no sympathy for Eugene Farley. The guy had everything—looks, polish, an impressive education, a great job—everything Ted wanted desperately but could only imagine having. Farley could have had someone like Tamara Peyton. Maybe even Charlotte Bishop. And he'd thrown it all away to embezzle money from Max Bishop so he could win back Viveca Cosgrove, an older woman and a gold-digger. Ted didn't even think she was pretty—she looked too styled, too stiff, too perfect, like a store mannequin. Max had brought in that high-powered outside accounting firm from Cleveland and they'd nailed Farley immediately. Oliver Peyton had done a piss-poor job of defending Farley—even Ted could see he was only half-trying. He'd been convicted. Then, weakling that he was, he had committed suicide. And here was Dee still grieving herself to near distraction over him.

Stealing from Max Bishop. What a fool.

Max Bishop. Oliver Peyton. What was the name of that accounting firm from Cleveland that discovered Farley's embezzlement? Martin, Goldstein, and *Hunt*. Richard *Hunt*, father of Warren Hunt.

"What's wrong?" Dee asked suddenly. "You look like someone just zapped you with the heart paddles. I'd say about 350 joules."

"I've got to call Meredith," Ted said. "*Now*."

I I

I

WEDNESDAY MORNING

"Ruth Meadows certainly seems nice," Natalie said casually. "Are you serious about her?"

Andrew St. John set down his coffee cup with a clatter. "Serious? Where do you get your nerve?"

"I think it's a perfectly appropriate question." Natalie took a small bite of toast and chewed calmly. "After all, if our positions were reversed, you would ask me the same."

"That is different."

"It isn't." Natalie grinned. "Besides, all this evasion answers my question."

"No it doesn't," Andrew said sternly. "I barely know the woman."

"Hear that, Blaine?" The dog looked up from a bowl of Alpo. "He barely knows the woman."

"It's true. Not that it is *any* of your business, but we have been out to dinner exactly three times and she cooked dinner for me once at her house."

"That's it?"

"Yes, nosy, that's it."

"I'm disappointed."

"Forgive me."

"No need. There's still time."

Andrew gave her a hard stare. "My darling girl, Ruth is a fine woman but I have no desire to change my life style."

"So you say now. Who knows? In three or four months—"

"About you and Kenny," Andrew interrupted. "What's going on?"

"Nothing."

"Balderdash."

Natalie giggled. "Dad, only characters in novels say *balderdash*."

"I'm the exception. Stop changing the subject. You and Kenny."

Natalie spread more jelly on her toast. "We had a fight."

"I guessed that much. About what?"

"I really don't want to go into it."

"Another woman. He was sleeping around." He paused. "Well, don't look so surprised. The first time I met him I knew he was the type."

"The *type*? Isn't that an unfair generalization?"

"Not when I saw him eyeing every woman who passed by when you weren't looking. I never approved of him. I especially disapproved of you living with him, which is probably why you did it."

"It is not!" Natalie flashed. "I loved him. *Love* him."

"You were right the first time. You don't love this man, Natalie. Don't go back to him."

"Don't tell me what to do!"

Andrew held up his hands. "Sorry. You're too old to take orders from your father. I'm at least entitled to give a little advice, though." He laid his napkin on the table. "I'm off to the hospital."

Natalie drew a deep breath, trying to calm herself. "Exciting day?"

"Appendectomy and gall bladder."

"Sounds thrilling. Tamara's visitation is from six to eight. You will be free by then, won't you?"

"I can be there by seven." He carried his plate to the sink, unobtrusively dropping a piece of bacon in Blaine's bowl. "I hate visitations."

"So do I, but it's a tradition. Of course it will be a closed coffin."

Andrew shook his head. "My God. That poor girl." He looked at Natalie. "You were at the sheriff's house until late last night."

"The housekeeper had to leave so I stayed with Paige while he worked late. A double homicide makes for a busy day."

"First Tamara, then Warren."

"And don't forget Charlotte."

"I took her tonsils out when she was ten. She was a most dislikable little girl."

"She was a most dislikable big girl. Except to Warren, apparently."

"Does the sheriff have any idea who the killer is?"

"No," she said, remembering that Nick had said perhaps Lily or Oliver killed Warren because they thought he had murdered Tamara. "Of course, I barely talked with him when he came in," she added.

"Hmmm."

"What does that mean?"

"Nothing. I simply thought it was *very* considerate of you to go out of your way to baby-sit last night."

"I went over to see about Paige's cat. Then this situation came up and she *is* a cute kid and—Dad, what are you smirking about?"

"Nothing except that Nick Meredith is single and goodlooking. I think he's a fine sheriff. Probably an excellent young man—"

"*Dad.*"

"As you told me, dear, there's always hope."

II

Andrew had just left when the phone rang. "Good morning, Nat. Feeling better about things?"

Kenny Davis. With everything that had been going on, she had barely thought about him the last couple of days. Well, more than barely. Less than constantly.

"By 'feeling better,' I assume you're asking if I've stopped being angry. I haven't."

"Come home. We can talk it out."

"I don't think we can talk this out, Kenny. You slept with another woman and it wasn't the first time."

"I'm not denying what I did. The reason *why* I did it is what we need to talk about."

"We already have. You said you panicked at the thought of commitment."

"But I'm over it."

To her surprise, Natalie laughed. "It took less than a week for you to overcome this deep-seated fear? Kenny, I'm not a fool."

"But I've done a lot of thinking since you left, Nat. I've missed you and I can't imagine my life without you."

"And after I've been back for a while and you've stopped missing me? What then?"

"You're not giving me a chance."

"Kenny, I told you I need time to think. *Time* doesn't mean five days—"

"Six."

"Okay, six. Whatever. Besides, a lot has been going on around here."

"I read in the newspaper about the murder of a Tamara Hunt in Port Ariel. Did you know her?"

"Did I *know* her?" Natalie burst out. "Kenny, she was Lily's sister. You've *met* Lily."

"Hey, don't get so mad because I didn't recognize the name of the married sister of someone I've met."

"You make it all sound so casual." Cold anger filled her. "Lily is my best friend. Tamara was her twin. I've known them since I was a child and I've talked about them *so* much since we've been together, but you don't remember. You weren't even listening to me."

"Of course I was listening. I'm just not good with names."

"Another lie."

"Why are you so *mad*?"

She sighed. "I repeat that I asked for time. Considering what you did, I think you might have the decency to grant it. Instead, this is the second time in less than a week you've called. I am *not* ready to talk."

"So I gather." He paused. "You only have one more week of vacation time. You'll come home then and we'll talk."

Home. Home was the condo she shared with Kenny. Could she possibly go back there and pick up where they left off?

I left off seeing Kenny in our bed with another woman, Natalie thought after hanging up the phone. Is that what he wants me to come *home* to?

A dull headache was forming at the back of her head. Tension. She could not take another round with Kenny. She turned on the answering machine to screen calls.

The doorbell rang. Natalie sighed. Now what? At least it couldn't be Kenny.

She opened the door. Ruth Meadows stood smiling at her and holding a pie dish covered with aluminum foil. "I couldn't sleep last night so I baked a few pies. Your father told me once that your favorite is cherry, so I brought one over."

"How nice of you!" Natalie was genuinely pleased. "I haven't had cherry pie for years." She stepped back. "Come in. Dad isn't here."

"Oh, I knew he wouldn't be," Ruth said. "Shall I put this in the kitchen?"

"Yes, please."

She followed Ruth into the kitchen. Ruth opened a drawer, pulled out a dishtowel, laid it on the counter, and set the pie on it. "It's still warm from the oven and I wouldn't want to damage this Formica. Such a lovely leaf pattern in these autumn colors."

"Dad had the kitchen remodeled last year. Nothing had been replaced since the house was built thirty years ago, but I was still surprised by the renovation."

"Your father is happiest when he's working. When he came to my house for dinner, he immediately decided the railing on my deck isn't strong enough and he plans to replace it soon. I told him I could hire a handyman, but he insisted."

"As you said, he's happiest when he's working." Natalie smiled. "And he likes you."

A slight flush came to Ruth's cheeks. "Do you really think so?" Then she laughed. "My goodness, I sound like I'm twelve."

"Well I shouldn't offer coffee to a twelve-year-old, but I put on a fresh pot not too long ago. Would you like some?"

"Please. I hate these nights when I can't sleep. I get up and do any work I can think of. The next day I feel dragged out. I could use some caffeine."

"Coming right up. Cream? Sugar?"

"Just cream. I gave up sugar a couple of years ago along with some pounds."

Natalie glanced at Ruth's trim body dressed today in aqua slacks that matched her eyes and a V-necked white knit top. At her throat hung a cameo on a gold chain.

Ruth reached up and touched the pendant. "My husband Walter gave this to me for our anniversary. He died four years ago. Cancer."

"I'm sorry."

Ruth accepted the coffee cup from Natalie. "It was a prolonged illness. That was in Virginia, right outside of D.C. Walter had a government job. After his death I stayed for a while, but I just couldn't enjoy our house or my old life."

"Why did you decide to move to Port Ariel?"

"Walter and I toured the Great Lakes in the early sixties shortly after we were married. We spent a couple of nights here. I liked it. As a matter of fact, we stayed at that lovely old hotel The Blue Lady. Such a shame it burned down."

"The dance pavilion is still standing."

"But it's closed and terribly unsafe, according to Andrew. I'd like to see it again, but I wouldn't take the risk, even if it weren't locked up. Besides, I've heard about those awful murders that happened at the hotel just a few years after my honeymoon. So frightening!" She shivered. "No, you wouldn't get me near that place."

A scary history and unsafe construction didn't stop me from going to the old place at night, Natalie thought uncomfortably. Not me and a nut claiming to be a dead woman.

"Anyway," Ruth went on, "I came to Port Ariel for a quick visit after Walter's death and I made an impulse move five months ago."

"So you're just getting used to the town."

"Yes. I've made quite a few friends through church and the suicide hotline—that's how I met Tamara, you know—but I'm ashamed to say I haven't unpacked all my boxes yet." They sat at the kitchen table and Ruth looked out the big window. "This is such a spectacular view."

"Yes, although today is overcast. The lake looks bleak."

Ruth's smile wavered. "A couple of weeks after I moved here I took a walk by the lake. It was late February and such a dismal day. The lake looked so vast and gray and lonely I felt overwhelmed by it. I gave serious thought that night to moving back home. The next day the sun came out and I felt better. I knew this was where I was meant to be."

Blaine padded into the kitchen. Ruth beamed and reached out a hand to the dog. "Here's the pretty girl! You've settled right in, haven't you?" The dog licked her hand and panted happily. Ruth looked at Natalie. "I saw your ad in the newspaper. Has anyone called about her?"

"No, thank goodness."

"You want to keep her, don't you?"

"Yes."

"Your father says you live in a condominium complex. Do they allow pets?"

Natalie hadn't given the problem a thought. Pets were not allowed at Kenny's place and she had no intention of giving up Blaine except to her owners. If I really intended to go back to the condo, wouldn't I have considered what I would do with the dog? she asked herself.

"I'm moving," she said abruptly.

"I didn't know. Are you planning to buy a house?"

"I'm not sure." Natalie took a sip of coffee. "My father has probably told you about my romantic relationship and living arrangement."

"No, dear, he hasn't," Ruth said mildly. "He's mentioned that you see a doctor from the veterinary clinic where you work and I get the impression Andrew doesn't care for him, but he's never said much."

"Oh," Natalie said in surprise.

"It's your personal business, dear. Andrew respects your privacy."

So her father might have something to say to her about every aspect of her life, but apparently he didn't broadcast his disapproval to everyone he knew. She had always assumed the worst, certain nothing she said to him was held in confidence. That hadn't been fair, she thought, especially because he never told her personal things about anyone he knew.

The phone rang again. "The machine will get it," Natalie said. She and Ruth sat in silence until after the second ring when Kenny's disembodied voice floated into the kitchen. "Nat, it's me again. I didn't like the way we left things. We need to talk more. If you're there, please pick up." Natalie sat perfectly still. "Okay, call me back later. I'll be home all day. Love you."

Natalie's gaze met Ruth's. "The reason I'm here."

"So I thought. Love can be wonderful. It can also be unbearably painful."

"Lately more painful than wonderful." Her headache was getting worse. She rubbed her neck.

"Tension headache?"

"I'm afraid so."

Ruth gave her a sympathetic smile. "I barged in on you before you even had a chance to get dressed. Why don't you take a couple of aspirins and a hot shower? You'll feel like a new woman. I'll be on my way."

"Oh, don't go," Natalie said, suddenly hating the idea of being alone with Kenny's calls fresh in her mind. "I'd love to talk with you more. I'll make the shower quick."

"Well, if you're sure you'd like for me to stay . . ."

"I am."

"Then take as long in the shower as you like. I'll have another cup of coffee."

Natalie went into the small bathroom beside her bedroom. She stood in the shower stall letting the hot water massage her stiff neck muscles for at least five minutes. She was rinsing shampoo out of her hair when Ruth tapped on the bathroom door.

"Natalie!"

She turned off the water. "Yes?"

"You just got a call from your friend Lily. She wants you to meet her. She says it's urgent."

In two minutes Natalie stood in the hall wearing an old terry cloth robe she'd found in the depths of her closet and a towel on her wet hair. "I was standing on the terrace with Blaine," Ruth explained. "The phone rang twice and of course I knew the machine would pick up. Lily left her message. When I heard her say *urgent* I rushed in, but she'd already hung up."

The light on the answering machine blinked twice. Natalie pushed the PLAY button. The first message was Kenny's. Then a breathless female voice began. "Natalie, it's Lily. Are you there? I'm at Tamara's. Meet me here. It's urgent."

"My goodness, she sounds half frantic," Ruth said.

"Yes. She didn't even wait for me to answer if I'd heard the call. I'd better hurry."

Ruth frowned. "Dear, do you think it's safe for you to go to Tamara's?"

"Safe?"

"Yes. The two people who lived in that house were murdered and Lily doesn't say what's wrong."

"Tamara and Warren weren't murdered in the house and Lily wouldn't ask me to come to a dangerous place."

Ruth looked concerned. "I'm not sure your father would want you to go."

"Dad would like for me to sit in the house and watch TV. But Lily needs me, Ruth. I *have* to go."

"I see I can't stop you," she said unhappily. "I want you to be careful, though. With all these awful murders, no one is safe." She paused. "I do wish you would give this a second thought. A lovely young woman wandering around by herself. Anything could happen. The world has turned into a dangerous place . . ."

Ruth continued to warn and fret until Natalie handed the woman her purse and nearly pushed her out the door. Then she rushed back to her room, slipped on a pair of jeans and a tee shirt, ran a wide-toothed comb through her wet hair, and pulled it back with a large clasp. She grabbed her shoulder bag and headed for the front door.

Blaine sat in the hall looking at her expectantly. "I'm sorry, girl. I promised you a walk this morning but something has come up." She opened the door, surprised by the cool air that wafted over her. A gray sky hung low like the lid on a box. She reached for a denim jacket hanging on the coat tree. Then she looked at Blaine again.

"I don't know why Lily wants me to go to Tamara's," she said. "You might be in the way, but I have this odd feeling . . ." The dog turned in excited circles as Natalie picked up her leash. "I don't want to go out there alone. It's your lucky day."

Blaine sat quiet and poised on the front seat, looking with interest at everything whizzing by. She left nose prints on the side window. Natalie flipped on the radio and stroked the dog's head as Linda Ronstadt's "Blue Bayou" played.

When she reached Tamara's house, she was surprised to find the driveway empty. No red Corvette. Maybe Lily had been delayed or had to leave suddenly.

She pulled in the driveway. Blaine jumped out behind her. Natalie held her leash although the dog clearly wasn't going off on her own. They climbed the porch steps. No note on the door. Feeling as guilty as a thief, Natalie turned the doorknob. Locked. She moved to the side and peered through the picture window into the living room. A book lay splayed on an end table as if someone had just put it down and would be right back. Only a week ago Tamara and Warren had lived in this house, Natalie thought. They'd slept, eaten, talked about their days, and now they were both dead. Not just dead—murdered, their throats slashed.

Soon other people would live in this house. Their furniture, their pictures, their clothing would replace the Hunts'. But some essence of Tamara and Warren would always linger here. No one would ever forget what had happened to them.

Natalie stepped off the porch and walked around the house. In Columbus, the daffodils and tulips already had disappeared, but here some faded blooms remained in Tamara's flowerbeds. Poppies and impatiens were just coming up. On the deck sat a glass-topped table with an umbrella. The green-and-white vinyl seat covers matched that of the glider and rocker. An expensive gas grill rested nearby. Leaves brought down in the storm the night Tamara was murdered littered the deck. If she had lived, every leaf would have been gone by noon the next day. Dear, meticulous Tam.

Tam. On the answering machine Lily had said Tamara but Natalie could not remember Lily ever calling her sister anything except Tam. Either my memory is faulty or Lily was really upset, Natalie thought. What on earth could be wrong?

She looked beyond the lawn to Hyacinth Lane. The dirt road was only visible for about a hundred yards until trees and vines obscured it from view. Her gaze drifted skyward.

Vultures.

"Oh, my God!" she cried, the image of Tamara's ravaged face flashing through her mind. "Lily!"

Natalie ran toward the road. She'd dropped Blaine's leash, but the dog galloped along beside her without a moment's hesitation. The last time Natalie had been out on this road, Blaine had run ahead to show her where Tamara's body lay. Today she thought if the dog ran ahead, then started furiously barking, she would faint.

Dirt and gravel crunched under her Reeboks. Much too soon her breath grew short. She used to run daily but had abandoned the routine months ago. Now she was out of shape. Blaine pulled ahead, then dropped back as if she sensed Natalie's need for a companion.

Natalie tried to keep her eyes straight ahead, but they drifted up again. The ugly birds circled. At least they weren't feasting. Yet.

A wave of nausea and breathlessness forced her to slow down. She was close now, but close to what? Oh, *please* don't let it be Lily, she prayed.

She saw a gray-white heap in the middle of the road. A hairy gray-white heap with a long bare rat-like tail. A dead opossum.

Natalie stopped abruptly and her vision blurred. She bent over, hands on knees, and drew deep, slow breaths. First she thought she would faint from fear. Now she thought she might faint from relief.

Blaine barked and drew closer. Natalie's head shot up. A man stopped in front of them, looking at Blaine with caution.

"I just wanted to see if you were all right," he said.

His voice was familiar. Natalie wiped away the perspiration dripping from her forehead into her eyes and blinked. Tall. Slender. Dark blond hair curling over the collar of his denim shirt. The man she'd met in Lily's store.

"Jeff Lindstrom?"

He smiled. "You remembered." He looked at Blaine. "Will you tell Lassie I'm harmless?"

"Her name is Blaine. She's *very* protective." Natalie was not sure this was true, although the dog was showing protective tendencies, but she suddenly recalled that the night Charlotte Bishop had been murdered she was seen arguing with a man who fit Jeff's description. She did not touch the dog, hoping Blaine would maintain her tense stance. "What are you doing out here?"

"Sightseeing. Someone told me about the Saunders house. I have to admit I was disappointed. They said the place was a little run-down. It's a wreck."

"So I've heard. My friends and I used to go there when we were kids. Back then it was run-down. I haven't seen it for ages."

"You and your friends?" He flashed the smile that at first had struck Natalie as open. Now it seemed studied. "Would that be Lily and Tamara Peyton?"

"Well, yes. How did you know?"

"When I was in Curious Things I could tell you were a good friend of Lily. Tamara was her twin. Simple deduction." The smile. "It really is terrible about Tamara. People in town have told me the details of her murder. She was found on this road, wasn't she?"

"Yes."

"By Lily and you." She nodded. "Hell of a thing. Who do you suppose would want to kill a lovely young woman like Tamara?"

"That's what the police are wondering."

"Then her husband and that Bishop woman. They must have been involved. Did Tamara know?"

"I have no idea," Natalie said faintly. She was growing alarmed. He was asking too many questions, watching her too intently. "I really have to be getting back."

"Why were you running? You looked like you were scared to death."

"Did I?" She forced a smile. "What you saw was strain, not fear. I haven't run for a long time."

"That wasn't a simple jog I saw. Tell me. What's wrong?"

You're scaring the hell out of me, that's what's wrong, Natalie thought. She wouldn't show it, though. "Nothing is wrong. I just ran too far too fast and I started to feel sick. I'm fine now."

"You don't look fine." He moved one step closer. "You're very pale."

Blaine emitted a low growl. Jeff barely looked at her. His gaze held Natalie's.

"I am *fine*." Turn around and *walk*, part of her said. Another part told her not to turn her back on this man. It would be easy for him to grab her and pull a knife neatly across her throat. "Did you drive out here? I didn't see a car."

"It's parked over there." He motioned vaguely toward the end of Tamara's street. "I've been around here for hours."

"Then you must be ready to go back. Walk with us."

"Wouldn't you like to see the Saunders house? You said you haven't been there for a long time."

No, dammit! she screamed inwardly. Should she chance it and turn away? He certainly didn't seem intimidated by Blaine and she couldn't stand here forever.

"Hi! How're you doin'?"

A kid's voice. Jeff looked past Natalie. She turned her head. A black-haired boy rode a bike toward them. "Hi!" she called gaily as if she knew him. He looked familiar. Wasn't he the boy who'd hung around the day they found Tamara's body?

"I saw you come out the road, Natalie," he said, grinding to a halt beside her and hopping off his bike. "You brought Blaine. Hi, girl."

Natalie? Blaine? How did he know their names? "She looks a lot better than the first time you saw her, doesn't she?" Natalie asked.

"She sure does." He looked at Jeff. "I'm Jimmy Jenkins. I live in that big blue house across from the Hunts."

"Jeff Lindstrom." Tight voice. Tight smile. "Nice to meet you, Jimmy."

"Do you live around here?"

"No. Just visiting. Natalie and I were headed back. Are you going to the Saunders house?"

Jimmy shook his head. "I don't care about that old house. I just came out to see Natalie and Blaine. I'll walk with you guys."

Bless you, Natalie thought. Jimmy grinned at her. He'd known something was wrong and he'd come to her rescue. She felt like throwing her arms around him.

When they reached the paved street, Jeff gave them an overly hearty farewell and began striding east. Natalie looked at Jimmy. "Thanks."

He shrugged. "No big deal. I saw him hanging around here eyeing the Hunts' house. Then he went out Hyacinth Lane. Then *you* came and I saw you take off running. I thought something was wrong."

"I was supposed to meet Lily here. When she didn't show up I got scared. I saw vultures flying around and . . . well, I thought of Tamara, but it was only a dead opossum."

"I've been around here all day and I haven't seen Lily."

Natalie frowned. "You couldn't have missed her?"

He flashed that grin again. In a few years he'd be a heart-breaker. "The way she drives her 'Vette? I couldn't have missed her screeching into the driveway."

"I don't understand," Natalie muttered. Then: "Jimmy, how did you know my name *and* the dog's?"

"Paige Meredith told me. We're friends."

"Oh, I see." Natalie remembered Paige mentioning a "Jimmy" four or five times last night. She obviously had a crush on him. "I'm certainly glad you came after me."

"I had to. There's something creepy about that guy." Jimmy looked at the ground and frowned. "I thought I saw something drop out of his pocket. There it is."

He pointed. Natalie bent and picked up an object. It sparkled in spite of the overcast day.

"What is it?" Jimmy asked.

"A silver and amethyst earring," Natalie said thinly. "It belonged to Tamara."

"You sure?"

"Yes. I gave these earrings to her for her birthday." Natalie frowned and asked slowly, "Could he have just found this on Hyacinth Lane?"

"Maybe." Jimmy looked at her solemnly. "Or else he's been carrying it around since the night Tamara got murdered."

12

The red Corvette sat in front of Lily's apartment. Natalie, Blaine standing beside her, knocked on the door. In a minute Lily appeared. She wore a robe and her eyes were red and slightly swollen. "Natalie," she said without inflection. "I didn't know you were coming."

"May I bring in the dog?"

"Of course. I love dogs." She shut the door. The draperies were pulled. The only light in the room came from a television. A soap opera played with the sound turned low. "Do you want something to drink? Juice? Soda? Coffee?"

"Wine."

Lily raised an eyebrow, a ghost of a smile playing around her mouth. "It's just past noon, Natalie St. John. What would your father say?"

"The same thing he'd say if it were ten P.M." She deepened her voice. "My darling girl, alcohol is not good for you."

"You obviously disagree," Lily said, pulling a bottle of wine from the refrigerator.

"At the moment it's exactly what I need. I've had quite a nerve-wracking morning, thanks to you."

"Thanks to me?" Lily poured white wine in a glass, then ran water into a bowl and set it on the floor. Blaine lapped loudly. "What did *I* do?"

"You called me," Natalie said, walking back into the living room and sitting down on the couch.

"I didn't call you this morning."

"Lily, your voice is on the answering machine. You said something like, 'Natalie, it's Lily. I'm at Tamara's. Meet me. It's urgent.' "

Lily stared at her for a moment. "Natalie, I did *not* call you. And I don't ever remember using the word *urgent*. And why would I be at Tam's? Why would I want you to meet me? What time did the call come?"

"Around ten."

"And it sounded like my voice?"

"Yes, but rushed and breathless."

"So it wasn't exactly like my voice."

"Well, no." Natalie paused. "And you said Tamara instead of Tam."

"*I* didn't say anything. I'm telling you, it wasn't me. Don't you believe me?"

"Yes, but I don't understand why someone wanted me to go to Tam's."

"*Did* you go?"

Natalie nodded. "You weren't there so I wandered around a bit. Then I . . ." She hesitated. She didn't want to remind Lily of the vultures. "I thought you might have gone down Hyacinth Lane to the Saunders house. On the way I ran into Jeff Lindstrom."

"Jeff Lindstrom?" Lily looked blank.

"The guy who was in your store yesterday morning. Lily, he was weird."

"He didn't seem weird in the store."

"Today he was like a different person. He asked me questions about Tamara and Warren and Charlotte."

Lily closed her eyes. "I suppose everyone is talking about them."

"These weren't the questions of someone expressing normal curiosity. He was so intense. He kept looking right into my eyes and coming closer. He asked if Tamara knew Warren was having an affair with Charlotte."

"The son of a bitch." Lily's tired eyes filled with tears. "My poor sister was pregnant at last and Warren was screwing around with Charlotte."

"Pregnant?" Natalie echoed. "You didn't tell me."

"Sheriff Meredith just told Dad and me after the autopsy. She was eight weeks along. Do you know how badly Tam wanted a baby?"

"Yes." Natalie reached out and touched her hand. "Lily, I'm *so* sorry. I know that doesn't help."

"Nothing can help. Tam is gone. The baby is gone." Lily shuddered. "Oh, God."

"Lily—"

She held up a silencing hand. "No. Don't indulge me. I have to pull myself together. I was doing better yesterday until I heard about the baby. I need to be strong, though. There's the visitation tonight and the funeral tomorrow." She drew a deep breath. "Tell me more about Jeff."

"Well, obviously he made me uncomfortable with all those questions. I said I had to go, but he wouldn't move. I was getting scared, when Jimmy Jenkins came flying up on his bike. After Jeff left, Jimmy told me he'd been hanging around Tam's house earlier."

"What do you suppose he's up to?"

"I don't know. I'm going to call Nick Meredith this afternoon and ask him to check out this guy."

"Good idea. He's not Tam's murderer, though."

"You don't know that."

"Oh yes I do," Lily said vehemently. "*Warren* killed Tamara. I *know* it."

"And left that note saying something about tombs?" Natalie said, careful to sound vague about the quotation. She had not told Lily about the anonymous phone call or the voice in The Blue Lady. As far as Lily knew, Natalie had only seen the quotation once, briefly, on a blood-stained note. "Why would Warren do that?"

Lily's attention quickened. "I think he left the note to throw off the police, to make them think some nut killed my sister. He was a psychologist—it's the kind of thing he *would* think of."

Natalie was taken aback. She hadn't liked Warren, but she knew he was extremely bright. If he were capable of killing Tamara to get rid of her, the murder would be carefully plotted. He'd already lied about his alibi for the night of the murder. He'd even somehow coerced someone into verifying the alibi. But *why* had he invented an alibi in the first place? Simply because he *had* no alibi and he was afraid he would be the number-one suspect? Or because he was guilty?

"If Warren killed Tamara, then who killed Warren and Charlotte?" Natalie asked evenly as the simmering hatred in Lily's eyes alarmed her.

"I don't know. I don't care. If I'd had any idea what Warren had been doing to my sister . . ."

"You'd have killed him yourself?"

Lily blinked and her expression grew guarded. "Now you think I'm a murderer? Natalie, I would have *felt* like killing him, but feeling and doing are different things."

For the first time in their long friendship Natalie felt a flicker of doubt about Lily. She hated the feeling. Would she be having it if Nick Meredith hadn't raised the possibility that Lily had killed Warren and Charlotte? Lily looked at her questioningly, and she realized she hadn't responded.

"I understand how you must have felt about Warren," Natalie said quickly. Then she thought of the other possible killer she had discussed with Nick. "How is Alison doing now that her beloved is dead?"

"Last night she was moving around like she was in a trance," Lily said, her face growing defenseless again. "Warren's father Richard stopped by. He has acquired this very young, flashy wife since you met him at the wedding. He also brought along his hulking younger son Bruce. Richard had already had a few too many drinks before they arrived, then he started in on Dad's brandy. He acts mad at Warren for getting killed."

"Well, they say anger is one of the stages of grief."

"It isn't that kind of anger. He was ranting and raving about how this was typical of Warren—he never showed good sense. What the hell was he doing with that Bishop woman? Did we *all* know about the affair? Did we all know what a complete *ass* Warren was making of himself? He was shouting and glaring at all of us. Alison started to cry. Her whole body shook. Viveca left with her. As soon as they were gone, Richard said Alison looked crazy. His wife told him to hush, but he just got louder and drank more and went on about what an idiot Warren was."

"I remember Richard Hunt from Tam's wedding. I thought he was awful."

"We all did. Thank goodness we haven't seen much of him and probably will never see him again after this mess is cleared up. As much as I detested Warren, I could see why he turned out the way he did."

"He certainly set off Alison for the evening," Natalie said, clumsily steering the conversation back to the direction she wanted. "Do you think she's worse?"

Lily looked away for a moment. "Yes. I hadn't really thought about it, but she's different than she was when Dad and Viveca began seeing each other."

"Do you think she's capable of violence?"

"Violence? Well, I've seen her throw a couple of tantrums that were pretty scary. She's stronger than she looks and her temper is fierce. She's been wandering around at night. I know Viveca is *really* worried."

"Alison is very unstable. *And* she had a wild crush on Warren." She paused. "Lily, Alison probably saw Tam as a rival."

Lily's eyes widened. "Do you think *Alison* might have killed my sister?"

"Maybe. And as for Warren—well, with her rival out of the way, Alison could have thought Warren would turn to her. But he didn't, of course. He ran straight to Charlotte."

"He did, didn't he? Two nights after his wife was murdered, he was with his mistress."

Lily suddenly sounded vague, detached. Was it because she'd

been profoundly shocked by the possibility that Alison killed Warren? Or was it because she *knew* Alison had not murdered him?

II

Natalie had brought no clothing suitable for a funeral. How could she have guessed a two-week visit home would include the murder of one of her closest friends? She'd never known anyone who was murdered. But no matter how she had died, the rituals of death would be observed for Tamara.

Natalie was never an enthusiastic shopper, but when she tried on clothes at the slightly antiquated local department store, she had to choke back tears. Lily never shopped for clothes in Port Ariel, but Tamara did. In a few months she might have stood in this dressing room trying on maternity tops. She would have been so happy.

Finally Natalie chose a short-sleeved black dress for the visitation and a navy blue suit for the funeral. She knew she would wear each outfit only once. The associations with Tam's death would always be too strong.

When she arrived home she felt as if she'd run a marathon. A telephone encounter with Kenny, the unnerving meeting with Jeff Lindstrom, a visit to Lily's, and a dreaded shopping trip had all occurred before three o'clock. To top it off, her head still hurt ferociously. She took two more aspirin and went to her bedroom, stripping to her underwear and slipping beneath the sheet and coverlet. Sleep came with the abruptness of a door slamming in her face.

"Coming to see me tonight?" Tamara asked. She sat in a wicker rocker, a filmy white gown flowing around her. On a small table beside her glowed a Tiffany-shaded lamp throwing soft colors over the perfection of her profile. Then the light brightened, and Tamara turned her head full face toward Natalie. The skin was checkered with bloody gashes, her eye sockets were empty. "Look what's happened to me, Natalie," she said sadly "Just look what's happened."

Natalie jerked up in bed, her heart throbbing, a strangled scream tearing at her throat. Alarmed, Blaine leaped onto the bed and leaned forward to lick Natalie's sweaty face. She put her hand on the dog's sleek head. "It's all right, girl," she murmured. "A horrible dream, that's all."

She swung her legs to the side of the bed and glanced at the clock. Five-fifteen. Less than two hours until Tamara's wake.

If Kenny were here he would be trying to cheer me up, she thought. He would be saying that Tamara had been happy in her twenty-nine years of life. He would tell me that everyone has a time to go and it was simply her time to go and that one shouldn't mourn over what fate has decreed.

He would be annoying the hell out of me, Natalie thought abruptly. Kenny never wanted to face the dark side of life. He'd never had the need. Nothing awful had ever happened to him. Her life had been different. No slick, superficial phrases had been able to wipe away the realization that her mother had walked away from her and barely looked back. She'd faced heartache and loss when she was young and although the experience had been rough, it had challenged her to do some deep thinking that Kenny had escaped.

A bit stunned by her realization, she absent-mindedly took another quick shower and dressed for the visitation, dusting powder over her face and adding some blush and lipstick to hide her pallor. The black dress made her look somber. She slipped on her watch and added small silver filigree earrings. Silver filigree earrings. She'd given Tamara dangling filigree earrings and one had fallen from Jeff Lindstrom's pocket this morning. Had Tam been wearing the earrings the night she was murdered? As soon as possible she had to tell Nick Meredith about Jeff and the earring. She hoped he would come to the wake.

At quarter to seven she headed to Leery's Funeral Home. The parking lot sat full of cars. Natalie opened one of the double doors and stepped in on incredibly thick forest-green carpet. Doleful organ music reverberated through the rooms. A tall, thin man with thick silver hair and melancholy expression descended on her. "Leonard Leery," he said just above a whisper. "This is my establishment."

"I know, Leonard. I'm Natalie St. John."

He squinted, then blushed. "Natalie! I didn't recognize you."

"It's been a long time."

"Yes. Not since Grace Peyton died." His melancholy expression intensified. "Oh, my, this is just awful. Dear Tamara. Such a fine woman. Oliver and Lily are devastated."

A short, plump woman appeared beside him. Leonard and Loretta Leery had always reminded Natalie of Jack Sprat and his wife. "Natalie, you sweet thing!" Leonard winced at his wife's fluting voice. "How slim you are!"

Natalie wished she could say the same for Loretta. Her black skirt was stretched tightly over a substantial girdled derriere and huge ruffles decorated her gray blouse, giving her the look of a pouter pigeon. She'd dyed her gray hair a brassy copper color and swept it up in a mass of hairspray-stiffened curls. "What do you think of my hair?" she asked, preening.

Leonard saved Natalie by saying softly, "Dear, I don't think now is the time to be discussing hair color."

Loretta smiled good-naturedly. "Lenny's right as always. I have the finesse of a rhinoceros. You go sign the guest register, Natalie. Then I'll show you your basket of flowers. They aren't the biggest, but they're one of the prettiest!"

Leonard blushed again. Loretta, wafting clouds of Opium perfume, hustled Natalie over to the register and then into the "slumber room." Candles glowed everywhere. "Here they are!" Loretta called cheerily as she stood beside a basket of glads and orchids. "The only basket like it! The mayor sent a dinky little planter—I'd be embarrassed—but the governor sent three dozen roses!"

"Oliver Peyton is close friends with the governor."

"Yes. The family's blanket was all carnations. I was surprised. Cheap. Doesn't make a good impression. I would have expected something like that from Warren, but Oliver?"

"I think carnations were Tamara's favorite flowers."

"Still . . ." Loretta said meaningfully. Then she frowned. "Of course, I shouldn't be throwing off on Warren even if I didn't care for him. Charlotte is another matter. I love Muriel Bishop. One of the sweetest women on this earth even if she is a bit dim. But that girl! Spoiled rotten. I told Muriel over the years, 'Muriel, you're spoiling that girl!' but she always gave that weak little smile and said, 'She only listens to her Max.' Max! Now *there's* a role model! No wonder Charlotte was so insufferable. Of course we'll be taking care of her. Do you think Paul Fiori will come to the funeral? Wouldn't that be exciting! Charlotte's coffin will be open, not like poor Tamara's. I tell you, Natalie, when they brought Tamara in I took one look at her and ran out of the room crying!"

"Loretta!" Leonard stood behind his wife, flushing to the roots of his exquisite silver hair. "Dear, I really could use your help with the mourners."

Loretta winked at Natalie. "He just wants me to quit blabbing, but I know you and I understand each other." Natalie wondered what would make her think so, although in spite of Loretta Leery's loose tongue Natalie had always liked her. "You're so much like your father, Natalie," Loretta said. "Thank goodness you take after him and not your mother."

Leonard turned fuchsia and looked as if he were going to pass out. Natalie almost laughed, marveling that someone as proper as Leonard, a mortician no less, had ever married the egregious Loretta, especially in his line of business. The only answer must be love, she decided. A great deal of love.

Loretta took her Opium-scented self over to another group while Leonard drooped back to the door. Natalie wondered if he'd ever walked jauntily, or had trudged solemnly even in the days of his youth, practicing for the time when he would inherit the family undertaking business.

"I didn't think she'd ever leave."

Lily stood beside her. She wore a dark blue long-sleeved dress and had skinned back her gleaming blond hair with a bow at her neck. She'd lost weight and with no makeup or jewelry, she'd also lost her glamour. Even her hazel eyes lacked their usual sparkle. Natalie felt a wave of pity and pushed down the treacherous doubts she had had earlier in the day about her best friend.

"Loretta is never at a loss for words," Natalie said, "but she means well."

"She's a sweetheart. Tactless but a sweetheart. She doesn't approve of the casket blanket I chose, but Tam loved pink and white carnations. Simple and unassuming." She rolled her eyes. "I sound like Warren talking about wine."

"No, Warren would have used words like *piquant, impertinent, imposing, provocative*." Lily grinned with a trace of her usual mischievous self. "Where is your father?" Natalie asked.

"He fell apart when we first came in. Viveca took him into a back room and *I* was sent away."

Bitterness edged her voice. Natalie had thought Lily resented Viveca because she was so different from Grace Peyton. Now she wondered if Lily might be jealous because Viveca had become so important to Oliver. Lily liked responsibility. She liked having her father and her sister lean on her. Now Tam was gone and Oliver had turned to Viveca, who would do everything she could to control him. It seemed to be working. He depended on her more and more. Natalie knew this would not have happened to her father. Andrew St. John would never let someone dominate his life.

"Please tell me Alison isn't here," Natalie murmured.

Lily shook her head. "Wish I could oblige. She's swathed in black, and I do mean swathed. She came in wearing a black lace mantilla on her head. She looks like something from the nineteenth century."

"Ariel Saunders?"

"Good call. She's definitely playacting."

Natalie lowered her voice to a whisper. "Are you getting any sense that she might have been responsible for Tam's death?"

Lily's eyes darkened with fury at the thought, but she hesitated. "I honestly can't say. She doesn't *look* or *act* guilty, but then she looks and acts so weird all the time, who could tell? I'm keeping an eye on her, though. I hope you will, too, when she finally emerges from seclusion with Viveca and my father. In the meantime, I'd better circulate. Looks like this dreadful little ceremony has been dropped in my lap."

"I see the Keatons coming in. I'll handle them. She'll want to go over every death in her family for the past twenty years."

"As if we haven't heard it all before. And there's Miss Ginsler. Can you believe she's still teaching second grade? I'm sure she was at least eighty when *we* were in her class."

Natalie grinned. "She's in a time warp. She's *always* been eighty. And a grouch. She couldn't bear me. She sent a note home to my father saying she thought I'd be in prison before I graduated from high school."

"You almost proved her right when you freed all those lab frogs when we were in high school." Lily smiled. "I'll handle her. Then I'm rousting out Dad, Viveca or no Viveca."

Half an hour later a gray-faced Oliver Peyton nodded solemnly to a few mourners. Loretta had dragged Viveca away from him to admire the flower tributes. Alison sat like a cold, sharp ice sculpture about two feet from the coffin. She watched it narrowly as if any moment she expected the lid to snap open and Tamara to pop up bursting with life. Was it fantasies or guilt that made her so vigilant? Natalie wondered.

Sheriff Meredith walked in. He still wore his uniform and he was the tallest man in the room. Voices quieted. People stared. Alison went rigid. Viveca's lips parted in either distress or surprise. Natalie strolled toward him. "You've dazzled your audience."

"So I see." He looked around self-consciously. "What's wrong? Have I sprouted horns? Grown fangs?"

"A lot of people immediately act guilty around the police even when they've never broken the law in their lives. I'm not so sure that can be said of this crowd. See anyone who looks suspicious?"

He smothered a smile and played along. "So far everyone

looks like they have something to hide. Have you picked up on anything?"

"I'm afraid not. Except for Alison. She's the one in the front row with long blond hair and yards of black cloth. She's acting very strange, but as Lily pointed out, Alison always acts strange. I thought Oliver was going to lurk in the back room throughout the festivities, but Lily dragged him out."

"Is Warren's family here?"

"I caught a glimpse of his stepmother, I haven't seen his father. Apparently he only came to Port Ariel to see what he could find out about Warren's death. I think he's showing terrible manners by not putting in an appearance tonight, but I don't think Richard Hunt gives a damn about manners. He certainly doesn't fit the stereotype of the mousy accountant."

"Who's that beautiful blond woman who keeps looking at Alison?"

"Her mother Viveca. I'm sure she's glad Alison isn't throwing one of her tantrums, but the statue act is almost as unnerving."

A look of reluctance passed over Nick's strong features. "I should offer my condolences to the Peytons."

"Yes. They're both staring at you."

"Be right back."

Neither Lily nor her father smiled at the sheriff. Natalie knew Lily didn't care for him—she liked Sheriff Purdue's down-home demeanor. Oliver Peyton liked Purdue because he was a puppet. Nick Meredith was no one's puppet.

Loretta was bearing down on Nick as he walked back to Natalie "Is there somewhere we can talk?" he asked suddenly. "Somewhere private?"

Loretta struck. "Sheriff Meredith!" She beamed, showing her perfect teeth. "I've been wanting to meet you. Loretta Leery. I voted for you!"

"Thank you," Nick said awkwardly.

"Loretta, is the back room empty?" Natalie asked.

"Need a cigarette?"

"I don't smoke," Natalie said, then could have bitten her

tongue for fumbling the perfect excuse. "I need to sit down. My shoes are too tight; my feet hurt."

"Right this way," Loretta answered, then glanced back in surprise as Nick followed them. "Do your feet hurt, too?"

"Uh, I thought you might have some coffee back there. I've been going since five this morning."

"Oh, you poor thing!" Loretta exclaimed loudly. People looked again. "Why, of course we have coffee. And some dough-nuts and Danish. The pastries were my idea. Leonard didn't approve, but I said, 'Leonard, people need a little boost to get them through ordeals like this.' And do you know that we received nothing but compliments on the addition of food? Sometimes I *do* have a good idea. I just have trouble making Leonard come around to my way of thinking. Well, here we are. Coffee, food, and the freedom to smoke."

"Thank you, Loretta," Natalie said as the woman hovered at the door. "We'll just be a few minutes."

"Take as long as you like." Loretta gave her an exaggerated wink of conspiracy indicating she knew Natalie's real intention was to get the handsome young widower alone. Natalie felt color tingeing her cheeks. Loretta the perpetual matchmaker. Naturally she would interpret the situation romantically. "Just relax, you two. Everything is in control out front, and it's *very* private in here."

She fluttered her fingers in farewell and rushed down the hall, no doubt to tell Leonard that something was going on with Natalie and Sheriff Meredith. It couldn't be helped and really didn't matter, Natalie told herself, although she hoped Nick hadn't been as aware of Loretta's sly looks and innuendoes as she had been.

Nick was already drawing coffee from the big urn. Natalie felt if she had any caffeine, she might shoot right through the roof. Her nerves tingled.

"Okay, what is it?" she demanded. "Don't tell me someone else has been murdered?"

He looked at her in surprise. "No. Sorry I scared you. I just wanted to talk to you. Hysell has an interesting theory about the connection among the murders."

"Hysell? *Ted* Hysell?"

"Yes. Don't look so shocked. He was more on the ball than I thought."

Natalie shrugged. "Will wonders never cease? What's his theory?"

"Do you remember Eugene Farley?"

Natalie took a deep breath. "He used to date Viveca Cosgrove. She was dating my father until she met him."

"Really?" Nick shook his head. "I didn't know about that."

"I was glad when Viveca stopped seeing Dad. Ever since her husband died she's gone through men like tissues. I was afraid he'd really fall for her and then she'd dump him. Well, she dumped him, but I don't think he felt anything serious about her." She frowned. "But you asked about Farley, not Viveca. Farley was head accountant at Bishop Corporation. He embezzled funds. He was tried and found guilty. Right after the trial he shot himself and died."

Nick sat down on a folding chair and took a sip of coffee, saying nothing. Natalie waited, then said impatiently, "I don't get Hysell's brilliant connection."

Nick looked at her. "Think about it. Oliver Peyton was Farley's attorney, and he lost the case. Richard Hunt was the accountant who exposed Farley. Max Bishop owned the company Farley stole from. He could have fired Farley and let things slide, but he brought up Farley on charges. Now a daughter of Peyton, the son of Hunt, and the daughter of Bishop have been murdered."

"They are all children of people involved in the Farley case," Natalie said slowly.

"Right."

"My God." Natalie sat down on a folding chair beside him. "That can't be the connection. It's too far-fetched."

"You'd chalk the connection among the victims to coincidence?"

"Saying it's a coincidence sounds just as far-fetched." Natalie thought for a moment. "But, Nick, these three people had more in common than being children of people who knew Eugene Farley. They were involved in a love triangle."

"In a case involving a love triangle only one or two people are murdered. If there's a third death, it's a suicide. None of these was a suicide." Natalie's forehead creased in thought and her gaze grew far away. "Today I called Constance Farley, Eugene's mother," Nick went on. "Her husband died just weeks after Eugene. She lived in Columbus at the time of the deaths, but six months ago she moved to Knoxville, Tennessee. I learned that tidbit from Ted, who is dating a woman who was involved with Farley."

"Good Lord, what an incestuous little town we are!"

Nick grinned. "I wouldn't go so far as to say incestuous, but it's hard for me to get used to all these relationships. I like it, though. It makes getting information easier."

"Who needs paid snitches when everyone knows everyone else's business and loves to talk about it? So what did you ask Mrs. Farley? If she'd been in Port Ariel slashing people's throats?"

"I tried something more subtle, but she got my meaning. She seemed shaky, but she told me she hadn't left Knoxville for months. She claimed she didn't know anything about the murders and she didn't want to know. She said, 'I just want to be left in peace.' "

"And you left her in peace."

"I didn't push it, but I called the Knoxville police and gave them the story. Very cooperative bunch down there. Two hours later they called back and told me they'd talked to Mrs. Farley's neighbors. Seems she's never been gone for even one day since she moved in almost six months ago."

"The neighbors have seen her every day?"

"Yeah. She has a dog and walks it rain or shine."

"How about when they can't see her? She could have come up here at night."

"It's approximately a sixteen-hour drive from Knoxville to here."

"She could fly."

"I thought of that, but the Knoxville police also told me Constance doesn't have a driver's license, which eliminates car rental. She'd have to fly into Cleveland and take a commuter flight to Port Ariel. The commuter flight schedules don't fit. She couldn't leave Knoxville at night and be back early the next day."

"You *are* thorough." Natalie tapped her fingers on her cup. "So Constance Farley hasn't been running back and forth to kill people in Port Ariel?"

"Seems not, and the Knoxville cops found the idea a stretch. I joked along with them, but I felt like a fool for suggesting it. When you *say* it, it does sound crazy, but I can't ignore the connection of the victims' parents with Eugene Farley, much as I hate to give up on the idea that Lily or her father had something to do with the double homicide." He paused. "You look uncomfortable. What is it?"

"This morning someone pulled another prank." She told Nick about the call from a woman claiming to be Lily and her meeting with Jeff Lindstrom. "You're going to ask if the voice on the machine sounded like Lily's," she said. "I saved the message and played it back twice. It's close, but it isn't Lily's voice. The enunciation and pace are right but not the quality."

"Did it sound like the voice you heard in The Blue Lady?"

"Yes, only more breathy."

"So you went where the voice asked you to go and you ran into Jeff Lindstrom, who'd been hanging around for hours and who asked you a lot of questions and acted like he might do something to you. Maybe he has more to do with this than we guessed."

"You think he could be the murderer? What does he have to do with Tam, Charlotte, and Warren?"

"Maybe Charlotte is the key. Maybe there was something between them before she came back here."

"She threw over Jeff for Warren? Well, that could explain him killing Charlotte and Warren, but why Tam?"

"I don't know. I'm just throwing out possibilities."

"What about my anonymous calls and the incident at The Blue Lady?"

Nick's face had turned tired and grim. "The voice on the phone and in The Blue Lady sounded like Tamara's. It couldn't have been Lindstrom unless he electronically altered his voice."

"I don't know how that works."

"It's fairly easy to come by the devices you need. Or he might have gotten someone to make the calls for him. How long did you walk on the shoreline before you went to the pavilion?"

"Around twenty minutes."

"If Lindstrom was watching you, that would have given him plenty of time to make a call on a cell phone and get someone to the pavilion."

"How could he know I'd go to The Blue Lady?"

"He could have lured you there—done something to set off the dog so she'd follow him and hoped you'd go inside. Hell, maybe he knew you actually used to go in there and might not be afraid."

"How could he know that?"

"He learned it from the woman who's making these calls for him, someone who's involved with him, someone who knows you."

"Nick, he hasn't been in town long enough to get seriously involved with anyone."

"We don't know how often he's been in this town, Natalie. This doesn't have to be his first visit."

"I guess you're right. Then there's the earring."

"Are you sure it was Tamara's?"

"If it's not hers it's one exactly like it and what are the chances of that? Two years ago I gave Lily and Tamara earrings for their birthday. Lily's had amethysts in a modern bezel setting. Tam's were the old-fashioned filigree." She reached in her pocket and withdrew the earring wrapped in a tissue. "The back is gone.

Also, Jimmy handled it, so there probably aren't any good fingerprints."

"You never know," Nick said, holding up the earring by the post. The small amethyst glittered in the light. "I'll check to see if Tamara was wearing only one earring. Some killers take trophies from their victims, you know."

"That would explain him carrying it around."

Nick stood. "I think I need to have a talk with Mr. Lindstrom." He set his Styrofoam cup down beside the coffee urn. "I'll call you tomorrow and tell you what I found out. I also need to talk to Viveca Cosgrove and Oliver Peyton."

"Why?"

"Farley stole the money because he wanted Viveca back. Peyton was his lawyer. They both have daughters who need to be careful."

"Do you really think this person might go after Alison and Lily?"

"Yes, I do." He paused. "Natalie, Farley didn't die immediately from the shot to the head. He was taken to the hospital. He died while your father was performing surgery, surgery someone claimed your father botched." He gave her a long, penetrating look. "And Andrew St. John has a daughter, too."

III

Andrew and Ruth arrived only minutes after Nick left. Andrew wore the haggard look that meant he'd done several surgeries. Ruth was bright-eyed and stylish in dark green and pearls.

"Sorry I'm late, honey," Andrew said to Natalie. "Harder day than I expected."

"That's all right. Even Oliver delayed his appearance."

"I thought I saw the sheriff in the parking lot," Ruth offered. "Has he learned anything else about the case?"

"I don't think so," Natalie said vaguely. Now was certainly not the time to go into Ted Hysell's theory about the connection among the victims. "He just stopped by as a courtesy. He'll probably come to the funeral, too. Come say a few words to Lily, Dad. She's not in good shape."

Andrew might have disapproved of Lily through the years, but he was all gentle concern tonight. Oliver did not unbend, looking at Andrew as if he'd never seen him before.

Viveca rushed over. Natalie cringed inwardly, but her father showed no emotion. Viveca might have bewitched Eugene Farley and Oliver Peyton, but apparently she had little effect on Andrew St. John. He introduced her to Ruth, and Natalie smiled inwardly as she noticed Viveca's blue eyes sweep over Ruth, quickly calculating the cost of her clothes and deciding whether the pearls were real. Ruth was probably ten years older than Viveca, but she held her own in the style department. Ruth looked calm and secure as she talked quietly with mourners. The woman had class, Natalie thought appreciatively. She also seemed to have made quite a few friends during her short time in Port Ariel, judging by the familiar way she talked to many of the guests.

The wake officially ended at nine o'clock. A few stragglers stayed behind talking about everything *except* the murder. "I'm going to take Ruth home now," Andrew told Natalie.

"All right. I'll stay and help Lily—"

"No you won't." Lily had materialized in front of her. "You look exhausted, Nat. Please go home. I feel drained, and I still have to get through the funeral tomorrow. I'll really need you then, so you'd better get some rest."

Natalie put up a feeble argument, then dropped it. Lily was right. She was tired, and tomorrow would be long and nerve-wracking. She needed to soak some of her tight muscles in a hot bath and try to drift into what she hoped would be a dreamless sleep.

Andrew had brought Ruth, who asked him to take her by his house so she could retrieve the sunglasses she'd left when she dropped by that morning. Natalie followed the couple in her car, and ten minutes later Blaine joyfully greeted everyone, her tail wagging at the sight of human company. Natalie realized she felt as if the dog had always been part of her life.

She talked Ruth into staying for pie and coffee. They all settled into the living room that glowed with soft lamplight to rehash the evening.

"So many people!" Ruth said. "Tamara had many friends."

"I think most were friends of Oliver and Lily," Natalie explained. "Tamara stayed to herself."

Ruth smiled. "So I've heard. I've been to Curious Things several times and met Lily. She seemed like an extrovert, a fun-lover."

"That's an understatement," Andrew put in. "I used to wish Natalie were closer to Tamara than Lily. Tamara might have curbed my daughter's rebellious streak."

"*You* weren't able to," Ruth returned tartly. "Frankly, I find high-spirited young women charming. I used to be one. Now I'm quite tame and boring."

"You aren't boring," Andrew announced.

"Church work and a cat. I *am* boring, just like most women my age." Except for my mother, Natalie thought sourly. "Local gossip tells me Tamara lived like someone at least twice her age, but everyone agrees she was goodhearted." Ruth sighed. "It's such a shame she had to die."

Natalie felt tears well in her eyes. She blinked furiously and stood. "More coffee or—" Her voice broke and she emitted a ragged, "Oh!"

Ruth stood and came toward her. "Natalie, you're a wreck." She patted Natalie's shoulder while Andrew looked at her apprehensively. He'd never known how to handle emotional scenes. After Kira left, Natalie had frequently burst into torrents of tears for her lost mother. Andrew always responded with an agony of blundering, ineffectual distress. Natalie had felt so bad about his misery at the sight of hers that she'd learned to save her tears for times when she was alone. Finally she had squelched them completely, pushing her grief far down and covering it with a blanket of resentment. Bitterness Andrew could handle, anguish he could not.

"I'm sorry," Natalie squeaked out around the lump in her throat. "This is so silly . . ."

"You're exhausted and upset," Ruth said. "You should get some sleep."

Andrew looked at Natalie warily as if he expected her to start jumping up and down and shrieking. "Would you like a sleeping pill, honey?"

"No. Kira was the one with a taste for downers, not me." That's better, she thought in satisfaction. Andrew appeared relieved that his daughter was issuing acid remarks instead of standing in the middle of the living room weeping. "I'll just clear up the dishes—"

"No, I'll do that," Ruth said, heading for the kitchen. "Off to bed and have golden dreams."

"I never heard of golden dreams before, but I'll try." Natalie managed a weak smile. "Good night, Dad."

"Good night, my dear. Do you have plenty of blankets?"

It was June, and even if it had been January with a blizzard howling in off Lake Erie, Andrew was not one to worry over bed linens. She must have really rattled him. Natalie tried not to let her amusement show in her eyes. "I'm fine, Dad. Come on, Blaine. Bedtime for us."

The dog obediently followed her into the bedroom. Natalie shut the door against the murmur of Andrew's and Ruth's voices, immediately kicked off her high heels, and sat down at her vanity table. She looked awful, hollow-eyed and pale-skinned. She removed her earrings and wiped off her lipstick. Tonight she wouldn't worry about dousing her face in her usual expensive cleansing cream she'd let a pushy saleslady at the cosmetic counter tell her she couldn't live without. Tonight a bit of equally expensive moisturizer would do. What *had* she been thinking when she bought this overpriced stuff? Kenny. She'd been thinking of looking like an eternal twenty-one-year-old for Kenny.

Disgusted with herself, she stood quickly and slid out of the unflattering black dress. She was unfastening her bra when suddenly Blaine trotted to the tapestry-covered bench beneath the window and jumped up. "No, no, Blaine," Natalie said. "Dog nails aren't good for the fabric."

Blaine ignored her. She nosed apart the curtains and stared intently for nearly ten seconds, then let out a low rumble.

Natalie went still for a moment, watching the black hair along Blaine's backbone rise and her stance stiffen. Someone was out there.

Without thinking, Natalie swiftly covered herself with her silk kimono, not from a sense of modesty but from fear, as if the delicate cloth could protect her. She turned off the overhead light and crept near the window. She peeked through the crack in the curtains Blaine had made and saw—

Nothing.

She squinted into the night. The carriage-style light mounted on a pole near the side of the house threw dim illumination over the rock garden Andrew had built for Kira thirty years ago. A few brave Grecian windflowers, crocuses, and grape hyacinths stood against the cool darkness. Near the rock garden a weeping willow tree.

The weeping willow tree. Had she caught a hint of movement? Blaine rumbled again, leaning forward until her nose pressed against the glass. Natalie's heart beat harder. Possibly the dog had seen an animal, although if it were a small animal it would have to be climbing *on* the tree to equal the height at which she'd noticed movement. Besides, she'd seen Blaine spot a squirrel on a branch yesterday. The dog had looked interested but not especially excited. Natalie did not think the sight of an animal had caused Blaine's raised hackles and stiff legs.

Her breath suspended, Natalie watched. She had inherited her father's sharp vision, better than 20/20. If anything—or anyone—was out there, she would see.

And there it was.

The glow of a cigarette tip. A lazy arc up, the brightening of the lighted ashes as someone inhaled, a lazy arc down. The watcher was calm and deliberate. How long had he been out there? What did he want?

Natalie jerked away from the window, startling Blaine who let out a sharp, loud bark. The yellow end of the cigarette shot away from the tree. Natalie rushed to the phone extension on her nightstand, called police headquarters, and reported the watcher. A slightly patronizing deputy told her not to worry as long as no one was trying to break into the house. "Is Sheriff Meredith in?" she asked.

"No ma'am, but we wouldn't need to bother the sheriff for some teenager trying to sneak a peek at a pretty lady undressing."

Anger flashed through Natalie. "Is Ted Hysell on duty?"

"Now, miss—"

"Is he on duty?" she demanded.

"He's not on duty, but he just stopped in—"

"Let me speak to him."

"It's not necessary—"

"Put him on the phone!" Damn, damn, damn! Precious time was slipping by. "Tell him it's Natalie St. John."

The deputy let out a furious sigh and yelled, "Hey, Hysell, some hysterical woman named St. John wants *you*!"

In seconds Ted Hysell asked, "Natalie? What's wrong?" She told him about the watcher with as few words as possible. "Be right there," he said and hung up.

Natalie clutched the kimono around her and rushed into the living room. Her father and Ruth had left. She ran to the front door to make sure it was locked, then went to her bedroom and pulled on a pair of jeans, a sweatshirt, and Reeboks.

Once dressed, she walked back to the living room and turned on every lamp, then sat down on the Boston rocker. Blaine sat beside her, frequently looking up at her face for signs of anxiety. Natalie had never been afraid in this house. Unhappy. Angry. Bored. Never frightened. But three people had been savagely murdered in Port Ariel during the past week. Three people who were children of people linked to Eugene Farley, just like her own father was. And now someone stood in the dark and watched this house.

She rocked faster. Where was Ted? Had he only been humoring her? Had he and the other deputy laughed over her panic as soon as he'd hung up? Maybe she should call Nick Meredith. Yes, that's what she should have done in the first place.

Natalie jumped up and was striding to the phone when she heard noises outside. She rushed to the window. Two men with flashlights, talking. They walked toward the house and in a moment knocked on the front door. She had already seen one in uniform. She swung open the door. "Ted! How long have you been out there?"

"About five minutes. No lights, no sirens. Didn't want to scare off the creep, but there's no sign of anyone."

"Ted, someone *was* out there under the weeping willow."

"Thought that's where he was. We found two cigarette butts and a crumpled Marlboro package. I got the cigarette package for prints."

Natalie smiled. "You don't know how glad I am you're taking me seriously. Sheriff Meredith told me your theory about the connection among the murder victims."

"He did? I figured he just blew it off."

"Well, he didn't. He even talked to Constance Farley today. Didn't he tell you?"

"It's my day off."

Which explained his jeans and work boots. The other deputy was in uniform. "I'm sure he'll tell you about it tomorrow. He doesn't think she's a suspect."

Ted looked disappointed. "I thought I was on to something."

"I think you are, in spite of Constance's alibi. So does the sheriff." She hesitated. "He respects your abilities, Ted."

The man's plain face slowly suffused with ill-suppressed surprise and joy. "He does?"

"Yes. He told me so." She didn't know what to say next. She might have already said more than Nick would like, but Ted had looked like he could use some bolstering. "Do you and the other deputy want to come in for some coffee?"

"No, no thanks," Ted said hurriedly. "Got to get back to write this up. Are you here alone?"

"Temporarily. Dad should be back soon."

"I'll have someone drive by once an hour anyway. 'Night, Natalie. Be sure to lock that door."

Oh, I certainly will, Natalie thought as she closed the door behind Ted. She had no doubt the watcher had been here before tonight and no doubt that he'd come again.

13

I

THURSDAY MORNING

Natalie awakened with a sense of dread she couldn't place. She opened her eyes and stared at her bedside clock. 5:55. She slipped out of bed and went to the window to look at the sky. A pale blue wave lapped at the dark shore of night. Birds chirped and sang. It would be a beautiful day.

A beautiful day for a funeral.

Natalie closed her eyes. How could she get through this awful day? She took a deep breath. As bad as this day would be for her, it would be much worse for Lily. Oliver, too, but he had Viveca. In fact, he seemed to have shut out Lily and turned to Viveca for strength and consolation. Natalie thought he was being cruel to Lily, but perhaps she shouldn't judge at a time like this. Still, the situation seemed odd. Oliver had always been so close to Lily—closer than to Tamara, much closer than to his delicate, retiring wife Grace. Natalie clearly couldn't ask Lily what had happened between them. In this case she would keep her own counsel. Maybe after the funeral the situation would right itself.

A cold, damp nose touched her and she jumped. Blaine. Natalie smiled and rubbed the dog's head. "It's early but I can't go back to sleep. I think it's time for coffee and dog food," she said.

When she reached the kitchen, Andrew was already sat at the table with a mug of coffee and a piece of toast in front of him. "What? Just toast? Not the usual breakfast of a prizefighter?" Natalie asked. "What's wrong?"

"What's wrong? We had a prowler last night and you didn't see fit to tell me," Andrew said coldly.

"How did you find out?"

"I couldn't sleep. When I saw a police cruiser creep by for the second time in an hour, my laser-sharp brain told me something was wrong. I flagged down the car and asked."

Natalie calmly poured coffee. "I didn't want to alarm you."

"Alarm me? Natalie, you seem to forget who is the parent here."

"And you seem to forget that I'm *twenty*-nine, not *nine*." She closed her eyes and took a deep breath. "Dad, I was going to tell you this morning. Last night you looked so tired I didn't see the point in disturbing your night's sleep, especially when the police were keeping an eye on the place. Was that so terrible?"

Andrew took a sip of coffee and gazed beyond her. "No, I suppose not. In theory."

"Okay. Let's drop it." Andrew still looked truculent, but she wasn't going to argue. "The funeral is at two."

"I know. I'm bringing Ruth. Will you be riding with us?"

"No. Lily might need me afterward so I want my own car."

"Suit yourself." Natalie could tell he was still seething. He rose, dumped his remaining coffee in the sink with a splash, and clumped out of the kitchen. Natalie sighed. An awful start to an awful day. What had she expected?

Her father left around seven-thirty to make rounds. Natalie called Lily to see if she needed anything. "Someone to lean on," Lily said plaintively. "My father acts like he's the only one suffering."

"Some people aren't capable of recognizing anyone's grief except their own," Natalie offered.

"Especially when they're encouraged to ignore everyone else by the likes of Viveca."

Lily's dislike of Viveca would be a real problem in the future if Oliver married Viveca. She felt she should say something placating, but nothing came to mind. Lily wouldn't listen anyway. "Don't think about Viveca today," she said. "Just concentrate on getting through the funeral."

"At least Warren won't be there. I guess I should be grateful for small favors." She paused. "I can hear your disapproval over the phone."

"I know you didn't like Warren, but he *is* dead."

"And even if he didn't kill my sister, he did have at least one affair. Do you know what finding out about that would have done to my sister? My pregnant sister? The bastard!"

The bastard who was killed hours after you found out your murdered sister was pregnant, Natalie thought. Nick's words came back to her: "Profound grief or shock can make you capable of things you never imagined."

"Natalie, are you there?"

The doorbell rang. Thank goodness, Natalie thought, overcome by guilt for even considering that Lily could be a murderer. "Lily, someone is here. I'll be at the church a little early, and I'll be at your house later."

"I appreciate it. And I'm sorry to be such a harridan today."

"Don't worry about it." The doorbell rang again. "I have to go. See you later."

She hoped Lily would turn down the virulence a notch before the funeral. Warren's father would probably attend, and though he didn't seem too fond of his son, he didn't need Lily popping off at him every five minutes. Natalie also didn't want Nick hearing Lily's rancor. If he seriously suspected her of murdering Warren, her hot temper could only make her look worse.

Natalie's mind was completely taken up with the problem when she opened the door. She blinked twice in the light before she recognized his tall, slim form. "Nick," she said flatly.

"Her heart pounds with enthusiasm for his unannounced visit."

Natalie smiled. "I didn't mean to be rude. I'm distracted about Tamara's funeral."

"And you also didn't get much sleep because of a prowler."

"You've talked to Ted."

"Yes. I wish you'd called me last night."

"You weren't on duty, and it was just a Peeping Tom."

Nick tossed her a skeptical look. "You don't seem like the kind of woman who calls in the cavalry over a Peeping Tom."

"You're right. After what you told me about a possible connection among the victims, I got spooked when I saw a guy watching the house."

"Did you get a good look at him?"

"No. I really only saw the cigarette burning."

"Then why are you sure it was a man?"

Natalie stared at him a moment. "The height of the cigarette, although it could have been held by a tall woman."

"Ted said they found two cigarette butts. He'd been watching you for a while."

"I'd only been in the bedroom a few minutes."

"His bad luck was that Blaine sounded the alarm before he could watch for long." She looked at him closely. "Ted gave me the details."

"Dad also got the details later in the night when he spotted a patrol car. I was going to spare him until morning. He's furious with me, and that's *without* knowing I might be on the killer's list."

Nick's thick eyebrows drew together. "He has to be told, Natalie."

"I will."

"If *you* don't, *I* will."

Irritation prickled through her. "This is *my* business."

"Not if you get killed. Then it's *my* business, and business has been too good lately."

Natalie felt slightly chastened. "I'll be careful."

"I have a feeling your idea of careful and my idea of careful aren't the same. I don't want anything to happen to you," he said fervently, then added as an afterthought, "or Lily or Alison."

"Who do you think the prowler last night was?"

"Jeff Lindstrom. Trudy at the diner told me he was staying at the Lakeview Motel. I checked last night, but he wasn't in. I went by again early this morning. No Lindstrom, no car, but he didn't check out."

"Then where did he go after he left here?"

Nick shrugged. "Maybe he figured he'd be the first person we'd suspect after you saw him at Tamara's and decided to lie low."

"He can't lie low forever."

"No, but he can leave town."

"Oh, great. Can't you find out where he is?"

"I can run prints from his room, although at this point I have no evidence for a warrant."

"It's a motel room."

"Rented to him, so temporarily it's his property. Natalie, this isn't television. Things don't just fall into place."

For the first time she noticed he had smudges under his dark blue eyes and lines of strain around his mouth. She also realized that, tired as he was, he was good-looking in a strong-boned, square-jawed way. Definitely not the male model type but definitely handsome.

"Why does everyone in this town stare at me?" Nick asked in amused exasperation.

Color rushed to Natalie's cheeks. She felt like she did at fifteen when she'd had a crush on seventeen-year-old Hart Sullivan. A crush? More blood rushed to her cheeks.

"Natalie, are you all right? You're flushed."

She blinked. She swallowed. She stretched her mouth in a semblance of a smile. "I'm fine. I'm just dreading today."

"Sure you are." He was all solicitous concern. She felt ashamed. Tamara was being buried today and she was sizing up the new guy in town. Worse still, he'd caught her doing it. "I'll be at the funeral," he said.

"I thought you would be." Natalie fought to regain some of her poise. "Still looking for potential suspects?"

"Unfortunately, yes. I also need to talk with Viveca Cosgrove and Oliver Peyton."

"Do you think the funeral is an appropriate place to do it?"

"No, but they've both made themselves unavailable to me," he said.

"That must be annoying."

"Annoying? It's pissing me off. This isn't a game."

"Oliver and Viveca don't realize Lily and Alison might be in danger."

Nick sliced his hand impatiently through the air. "So what? I'm the sheriff, dammit. I'm trying to solve three murders, one of them Peyton's daughter's. The Cosgrove woman is supposed to be in love with him and to care about Tamara. I shouldn't have to chase them down. They should be eager to help me in any way they can instead of acting like I'm some nosy pest."

Natalie looked at him sympathetically. "They're both really high-handed."

"Well, they can get off their thrones voluntarily or I'll damn well drag them off. I'm getting sick of people like Oliver Peyton and Max Bishop."

"Max Bishop won't talk to you, either?"

"I stand corrected. He will. He called yesterday to yell that I'm not doing my job. His body may be debilitated, but his voice is in fine working order. He says Purdue would have had this whole thing solved in twenty-four hours."

"Purdue wouldn't have known what to do if the killer walked right up to him and confessed," Natalie said scornfully. "Real police work scared him to death, sent him straight to his office for a shot of courage he thought no one knew he kept in his desk drawer. Nick, you have to realize that Oliver Peyton, Viveca Cosgrove, and Max Bishop are big fish in a very little pond called Port Ariel and Purdue was their flunky. Don't let *any* of them run over you because you're trying to fit in around here. You'll never fit in like Purdue did and most people in this town thank God that you don't."

Nick relaxed slightly and grinned. "Thanks, coach."

"I didn't mean to preach."

"I needed a sermon. You're right—I can't let these people get to me. If I do, I can't think clearly."

"Well, I for one want you thinking as clearly as possible, Nick, because without you, this killer will go free." Natalie shivered. "And I think he'll kill again. I can feel it."

II

Natalie could not remember enduring a longer funeral service. Lily looked as pale as death itself. Oliver sat frozen-faced, his black-and-silver hair slicked into place, his dark gray suit exquisite, although he looked as if he'd lost ten pounds; the suit was too big in the shoulders. Beside him Viveca posed in equal sartorial splendor, diamond studs glistening on her earlobes. Alison slumped in her pew, her face vacant, her restless hands twisting strands of her flaxen hair. Several times Viveca reached up to gently stop the nervous movement.

Lily shot Viveca and Alison scalding glances, clearly resenting their places with the family while aunts, uncles, and cousins were relegated to more distant pews. Warren's father had not come, although his young wife fidgeted in stylish boredom beside Warren's hulking brother who seemed to be dozing.

Natalie sat with her father and Ruth. Every time Andrew kneeled, his knees popped and his face reddened. Ruth cast him a couple of encouraging smiles. Natalie wondered how serious they were. They hadn't been seeing each other long, and Andrew swore he "barely knew" Ruth, but they seemed close. Natalie wished he would find someone. He'd been alone too long.

Suddenly she realized she was thinking of everything except the service. Deliberately. If she didn't, she would cry and she didn't want to cause a scene. Long ago Natalie had learned to shed tears in private. She would do the same today.

At last the service ended. As they filed out of the church, Ruth let out a tiny gasp and dropped her purse. Startled, Natalie bent to retrieve the purse while Andrew firmly took Ruth's arm. "What's wrong?" he muttered.

"I . . . I don't know. Everything went black for a moment." Ruth managed a twitchy smile, although her face was dewy with perspiration. "I'm fine."

"You're not." By now they had reached the door of the church. "Natalie, I'm taking Ruth home."

"Oh, no," Ruth protested. "You'll want to go to the gravesite . . ."

"I don't," Andrew said emphatically. "I want to take you home and have something to drink and a quiet talk."

"Andrew—"

"There's no point in arguing with him," Natalie said.

"It never stopped you," Andrew retorted without sarcasm. Ruth smiled. "Come on, Ruth. You're pale and your hands are trembling. It might be an attack of hypoglycemia, in which case you need nourishment." Or the service might have been a reminder of her husband's funeral, Natalie thought. Her father looked at her. "We'll see you later, dear."

With that they were heading for Andrew's car. Natalie watched them. A handsome couple. Andrew's concern for Ruth was obvious. He would take care of her, even though her attack was probably nothing serious.

As she walked toward her car she saw Nick Meredith almost running toward a light blue car. He wore a suit and had driven his own car to the funeral, but she knew he was on the job and something was wrong. She stood by her car, fingers touching the door handle, watching Nick tear out of the parking lot and make a fast right onto a busy street. Who was he chasing? It had to be someone he'd seen at the funeral.

III

If Nick had not turned at that exact moment, he would have missed Lindstrom, head bowed, creeping out the door of the church. He was trying to lose himself among the other mourners. He failed.

By the time Nick pushed his way through the sedate line of people in front of him, Lindstrom had made it to a white Cavalier. He cast cautious looks around him and met Nick's gaze. Their eyes locked for a significant instant before Lindstrom swung his long legs in the car and turned on the ignition. Nick ran. He was already firing up his car as Jeff Lindstrom spun away from the Sacred Heart parking lot.

Nick had left his car unlocked. As he climbed in, he saw Natalie St John standing beside her car, looking at him. Her long black hair lifted gently in the breeze and her dark eyes filled with curiosity. He didn't know if she had seen Lindstrom— probably not—but she knew something was wrong. No time for explanations. Catching Lindstrom would be explanation enough. The creep may not have killed three people, Nick thought, but he'd terrified Natalie on Hyacinth Lane and spied at her through her bedroom window.

Spied on her. Lain in wait for her. Nick's foot pressed the accelerator. This bastard wasn't getting away from him.

He was one car away from Lindstrom. The elderly man ahead puttered along in an old, rusted Cadillac that put out a cloud of smoke. Every time Nick tried to pass, the car weaved toward the left. Nick honked the horn to indicate he needed to pass. The old man gave him the finger. Surprised and infuriated, Nick checked oncoming traffic, then roared by the ancient Cadillac. The guy gave him the finger again and laid on the horn. Nick quelled the impulse to return the obscene gesture, but he couldn't resist blasting his own horn. He wanted to pull the guy over, but he had to concentrate on Lindstrom, who was getting away.

The Cavalier shot around a pickup truck, nearly colliding with a car coming in the opposite lane. Nick nosed near the pickup, whose bed was loaded with a couch, a chair, a dresser, a stained mattress, and dozens of boxes. The guy deserved a ticket. Nothing in the bed of the truck was secured properly and looked like it could come flying off at any moment.

Which is exactly what happened. Nick had drawn close, watching for a break in traffic so he could pass, when a box took flight. He saw it coming and flinched even before it slammed against his windshield. Pillows, sheets, towels, and underwear engulfed his car. He swerved right, his front tire hitting dirt and sending gravel spitting through the air. He eased back onto the pavement, mentally taking down the license number of the pickup. The driver would be receiving a citation tomorrow.

Smaller debris shot from the truck as Nick pulled to the left and accelerated. When he passed the driver's window, he saw a moon-faced man with a vacant expression bobbing his head and singing. Nick blasted his horn and rolled down the opposite window. The sound of a Garth Brooks song blared from the pickup. The driver looked at him blankly.

"Stuff is falling off your truck!" Nick shouted. The guy nodded and smiled amiably. "Pull *over!*" This time another amiable smile accompanied by a thumbs-up signal. What the hell did that mean? Nick jerked his badge from beneath his suit jacket and held it up. "Listen, shithead, stuff is falling off your truck!" he yelled at the top of his voice. "Pull OVER!"

The guy's benign smile faltered. He looked in his rearview mirror. Then he slowed and began creeping off the road, leaving a trail of household items behind him. Nick didn't have time to fool with him, either. Dammit, where was the highway patrol when you needed them?

Lindstrom's Cavalier sped at least ten miles over the speed limit. He passed another car and gained even more speed. "Damn!" Nick muttered as traffic grew heavier. He'd probably never catch the jerk now. While cops on television never missed an opportunity to launch a high-speed chase, real-life cops were more careful in traffic. The danger of killing innocent people was too great.

Then the white Cavalier wavered and shot violently to the right, tilting slightly. "Blew a tire!" Nick shouted in glee. The car slowed and edged off the road. Two cars passed before Nick whipped up behind it. He leaped out of his car as Lindstrom slowly climbed from his. Lindstrom gave Nick an uncertain look, then threw him a guileless smile. "Thanks for stopping to help. I never was too good at changing tires."

"You know damned well I didn't stop to help with your tire."

Lindstrom's smile disappeared. He tried to look wary. "Hey, what's your problem?"

"My problem is that I'm the sheriff and I've been trying to get you to pull over since you left the church."

"I didn't know you were the sheriff!" He glanced at Nick's Intrepid. "That's not a police cruiser. I thought you were some nut trying to run me off the road."

He was lying. He'd seen Nick at Lily's store. Then at the church his gaze had directly met Nick's before he'd jumped in his car and taken off as fast as he could. But Nick had no proof, so he had to let the matter drop. "Why were you at Tamara Hunt's funeral?"

"I . . . well . . . curiosity." Nick stared at him hard. "Okay, I know how sick that sounds, but hear me out. I'm a reporter with the *Cincinnati Star*. I'm on vacation, and I came up here to see what I could find out about these murders. I've always wanted to write a true-crime book like *Small Sacrifices*. Ever hear of it?"

"Ann Rule."

"Hey, you read!" Jeff grinned.

"Learned in elementary school."

"I didn't mean it that way," Jeff said quickly. "I just meant that . . . well, maybe you didn't have time to read."

"I don't care what you meant. So you want to write a book. Is that why you've been asking so many questions about Tamara and Warren Hunt and Charlotte Bishop?"

"Yes."

"That's why you cornered Natalie St. John on a deserted road and gave her the third degree?"

"I didn't *corner* her," Jeff said hotly. "I just ran into her. It was daylight. Did she tell you I tried to hurt her or something?"

"No, but she said she had a hard time getting away from you."

"Maybe I talked too much. Hey, she's a good-looking woman, don't you think?" Nick stared at him expressionlessly. "Look, I didn't mean to scare her. I was just talking."

"You were asking a lot of questions." He paused. "And what were you doing with Tamara Hunt's earring?"

"Earring? I don't know what you're talking about."

"It fell out of your pocket while you were *just talking* to Natalie. Where did you get it?"

"Oh, the earring. I found it. Out on that road."

"And what are you—a bag lady in disguise? You squirrel away bits and pieces of things you find?"

Jeff glared at him. "No, Sheriff. Frankly, I did think it might be Tamara's. I was going to bring it to you."

"Oh, were you?"

"Yes."

"But when you discovered your pocket was empty, you didn't call me up and say, 'Sheriff, I found an earring on Hyacinth Lane that might have been Tamara Hunt's, but I lost it. It's probably still out there somewhere.' "

"What would have been the point of that?"

"If you're such a fan of true-crime novels, you'd know we might have learned something from that earring. I don't think you ever had any intention of turning it in to the police."

"Think what you want," Jeff snapped.

"Did you talk to Charlotte Bishop the night of her murder?"

"*What?*"

"You're not hard of hearing, Lindstrom."

"No, I didn't talk to her."

"Her mother says she saw Charlotte talking with someone fitting your description right before she left the house that night."

Jeff raised his arms helplessly. "I didn't know Charlotte Bishop."

"That isn't what I asked."

"Why would I be talking to her?"

"Your book."

"What would she have to do with my book? She hadn't been murdered when I was supposedly seen talking with her. I don't know what the hell this is all about, but—" Lindstrom seemed ready to burst into a tirade, then got control of himself. He flashed the grin that was beginning to grate on Nick's nerves. "Sheriff, doing this book means a lot to me. I'm sorry if you don't like me asking Natalie St. John questions. I'm sorry I didn't mention the earring. I'm new at this stuff." The grin. "But can't you cut me a little slack? How about letting me in on this investigation? When the book comes out, you'll be prominently featured in the acknowledgments. I promise."

"I don't care about your book," Nick said coldly. "Just stay out of my way."

Jeff's grin vanished. "I didn't have any intention of getting in your way, but you can't stop me from asking questions and doing a little digging of my own."

"I've given you a warning." Nick looked at him chillingly. "You ignore me, and I'll have you arrested for interfering with a police investigation."

"I've got rights," Jeff called as Nick walked back to his car.

"You just keep telling yourself that, Lindstrom, when you're sitting in a dark, little jail cell with one of our less civilized citizens staring at you like you're a prime piece of fresh meat."

IV

Thankfully the graveside service was short. Lily and her father dropped flowers onto the coffin. Then Lily made a beeline for Natalie. "You're coming back to the house with me, aren't you?" she asked almost desperately.

"Of course. I told you I would."

"I know. I'm just so . . . Oh, I don't know. Sad. Confused. Bitter. I've lost my sister *and* my father."

"You haven't lost your father."

"Not physically. But that damned Viveca and her nutty daughter . . ."

"Speaking of your father, he's shooting meaningful looks in this direction."

"I suppose I'm not presenting a suitable picture of family solidarity."

"Lily, don't you think you're being a bit hard on him?"

Lily's hazel eyes flashed. "No, and please don't lecture. I need a friend, not a . . . a . . ."

"I get it." Natalie put on her sunglasses. "I'll meet you at your house, and no lectures, I promise."

Fifteen minutes later she pulled up to the Peyton home. Cars lined the elegant street for a block north and another south of the house. Natalie wondered how many of these people really knew Tamara and how many were here because their familiarity with Oliver allowed them in the door to slake their avid curiosity. Inside she recognized few people and decided that unfortunately many were here out of curiosity alone. Ghouls. But maybe she wasn't being fair. Perhaps some of these people were friends Tam made through Warren. Natalie doubted it, though. She'd never heard Tamara mention parties or conventions she'd attended with Warren. It seemed he'd usually left his pretty, shy wife at home. Natalie had no doubt he'd always been unfaithful. How many women like Charlotte had there been?

She was making herself angry, she thought as she approached the front door. There was no sense in going over how Warren might have wronged his wife. That was what Lily was tearing herself apart over and for what? It wouldn't bring back Tamara. And Warren had certainly paid a heavy price for his wrongs. Someone had evened the score.

Someone had evened the score. The sentence tolled in Natalie's head. Was someone trying to even the score for Eugene Farley by killing the children of people who'd been involved in his downfall? Or had Warren died because someone thought he had killed Tamara? Who would feel passionately enough to exact revenge for Tam's murder? Oliver or Lily?

"Natalie, thank God you're here!" Lily stood in the doorway, her blond hair escaping from the bow, her eyes anxious. "I *cannot* get through this without you."

Natalie swallowed. She couldn't manage a smile when ten seconds earlier she'd been wondering if her best friend murdered Warren. Slashed his throat. And Charlotte's.

"Nat, what's wrong?" Lily reached out with her strong, long-fingered hand. "You look . . . *frozen.*"

"It's just a weird day." What a creative answer, Natalie thought. "I need a drink."

"You've come to the right place. I feel like I'm at Truman Capote's famous Black-and-White Ball. Viveca has outdone herself."

When Natalie walked in the house, she had to agree with Lily. None of the somberness of other funeral receptions she'd attended prevailed here. Instead, waiters circled with trays of canapes. Vivid flower arrangements flourished. Candles burned and music played loudly in the background. An open bar operated in the dining room. Natalie felt almost dizzy.

"Lily, isn't that the waltz from *Die Fledermaus*?"

"Yes. Any minute I expect someone to start dancing. Either that or the next musical selection will be 'Bolero.' I don't know what Dad is thinking. Or even *if* he's thinking. He has to know Tam would hate this. And my mother would be turning in her grave!"

Natalie shook her head. "You're right, I don't understand. Viveca usually has good taste."

Lily emitted a modified snort. "From what I've heard she threw a similar shebang for her husband. Former lover Eugene Farley didn't rate the same treatment."

Natalie stiffened at the mention of Farley. She didn't want to talk about him, but Lily had just given her a perfect opening. She girded herself emotionally. "Did you know Eugene?"

"Yes, a little."

"Tell me about him."

Lily gave her a bemused smile. "Are you trying to take my mind off all this?" Natalie smiled back enigmatically. "Well, whatever. Let's see. He was extremely good-looking. Pretty-boy good-looking. He came into the store once right after he moved to town. He said he wanted something for his mother. He bought a cameo pendant. He was friendly and somehow seemed younger than his age. He also talked a *lot* about his mother. Anyway, the second time he came in he wanted more jewelry. I asked if it was for his mother and he said no, someone younger.

He actually *blushed* when he said it. I'd heard he was seeing Dee Fisher. I couldn't imagine I'd have anything *she'd* want. He chose an antique garnet brooch set in eighteen-carat gold. It was pretty expensive. I remember he put it on a credit card. I know now it was for Viveca."

"Did you like him?"

"He was okay. Too shy and formal for my taste. Of course, you know me—I always go for the dangerous types that break your heart." She paused. "I hope Viveca didn't break your father's."

"I think she barely fazed him, which must have bruised her ego. Maybe she turned to Eugene because she wasn't having the desired effect on Dad. He's wary of women after Kira. I'm surprised he dated her at all."

Lily shrugged. "Maybe he was just amusing himself or trying to show the town he hadn't turned into some weird old misogynist. By the way, how are he and his new lady friend getting along?"

"I haven't quite gotten a bead on that relationship yet. Dad is being even more cagey than usual. Ruth certainly seems nice."

"You like her."

"Yes. And I don't want Dad to be alone, but he's spent so long dodging serious relationships I don't have a lot of hope."

Lily smiled mischievously. "Well, if things don't work out for them, I want Ruth for Dad."

Natalie glanced up. Viveca stood right behind Lily. She raised a carefully penciled eyebrow and swept away, her head high. Had she been hurt by what she'd overheard or merely insulted? "Lily, Viveca heard that," Natalie murmured.

"Who cares? She knows I don't like her."

The front door opened again. Nick Meredith stepped in. "What do you know?" Lily said. "The heat has arrived."

Natalie excused herself and walked toward Nick. His cheeks were flushed, his gaze restless. "Why did you leave the church so fast?" she asked bluntly.

"Nothing gets by you, does it?"

"I usually notice cars speeding away from funerals. What was it?"

Nick lowered his voice. "I saw Lindstrom."

"At the funeral?" she blurted.

"Don't announce it to the whole room," Nick said. "Yes, at the funeral. I saw him leaving."

"Killers come to funerals."

"Now don't get carried away with all those murder mystery clichés. *Sometimes* they come to the funeral."

"What other reason could he have?" Natalie asked. "He didn't know Tamara. What excuse did he give you?" She paused. "You *did* catch him, didn't you?"

"Yes. He said he wants to write a book about the killings. You know—true crime."

"And you believe him?"

"He claimed to be a reporter with the *Cincinnati Star*. I checked it out. He *was* a reporter for them until about three weeks ago. The editor said he'd left, but even though the guy wouldn't discuss details, I got the impression Lindstrom was fired."

"So he lied. What about the earring?"

"He says he found it on the road. Thought it might be Tamara's, was going to bring it to me, but when he got home he didn't have it. *And* he didn't mean to scare you out on that road. Says he was just curious. Also got a little carried away with himself because you're pretty and he didn't want to end the conversation."

"My looks had nothing to do with the way he was acting, Nick."

"Probably not. Not to underestimate your considerable looks."

"I wasn't fishing for a compliment."

"I know. If you had been, I wouldn't have given you one."

Natalie grinned. "Goodness, you're a hard case."

"Tough as nails, lady."

"What about Mrs. Bishop saying she saw him talking to Charlotte?"

"Mrs. Bishop didn't say she saw *Lindstrom*. She just gave a vague description of someone resembling him. Of course, he says he didn't know Charlotte and didn't have any interest in her at that time."

"Why no interest?"

"She wasn't a corpse, yet. Anyway, after all this bullshit he had the damned nerve to ask if he could be part of the investigation. Promised me an acknowledgment in his book."

"And your heart of steel melted."

"I was putty in his hands."

"The truth, please."

"I told him if he didn't butt out, I'd have him arrested."

"Do you think you scared him off?"

"Hell, no. He knows I can't stop him from asking people questions, and so far that's all he's done."

"So far?"

"I've met a hundred guys like him, Natalie. He's a sleaze, but he's cool enough under pressure to tell lies without blinking an eye. I don't trust him."

"You don't trust who?"

Natalie and Nick looked up at Alison. They were both so startled by her smiling face they stared. "Cat got your tongues?" she asked archly. "Do you like cats? *I* do."

"I have a cat," Nick said, then looked surprised at the sound of his perky voice. He sounded as if he were speaking to a child. "His name is Ripley."

Alison frowned. "Why Ripley?"

"She wasn't supposed to, but my daughter saw the movie *Aliens*. It scared the daylights out of her, but she loved the main character Ripley."

Alison looked at him as if he'd lost his mind. "Sigourney Weaver played Ripley. Ripley is a *woman*. Wow, didn't you *get* that?" Nick colored as Alison's voice rose. "Your *male* cat is named after a woman!"

"My daughter liked the name," he muttered. "I don't believe she really thinks about sex."

Alison leaned toward him confidentially. "*All* girls think about sex."

"My daughter is eleven," Nick returned stiffly.

"Far beyond the age of innocence," Alison sneered. She winked at Natalie. "Am I right?"

Natalie was flummoxed. "I guess it depends on the girl."

"Well, with a mother like *mine* . . ." Alison rolled her eyes. "Hey, what's the difference between a whore and a courtesan?"

"A . . . *what*?" Nick blundered.

"C-O-U-R-T-E-S-A-N," Alison spelled loudly. "So? Anyone know?"

"I . . . well . . ." Natalie longed for another good, stiff drink. Nick looked like he was considering plunging out a window. Alison gazed at them with a twelve-year-old's innocent face and avid, ferreting eyes. "Let's talk about something else," Natalie managed finally. "You said you like cats. What about dogs? I have a dog."

"I *love* animals, but my mother never let me have one. I know about yours, though. You have the dog that stayed with Tamara when she died. I'm not supposed to know that." She gave each of them a canny look. "However, I know *all* kinds of things I'm not supposed to know."

"Alison, darling, I've been looking for you." Viveca appeared behind her daughter, placing her hands on each of Alison's thin shoulders. "Have you had anything to eat?"

All the air seemed to flow out of Alison. "I'm not hungry."

"Nonsense. There is some lovely *foie gras*—"

"I-am-not-hungry," Alison said through clenched teeth. "You only want me to eat so I'll be quiet."

"Darling, that's not true—"

Alison uttered a guttural sound and flung away. Viveca looked at Nick and Natalie, shrugged, and emitted a high-pitched trill of laughter before darting after her daughter. "Good God," Nick muttered.

"Never a dull moment around here. My father dated Viveca. Alison could have been my stepsister."

"What saved you?"

"Viveca dumped Dad for Eugene Farley, then Eugene for Oliver. I think she might marry Oliver. Lily will be furious. She hates Viveca."

Nick frowned. "Tell me about her husband."

"Alison's father was Damon Cosgrove." Nick's eyebrows raised. "Yes, the writer. Two critically acclaimed best sellers. Then the poor sap came to his aunt's summer cottage in Port Ariel and met Viveca. They married, had Alison, and he never published another book. Not even a short story."

"Why not?"

"I don't know. Maybe he was just one of those writers who only has one or two books in them. Or maybe he felt overwhelmed by Viveca. I think she was about ten years younger than he but still quite the *femme formidable*, as my Grandmother St. John would say. Damon died when Alison was five or six. He was electrocuted to death in front of her."

Nick cringed, thinking of a five-year-old Paige seeing something so ghastly. "Viveca blames Alison's problems completely on the accident," Natalie continued, "but I've heard she wasn't exactly a well-adjusted child before it happened." She took a deep breath. "And now I'm guilty of pernicious gossip but I comfort myself with the thought that the more you know about us, the quicker you might find the killer."

"It's true that the more I know, the better, especially because Alison is directly involved as a potential victim *and* a suspect."

The music changed to "Try to Remember" from *The Fantasticks*. Nick looked around with a mixture of bewilderment and humor. "Viveca's idea," Natalie said. "She seems to think we're mounting a Broadway play."

"This whole thing is like a play," Nick grumbled. "And the more time I spend waiting for all this nonsense to end, the more I put Lily and Alison and *you* in danger. I want to talk to Viveca and Oliver now."

"Now? Can't you wait until all of this is over?"

"This could go on for hours. There's Viveca hovering over

Alison. Find Peyton for me, Natalie. Tell him I want to see him and Viveca."

Natalie didn't know Nick well, but she could already tell when he was deadly serious. She also knew he was not someone to be argued with when he'd made up his mind.

"Mr. Peyton, the sheriff would like to speak to you," she said softly when she located Oliver speaking to the mayor.

Oliver made a swatting motion as if she were a gnat. "I'm busy. I'll speak with him later."

"He wants to talk to you now."

Oliver's lips pressed together. "Young lady, I don't mean to be rude, but I have said later and I mean *later*."

"Mr. Peyton, it's important."

Oliver Peyton gave her a coldly furious look. Then Lily said in a steely voice, "If Natalie says it's important for you to speak to the sheriff, then it's important." She gave the mayor a polite smile. "I'm sure you understand."

"Of course," he said. "Go right ahead, Oliver."

Oliver walked beside his daughter, frowning furiously. "I think you've lost your mind," he snapped at Lily. "I do not answer to Sheriff Meredith *or* Natalie St. John!"

"Please save the high-and-mighty act," Lily said tiredly. "You don't scare me like you did Tam, and you certainly don't scare Meredith. He and Viveca are waiting for you in your study."

"Viveca!" Oliver exploded. "What does Viveca have to do with this? Lily, I know you don't like her, but if you are talking your friends into bullying her—"

"No one bullies Viveca, Dad." Lily opened the door to the study. "Here's your shrinking violet now. I'll leave you alone."

"Lily, I'd like for you and Natalie to stay," Nick said. "Close the door, please."

"My daughter—"Viveca began.

"Your daughter will be fine for a few minutes, Mrs. Cosgrove," Nick said. "I don't want her to hear what I have to say."

"Hear what?" Viveca asked. "What can't she hear?" She leaned toward Oliver and clung to his arm, frightened and helpless. Natalie exchanged looks with Lily. What an actress. Viveca Cosgrove could organize and lead an army into battle. "Oliver?" she implored tremulously.

"This is ridiculous," Oliver burst out. "You are alarming Mrs. Cosgrove. What is this all about?"

"If you'll all be quiet, you'll know what it's about," Nick said repressively. "I believe I see a possible connection among these murders." He then calmly, almost tonelessly, laid out the story of Eugene Farley and how Viveca and Oliver played into the drama of his death. "Therefore, you need to be especially careful about the welfare of Lily and Alison."

Viveca and Oliver stared at him for a moment. Then Natalie watched color slowly drain from Oliver Peyton's face. Even his lips paled. He looked ill and touched his left arm. For a moment she thought the man might be on the verge of a heart attack.

Viveca paid no attention to her supposed great love. She, too, had grown pale, but she came out fighting. "I think this theory of yours is absurd, Sheriff Meredith. *I* never did anything to Eugene." Nick stared her down. "Oh, we dated some and it didn't work out, but beyond that—"

"Beyond that he embezzled two hundred thousand dollars from Bishop Corporation to win you back," Lily lashed out.

"Well, that wasn't *my* fault!" Viveca returned hotly. "*I* didn't ask him to do it. And poor Oliver here *defended* him."

"And lost the case," Nick said.

"Once again, that was not his fault!" Viveca retorted. "It's ludicrous to hold us responsible for Eugene Farley's death!"

Nick looked at her coolly. "Mrs. Cosgrove, *I'm* not holding you responsible for Farley's death. I think someone else holds you responsible."

"I don't understand. Oliver, why don't you say something!"

"Maybe he's afraid to." The door had opened quietly and Alison stood there, glaring at Oliver Peyton. "Why don't you tell them what *I* know?"

"I . . . I don't know what you're talking about," Peyton stammered.

"Alison, go in the other room!" Viveca ordered.

"No." She looked at Nick. "People in this town were *awful* to Eugene. He was wonderful—handsome and sensitive and kind, and *they* caused his death." Tears streamed down her cheeks. "They *all* caused his death!"

"Alison, you don't know what you're talking about," Viveca said in the harshest voice Natalie had ever heard her direct toward her daughter. Her gaze flashed back to Nick. "If you're looking for someone who's bitter about Eugene's death, look to Dee Fisher. She's that trampy nurse he dated when he first got to town. She stole drugs from the hospital. She even accused Andrew St. John of negligence and claimed he let Eugene die during the operation. She's crazy! She was also obsessed with Eugene. She threatened me when I was seeing him. She told me I'd pay for taking him away from her! She's crazy, I'm telling you!"

"Yes, you've told me twice," Nick said mildly. "And I'm aware of Dee Fisher's possible involvement in all this. But I'm not here to talk to you about my suspects. I'm only warning you and Mr. Peyton that Alison and Lily might be in danger."

"And what about Natalie?" Viveca demanded.

"Natalie, too. She knows that. So will her father. Right now I'm *trying* to talk to you about *your* daughter."

Viveca looked at Alison, who still hovered in the doorway, thrumming with tension. "Dear, go into the other room."

"I *won't*" Alison's eyes narrowed. "You're all covering up about Eugene!"

"What about Eugene?" Nick asked.

"Nothing!" Viveca nearly shouted. "She knows nothing! Leave her alone!"

"I know *everything!*" Alison shrilled. "You *all* killed him and you'll *all* pay!"

Her body tensed. Viveca jumped up and rushed to her as she began to shake and her accusations dissolved into babbling. Her arms flailed. Viveca tried unsuccessfully to control her daughter. She looked helplessly at Oliver, who sat like a rock. Nick flew into action, wrapping his strong arms around the girl. Even then she continued to writhe with amazing strength.

"I'm calling the emergency squad," Lily said.

"I don't want her to go to the hospital!" Viveca wailed. "Everyone in town will know. The talk—"

"Oh, for God's sake, Viveca!" Lily erupted and dashed to the phone.

"No!" Alison screamed. "Not the hospital! I'll kill myself!"

She picked up a glass vase, broke it, and tried to drag it across her wrist. Nick wrested the jagged glass from her hand while Alison continued to howl.

"She means it," Viveca cried. "She *will* do something to herself. I have to get her home."

"She needs a doctor," Nick insisted.

"Not the *hospital*—"

"Viveca, will you let my dad see her?" Natalie interrupted.

"Andrew?" Viveca frowned, then looked at Alison. "Darling, may Dr. St. John visit you? You like him."

Alison slowly stopped shrieking. "Johnny? He was nice to me."

"Yes, darling, Johnny was nice to you." *Johnny?* Natalie thought in amazement. "If we go home, will you let him give you something to make you feel better? Please?" Viveca begged.

Alison's breath labored in her narrow chest. "Yes. Okay. But only Johnny. Do you hear me? Only Dr. Johnny. And not *here*. I want away from *here*. I want to go *home*!"

Natalie took the phone from Lily. No one answered at her house and she panicked. Then she thought of Ruth. Directory assistance gave her the number, and Ruth put him on the line. With as little explanation as possible Natalie told him Alison needed him and would be at Viveca's. "I'll go there immediately," he said and hung up.

Alison looked venomously at Nick. "I can't bear for strange men to touch me. Let *go*!"

He released her and she sagged. Lily came forward to help. Remarkably, Alison draped an arm over her shoulder as her eyes began to glaze. Mentally, she was no longer with them.

Three minutes later Nick and Natalie stood alone in the room. Lily had helped Viveca get control of Alison, who had begun to scream methodically and tonelessly. They led her out to Viveca's car. Oliver had tottered out behind them looking like a man in shock. Natalie felt chilled to the bone by the awful scene. She stared at Nick. "What in the name of God was all that about?"

"I don't know," Nick said slowly, "but I'm afraid if Alison Cosgrove isn't our killer, she just signed her own death warrant."

14

Nick pressed the doorbell for the second time. A lamp burned in the living room and another in an upstairs room. He heard faint sounds of a television rattling on. He looked at his watch. 9:05. Too early for most people to be in bed. He raised his hand to ring the bell again when the door flew open. A hawk-faced woman with white hair in pin curls glared at him. "Yeah? What is it?"

"Mrs. Fisher?"

"What if I am?"

"I'm Nick Meredith, the sheriff, and—"

"I knew it! What's she done *now*?" the woman demanded fiercely. "As if I don't have enough to worry about!"

"Ma'am, I wonder if I might come in and speak with you."

"You can talk from out there on the porch."

Mosquitoes and moths floated and fluttered around the porch light next to Nick's head. Besides, the woman looked ill and not too steady on her feet. He thought she needed to sit down. "Please, ma'am, I think we'd both be more comfortable inside—"

She began to cough violently. He reached forward, not knowing what to do besides pat her on the back, but she smacked his hand. "Night air," she choked out.

"Do you need a doctor?"

"I'm sick of doctors. I.D."

"What?"

"Show me some I.D. and you can come in."

Nick flashed his badge and photo identification. She nodded and allowed him inside. She clutched a worn flannel robe around her scrawny body with one hand and coughed into the other. Nick stood watching, feeling alarmed and utterly useless. "Mrs. Fisher—"

She glowered him into silence. He watched uncertainly as she hacked for another minute, then trailed off into a series of gulps and snorts. Finally she slammed the front door behind him and motioned him into the living room. "You can sit down but I'm *not* turnin' off the TV," she announced in a grating, truculent voice. "This is my favorite show. It's a rerun of *The Mary Tyler Moore Show*. This channel shows all reruns. I don't like modern shows. They don't make any damned sense. What about you?"

"What do I like to watch?"

"*No!* What about you bein' here? It's about Dee, right?"

"Yes, Mrs. Fisher."

The woman had sat down on the ratty armchair directly in front of the television. Nick started to sit on the plastic-covered couch when she yelped, "Stop!" He halted halfway down. "While you're up, get me a beer. I drink right out of the can. No use dirtyin' glasses if you don't have to. Get yourself one, too. I don't care if you're on duty. I won't tell no one."

"I'm not on duty and I'd like a beer."

"Yeah, whatever," Mrs. Fisher said absently, transfixed by the character of Mary Richards wailing "Mr. *Grant!*" Nick went in the kitchen with its worn linoleum and myriad of handicrafts hanging on every available wall space. The entire lower shelf of the refrigerator held a cheap brand of canned beer. Nick removed two cans and carried them back to the living room. Mrs. Fisher took hers without looking at him. "Thanks. Nothing like a cold beer before bed, I always say."

"Yes, I enjoy an occasional beer in the evening myself." Nick wasn't sure why he sounded so prissy, but Mrs. Fisher cast him a suspicious look from behind her bifocals. To make up for it he took a hearty swallow and let out a loud, appreciative sigh.

"Damned good!" Well, that was even worse. Mrs. Fisher cast him another dubious look. So far he wasn't off to a good start with her. It would be better to forge ahead bluntly rather than keep trying to play up to her. At this rate she'd throw him out.

"Mrs. Fisher, your daughter Dee lives here, doesn't she?"

"You know that or you wouldn't be here. What's she done?"

"Nothing." Mrs. Fisher emitted something between a burp and a disbelieving grunt. "I'm telling you the truth, ma'am."

"If she hasn't done nothin' then why're you here interruptin' my show?"

"I'm sorry about my timing. Dee isn't here now, is she?"

"What makes you think so?"

"Because I know you're not well but you came to the door."

Mrs. Fisher's thin mouth twisted. "Not *well*. That's a good one. Lung cancer. I'm dyin'. I got four months, tops."

"I'm sorry."

"My doctor bitches at me 'cause I smoked all those years. Well, I'll tell you same as I tell him. Them cigarettes was about the only joy in my life. Them and my beer."

"Not your family?"

"I had two husbands run out on me. Left me all alone with three kids, Dee bein' the youngest by the last no-good. I tried with them three, but not a damned one turned out worth a grain of salt."

"Dee is a nurse. She takes care of you."

"For free room and board. She doesn't fool me none. That's all she hangs around for, though sometimes she tries to be nice. Tells me she appreciates all I went through for her. But it's pure *bullshit*!"

"Are you sure about that, Mrs. Fisher?"

"Yes, I am sure, Mr. Policeman who comes in here drinkin' my beer, interruptin' my TV, and doesn't know *nothin'* about me!" She stared at the television hard for a moment, then let out a cackle as the character Ted Baxter bumbled through the newscast. "I swear he's a case!"

"Yes, the show is a classic," Nick said vaguely. He'd made her mad, temporarily losing her. Maybe the way to get her back was through the sitcom. "Who do you like best? Mary or Rhoda?"

"Mary! Rhoda wears gaudy clothes and those silly scarves on her head." She looked at him. "Why? Is Rhoda *your* favorite?" It wasn't a question—it was an accusation.

"Oh, no." Actually, when he was young Rhoda *had* been his favorite. She seemed like more fun. "Mary is so . . ."

"Perfect." Mrs. Fisher smiled in approval. "I hoped Dee would grow up to be like her, but Dee has a bad streak like her daddy."

"A bad streak?"

"Well, don't tell me you haven't heard about her stealin' them drugs from the hospital. Lord, was I embarrassed when she got caught! *Everyone* knew. Then she started raisin' hell about Dr. St. John. That's 'cause he's the one blew the whistle on her." Her voice softened slightly. "She *was* off her head about that Farley boy dyin'."

"Eugene Farley?"

"Yeah. I met him once. Handsome as the devil. Manners like you've never seen. Treated me like a real lady. He had class." She shook her small head with its helmet of pin curls. "I knew he'd never stay with Dee. She was way outta her league. I told her over and over."

I'll bet that did a lot for her ego, Nick mused with a twinge of sympathy for Dee.

"When he gave her the heave-ho, I thought she'd lose her mind," Mrs. Fisher went on. "Like scared me to death 'cause I was already gettin' sick, and if Dee went to pieces, who'd look after me? Gave me quite a few sleepless nights, I can tell you."

Because you were worried about yourself, not your daughter, Nick thought scornfully. If Paige had been on the verge of a breakdown, the last thing her mother would have been worried about was her own welfare. He forced himself to sound polite. "But everything turned out all right and Dee is taking good care of you."

"Good care? Hah!"

"She's not taking good care of you?"

"If she was, would I be sittin' here all by myself at night? She's always out lately."

"With Hysell?"

"Who? Oh, that deputy. He won't marry her either. I told her. But she's not with him. I know 'cause he called here for her not half an hour ago. There've been other times he's called when she's out."

"You don't know where she goes at night?"

"No. She makes up excuses, but I can always tell when she's lyin'."

"How long has this been going on?"

"A week. Maybe two. She's been havin' lots of hush-hush conversations on the phone, too, and they ain't with that deputy."

"Then who?"

Mrs. Fisher shrugged. "Beats me." She pointed at the television. "There's Rhoda in one of them scarves! Can't she see herself in a mirror? Doesn't she know how stupid it makes her look?"

And don't you know this is a TV character from almost thirty years ago, not a real person? Nick thought. How reliable was anything she said if she couldn't distinguish fiction from reality? "Mrs. Fisher, do you think your daughter is going off at night to meet a man?"

"How should I know? Seems like the kind of trashy thing she'd do, though. Be just like her to start seein' someone respectable like the deputy and then sneak around behind his back." Her face contorted and she fell into another coughing fit. Nick rose nervously as she convulsed forward, sounding as if she were going to spew forth her lungs.

"Mrs. Fisher, please let me call the E.M.S."

"*No!*" she choked. "My *show's* on!"

"You're turning blue! I *am* calling the emergency squad."

Her tear-filled eyes looked huge as she glared through her bifocals. "You do and I'll tell 'em you broke in here and tried to *rape* me!" she snarled in a cough-ragged voice. "They'll believe me, young feller out prowlin' late at night, me here all alone and barely dressed!"

Good God, Nick thought. What was wrong with the women in this town? First Alison demanding he not touch her, now the irresistible Mrs. Fisher in her faded flannel and pin curls threatening to yell rape. She was spluttering to a halt. "All right, ma'am," he said in a placating voice. "I was just worried about you. I didn't mean any harm."

"You're gettin' on my nerves."

"I'm sorry. I'll leave now."

"Good," she rasped. "You got a cigarette on you?"

Nick looked at her, astonished. "No. I don't smoke."

"Well, hell." She sighed as if at the general unfairness of life. "Even if you had one, you probably wouldn't give it to me, like it would make any difference." Nick gazed at her silently. "All right. Before you go, Mr. Policeman, the least you can do is get me a beer."

Obediently Nick fetched a cold can of the cheap beer and popped the top. When he placed it in Mrs. Fisher's heavily veined hand, she didn't glance at him or the beer. She was smiling happily at the imaginary world on her television.

II

Paige hung off the bottom branch of the oak tree, then dropped. "You're getting better at climbing," Jimmy said.

Paige blushed with embarrassment, both from the compliment and from the memory of the first time she'd tried it and fallen on her head at Jimmy's feet, promptly bursting into tears. "Thanks. What's the big emergency?"

"We were going back to the Saunders house and take a picture of the serial killer. I got my Dad's Polaroid." He held it up proudly.

"You want to go *tonight*?"

"Sure. We can't wait forever. He could kill more people."

"Well, yeah, but . . ."

"But what?" Jimmy asked impatiently. "Your dad's car isn't here, so you don't have to worry about him."

"He called and said he'd be late. Mrs. Collins got all huffy. Not to *him*, but she called one of her friends and went on about how she can't spend so much time here because she's got all this church work. They're getting a new preacher and there's gonna big this big dinner for him—"

"I don't care about the church party!" Jimmy turned his head. "Oh, great," he moaned as headlights flashed across the yard. "Duck!"

They both hit the dirt. "It's my dad," Paige hissed. "He'll come right upstairs to check on me."

"Then climb up the tree and get in bed. I'll wait for a while."

"And if I don't come down you'll go without me?"

"I'll have to think about it," Jimmy said importantly. Actually he had no desire to revisit the creepy Saunders house by himself, but he'd never admit it. "Hurry. Your dad's going in the house."

Paige jumped, grabbed the low branch, and began a quick ascent. She'd come a long way since she first started climbing the tree, Jimmy thought proudly as if he'd had something to do with her progress. He sat down in the shadow of a tree to wait.

Paige was clambering over the window sill when she heard her father explode, "Dammit, Ripley!"

She tore across her room and down the hall. "What's wrong, Daddy?"

Nick rubbed his neck while Ripley sat in humped, green-eyed wariness halfway up the stairs. "Your pain-in-the-ass cat jumped off the newel post onto my back."

"Daddy, he is *not* a pain in the ass, and Mommy used to tell you not to say things like that around me." She rushed to Ripley and cuddled his stiff black body. "You've hurt his feelings."

"His claws hurt my back."

"He's sorry, but it's his favorite trick."

Nick looked at his daughter's beautiful, distressed little face and melted. "Okay, I'm sorry I yelled. But I wish he'd find another trick."

"We'll work on one," Paige assured him earnestly.

Mrs. Collins hovered near the door. "I guess I'll be on my way, Sheriff. It's very late—" She was warming up to complain, but Nick's stormy face stopped her cold. "I'll see you tomorrow, Paige."

"Yeah, bye," Paige said absently as her father closed the door behind the woman. "You look awful tired, Daddy. Are you going to bed?"

"It's not ten o'clock yet." Nick's eyes narrowed slightly. "Why the rush to get me out of the way?"

"It was just a question."

"Yeah, sure." Nick rubbed his neck again. "I'm staying up. I have some things to think over. It's time for *you* to get ready for bed, though. I'll be up in a little while to tuck you in."

Fabulous, Paige thought dismally. How long was "a little while"? Paige slumped up the stairs holding a reluctant Ripley. Shortly after eleven Nick gave his sleeping daughter a kiss as Jimmy Jenkins crept silently from the lawn and began pedaling for home.

There would be no trip to the Saunders house tonight.

III

At the clinic Natalie often put in eighteen-hour shifts that included performing three or four surgeries. Even after one of these days, she did not feel as tired as she did when she and Lily said good night to the last of the mourners, finished cleaning up the kitchen, coaxed a silent Oliver away from the stereo and into bed, and fixed a pitcher of martinis to take to the big, old-fashioned back porch.

They both kicked off their shoes and relaxed on old, slightly musty chaise longues. "This is the only place in the house Viveca hasn't remodeled," Lily said, wiggling her toes. "I remember when Mom bought this furniture for the porch. Ten matching pieces! She was horrified by her extravagance but at the same time so excited. That wasn't too long before she was diagnosed with multiple sclerosis." Lily took a deep breath and added fiercely, "I will *never* allow Viveca to get rid of this stuff, even if I have to pile it all up in my basement."

"I'm sure Viveca wouldn't trash it if she knew how much the furniture means to you."

Lily gave her a long look. "I asked you not to be sweet and reasonable."

"I thought I'd give it a try." Natalie took a sip of the chilled gin and vermouth. "Okay. If she even attempts to remove it, I promise to come and lash myself to this chaise longue. If it goes to the dump, so do I. How's that?"

Lily burst into laughter. "I appreciate the passion, but it might be wasted. Viveca would have you both hauled off. She doesn't like you any better than she does me."

"Does she like any females besides Alison?"

"I think she liked Tam."

"Really? Did she know Tam didn't like her?"

"I don't know. Tam was always polite. Too polite. Viveca had begun to push her around. I wish Tam hadn't been so gentle. If she'd had more spirit, she would have left Warren and she wouldn't be dead."

Natalie tensed slightly but forced herself to sound casual. "I thought you were considering that Alison might have killed Tam."

"If she did, it was because of Warren. But Dad won't even consider the idea that she's guilty. He's convinced Warren murdered Tam."

Natalie let silence spin out for a few moments while she and Lily each sipped their drinks and looked at the fireflies glittering around the large lawn. "What do you suppose Alison meant when she said she knew things?" Natalie asked finally.

"Nothing. Alison is crazy."

"But your father looked so upset."

Lily flashed her a stormy look. "Of course he was upset! He's cut to pieces over Tam. Then the day of Tam's funeral here's Alison making a scene, trying to *kill* herself!"

"That suicide attempt was nothing but melodrama."

"Probably. But she would have *hurt* herself and she's Viveca's daughter and Dad loves Viveca, although why in God's name I'll never know and . . ." Lily wiped at her eyes with the back of her hand like a child. "Tam's murder did something to Dad, Natalie. I mean, of course he's devastated with grief, but he's also just different. I can't explain how. I do know he'll never be the same."

"No one is the same after suffering a tragedy."

"You don't understand what I mean."

But Natalie did understand. Tamara had not died in a car wreck or of a disease. She had been viciously murdered, causing something fundamental in Oliver Peyton to change. Was he now capable of murder, too? Is that what Lily was saying?

Lily swiped at more tears. Natalie believed if she pushed her any further, she would fall apart. "I hope you're not going in to work tomorrow, Lily."

"I am. I can't bear sitting around by myself all day."

"We could do something."

"I need to go back to the store, Natalie. I need my routine."

"You look exhausted, but I won't argue with you. Work is the best panacea for some people." Lily didn't answer, her mind clearly elsewhere. "I think I'll go home now. I'm tired."

Lily forced a wan smile. "Thanks for your help today and all through this."

"We're friends. I'm always here for you."

Natalie left Lily sitting on the porch having a second martini. When she got in her car, though, she realized that in spite of her fatigue, she didn't want to go home and thresh out the day with her father. She felt like driving.

The night was cool but still held a note of summer's sultriness. Natalie rolled down the car windows and listened to music as she cruised through the quiet streets of Port Ariel. In winter the downtown section was deserted at night. In summer many stores stayed open and tourists peppered the sidewalks. She noticed three standing in front of the beautifully lighted bay window of Curious Things. Farther down the block a few people trailed into Trudy's Diner. Probably locals, Natalie thought. Tourists liked the more expensive restaurants along the shore, although the food was no better and not so plentiful.

After a while she glanced at the car clock and was surprised to see she'd been driving in a big circle for forty-five minutes. Someone would surely call the police to report a car repeatedly driving by. Besides, she was getting sleepy.

On her way home, Natalie passed The Blue Lady. She slowed down, staring at the big, dark pavilion. "I don't want to be alone anymore, Natalie," she remembered the eerie, disembodied voice saying with a note of threat. "I want you to join me."

She shivered. Who would have hidden in the dance pavilion and threatened her in Tamara's voice? Clearly it couldn't have been Jeff Lindstrom. He could only have enlisted the aid of someone else. Who? That light, lovely voice. She'd already considered Alison. Her voice had the same pitch as Tam's and she'd been around Tamara enough to know how she sounded. Who else could it have been? Dee Fisher, whom her father had accused of stealing drugs and Viveca had suggested as a murder suspect? Natalie vaguely remembered Dee from high school. She'd always been surly and unfriendly. Natalie had barely spoken to her then and had no idea what her voice would sound like now. Maybe she *could* make it sound like Tamara's.

And of course there was Lily. Who better to imitate Tam's voice but her twin sister? But that was impossible. Why on earth would Lily want to scare her?

She shook her head as if she could shake away the confusion and turned into the driveway. It was empty and the open garage door showed that it was empty inside, too. Her father wasn't home. Earlier he had called Lily and told her he'd given Alison a mild sedative. She was sleeping at home. He wouldn't still be at Viveca's, Natalie thought. Maybe Ruth's. She smiled, trying to think of how he would explain himself if he spent the night. She wouldn't make it easy on him in the morning. She would ask a lot of questions and demand answers, turning the tables. She could almost see him red-faced and stumbling for words, then blustering in outrage.

Natalie climbed from the car and walked to the front door, taking in a deep breath of lake-scented air. Looking over her shoulder, she saw the moon reflected almost perfectly in the still water. In fact, the night seemed unusually quiet, almost breathless, as if it were waiting for something to happen. Something cold and dark settled in Natalie's chest and the nerves along her neck tingled. Something didn't feel right.

Ridiculous. This wasn't The Blue Lady. This was home. She was just tired and her imagination was running away with her. Still, she jangled her keys, trying to find the one that usually came immediately to her fingers. She looked over her shoulder again. A long stretch of empty lawn ran downhill to the moon-silvered water. No one walked along the shore. No sounds or lights came from Harvey Coombs's house a hundred yards away. Nothing was strange, yet she was frightened. She felt as if something in the dark watched and *hungered*.

Hungered? What had brought that word to mind?

Beads of perspiration were popping out on her forehead when she swung open the door. "Blaine?" she called shrilly. The dog usually raced to greet her. Tonight there was no sign of her. "Blaine!" Quickly she stepped inside, slammed the door and locked it.

"Lock the bad thing out," she muttered breathlessly, then closed her eyes. What was she saying? She sounded like a child. Still, her palms slicked with perspiration and her heart raced.

Finally her cold fingers found the switch for the entrance hall light. She flipped it on and gasped. At her feet lay the black dress she had worn to the wake last night, ripped and torn into an almost unrecognizable mass of cloth. Beside it was a small pool of red. She bent and touched it, then sniffed her finger. The coppery smell of blood.

"Blaine!" she called loudly, springing up on shaking legs. "Blaine, where are you?"

A trail of red spots down the hall toward the bedrooms.

Natalie took a few more hesitant steps. Her shoe touched a broken picture frame. She picked it up. The glass was shattered. Inside the twisted frame were scratched remains of a photo of her and the dog Clytemnestra that had sat in her father's study for over twenty years. In the photo her eyes had been gouged out. Just like Tam's, she thought in frozen horror.

A calm, distant voice told her she should turn and leave the house immediately. The voice of reason. Instead she followed the spots of blood like one hypnotized, certain they led to Blaine. Was the dog merely injured? Or was she dead?

Pain shot through Natalie at the thought of the gentle, amber-eyed dog lying motionless as her life drained from a slit throat. Anger followed the pain, white-hot fury at someone who would come into this house and hurt—

She halted in her bedroom doorway, her gaze flashing to the flickering on her vanity. Four fat candles threw wavering yellow light around the room.

On the bed lay her silk kimono, carefully spread without a wrinkle, the sash tied in a neat bow. At the neck of the kimono rested a clean, hollow-eyed human skull, a fresh red rose caught between its clenched, yellowed teeth.

15

Natalie stood transfixed for what seemed an endless time. Then she snapped back to reality. She turned on the overhead light, blew out the candles, and called police headquarters. Then she unlocked her suitcase, withdrew the gun she'd promised Nick she wouldn't use, and went in search of Blaine.

She felt eerily composed as she moved slowly down the hall, passed through the seldom-used dining room, and crossed the living room, flipping on lamps as she went. When she came to the sliding glass doors leading to the terrace, she turned on the outside lights and finally drew a deep breath.

Blaine stood chained to the metal lamp pole. A muzzle covered her face. She trembled and crouched in fear.

Natalie covered her hand with the edge of her suit jacket so she wouldn't disturb fingerprints and pushed open the door. She rushed to the dog, removing the muzzle that was much too tight, then hugged her and murmured to her as she ran expert hands over the dog's body searching for injury. Blaine winced when Natalie touched her left side. She didn't believe a rib was broken, but perhaps it was cracked or bruised. The dog must have put up a struggle, although there was no blood around the mouth. Apparently she hadn't bitten anyone.

"I'm so sorry," Natalie crooned. "I wish you could tell me who did this to you."

Blaine jerked and looked over Natalie's shoulder. Natalie grabbed the gun and still crouched, spun and aimed.

"Natalie!" Andrew St. John froze. "My God, what's going on here?"

Natalie lowered the gun. "We've had an intruder."

Andrew gazed at the gun. "Where did you get that thing?"

"I've had it for a few months. Don't worry—I know how to use it."

"That's exactly what *does* worry me. You handle the damned thing like it's second nature to you. Natalie, I hate guns. Do you know what a bullet can do to the body?"

"Yes. I also know what a long-bladed razor can do to the body. Someone has slashed three throats lately. I'm not going to apologize for arming myself." Andrew continued to stare at the gun. "I've called the police."

"Yes, that was the right thing to do. There's blood in the hallway, you know. Come in out of the cold." It wasn't cold but Andrew looked slightly dazed. Blood in the hall, his daughter pointing a .38 at him. It had been too much, Natalie thought. He nodded at the gun. "Put that thing away before the police get here, or you might get in trouble."

She'd already been in trouble over the gun, but she couldn't tell her father about the night when Nick found her in The Blue Lady. "I'm not going to put it away. I have a permit for it," Natalie said casually, "and I'm not sure someone isn't still in the house."

Her father grew motionless. "Still in the house?"

"I didn't check every room, Dad. I just went back to my bedroom and then in search of Blaine."

"That was very foolish of you. You should have run out of the house as soon as you saw the mess in the hall."

"Dad, before I came in I had a feeling I was being watched. Harvey and his wife aren't home—no one would have heard me if I'd screamed. I got inside as fast as I could and locked the door behind me. Once I saw the havoc in the house, I went for my gun."

"You went for your gun. Dear God."

"Dad, the fact that I have a gun is hardly the big problem here." Natalie stood up. "Someone has invaded our home."

"I should never have left you alone."

"Have you been with Alison all this time?"

"No. I sedated her and left her sound asleep. Then I went back to the hospital to check on some patients." He paused. "The blood in the hall and the shredded clothes and picture. Is that all the damage?"

"Well, there's a skull with a flower in its teeth on my bed."

"A skull? A *real* skull? A *human* skull?"

"It's human and I'm fairly sure it's real."

"Natalie, how can you act so calm?" Andrew finally thundered. "What's wrong with you?"

"Nothing is wrong with me. Would you be happier if I were standing here shrieking my head off?" Andrew slowly shook his head. "I will never understand you if I live to be a hundred." A car pulled into the driveway. He looked out the window. "Not the police. No light bar flashing on top."

"I asked them not to flash the light. There's no sense in disrupting the whole neighborhood."

"Natalie, you act as if this kind of thing happens to you every day!"

Something *has* been happening to me almost every day, Natalie thought. "I have delayed reactions, Dad," she said gently. "Half an hour from now I'll be shaking like a leaf." Andrew looked relieved at the promise of what he considered a normal response. "You'd better open the door for the police."

Natalie led Blaine inside and watched the police enter. She was relieved to see Nick with Hysell following close behind. Nick looked controlled, but Ted was nearly vibrating with excitement. "A little trouble here, Dr. St. John?" Nick asked calmly.

"Shredded clothes and picture. Something that looks like blood in the hall."

"And some real creativity in my bedroom," Natalie said. "I didn't touch anything except some light switches. I haven't checked all the doors and windows to make sure they're locked, but they usually are. The sliding glass door to the terrace was unlocked, but the intruder had put Blaine out there and might simply have left it unlocked. I covered my hand when I touched the door handle."

Nick looked at her approvingly. "Sounds like you know how to handle yourself in this kind of situation. Careful not to disturb evidence."

"I watch a lot of those television police shows you don't like."

Nick glanced at Blaine. "Dog all right?"

"Yes. She was chained to the light pole on the terrace and muzzled. She's scared but not seriously injured."

"How much of a fight would she put up if a stranger broke in?"

Natalie shrugged. "I don't know. I've had her such a short time. She's slightly hurt—she received a blow to her left side. I don't think anything is broken, and I don't believe she bit anyone."

"Sheriff, take a look back here," Hysell called from the direction of Natalie's bedroom. Nick disappeared down the hall. Their voices lowered. Then Natalie heard the click of Hysell's ever-present camera. Someone's handiwork would be immortalized. Is that what the intruder wanted?

Natalie and her father sat silently in the living room. No damage had been done here. Blaine still trembled slightly but was gradually calming down. They could hear Meredith and Hysell going from room to room, searching, testing windows. At last they returned. "All the windows are closed and locked except for a small bathroom window. There's some undisturbed dirt in the grooves holding the screen," Nick said. "No one came in that way. Natalie, you said the sliding glass door was unlocked. Do you normally lock it when you leave the house?"

"Always," Andrew said.

"Dr. St. John, who else has keys to this house?"

Andrew looked blank for a moment. "Keys? Well, Natalie of course. Then there's a set I keep in my office at the hospital."

"Is the office always kept locked?"

"No. During the day it's usually open."

"Even when you're in surgery?"

"Yes. But there's a secretary in an outer office. Mrs. Rosen. Ralph Harkins and I share her."

"As a secretary?" Hysell interrupted.

Nick's lips tightened in irritation. "Of course as a secretary," Andrew said indignantly. "What else?"

"I don't know. Maybe a nurse or something."

"She isn't a nurse."

"Well, I just thought—"

"Does anyone else have a key?" Nick plowed on.

"Let's see . . ." Andrew frowned. "Harvey Coombs."

"Harvey Coombs!" Ted burst out. "You trust old Harvey with a key?"

Andrew shot him a paralyzing look from steel-gray eyes. "Harvey has been my friend for thirty years. He's had some problems lately, but that wasn't always the case."

"I see," Ted said loudly, then mumbled, "but I wouldn't let him have a key to *my* house."

Nick took control again. "We'll have to talk to Mr. Coombs."

"*He* didn't break into my house," Andrew protested.

"I'm sure he didn't, but I want to make certain he still has the key," Nick said. "He could have lost it or loaned it to someone."

"He wouldn't have loaned it." Andrew paused. "He could have lost it, though. He's had it for over twenty years."

"So he lost it five or ten years ago and it just happened to fall into the hands of a killer?" Ted asked.

"A *killer*!" Andrew thundered. "Why do you think whoever did this was a killer?"

"Because of your connection with Eugene Farley and Natalie being your child," Ted explained earnestly.

Andrew fixed Nick with his piercing gray gaze. "What in hell is this man talking about?"

"Hasn't Natalie told you?"

Andrew sighed. "Sheriff, my daughter has a lifelong habit of forgetting to tell me things. Why don't you fill me in?"

Ted looked as if he were dying to tell the tale, but mercifully

Nick cut him off, outlining the Farley theory concisely and dispassionately. When he finished, Andrew stood and walked around the room, his head down. Finally he looked at them and said, "Well, what are you doing to protect Lily, Alison, and Natalie?"

Natalie was stunned. She had thought her father would first declare the theory absurd, then demand to know why she hadn't told him sooner. It seemed she didn't understand him any better than he understood her.

"I've only warned Mrs. Cosgrove and Mr. Peyton and Lily," Nick said. "We don't have the manpower to guard three people. Of course, Alison stays home most of the time. I believe a house-keeper is with her during the day."

"Yes," Andrew said. "In spite of her mental condition, she's probably not as much trouble as Lily Peyton and my daughter."

"Thank you, Dad," Natalie said dryly.

"It's true. You've always been headstrong and reckless."

"This gets better and better." Natalie looked at Nick. "I've told you I'll be careful. I'm sure Lily will, too. Now what about the havoc in this house?"

"I'll call our tech team, such as it is. Have you moved anything?"

"No. I do know that's real blood in the hall, but I'm not sure if it's animal or human. And I think the skull on the bed is real, although I can't imagine where someone would get a real human skull."

"Can't be real," Ted pronounced. "Not unless we've got grave robbers in Port Ariel."

"Given everything else that's been going on, I wouldn't rule it out," Natalie said wryly.

The phone rang. Andrew answered, his expression distracted. Then his face tensed. "Certainly she isn't here. I would have called you." He paused and looked at Nick Meredith. "It's Viveca Cosgrove. Alison has been missing for over two hours."

II

"I thought you sedated her," Nick said.

"I did. Not heavily, though. She's been off all medication for a year, so I thought her tolerance was low. I administered a small injection of Ativan, and she quickly fell asleep." He shook his head. "Too quickly. She was acting. The injection no doubt calmed her but didn't knock her out."

Nick had spoken to Viveca and then made a quick call to headquarters, dispatching two deputies to search for Alison. "Do you think she could have broken into your house?" he asked Andrew.

"Alison? *Why?* I thought you were worried about her, not suspicious of her."

"I'm both," Nick said. "Anyone have any idea where this girl might go?"

Natalie lifted her hands. "I barely know her. Dad?"

Andrew had begun pacing again. "I didn't really know her, either. She was shy around me. But she was in better shape when I was seeing Viveca than she is now. She was on medication—medication she desperately needed. I don't know why in God's name Viveca turned her over to Warren Hunt. Oh, hell, this is my fault. I should have given Alison a stronger dose of Ativan."

"No, her mother should have been watching her more closely," Nick said firmly. "Viveca's lack of vigilance isn't our problem, though. Finding Alison is. If she did this to your house, God knows what else she might do tonight. If she *wasn't* here, she's wandering around alone, drugged, and the perfect target for a killer."

III

Andrew insisted Viveca should not be left alone. "Well, Oliver certainly isn't up to baby-sitting her," Natalie said. "And don't even suggest Lily." Andrew looked troubled. "You go, Dad. I can tell you want to."

"I can't leave you."

"I'll be fine. The technicians will be here soon to collect evidence."

"And when they're finished, you'll be alone again in a house that's already been violated tonight. We'll both go to Viveca's."

"Count me out. I wouldn't be any help. She doesn't even like me."

"You don't like *her*. That's why you don't want to go." Andrew gave her a determined look. "But now is not the time for you to indulge your childish antagonism toward this woman. You cater to unfeeling egomaniacs like Kenny Davis. Can't you find an ounce of compassion for a woman who's distraught over her deeply disturbed missing daughter?"

"Don't you think that's a little harsh?" Natalie bristled.

"Maybe. But it's true."

Natalie wanted to stay angry because her father had called her childish and criticized her relationship with Kenny, but she couldn't, because he was right. Whatever Viveca's faults, the woman did love her daughter.

She stood. "Blaine, come along. We're going visiting."

Andrew shook his head. "Viveca doesn't like dogs."

"I'm not going without her, not after what happened to her earlier this evening. She's frightened." She gave her father a hard stare. "It's both of us or neither of us."

He stared back for a moment, then slowly smiled. "You bend, but only so far. You're very much like my mother."

"Grandmother?" Natalie was shocked. "You've never said that before."

"I'm enigmatic. Never say everything I think. It's part of my charm." He winked at her. "Get Blaine's leash, my stubborn one, and we'll be off."

The evidence technicians were arriving as they left. Andrew gave them Viveca's number and told them to lock up when they left. "And you *will* be sure to lock up, won't you?" he asked.

One of the men looked at him stonily. "We're the police, sir. Of course we'll lock up."

"Locking up hardly matters, Dad," Natalie said in the car. "After all, whoever came in did it with a key."

"A key we'll have to locate," Andrew answered.

As Natalie expected, Viveca had worked herself to near distraction. "Where can she *be*?" she kept demanding of Natalie and Andrew. "Where can my baby have gone?"

"You would have a better idea of that than we would," Andrew said gently. "Just calm down and think."

"I *can't* think with that dog looking at me!"

"That's absurd," Natalie retorted. "Blaine isn't bothering you."

"Andrew?" Plaintively. "Does the dog *have* to be here?"

"Forget the dog, Viveca," Andrew said gently. "Think about where Alison might have gone. Does she have any favorite spots?"

Viveca sat down on the piano bench, rubbing at tiny vertical lines between her brows. "She likes a few shops. That nice little bookstore called The Alcove. Lawson's Music. Curious Things."

"Those places are closed at this hour," Natalie said. "Besides, I don't think she ran off to a store."

Viveca's eyes blazed. "Don't be sarcastic!"

"I didn't mean to be sarcastic. What other places does she like?"

"Not many. There's a little restaurant by the lake. Her father took her there the day he . . ." Her eyes filled with tears. "I can't remember the name. It's rather tacky—"

"The Lantern," Andrew supplied. "It closed last summer."

"Oh. I don't know of anywhere else." She looked around helplessly.

"How about the library?" Natalie suggested. "I think it's still open. Did she ever go there?"

"No. She said it was cold and unfriendly."

"Did she have any friends?" Andrew asked.

"No. Only Eugene. She got sick after he killed himself."

In that same gentle tone, Andrew said, "Viveca, she was sick long before Eugene Farley died—"

"Don't you think I know that! She's been sick for nearly twenty years! Her father died in front of her and *I* wasn't here! I wasn't *here*! Oh, God!"

While Viveca poured forth a torrent of misery and guilt, burying her golden head against Andrew's chest, Natalie crept up the stairs with Blaine. They walked slowly, down the hall until they came to what Natalie knew must be Alison's room. Inside, the dog walked around slowly, sniffing the ruffled bedspread, the collection of stuffed animals, a delicate crocheted sweater tossed over a chintz-covered chair. She reacted with nothing except casual interest.

After a few minutes, Natalie knew absolutely that Alison Cosgrove had not invaded the St. John house and terrified this dog just a few hours ago.

16

"Haven't seen him since yesterday afternoon," said the teenage desk clerk of the Lakeview Motel.

"What time?" Nick asked.

"I don't know. Maybe one." The boy scrunched his acne-spotted face in thought. "Yeah, around one 'cause the mailman was here. Lindstrom came in to tell me the ice machine wasn't working. Piece of crap only works half the time. Anyway, he had on a suit. I said, 'Hey, you goin' to a funeral?' He said, 'Matter of fact, I am.' "

Jeff Lindstrom had been headed for Tamara's funeral, Nick thought. "And you didn't see him come back?"

"No. I already told you."

"How late do you work?"

"Midnight." He threw Nick a long-suffering look. "My old man died two years ago. Place ain't doin' too great, so in the summers my mom has me doing slave labor. Didn't you come here looking for him before?"

"Yes, but he wasn't around. Did you talk to him much?"

"Sort of. Mostly he asked questions." He laughed. "Like you."

"Asked questions about what?"

"The murders. Only exciting thing that's happened around here for years. And he asked about a few other people I didn't really know."

"What people?"

"The Hunt woman's sister. The one that has a store down-town. Don't know her. That doctor's daughter—somebody St. John."

"Natalie."

"Yeah. Don't know her, either, but I kind of met her old man. He took out my spleen after the car wreck I was in that killed my dad. He was driving," the boy added quickly. "And Alison some-body and that Farley guy that killed himself. Now that *was* something fairly exciting around here. Probably the last thing till these murders. Anyway, that kind of stuff. Once in a while he'd ask something about me, but he was only being polite. Thought I couldn't see through him."

"You didn't like him?"

"Smiled too much. Mom thought he was charming." He rolled his eyes again. "He was the kind of guy that, you know, women think are *charming*." Apparently to this kid *charming* was an epithet.

"Could Lindstrom have come back without you seeing him?"

"Hey, this ain't the Hyatt. Just a little strip motel. I can see every car from this office. Never saw his. Never saw him. The room was dark all evening, too."

"Sounds like you keep a close eye on the guests."

"Not much on TV last night. 'Course, all I got in here is this crummy little thirteen-inch set. Can't wait to get one of those high-definition jobs. Gonna get one with a big screen—maybe forty-six inches. And a really dynamite surround sound system."

"Pay must be pretty good here."

The clerk scoffed. "Yeah, in my dreams. No, I'm not spendin' my life in this dump. I'm gonna get one of those high-payin' computer jobs."

"Know a lot about computers, do you?"

"I'm hell on those games, and I surf the Net all the time."

A regular computer prodigy, Nick thought in amusement. He'd better not count on getting that expensive television anytime soon. "How long has Lindstrom taken the room for?"

"He was paid up till noon today."

"Today!" Nick repeated. "Noon? It's eleven forty-five."

"Yeah." The clerk looked at him closely, obviously noting Nick's agitation. "What's the deal?"

"The deal is that if he hasn't paid for the room, I don't need a warrant to search it."

"That so? Cool! I'll get the key."

"Not yet. I'm waiting until noon. If I find anything incriminating, I don't want it thrown out of court because I searched the room fifteen minutes too soon."

"Incriminating evidence?" the clerk asked excitedly. "Hey, what's this guy done?"

"Maybe nothing. I can't discuss it." The clerk turned sullen until Nick said, "But if this does ever come to court, I might need you to testify that I didn't enter the room until after noon. You're my witness."

"Me, a *witness*? Cool!"

Twenty minutes later Nick entered Room 11 of the Lakeview Motel. "Need me to stand guard?" the desk clerk asked anxiously.

"Stand guard against what?"

"I don't know. Maybe Lindstrom will come back and go ballistic. I could protect you."

Nick looked at the teenager's reed-thin body, the narrow chest covered by a KISS tee shirt. Lindstrom was a couple of inches taller and at least twenty pounds heavier than this kid. "Your mother expects you to handle the desk, but you keep an eye on the room from the office," Nick said diplomatically. "If Lindstrom shows up, you come running."

"You bet!" the kid said happily. "I won't let you down."

Another Jimmy Jenkins, Nick thought. "Do you watch *Street Life*?" he asked impulsively.

"Never miss it. Eddie Salvatore is *cool*."

"Yeah. Well, you head back to the office. Thanks for letting me in."

Nick grinned as the kid loped off. Had he ever been that young and eager? Had he ever been that goofy? Yes to both, he decided.

Jeff Lindstrom's room didn't look as if the man had been preparing to leave. Jeans, denim shirts, and tee shirts were thrown over the two chairs pulled up to a circular table in front of the window. Papers lay on the table. Newspapers and photographs, Nick realized when he looked closer. Polaroids. Oliver Peyton's colonial. The Hunts' Cape Cod. The slightly modernistic stone home of Andrew St. John. Nick lingered over this one. The photo gave a clear view of the weeping willow where they'd found the cigarette butts and Marlboro package the night after Natalie had reported a Peeping Tom. Nick felt himself getting angry again and moved on. Viveca Cosgrove's white two-story. He frowned, holding it closer to the light. A pale figure stood in a second-floor window. She had waist-length blond hair and faced fullly forward, smiling. She was naked.

Nick remembered Alison's references to sex after Tamara's funeral and Natalie's claim that Alison was fixated on Warren. Along with all her other problems, was Alison a nymphomaniac? Nick wondered. He flipped to the next photo. A shot of a townhouse apartment in a complex. He knew Lily Peyton lived here. Next was a huge, crumbling old house peeking from behind a shroud of ivy and overgrown shrubbery. He should know this place, but for the moment he was blank. A day shot of The Blue Lady dance pavilion. In the sunlight it looked even shabbier than at night. Last, a shot of Natalie on the patio with the dog. A garden hose lay beside her, and her long, shining hair hung over one shoulder as she ran a towel down the dog's side. An older woman stood in the doorway watching her.

Beside the photos lay a magnifying glass, an empty Coke can, a telephone book, and an ashtray holding three Marlboro cigarette stubs. The same kind of stubs as under the St. John weeping willow tree. No doubt Lindstrom had stood staring into Natalie's bedroom. Had he also entered the house, shredded Natalie's dress, and left a skull on the bed? If so, why? Was he trying to cook up more drama for the book he claimed to be writing?

Nick wandered around the room looking for anything

interesting. A few toiletries in the bathroom. A copy of *Bitter Blood* by the bed. Maybe the guy really was serious about writing a true-crime novel like this one. A legal pad on the dresser with most of the paper torn away. The few remaining pages were blank.

He riffled through an open suitcase. Some underwear and socks. A copy of *Penthouse*. Next to the suitcase lay a briefcase. Luckily it was unlocked. Inside were two manila folders filled with newspaper clippings. The thinnest collection concerned the recent murders in Port Ariel. The other bore stories about the arrest, trial, and suicide of Eugene Farley.

Under the folders rested an address book. Nick flipped through it hurriedly. Apparently the guy didn't have too many friends. Most pages were empty. Then he came to the *F* section and an address jumped out at him: 224 Dobbin Street, Knoxville, KY. Knoxville? And the name above the address? *Aunt Constance.* Constance Farley lived in Knoxville.

"I'll be damned," Nick muttered. "Eugene Farley was Jeff Lindstrom's cousin."

II

"The contractor who renovated the kitchen last summer swears he gave back the spare set of house keys," Andrew told her. "Unfortunately, I can't find them."

"Do you remember him giving them back?" Natalie asked.

"No. But I was extremely busy at the time. I had a heavy load at the hospital, and this place was a mess with the remodeling. I just don't recall."

"Okay. Let's go talk to Harvey before the police do. I don't trust him to tell the police the truth."

It was just past noon and Harvey Coombs opened the door with a gin and tonic in his hand. "Andrew!" he boomed. "And Natalie! My goodness, you've grown a foot since I saw you last."

"Nonsense, Harvey," Andrew said. "You saw her just last year and she's been this height for over a decade." Harvey frowned in thought. Natalie wasn't sure whether he was trying to remember when he'd seen her or how many years were in a decade. "May we come in?"

"Hell, yes! The wife is at the grocery store. Or aerobics class. Or garden club. I think she invents places to go to get away from me." They trailed behind Harvey into a sun-filled living room where Dean Martin sang on the stereo. Natalie suddenly remembered that Harvey used to constantly sing Dean Martin songs, and when she was a child, he'd taught her "That's Amore"

"Still like Dean, Natalie?" he asked her.

"Sure. Such a mellow voice."

"Another Ohio native, you know. We went to high school together."

"Harvey, Dean Martin was over twenty years older than you," Andrew returned irritably.

"Oh, I must be thinking of someone else," Harvey said vaguely, then immediately brightened. "Get you something to drink? We have some nonalcoholic beverages around here for the little one."

Natalie assumed she was "the little one." "No thank you, Harvey," she said. "We need to talk to you."

"Good. I'm lonely and there's nothing like a pretty girl to brighten my day. Have a seat on the couch. What can I do for you?"

"We had some trouble at the house last night," Andrew said. "Someone broke in."

Harvey lowered his glass and his bloodshot eyes widened. "My God, that's awful! Did they take anything?"

"No. They just tore up a few things."

"Home invaders!" Harvey pronounced. "Right here in Port Ariel. You're not safe *anywhere* anymore!" He drained his drink to soothe his outrage. "Police get them?"

Natalie shook her head. "Did you see anything?"

"We went to my daughter's for dinner. The one married to the Baptist minister. Nice guy but dry as dust. So was the evening. No alcohol, naturally, *and* I got a lecture about my drinking. Anyway, we left around six and got home near ten. Late hour because of the lecture. *And* an endless prayer for me. One of the longest evenings of my life. That's why I remember the time. Damn, I wish I'd been home. I would have shot those bastards!"

"Then I'm glad you weren't home," Andrew said. "We wouldn't want you up on murder charges. The interesting thing is that the house wasn't broken into. Someone had a key."

"Son of a bitch!" Harvey exclaimed, then headed into the kitchen. "How did someone get your key?" Natalie heard ice clinking in a glass. "Lose it someplace?"

"That's what I wanted to ask you about," Andrew called. "I gave you a key to the house a long time ago. Do you still have it?"

Harvey strode back into the living room. "You think I broke in your house?"

"Good heavens, no, Harvey. I'm just trying to track down all the keys."

"Oh." Harvey sat down. Sunlight fell harshly on his reddened, flabby face, and a pain shot through Natalie when she remembered how handsome he'd once been. "Sure, I've got your key. A good thing, too. That cable repairman needed it a few days ago."

"Cable repairman?" Andrew repeated. "There's nothing wrong with my cable."

"Well, no. He fixed it." Harvey laughed. "Nice fellow."

"Did a man come here claiming to be a cable repairman?" Natalie asked, understanding what Harvey did not.

"No. He didn't come *here*. I saw him standing outside your place. I went over to see what was going on and . . ." Harvey took another sip of his drink, ". . . and he said he was supposed to be here but no one was home, and I said, 'I bet the cable is out,' and damned if I wasn't right!"

Wonderful, Natalie thought. Harvey had provided a possible intruder with an excuse for getting in the house. "What did he look like?"

"Look like? I don't know. Average. My height. Maybe thirty. Light hair."

"How long did he have the key?" Andrew asked.

Harvey looked blank. "About an hour, I guess."

"You guess?"

"Well, hell, I didn't have my stopwatch, Andrew. What's so important about it, anyway?"

Andrew asked quietly, "Would you get the key?"

Harvey sensed that he'd done something wrong and swung into loud defensiveness. "Sure! Nothing to me!" He crashed his glass onto an end table, sloshing gin onto his hand. "I don't want your damned key. I was only trying to help."

He disappeared into the kitchen again, muttering and cursing. Drawers slid out and slammed. Cabinet doors opened and slammed. Natalie and Andrew exchanged looks. Finally Harvey returned to the living room and said weakly, "Can't lay my hands on it right now."

Andrew sighed. "Harvey, do you *remember* the young man bringing back the key?"

"Sure! Well, actually . . . not really." He looked sheepish. "I think I took a little nap when he was over there."

"He never returned it," Andrew said flatly.

Harvey's shoulders slumped. He looked old and defeated and completely demoralized. "I screwed up, Andrew. I'm sorry."

"Don't feel bad, old friend," Andrew said quickly. "I think I lost one of the keys, too."

So two house keys were unaccounted for, Natalie thought. Which meant any number of people had easy access to the house.

III

FRIDAY AFTERNOON

Nick dialed Constance Farley's phone number and leaned back in his chair. She picked up on the third ring.

"Mrs. Farley, this is Sheriff Meredith in Port Ariel again."

"Good gracious," she fluttered. "What's wrong now?"

"Do you have a nephew named Jeff Lindstrom?"

A short silence. "Unfortunately, yes. My sister's boy. What do you want to know?"

"He's here in Port Ariel."

"You've talked with him?" she asked anxiously. "Did he tell you about me?"

"I've talked with him, but he never mentioned his relationship to you."

"Oh." She drew a breath. "Sheriff, I really don't understand. If he didn't tell you of our relationship, then why are you calling about him?"

"I found your number in his address book."

"Address book?"

"Yes. Let me explain. Lindstrom has been nosing around town for about a week. He's been asking a lot of questions about the murders we've had. Frankly, he's been bothering people, and I told him to back off."

"He's an awful boy," Constance pronounced. "Pushy. Unprincipled. I think he's a little crazy."

"Crazy? How is he crazy?"

"There have been things over the years, things I don't think my sister would want me to discuss. But he's awful, I tell you."

At least he didn't have to worry about offending the woman, Nick thought. "He claimed he was doing research for a book."

"A book? I wouldn't know anything about that."

"Anyway, I need to talk to him again, but he seems to have disappeared and—"

"Disappeared? What do you mean *disappeared*? He left town?"

"If so, he left without his luggage. He hasn't been in his motel room since yesterday afternoon. That's where I found his address book."

"Oh. Well . . . well, I don't see what this has to do with me."

"I thought since your number is in his address book, you might be in touch with him. You might know where he is."

He had not called because he thought Constance might know Lindstrom's whereabouts. He'd called to get information about their relationship. All the murder victims were connected with Eugene Farley. He had first suspected Constance Farley, but her neighbors confirmed she'd never left Knoxville. Now he found out her nephew was in town and he seemed to be stalking potential victims. Could this woman have dispatched Lindstrom to do her dirty work? That would mean they were both crazy. She said *he* was crazy. Were they both *that* crazy? Improbable. Not impossible.

"I don't know why you think I'd know where that boy is," Constance returned. Her voice shook slightly as if she were controlling her anger. "I didn't even know he was in Port Ariel. I'm not close to him at all. And frankly, Sheriff, I'm getting really tired of these calls. My life hasn't been easy the last two years, but I'm trying to hold on. I was doing fairly well and then you start this . . . this . . . harassment!"

"I didn't mean to harass you, Mrs. Farley."

"Really? You had the police question my *neighbors*! How humiliating!"

"I'm sorry."

"You should be." Tears in the voice. "I don't know why Jeffrey is there, but believe me, he's a terrible person. Don't talk to him. Don't give him any information."

"I have no intention of giving him any information about this investigation."

"Or about Eugene."

"Mrs. Farley, I didn't know Eugene. I didn't even live in Port Ariel when he . . . died."

"I see. Well, I don't mean to sound like a harridan, but I'm just so *tired*, so *nervous*, and now *he's* causing trouble—"

"Mrs. Farley, you just calm down," Nick said kindly. "I'll take care of Lindstrom."

"What will you do to him?"

"Chase him to the town limits."

"Good!"

Nick had been trying to strike a lighter note. Did the woman really think he could run someone out of town? "I'm sure I'll locate him soon," he began more seriously. "Everyone involved in this case knows not to talk to him."

"No, don't talk to him."

She was certainly adamant about no one talking to Lindstrom, he thought. What was she afraid he'd say? "He won't be a problem for long, Mrs. Farley."

Nick wished he believed that last sentence. He hung up the phone and rubbed his eyes. Too little sleep since this mess started. Even when he slept, he didn't *really* sleep. He dreamed of Meagan lying white and frail in a hospital bed connected to blinking, beeping machines as her lively gaze dulled to emptiness. Last night he'd dreamed of Natalie St. John sitting at a table in a dark room. A big, mirrored ball twinkled overhead and a band played. He'd walked over to her table and asked her to dance. She'd smiled sadly and lowered a lacy shawl to expose her neck. "I'm sorry," she'd said. "I love this song, but as you can see, someone has slit my throat."

"Sheriff?"

"Damn!" Nick shouted, startled out of a half-sleep and a return to the horrible dream about Natalie. "What is it, Hysell?"

"Some kid from the Lakeview Motel insists on talking to you. I told him you were busy, but he wouldn't spill his no doubt earth-shattering information to me."

"Okay, Ted. He's a good kid, just a little overeager. I'll take the call."

He lifted the receiver and spoke. An ebullient voice announced, "Hey, Sheriff, it's Wade Hanley at the Lakeview."

He hadn't even caught the kid's name earlier in the day. "So, Wade, has Lindstrom come back?"

"No. Haven't seen him."

"What did you need to tell me that you couldn't tell Deputy Hysell?"

"Something I remembered a few minutes ago. I didn't think Lindstrom was here last night, but I saw a woman leaving his room around ten, so he must have been."

"A woman? Anyone you know?"

"Yeah. That's why I didn't want to tell Hysell. I remember her from when I was in the hospital. The woman was Dee Fisher. I've heard she's Hysell's girlfriend. At least she used to be. Did they break up?"

"Not that I know of," Nick said with interest. "What else can you tell me about her visit?"

"Nothing. I just saw her coming out of his room to a car. She was alone. She looked awful—scared or mad or something. All worked up."

"Has she been back today?"

"No."

Nick suddenly recalled telling Natalie that perhaps this was not Lindstrom's first visit to Port Ariel. If he *were* having a woman make calls for him, it could be someone he'd gotten to know here. "Got another question for you, Wade. Has Lindstrom ever stayed at the motel before?"

"Gotta think on that one a minute. You know during school I don't work as much, don't see as much. I don't remember him especially, but . . ."

"But?" Nick prompted.

"But there's something kind of familiar about him. First time he came in the office I thought I might have seen him before."

"Think on it some more. And thanks, Wade. You've been a big help."

"Hey, I'm lovin' all this mystery. I'm gonna stay up all night and see if Lindstrom comes back."

Hysell burst into the office just as Nick was hanging up and frowning over this latest development. "I know you don't think much of our tech department, Sheriff, but they did some pretty good work at the St. John house." Ted slapped down a report on Nick's desk. "No fingerprints except Natalie's, the doctor's, that woman he's seeing, and a cleaning lady who comes in once a week. I guess St. John doesn't entertain too much. The blood in the hall was cow blood. Sort of watery like it might have come from a package of beef. Not too creepy. The skull's a different matter."

Ted lapsed into one of his dramatic pauses that drove Nick wild. One day he'd snap, draw his gun, and shoot the deputy. Then he'd be arrested and thrown in his own jail. Until that day he would force himself to smile placidly and ask the expected questions. "What about the skull, Hysell?"

"It's *human*. Male." Ted leaned over the desk, flipped through the pages of the report, and emphatically tapped his fingers on a photo of the skull. "According to the M.E. about fifty years old."

"Is it the skull of a fifty-year-old male or a fifty-year-old skull?"

"Huh? Oh, he didn't say. Anyway, there's not a bit of dirt on it. He said it was a fine specimen—almost *antiseptic*. His word."

"Interesting."

"Just 'interesting'? Sheriff, it was once somebody's *head*," Ted said portentously.

"Most human skulls were."

"Yeah, but you don't find them laying around everywhere. Who do you suppose dug this up?"

"I don't believe anyone dug it up." Nick held the photo of the skull under his desk light and looked at it closely. " 'Alas, poor Yorick! I knew him, Horatio, a fellow of infinite jest, of most excellent fancy.' "

After a moment Ted said carefully, "Sheriff, you think you know who this person was? Some guy named Yorick?"

Nick exploded into laughter. Ted recoiled, stung. "Sorry, Ted, I'm so tired I'm giddy. I was quoting the little bit of Shakespeare I know."

"Oh, Shakespeare," Ted said disdainfully. "I never liked him myself. He took forever to say anything. I mean, why didn't he just *say* it instead of talking in circles? I think he must have been getting paid by the word."

"So you don't read Shakespeare's sonnets to Dee?"

Ted relaxed and smiled. "She'd kick me all around the room if I tried anything so sissy. Besides, I only know one poem. 'The Charge of the Light Brigade.' Had to memorize it in eighth grade and I never could get rid of it."

Ted made the poem sound like a bad cold he couldn't shake. " 'Charge of the Light Brigade' isn't too romantic. Better to stick with flowers and candy."

"Yeah. Maybe I should try some flowers," Ted said unhappily. "She might like flowers."

Nick looked at him sharply. So Ted already sensed there was trouble in Paradise. Did he know the trouble involved Jeff Lindstrom?

IV

"Where's your dad tonight?" Jimmy asked.

"Out looking for that girl. Alison something. Mrs. Collins was talking on the phone and she said Alison was crazy as a loon. I read about loons in the encyclopedia. The article didn't say anything about loons being crazy."

"I told you not to read so much and who cares about loons, anyway?" Jimmy held up the Polaroid. "Got my dad's camera again. Tonight's perfect for going to the Saunders house and getting a picture of the killer."

Paige ran the toe of her tennis shoe over a clump of crabgrass. "It's kind of early."

"Yeah, but it's been a gloomy day. It's almost dark an hour earlier than usual. Besides, your dad's gone and Mrs. Collins will be jabbering on the phone for hours about this crazy Alison person. It's the perfect time." He paused. "Unless you're too scared."

Paige's blue eyes flared. "I told you I'm not scared!"

"My mom says actions speak louder than words. If you're scared, you can just stay here and I'll tell you all about taking a picture of a *murderer*. It won't be as exciting as *being* there . . ."

"I have a feeling I'll get caught."

"You always have a feeling you're gonna get caught and you never do." Jimmy draped the camera strap around his neck and hopped on his bike. "Are you coming or not?"

Paige looked up at the dreary, pewter sky. All day Mrs. Collins had predicted rain, but it had never come. The hours had simply spun out in gloomy endlessness. She was bored. She wanted to please Jimmy. Getting a picture of a mad killer *was* the chance of a lifetime.

"Okay, I'll come," Paige sighed.

She climbed on her bike and pedaled behind Jimmy. As she passed the lighted kitchen window, she saw Mrs. Collins sitting at the table talking animatedly into the phone receiver. She'll never miss me, Paige thought.

V

Andrew had been called back to the hospital for an emergency surgery at six. He hadn't wanted to leave Natalie alone and suggested she come with him. "Dad, you could be in surgery for *hours*," she'd said. "I don't want to spend the whole evening sitting in your office. I'll be fine here." He'd fussed because the locks had not yet been changed but at last gave up when he saw she was determined not to accompany him.

Now she rinsed the plate from which she'd eaten her elaborate dinner of a grilled cheese sandwich and potato chips. Blaine sat nearby, alternately gazing at her and the package of jerky strips lying on the counter. "You've already had dinner, so two jerky strips for dessert. That's it," Natalie pronounced, knowing that before bedtime Blaine would be enjoying at least two more strips and a couple of giant biscuits. She needed to gain five to ten pounds before she reached normal weight.

After giving the dog her treat, Natalie wandered into the living room and turned on the television. Kenny used to annoy her by flipping from channel to channel. Now she did the same. Fifty channels and she couldn't find one program that interested her. She was too restless to concentrate.

The phone rang. It was Nick calling to tell her Jeff Lindstrom was Constance Farley's nephew, but he hadn't been seen since Nick chased him down after Tamara's funeral over sixteen hours ago. Alison had been missing almost as long. Maybe a coincidence. *Hopefully* a coincidence. "I'll be working all night," he said tiredly. "Mrs. Collins is thrilled."

"And Paige will be just as delighted to be spending the evening with *her*," Natalie pointed out. "I have an idea. Your daughter doesn't go to bed early, does she?"

"Only under duress. I don't worry about it too much when she's on summer break from school. I guess that's lax of me.

"I never had a set bedtime."

"And just look how you turned out," Nick said dolefully.

"You are a laugh riot, Sheriff. Anyway, I promised Paige a guitar lesson. Since I'm alone and she's probably bored, how about my giving a lesson tonight?"

"She'd love it. And I'd love knowing you were with her. With everything that's going on . . ."

"There's safety in numbers," Natalie finished for him.

After they hung up she called the Meredith house and got a busy signal. Ten minutes later she tried again. Still busy. Probably Mrs. Collins. She decided to simply get her guitar and go.

Blaine watched her rummage in a storage closet for the first guitar she'd ever owned—a Yamaha compact classic. Kira had given it to her for her sixth birthday. She'd been thrilled, so thrilled she not only practiced constantly but actually tried to sleep with the guitar. Her talent and devotion to the instrument pleased Kira. "Yeah, it pleased her so much she took off five months later," Natalie muttered, then forced her thoughts away from her mother. She scribbled a note for her father and grabbed her coat. Blaine drooped behind her to the door, gazing at her with tragic eyes. "Okay, Sarah Heartburn," Natalie laughed. "I have *no* idea how you and Ripley the cat will get along, but I guess we'll find out. Besides, I don't like the idea of leaving you alone in this house again."

Blaine immediately perked up at the sight of her leash and trotted happily to the car. Natalie felt as if she'd always owned the dog, and Blaine acted as if Natalie had always been her mistress. But she had placed the lost dog ad less than a week ago. Someone could call tomorrow and reclaim Blaine, Natalie reminded herself. Could she bear to give her up? If this were a beloved dog that had gotten lost, she would have no choice. But if she sensed the dog had been dumped . . .

"If you were dumped, the person who dumped you won't call," Natalie said as they drove toward the Meredith house. Blaine cocked her head as if she understood every word. "And if you merely got lost from a loving home, I don't think you would have bonded to me so quickly." She sighed. "You're a mystery, Blaine, one of many lately, and I've found out they're more fun to read about than to live."

Lights glowed in the picture window and one upstairs window of the two-story Meredith house. Natalie knew the place had been vacant for nearly three years before Nick Meredith bought it. The former owner had demanded an unreasonable price and refused to negotiate until his business hit a giant snag and he needed the money. Nick had made a few repairs to the place and added a fresh coat of white paint, but the shrubbery and flower-beds needed work. That might be a project for her and Paige as the summer wore on.

Natalie stopped abruptly on the sidewalk leading to the porch. A summer project? She had a job in Columbus she'd return to in a week. She also had a relationship to work out. After all, in spite of what had happened between her and Kenny, he was more important to her than a precocious kid, or the precocious kid's attractive, dominating, funny, workaholic father. Wasn't he?

Enough of this ridiculous thinking of summer projects, she told herself sternly. She walked determinedly forward, rang the bell, and looked around the porch. Two green plastic lawn chairs and a pot of bedraggled geraniums. In a town where people took pride in creating lovely porches, Nick Meredith wouldn't win any awards. The house had the air of a stopping-over place, as if no one meant to stay. Or maybe it simply lacked the touch of someone who thought of it as a true home.

Natalie was raising her hand to ring the bell again when Mrs. Collins's broad face peeped through the sheer curtains. She looked blankly at Natalie. Natalie smiled encouragingly. "I come in peace," she felt like yelling. Mrs. Collins blinked a couple of times then pulled away from the window. At last the door opened slowly.

"Hello. Remember me? Natalie St. John. I stayed with Paige the other evening."

"I remember you." The woman flushed. She probably also remembered Nick chewing her out for discussing the murders of Charlotte and Warren in front of Paige. She looked at Blaine, then at the guitar case. "Did you want something?"

"I promised Paige a guitar lesson. Sheriff Meredith said tonight would be fine." She paused. "He also said I could bring my dog." A lie, but she didn't think the woman was going to let them both in.

"Well, I guess it's all right if the sheriff said so. I *try* to take very good care of Paige. I treat her like my own daughter, but my girl was more manageable. Less sassy. Paige was born in New York City, you know."

Apparently Mrs. Collins thought being born in New York City explained any undesirable personality traits Paige might exhibit. Natalie and Blaine stepped past her. The woman continued to stare inhospitably. "Paige *is* here, isn't she?" Natalie asked.

"Of course she's here!" Mrs. Collins burst out. "Where else would she be? It's night!"

"I just thought she might be sleeping over with a friend."

"With a murderer on the loose?" Mrs. Collins demanded. "Besides, she doesn't have any proper friends. Just that young Jenkins hooligan. His mother should keep a closer eye on him and the sheriff should forbid Paige to see him. If she were my girl—"

"Is she upstairs?" Natalie interrupted to stem the flow of unwanted opinions.

"Yes. In her room."

"I'll just go up then. Second room on the left, right?"

She dashed up the steps, Blaine trotting behind her. She

really shouldn't have come here, she thought. Clearly her visit annoyed Mrs. Collins, and even though Paige didn't have a set bedtime, she was probably getting sleepy by now. A guitar lesson might simply be disruptive. She'd been thinking of herself when she came, not what was best for Paige. Maybe she wouldn't be any better at mothering than Kira had been. She'd make the guitar lesson short.

Natalie tapped lightly on the closed bedroom door. Her knock went unanswered. She tapped again. Nothing. Could the child already be asleep?

She turned the knob slowly and swung open the door. A small lamp glowed on the nightstand providing the light Natalie had seen from outside. A flowered quilt stretched over a small form whose auburn hair spread across a pillow. A pair of luminous green eyes stared from atop the chest of drawers. Ripley.

Something didn't feel right. Didn't Nick say Paige didn't go to bed early? And hadn't Paige told her that Ripley always slept on the bed with her? Maybe the cat left the bed after Paige went to sleep and she never knew it. Or maybe he was spooked by Blaine and had jumped to the safety of a high place. But he didn't look scared. And the auburn hair on the pillow had the metallic sheen of artificial hair. She walked over and pulled down the quilt.

Mrs. Collins had followed her up the stairs. "A *doll!*" she screeched as if saying, "A *body!*" Ripley stiffened, his tail snapping around to firmly cover his paws. Natalie walked to the window, which was raised. An arm's length away hung the sturdy limb of an oak tree. "Looks like Paige has escaped."

"Oh, my! Oh, Lord! Oh, gracious! Heaven help me!" Mrs. Collins bleated. "This is *not* my fault! It's not *my* fault! It is not my *fault!*"

"You were supposed to be watching her," Natalie said harshly, galled by the woman's concern for herself rather than the missing child. "How long has she been gone?"

"I have no idea." She met Natalie's incensed stare. "Well, I can't keep my eyes on her every minute!"

"Especially when you're spending all your time on the phone."

"I wasn't on the phone!"

"I tried to call twice before I came by. The line was busy and clearly Paige wasn't tying it up because she wasn't here. Now when was the last time you saw her?"

Mrs. Collins threw her a venomous look before her eyes filled with tears. "You're right. I was on the phone much too long. I just never thought she'd do anything like this."

"I understand," Natalie said in a milder tone. Soothing the woman was necessary to make her concentrate on what was important. "Calm down and try to remember when you saw her."

Mrs. Collins took a deep breath. "All right. Let's see. We ate dinner at six. She went up to her room for a while, then she came back down and watched something on television. I don't remember what. Then she went back up. That must have been around seven-thirty."

Natalie glanced at her watch. "It's 8:48. Over an hour unaccounted for, but I'll bet she didn't scoot out that window until nearly dark. It's been dreary all day, darker than usual . . ." Mrs. Collins nodded in vigorous agreement. "Do you have any idea where she might have gone?"

"The Jenkins house?"

They looked up the number and called. A harried Beth Jenkins told Natalie she hadn't seen Paige for days. Was Jimmy home? Natalie asked. Beth dispatched her husband for a five-minute search that included a few gusty bellows of "Jimmy, where the hell are you?" Another child wailed in the background. They couldn't find Jimmy, Beth finally said. It was summer and he was always running around, but she was *sure* it wouldn't be after dark with a little girl. After all, Jimmy wasn't some kind of pervert. Is that what Sheriff Meredith thought?

Natalie assured her Sheriff Meredith liked Jimmy. She liked Jimmy. Jimmy was a fine boy. Natalie grimaced as she spent more time reassuring than gleaning information. When she hung up, she checked the time again. Nine. Far too late for Paige to be wandering around without adult supervision. "I'm going to look for her," she told Mrs. Collins. "You call Nick and tell him she's gone."

The woman shrank. "Oh, no! I don't think we have to tell him yet. She could walk in that door any minute."

"Or she could *not* walk in all night, and then what would the sheriff do if no one had told him his daughter was missing?" Natalie asked severely. "You must call him. *Now.*"

The woman sighed shakily and plodded toward the bedroom extension as if headed for the guillotine. Natalie looked around Paige's room, then picked up an errant sock peeking from beneath the bed. Mrs. Collins was meekly asking to speak with the sheriff as Natalie left the room with the sock in one hand and the dog's leash in the other.

Natalie sat in her parked car, her hands on the steering wheel as she stared ahead, thinking. "Where would an eleven-year-old girl go on a summer night?" she asked Blaine. "Lily and I used to walk on the shore and go sit in The Blue Lady. A big, deserted place. Very daring of us, we thought." But The Blue Lady was three miles from the Meredith house. Quite a distance to cover on foot or a bike. And Paige was probably with Jimmy. No doubt because she was the relative newcomer to the town, he'd taken her somewhere familiar to him. But where would that be?

Natalie closed her eyes to concentrate. Where did Jimmy live? Across the street from Tamara. Natalie remembered the night she'd watched *Jane Eyre* with Paige. "Jimmy thinks Ariel Saunders's house is *huge*" she'd said, "but it's nothing compared to Thornfield Hall." Beside Tam's house ran Hyacinth Lane, which ended at the Saunders house. Paige had seen the house and Jimmy had been her guide.

"I'm having a brainstorm," she said to the dog as she turned the key in the ignition. "Ready for a trip to your old stomping ground?"

Blaine panted. Clearly a *yes* to her brilliant idea. Her only idea.

Natalie took a shortcut to Hyacinth Lane, one that cut the trip to less than half a mile and one she was sure Jimmy knew. She turned onto the lane, not looking at the darkened windows of Tam's house. Too depressing. Halfway up Hyacinth Lane the ruts and potholes threatened to knock the car out of alignment. She stopped. "Rest of the way on foot and paw, Blaine." She opened the glove compartment and withdrew a flashlight. Then she picked up Paige's small sock and held it under Blaine's nose. The dog sniffed obediently and thoroughly. "Okay, girl, show me what a good tracker you are," Natalie said. "Find Paige."

She unhooked the leash and opened the car door. Blaine jumped out, looked around, then loped a few feet in the direction of the Saunders house before looking back at Natalie as if to say, "Well, come on!" Natalie followed, careful to act calm and be silent so she wouldn't distract the dog. Disappointed, she saw that Blaine did not sniff the ground. She acted as if this were merely a casual walk. Maybe it was useless. Perhaps the dog did not track. Perhaps Paige had not been on Hyacinth Lane.

Natalie caught up with Blaine and held the sock under her nose again. She sniffed. She looked around. She ambled forward. Then, abruptly, she dipped her head, touching her nose to a fallen leaf. Her ears perked up and she galloped forward.

Natalie picked up her pace. The gloom of the day lingered, dulling the night. A weak moon cast murky light on the rutted lane being strangled by flourishing honeysuckle vines and multiflora roses. Chills rushed down her arms and she wished she'd remembered to put on a sweater as cool lake winds whispered through the trees.

But the whispering wind wasn't the only sound in the darkness. Natalie slowed, feeling as if her own ears were perking up like Blaine's. Music. Not the slow, haunting music that would be in harmony with the somber evening. Loud, rollicking music, electric guitars blasting into the darkness, powerful male voices wailing a warning into the night:

Don't close your eyes,
He's waiting for you . . .

"What on earth?" she muttered, listening as the music rose, shuddering through the woods. Two birds soared in tandem, startled from sleep, and something rustled in the brush to her right. Her gaze darted sideways, expecting to see an animal rushing toward her. Instead the rustling moved in the opposite direction as she spotted moonlight shining on metal. She moved closer. Two bicycles. Her hunch had been right. Paige and Jimmy had gone to the Saunders house—the house from which rock music roared.

Natalie's breath came quick and shallow as she ran, keeping her gaze on the lane so she wouldn't step in a hole and twist her ankle. The dog raced ahead with enviable canine speed. She tried to search for possible explanations for the music, but nothing would come except the image of two faces—Paige's and Jimmy's, both bright-eyed, eager, and inquisitive. Maybe too inquisitive. Maybe fatally inquisitive.

No. She wouldn't think that way. She would concentrate on her breathing, her footing—

A high-pitched shriek froze her heart. She plunged forward, every ounce of her energy directed to her flight. Then she saw forms ahead on the lane. Blaine bouncing around excitedly. A boy saying, "It's just a dog, Paige! Come on!"

"Paige! Jimmy!" Natalie called breathlessly.

"Oh, *no!*" Natalie heard Paige exclaim.

"It's Natalie," she huffed. Blaine ran to her, then back to the children twenty feet away. "Are you all right?"

"Natalie?" Paige wavered. "Is my dad with you?"

"No." Natalie stopped in front of them. "I went by your house and you were missing. I came looking for you by myself. What are you doing here?"

"The killer is in the Saunders house!" Jimmy burst out. "We saw him before. It's a great hiding place. We came back tonight to get a picture. And we did!" He waved a rectangle of paper in front of Natalie. "Look!"

"The killer? A *picture*?" Natalie took the photo and flipped on her flashlight. She saw the blurred image of someone in a white robe. "What's he doing?"

"Dancing to that music! And it's a *she*. Real long blond hair."

"Long blond hair?" Natalie repeated. "Is she young—"

The booming music stopped so suddenly that all three jumped. The woods fell eerily silent. Paige tensed. "She's coming *after* us! She's gonna *kill* us!"

A scream ripped through the night. Not the shrill yelp of surprise Paige had emitted when Blaine had rushed toward her in the darkness. This scream vibrated with pure, depthless terror. Another followed, then another, each more shattering than the last.

Blaine barked. Paige clutched Natalie's arm. Even the indomitable Jimmy quailed.

"What's that?" Paige whimpered.

"Someone in bad trouble." Natalie looked at Jimmy. "Grab your bike, go home, and call the police. Take Paige with you."

"What about you?" Jimmy managed.

Another scream rent the night. "Just go! *Now!*"

The children darted around her and pounded down the lane toward their bikes. Natalie hesitated. She should go with the children. Or stay where she was. God knows what was going on in that house.

Another chilling, agonized scream. Blaine barked frenziedly and lunged forward. Without thought, Natalie followed.

She hadn't realized how close she was to the house until within seconds its bulk loomed ahead of her. Flickering light spilled from the windows onto the ragged growth that had once been a lawn. Candlelight. No. The light didn't flicker, it *leaped*. Bigger flames than candles could create.

Blaine was ahead of her, running back and forth in front of the house, barking wildly. Natalie hesitated again as the shadow of the house fell over her. Then she thought of what the children had said. The killer was a *she* with long blond hair. Alison. She *knew* it. But there had been the screams and now the fire. What if Alison wasn't the killer but the victim?

The door of the house stood open. Natalie stepped cautiously into a musty hall. To her left was a darkened room. To her right light glimmered through the doorway of another room. She moved toward it, her heart thudding. A thin veil of smoke floated toward her, enough to sting her eyes and nose, not enough to make her cough. She put her hand over her nose, took a deep breath and held it. Then she crept into the room.

Candles everywhere. A body lying facedown on the floor, pale blond hair spilling around the head, flames eating at a long, white gown.

Natalie rushed forward, grabbing up a small rug as she assessed the extent of the fire. Not bad. She slapped the rug down on the burning edge of the robe. Once, twice, three times. Then the overturned candle beside the body, then the small pillow whose foam rubber stuffing puffed most of the smoke. The wooden floor below, dampened by long years of moist lake air and no heat, merely smoldered.

Natalie tossed the rug onto the wood and stepped on it a few times. Satisfied that she'd extinguished all of the minor fire, she pulled the body away from the scorched flooring, turned it over, and swept back the blond hair. Alison Cosgrove's eyes remained closed, her face deathly white, as blood oozed from the ugly gash on her delicate neck.

17

I

Sirens. Flashing lights. Police cars. An ambulance. Emergency technicians. Cops. A frantic, shouting Nick Meredith.

"Where is my daughter? Is she all right? What are you *doing* here, Natalie? Do you have a death wish or something?"

"Will you just calm down?" Natalie begged. "No one can tell you anything while you're standing here bellowing."

"Pardon me for raising my voice, but I want to know WHAT THE HELL IS GOING ON!"

Natalie flinched. "I will tell you what the hell is going on if you promise not to say one more word until I finish explaining." Nick glowered. "I mean it."

"All right," he ground out.

Natalie took a deep breath. "I stopped by your house. Paige was gone. I came looking for her—"

"I know that much. What I *want* to know is—"

"Nick, be quiet. You promised." He stared hard at her for a moment, then nodded. "Something Paige had said to me made me think she'd been to the Saunders house. When we got to Hyacinth Lane, Blaine started tracking her. We ran into her and Jimmy. They babbled something about the killer being in the house and showed me a picture. Then we heard screams. I sent the kids to Jimmy's and I came to the house."

"So Paige is at Jimmy's?"

"I'm sure Beth Jenkins wouldn't have let her leave."

Emergency technicians carried Alison from the house. She lay motionless, covered with a blanket and strapped to the gurney. An oxygen mask covered her face and an IV bag dangled above her head. "Is she alive?" Nick called.

"Yes. Barely. She's in shock. Only first-degree burns on her legs," one of the E.M.T.s answered. "The throat is another story. If she'd been found just five minutes later by someone who didn't know exactly how to apply pressure, she'd be gone."

Nick looked at Natalie. "You saved her life."

"You say that like an accusation."

"No. I just want to be mad at you, but how can I when you saved a life?"

"You can't and I'm freezing, so why don't we go to the Jenkins house, make sure Paige is safe, and find out what the kids saw?"

"It's not that cold. You're scared." Nick took off his jacket and handed it to her. "Hysell, you know what to do here," he called. Ted looked surprised, then immediately began bawling orders, even to people standing next to him.

Ten minutes later two wide-eyed children stood in front of the sheriff. Paige's freckles stood out against her milkwhite skin. Jimmy had lost most of his swagger. Nick had pulled himself up to his full six-feet-two, and even Beth Jenkins and her balding husband looked frightened. Blaine lying at her feet, Natalie let herself be swallowed by an overstuffed recliner. She still wore Nick's jacket and with both hands she held the hot mug of coffee Beth had shoved at her as soon as she came in. Natalie felt oddly detached, almost as if she were floating high above the tableau. She did not let herself think about Alison.

Nick pinned the children with a dark blue glare. "I want to know what you two were doing at the Saunders house," he said in a deliberate, loud voice. "No lies, no evasions."

"I go over to the Saunders house all the time," Jimmy volunteered. "I'm allowed."

"Not at night. And *not* with a little girl," his father blustered. "What were you thinking? Are you out of your *mind*?"

Nick held up his hand for silence. "Paige?"

"I . . . well . . . I wanted to see the house."

"But you sneaked out to do it," Nick said severely. "And this is not the first time."

"Well . . . no. I've been there once before."

"You sneaked out of your room and came with Jimmy."

"Yes," Paige said miserably.

"But Jimmy didn't *force* her to go, did you Jimmy?" Beth interrupted anxiously.

Nick looked at her. "I'm sure he didn't *force* her. He no doubt *persuaded* her. But I'm not putting the blame entirely on Jimmy. Paige knows better than to pull a stupid trick like this."

Paige's face went from white to crimson. Wretchedness shone in her beautiful eyes. Natalie knew the child had done wrong, but she empathized with her. She would have done the same thing at Paige's age. She probably had *no* influence with Nick Meredith, but she would try to make him see that under normal circumstances what Paige had done would not be the end of the world. Of course having a murderer on the loose wasn't a normal circumstance for Port Ariel, as Paige well knew. Calming down Nick would not be easy.

"We'll deal with the lectures and punishments later," Nick continued evenly, although Natalie expected any moment to see steam explode from his ears. "Right now I want to know everything you saw. Jimmy, you first."

"Yes, sir." Jimmy stepped forward, suddenly military in his bearing. "We arrived at the Saunders house at 8:25. I looked at my watch because we were doing something real important and I knew you'd want me to get everything right."

"You were going to tell me about this?" Nick asked incredulously.

"Oh, yes, sir. Well . . . not *everything*. I wasn't going to tell you about Paige being with me. See, I sort of made her go."

"Jimmy!" both elder Jenkinses barked as Paige threw him a grateful look.

"How did you *make* her?" Nick demanded.

"I kinda embarrassed her into it. I said she was too scared. A little girl. She hates that."

"Jimmy, you're never going to set foot outside this house again!" Beth began shrilly before she spotted another junior Jenkins peeking around the door facing and went after him, shouting.

"Go ahead, Jimmy," Nick said. "It was 8:25 and . . ."

"And nothing happened for a few minutes. I knew it would, though. I had a *hunch*. So then someone started lighting candles, and then the music came on real loud. I went up to the window because Paige and me wanted a picture of the killer we saw the other night at the house." Nick frowned ferociously. Paige shrank. Jimmy hesitated, then plunged on. "Someone was wearing a long white thing and dancing. I was surprised. I thought it would be some awful-looking guy, but it was a girl with blond hair. I took the picture. She saw me. She ran out of the room, and Paige and me took off. Then Blaine and Natalie caught us, and you know the rest."

"The girl was alone?"

"Yeah. Dancin' like I said."

"You didn't see anyone in the room with her?"

Jimmy shook his head. "Just about a hundred candles."

More like ten, Natalie thought, but Jimmy was excited. He blinked at the sheriff, clearly expecting more questions, but Nick's attention had turned back to Paige.

"Is that what you saw?"

"I . . . I didn't go up to the window. I was standing closer to the front door. And I saw something else. Somebody came out of a room and crossed the hall to where the girl in the white robe was."

Nick leaned forward. "What did this person look like?"

"It was dark and I couldn't see real good. There was this thing like a . . ." She searched for the word. "I think they call it a poncho. With a hood. I couldn't see the face. I'm sorry," Paige ended meekly.

Natalie knew the apology was two-pronged. Paige was sorry for not seeing who was wearing the poncho. She was also sorry for sneaking out. She sounded so pitiful Natalie didn't know how Nick could stay angry with her, but he didn't look as if he were softening.

"So you kids have seen someone at the house before, someone burning candles and dancing to loud music, but you never said a word about it," Nick accused.

"We didn't think you'd believe us," Jimmy explained. "It was so weird—the candles and the music and the person in a robe."

"A girl named Alison Cosgrove is Ariel's descendant," Natalie said. "I think she's been dressing up and going to that house at night, pretending to be Ariel."

Paige's eyes widened. "You mean that girl we saw is the killer?"

Nick said harshly, "I don't think so. The person wearing the poncho is the killer. He cut Alison's throat."

Jimmy's face slackened and Paige cringed. "Is she dead?" she asked timorously.

"No, but she could have been. So could you. You have *no* idea of how much danger you were in." Nick's voice rose. "If you hadn't run away when you did . . . If Natalie hadn't come along, I don't know *what* might have happened!"

Hearing the agitation in his voice, Blaine jumped up and barked. "I think everyone gets the idea, Sheriff," Natalie said calmly. "Paige needs to go home now—"

"*I'll* decide what my daughter needs," Nick snapped.

"Okay. What do you think she needs?"

Nick hesitated. "To go home. Will you take her? I have to get back to the Saunders house."

"I'll be glad to take her." Natalie stood and suddenly realized how weak her legs felt.

On the ride home, Paige began to cry quietly. Blaine nudged her and she wrapped her arms around the dog's neck. "Are you all right?" Natalie asked.

"Yeah, I guess." She sniffled. "I've never been so scared."

"I haven't, either."

"Really? You don't act like you're scared."

"Sometimes it takes our bodies a while to register how scared we've been. We look all right, and then we fall apart."

More sniffles. "Do you think my dad still loves me?"

"Of *course* he does! He's angry because you sneaked out and he's frightened when he thinks about what might have happened to you, but he will always love you."

"Maybe," Paige said doubtfully. "Do you think he hates Jimmy?"

"No. He's mad at Jimmy for luring you out, but he doesn't hate him."

"How do you know?"

How *did* she know? Lots of parents would turn Jimmy into a villain, bad-mouth the child all over town, forbid him to come within fifty feet of his daughter again. "I haven't known your father long, but I have a feeling he's a fair person," she said carefully. "He will realize Jimmy isn't an adult. He's an impulsive kid who probably learned an important lesson tonight."

And I hope all that's true, Natalie thought. Otherwise, Paige will be disappointed in her father. And so will I.

"Do you know the girl that got her throat ..." Paige shuddered.

"Yes, a little."

"You said her name is Alison. Is she the crazy girl Mrs. Collins was talking about on the phone today?"

Mrs. Collins, who gossiped incessantly around Paige. Nick must replace that woman. "Something awful happened to Alison when she was much younger than you and she never recovered. She's what they call *unstable*." And *you* have called *her* crazy, Natalie thought with a stab of guilt. "She's been missing since last night and everyone has been terribly worried."

"If I'd known it was her we saw at the Saunders house, I would have told someone," Paige said earnestly.

"I'm not absolutely sure it was her. I'm just guessing because I know she loves the story of Ariel and she loves rock music. I know you would have told someone about someone being at the house playing music, though, if you hadn't been so scared."

Paige was silent for a few minutes. Then she said in a tiny voice, "Natalie, I didn't tell my dad the *complete* truth."

Natalie felt a cold tingle in her neck. "The complete truth about what, honey?"

"About the person in the poncho. The person that cut Alison's throat and maybe killed all those other people."

Natalie asked urgently, "What is it that you didn't tell your father?"

"I told Daddy I didn't get a good look at the person's face because of the hood and that was the honest truth. I didn't even tell Jimmy. But the person in the poncho looked right at *me* and I didn't have a hood on. He *saw* me, Natalie, and he prob'ly thinks I saw *him*!" Paige's voice rose to a wail. "Now he's gonna hunt me down and cut *my* throat!"

II

Natalie lay staring at the ceiling. It was one A.M. and she didn't think she could sleep, but at least she could rest. She could try to slow her heartbeat. She could make herself breathe slowly and evenly. She could force the image of a slashed and burning Alison from her mind.

When the phone beside her bed rang, she almost shrieked. Fumbling in the dark, she picked up the receiver before the second ring. "*What?*"

"Nat—is that—Natalie?"

"Yes, Viveca. How is Alison?"

"Still in surgery. It doesn't look good. That's what the doctor told me. Can you believe that? How insensitive of him to tell me that right before she goes into surgery."

"He's not insensitive. He's just trying to be honest with you in case she doesn't make it."

"I don't like him. I wish Andrew were doing the surgery. I want him here."

"He got home two hours ago, exhausted after a long surgery," Natalie said. "I didn't tell him about Alison. He needs sleep."

"But I need him. Alison may be dying."

"If she is, my father's presence can't change anything. Where's Oliver?"

A moment of silence. "Home." Viveca's voice trembled. "He said he couldn't face another dead girl."

"The cold bastard."

"Oh!" Viveca sounded startled by Natalie's vehemence. Then she added halfheartedly, "He's been through a lot."

"You're going through a lot, too."

"Yes, this is very hard," Viveca said softly. "Natalie, will you talk with me for a while? I just can't sit here staring at the wall any longer or I'll start screaming."

"Isn't anyone with you?"

"No. I don't have anyone besides Oliver I could ask to sit up half the night with me."

I can't believe I'm going to ask this, Natalie thought. "Do you want me to come to the hospital and be with you?"

"That's not necessary. From what the sheriff said, you've had a pretty rough evening yourself."

"It's one I won't forget."

"He said you saved Alison's life. Thank you, Natalie. Thank you so much."

"I'm glad I got there in time."

"Will *you* tell me what happened? I got the sheriff's version, but he never explained why you were at the Saunders house."

Natalie propped her pillows against the headboard and settled in for a long chat. After all, it wouldn't kill her to keep Viveca company, if only over the phone, while the woman waited to hear if her daughter would survive. She described finding Paige missing and ended with the E.M.S. taking away Alison.

"I don't know if it was chance or destiny that put you there in time to save Alison," Viveca said. "My husband always said the universe was chaotic. I like to believe everything happens for a reason."

"I'm not sure where I stand on that issue. Viveca, why do you think Alison was at the Saunders house?"

"Alison used to fantasize that she was Ariel. I thought she'd grown out of it, but lately she's been talking about Ariel again. She has some books on reincarnation. I believe she thinks she's the reincarnation of Ariel. I've suspected she's been going out at night." This Natalie already knew. "I think she was going to the Saunders house pretending, or maybe actually *believing*, she's Ariel."

"That makes sense," Natalie said slowly. "Did the sheriff tell you Paige and Jimmy saw her there a few nights ago?"

"No, but I'm not surprised. I should have kept a closer eye on her, but she resents the amount of supervision she *does* have. Mrs. Krebbs during the day, me at night. But I can't stay up *all* night. I have a job. I should have hired a nurse. That's what your father told me to do. I was considering it when suddenly she improved during the time I was seeing Eugene."

Natalie couldn't resist plunging on. "Viveca, why did you stop dating Eugene?"

Natalie could feel the woman's hesitation. "Because of Alison."

"But you said she improved during your time with him."

"She did, but . . . well, there were complications. She seemed to like Eugene too much." Viveca sounded pained. Had Alison actually tried to seduce Eugene? Natalie wondered. "I think Alison has only been slipping out at night for a couple of weeks," Viveca rushed on. "She's been so much worse lately."

"My father thinks she needed medication, but Warren couldn't prescribe. Why did you let him treat Alison?"

"She refused to see anyone else after she met him."

"She had a crush on him, didn't she?"

Viveca sighed. "I suppose so. But it was only slight, a little girl thing. Nothing serious."

I wouldn't be too sure about that, Natalie thought. "Whether it was serious or not, you don't have to worry about it anymore. Now that Warren is gone, Alison will be seeing someone else, and I think it should be a psychiatrist this time."

"It will be. *If* she makes it."

Natalie had never been one to spout false optimism, but Viveca sounded desolate. "Alison is young and physically healthy. Those things are certainly in her favor."

"Yes, she's in *very* good health," Viveca said hopefully. "Flu and a few colds. That's all she's ever had. Never even measles."

"She must have a strong immune system." Probably because she never went to school like most kids, Natalie thought, she hasn't been exposed to many contagious illnesses. "Her burns are minor."

"It's just the slashed throat that bothers me." Viveca gave a brittle laugh, then swallowed hard. "I'm sorry."

"You're entitled."

"Natalie, you don't know who did this to Alison?"

"If I did, I would have told the police. The attack was over when I arrived."

"If only you'd gotten there a few minutes earlier."

"I know. Maybe I could have stopped the whole thing, but at least the kids were there. I have a feeling the attacker was flustered, hurried, so he bungled what otherwise would have been a murder."

"Well, thank God for that. You're sure the children didn't see this person?"

"No, they couldn't possibly identify him," Natalie said forcefully. When she'd told Nick that the would-be killer had looked directly at Paige, he'd turned ghastly white and immediately ordered round-the-clock protection for her and for Jimmy. But he told Natalie to emphasize that the kids had seen nothing. The more people who heard this, the better. Word spread fast in Port Ariel. The killer *must* be made to think he was safe.

Otherwise, Paige and Jimmy could be the next victims.

III

His head pounded and he was desperately thirsty. Jeff Lindstrom was also desperately afraid.

He had no idea how long he'd been here in the dark. Until

what he guessed to be an hour ago he'd been unconscious from the last injection. Yesterday—or was it the day before?—he was standing by a window, grinning with satisfaction as he looked out to see a bright red cardinal flying past, when pain suddenly erupted in his head and blazed down his neck. It had just reached his back when his vision blurred and he crashed to his knees, then slid into oblivion. And now he was here.

But where was *here*? He sat on a concrete floor. The chill of it penetrated his jeans and his hips already hurt from the long contact with the hard surface. A slightly musty, dank smell reached his nostrils. He felt chilly in his suit pants and long-sleeved cotton shirt. His jacket was gone and so was one shoe. Dried blood clung to the ragged heel of a gray sock.

A tight blindfold covered his eyes. A strong cloth had been twisted, forced between his teeth, and tied behind his head. His mouth was abominably dry, his lips cracked. Metal hand-cuffs secured his hands behind a pole. He flexed his ankles against the cuffs shackling his feet. He bent his legs at the knees, planting his feet flat on the floor, and pushed himself against the pole as he rose painfully. He felt as if he'd been kicked all over. He was certain at least one rib was broken. His legs trembled.

Panic rushed over him. He heard a long, rough sob and realized it came from him. He would have been embarrassed, but no one was around to hear. At least he didn't think anyone was near. He couldn't see. But he could hear. He went perfectly still, forcing his breath through his nose rather than his mouth. No sound.

He squeezed his eyes behind the blindfold. Just this morning he thought he had it made. No one in the family thought much of him. Most family members wouldn't socialize with him because they thought he'd hit them up for money. And he usually did. He'd always acted like none of it mattered. After all, who cared what the family thought of him? he asked himself in the mirror each morning. Who cared what his idiot ex-wife thought of him?

But he did care and it made him feel hopeless. Until lately. At last all the failures, the family scorn, the loss of the pretty, bubble-headed wife he'd inexplicably loved— none of it mattered because he was going to even the score. Not even the run-in with Meredith had bothered him. The big man with his righteous outrage. The sheriff didn't have a clue what was really going on. It had been funny.

But not any more.

Jeff couldn't believe this was happening to him. Life sure hadn't been any bowl of cherries. He'd always had lousy luck, things had always gone wrong for him, but not *this* wrong. Not—

A noise. He cocked his head. A door opening and not too far away. His breath quickened, whistling around the narrow gag. Footsteps. He tried to speak, but nothing came out except unintelligible grunts.

"Be quiet. I can't understand anything you're saying and I don't want to."

Jeff fell silent for a moment. Then a wave of fury mixed with fear overcame him and he burst forth again with a series of staccato grunts. A hand slammed against his face. The sting brought tears to his covered eyes.

"I told you to shut up." A sigh. "But I suppose it doesn't matter now."

"Why doesn't it matter?" Jeff screamed inwardly. He lunged forward. The handcuffs clanged against the metal pipe and pain raged through his shoulders.

"Now that was stupid. Useless."

Jeff tried to kick. The shackled right foot pulled the left out from under him. He slammed to the floor so hard his teeth snapped on the gag. He sat in shock for a moment before the pain registered. A breathy moan escaped him.

"Stop thrashing around. You're only hurting yourself and there's no need for pain."

No need for pain? Jeff thought with a surge of hope. He wasn't going to be hurt. But if he wasn't to be hurt, then what?

"You've wet your pants." A hint of amusement, a hint of

disgust. He pictured the ghastly smile he'd seen for just an instant before he'd been knocked unconscious what seemed an eternity ago. "Not attractive. You wouldn't set any female hearts aflutter now. Natalie St. John wouldn't wipe her feet on you." Pause. "You *do* want her, don't you?"

A needle jabbed into his arm. Something stung its way into his body, something that robbed him first of muscle control, then of consciousness.

His eyes were closing as a soft, insidious voice said in his ear, "I guarantee, Jeff, that Natalie St. John will never forget *you*."

IV
SATURDAY MORNING

Natalie awakened with a sense of dread. Something is wrong, her mind seemed to say before she'd fought her way completely through the last level of sleep. What was making her want to squeeze shut her eyes, hold Blaine tightly, and pull the covers over both of them for the rest of the day?

Viveca had called back at four to say Alison had survived surgery and was now floating in and out of consciousness, mumbling "magic midnight, golden dreams." "Her father used to say 'magic midnight,'" Viveca explained. "And Eugene Farley once told her to have 'golden dreams.' Sad memories, but I think it's encouraging that she *does* remember the phrases, don't you?"

Natalie agreed heartily that it was very encouraging. She put her father on the phone to discuss Alison's condition in more detail. This time the killer had been unsuccessful. But what about the next time? And *who* was next? So far Ted Hysell was right—all the victims had been children of people involved in the Eugene Farley tragedy. Tamara, Warren, Charlotte, and now Alison. That left her and Lily.

Andrew had been outraged that Natalie hadn't told him immediately about Alison. He didn't know until Viveca called with the news that Alison would survive. He wanted to go to the hospital immediately and urged Natalie to come with him so she wouldn't be alone. "Dad, I'm too exhausted to move," she'd protested. "You go. It'll be daylight in a couple of hours and I'll be fine."

So off he'd gone and she'd lain in bed until dawn broke, then fallen into a deep if brief sleep. Now the clock told her it was eight. At nine o'clock the locksmith would be here. Time to rise no matter how much her tired body protested.

The coffee smelled especially delicious as it dripped with maddening slowness into the pot. Natalie poured a mug before the pot finished filling, took a bagel from the toaster, spread it with cream cheese, and sat down at the kitchen table. Yesterday had been gray and dismal. Today a periwinkle-blue sky lay above the calm waters of the lake and a pale yellow sun warmed the tender green grass of early summer. Once again Harvey Coombs sat out in his rowboat, ancient hat jammed on his head as he fished for famous Lake Erie perch. The scene looked like a calm, lovely painting. Murder had no place here.

But it *was* here.

"I will not think about it this morning," Natalie said to Blaine as the dog finished her breakfast and Natalie went to the front door. The newspaper lay on the lawn. She sighed. The paperboy was a star pitcher on the high school baseball team, but he could not seem to get the rolled newspaper anywhere near the front porch. Ever. Natalie clutched her robe around her and padded down the front walk on bare feet. A white car was parked across the street. A man sat behind the wheel. He paid no attention to her, but embarrassed in just her robe, she turned and quickly ran inside.

She sat down at the table with a second cup of coffee and unrolled the paper. Headlines screamed the news of Alison's attack. The story was scanty—reporters had had barely enough time to gather a few details before the paper was put to bed at ten o'clock. By now they were besieging Viveca at the hospital. Natalie could imagine her distress as reporters dug for details of Alison's background and mental history, and she was oddly relieved that her father was there to help Viveca, since Oliver seemed to have stepped out of the picture.

She glanced up at the kitchen clock. 8:45. The locksmith was due at nine. Natalie hurried through a shower and pulled on jeans and a tank top. Her hair hung long and wet as she rushed to answer the doorbell. A middle-aged man with graying curly red hair and a gold front tooth faced her. "Gary of Gary's Locksmiths!" he announced, grinning ferociously. A locksmith on speed, Natalie thought. Or maybe he just loved his job. Or perhaps he was showing off his gleaming tooth. Whatever the case, Andrew had described Gary to her, so she didn't worry that he was the killer posing as a locksmith. "Come right in," she said. "We need a new lock on the front door, the back door on the garage, and the sliding glass doors leading to the patio."

"Yep. Doc already told me. I'm gonna put a bolt on the sliding glass doors. Slickest thing you've ever seen." Gary grinned again, looking expectantly for an ecstatic reaction to his amazing sliding glass door bolt. "I'm rarin' to go!"

Good Lord, Natalie thought. She motioned him in, glancing at the man in the white car. He sat perfectly still, looking straight ahead with his head tilted slightly to the left. Maybe he was waiting for the young couple who had recently moved into the gray house across the street. But he'd been waiting for twenty minutes.

And he hadn't moved a fraction.

Natalie stepped past Gary onto the front walk. She gazed at the man, transfixed as an icy feeling settled in her stomach, radiating shuddery cold. Suddenly she felt as if she could stand under a white-hot desert sun for hours and still not feel warm.

Slowly she walked toward the car. From what seemed a great distance she heard Gary yapping about replacement pins and tumbler cylinders. Natalie ignored him. If he'd started shouting at her she still wouldn't have turned around. Something waited for her in that car. Something as irresistible as it was awful.

Natalie halted at the car and stared in the window. No movement. The unnatural angle of the head. The white shirt with a blood-soaked collar.

Unable to stop herself, she clasped the door handle. Pausing, she drew a deep breath, then opened the door.

The body of Jeff Lindstrom tumbled from the car, landing at her feet, his glassy brown eyes staring up at the beautiful blue sky.

18

I

"Good God Almighty! What the hell! Is he drunk?" Gary blustered from the doorway. Harvey Coombs's wife Mary had materialized in the street. She took one look at the gaping neck wound, gagged, and ran for home. Natalie kneeled and lifted a wrist searching for a pulse. The arm was beginning to stiffen. Given the temperature, she would say Jeff had died about three or four hours ago. She glanced in the car at the congealing blood covering the cloth upholstery seat. So much blood. His throat had been slashed in the car where he'd been left to bleed to death.

All of this ran through Natalie's mind as she pressed lightly on his lids, closing his eyes. She knew she shouldn't touch the body, but she could not leave those sightless eyes open, vulnerable like Tam's had been.

She looked up. Gary still stood gaping at the front door. "Call the police," she yelled. He didn't move. "Gary, call the police! Ask for Sheriff Meredith or Ted Hysell. Tell them to get here immediately." Gary was frozen. "Gary, *now!*"

Gary jerked as if jolted by electricity. The young couple from the nearby house appeared on their front walk, dressed in identical red-white-and-blue running suits. Both were tall and blond and looked like brother and sister. The young man walked toward Natalie. "What's going on?" He circled around the front of the car, looked down at the bloody body and quailed, all color draining from his ruddy face. "Did *you* do this?"

The absurdity of the question snapped Natalie out of her numbness. "Do you think I'd cut this guy's throat, then leave him outside my house so I could stand over him, gazing at my handiwork?" she asked coldly.

The young man backed off, obviously considering more strongly the possibility that this loony woman had indeed killed the man. "I was only trying to help."

"I didn't hear any offer to help." Tears suddenly filled Natalie's eyes and she began to tremble. "Do you have a blanket we can throw over him?"

He turned and ran back to his wife. After a murmured exchange she exclaimed, "I'm not ruining one of my good blankets!" In measured strides they retreated to their house and firmly closed the door. In less than a minute their faces appeared at the front window.

"Love thy neighbor," Natalie muttered as she sank down beside Jeff's body, suddenly dizzy. Three times in one week she had stood guard over the victims of savage violence. It was absurd. It was horrible. She felt as if she'd fallen off the edge of the world.

Mary Coombs dashed out of her house bearing a blanket that she tossed over the crumpled form of Jeff Lindstrom. Then she sat down on the pavement beside Natalie and poured a cup of coffee from a Thermos. "Drink this, honey. You're shaking like it's thirty degrees out here."

The coffee was thick with cream and sugar. Natalie liked her coffee black, but she drank obediently. Mary put her arm around Natalie's shoulders, and slowly the shaking began to subside. "Did you know him?" Mary asked.

"Slightly. He wasn't a friend." She shuddered. "He was left here for me to find."

"Now, Natalie, you're just scared."

"I know what I'm talking about." She looked at the pleasantly weather-worn face of the woman who'd offered love and sympathy ever since Kira deserted her so long ago. "Mary, did you see his throat?"

"Yes, horrible. This is nasty business, Natalie, but it doesn't have anything to do with you. Not a thing in the world."

But it did. Natalie knew with sickening certainty that it had everything to do with her.

She wasn't sure how long she and Mary sat silently beside the white car before the first police car arrived. Nick Meredith emerged, his expression grim, his eyes surrounded by bluish circles. Natalie doubted if he'd gotten a full night's sleep since the murder of Tamara. He looked at the blanket, then at Natalie. "Know who it is?"

"Jeff Lindstrom."

He drew in a quick breath. "Okay, besides Natalie, how many people have trampled on the crime scene?" he demanded.

"Only me," Mary returned indignantly, "and I didn't *trample.*"

"The guy who lives in the gray house was here," Natalie told him. "He didn't come within six feet of the body, though, and I didn't see him touch anything."

Nick looked around. "Pretty boy standing at his window clutching a woman?"

"Yes. Gary didn't come over."

"Who's Gary?"

"The locksmith gawking at you from the doorway of my house. He made the call after I found the body."

Nick turned to a deputy hovering nearby. "Get the tech team."

"Runnin' them ragged lately," the deputy muttered as he headed for the patrol car.

"And keep everyone else away from the area," Nick added. He pulled on a clear, latex glove and lifted the blanket. After gazing at the neck wound for a moment, he withdrew a wallet from Jeff's pants pocket. He flipped it open and read from the driver's license. "Jefferson R. Lindstrom. 2020 Madison Street, Cincinnati, Ohio."

Mary looked at him sternly. "Certainly you don't need Natalie to stay here and watch whatever you do with a body. She needs to go inside."

"She does indeed." Nick reached down and took Natalie's arm. "Let's go in and you tell me what happened."

Mary insisted on following, casting suspicious looks at Nick. He told Gary to go about his business, but Gary wasn't breaking any records. He worked slowly and quietly as he eavesdropped on Natalie's account of the morning up until she'd opened the door of Jeff Lindstrom's car.

As soon as she finished, someone began pounding on the front door and shouting, "What the hell is going on? Are those home invaders back?"

"Oh, Lord, it's Harvey," Mary groaned. "He was fine when he went out to fish, but it sounds like he got into the liquor before he came over."

"Would you mind taking him home, ma'am?" Nick asked politely. "We have all the confusion around here we need."

"Yes, I'll take him home," Mary said with suppressed fury. "If we hadn't been married since we were nineteen, I'd divorce him, the old fool."

She marched off and, after a brief but loud altercation on the front porch, Natalie heard her leading away a protesting Harvey. "Poor guy," she said. "He used to be brilliant and so charming."

"Last week he spent the night in jail," Nick told her. "I thought Hysell was going to cry when I arrested him, but I can't have him sitting out in his boat yelling to a crowd of tourists that he hid a bomb on shore."

Natalie smiled faintly. "I appreciate the effort, but you don't have to keep prattling about Harvey. It's not going to take my mind off Jeff."

"I know, but you're so pale I thought I'd give you a minute to recuperate." Nick sat down and to her surprise took her cold hand in his. "Where's your father?"

"At the hospital. He's always spent more time there than at home."

"Even when you were a little girl?"

"Yes." She looked at him. "He couldn't help it. He's needed."

"I wasn't criticizing. When I think of how little time I've spent with Paige lately . . . well, never mind. Are you all right?"

"I honestly don't know. I keep finding bodies. It's almost funny. I feel like a bloodhound." Abruptly she started laughing. The laughter lasted for thirty seconds until suddenly it turned to ragged sobs. "I just don't understand, Nick. I thought Jeff might have killed Tam, but now *he's* been murdered. I guess this blows Ted's theory. Lindstrom didn't have anything to do with Eugene Farley."

"Yes, he did," Nick said slowly. "His mother is Constance Farley's sister. Eugene was Jeff's cousin."

Natalie looked at him in disbelief. "His *cousin*! How do you know?"

"I spoke with Mrs. Farley. She was really upset when she found out he was here. She said he was, and I quote, 'an awful boy' and 'crazy.' "

"Crazy how?"

"She didn't elaborate, but she was adamant that I not cooperate with him. She was especially freaked out over the possibility that I might discuss her or Eugene with him." He smiled. "She wanted me to run him out of town."

"Tar and feathers?"

"I didn't suggest it, but if I had, she would have jumped at the idea."

Natalie wiped at the tears streaking her face. "What do you suppose he was really doing here?"

"I don't know. I considered the possibility that Mrs. Farley might have dispatched him to do her killing for her, but that seems too extreme. Then there's the possibility that he really was interested in doing a true-crime novel and in his investigation he found out more than I did. Maybe he thought he knew who the killer was."

"And?"

"And he made the mistake of confronting that person. He could have had plans to triumphantly drag the killer into the headquarters of the stupefied police. Or he could have had plans to blackmail the killer. Lindstrom was cocky as hell, Natalie. He was the type who thought he could outsmart, outmaneuver anyone." Nick looked into her eyes. "But maybe he met his match."

II

The door swung open and Mrs. Fisher looked at Nick belligerently. "What is it now?"

"I need to speak with Dee."

"I need to *speak* with Dee, too, but she's not here." The woman clutched her flannel robe around her. She'd combed out her pin curls and her white hair formed a thin, frizzy halo around her wizened face. "I haven't seen her since yesterday afternoon. No one to fix my dinner! No one to fix my breakfast! I could have *died* in the night and laid in my bed till I *rotted*!"

Her face reddened and Nick feared she was working herself into another coughing fit. "Is there anything I can do for you?"

Her gaze narrowed. "Always tryin' to get into this house, aren't you?"

Oh, God, not this again, Nick thought. "Mrs. Fisher, do you have any idea where Dee might be?"

"If I knew, I'd sure as hell tell you so you could drag her back by the hair to take care of me like she's s'posed to. Free room and board I give her! And for what?" Her pale eyes pinned Nick. "Why're you here lookin' for her? She's done somethin'. Don't try to fool me. What is it?"

"I don't know that she's done anything. I just want to talk to her."

"About what?"

"I can't discuss it with you."

"Well, to hell with you then!" Mrs. Fisher slammed the door.

Nick stood on the porch for a moment, thinking. Dee Fisher had been acting strangely for over a week. According to her mother she was often gone at night and had received a number of secret phone calls. Wade at the Lakeview Motel had seen her coming out of Lindstrom's room the night after Tamara Hunt's funeral. She was upset. Lindstrom was never seen again. And now he was dead.

And what about Alison Cosgrove? She'd been attacked around ten last night. Mrs. Fisher said she hadn't seen her daughter since yesterday afternoon. That left nearly twenty-four hours unaccounted for. Twenty-four hours missing from the life of a woman who had loved Eugene Farley and never gotten over his death.

As much as he hated to do it, Nick knew he had to talk with Ted Hysell about the possibility that his girlfriend was a killer.

III

The paramedics had taken Jeff Lindstrom away over an hour ago. A couple of reporters prowled the street, but everyone had sequestered themselves in their houses, refusing comment. Just twenty minutes ago Natalie had spotted a particularly pushy female reporter for the local newspaper standing on the patio peering in the sliding glass doors at her. Natalie had drawn the vertical blinds with a crash and uttered an expletive loud enough to be heard through the glass.

Now, numb from the shock of finding the body, she sat on the floor with her guitar and strummed absently, Blaine by her side. She hit ragged chords. Her voice quavered. She broke a string.

The phone rang. Kenny's disembodied voice floated from the answering machine. "Natalie, I know you're there, so pick up. I want to talk to you. Let's work this out. Natalie?" A pause. "Well, I love you, hon."

Nothing about having read of more murders in Port Ariel and being worried about her. Nothing about thinking of her sadness after Tamara's funeral. "Let's work this out." He was bored, temporarily at sea without her. And, "I love you, hon." Two weeks ago her heart would have beat faster at hearing those words. Now they sounded hollow. No feeling ebbed behind them. Had it ever? Or had she been nothing more to Kenny than the woman of the moment, someone convenient and eager to please?

She began to play and sing, launching into "I Can't Make You Love Me," by Bonnie Raitt. Tears were gathering in her eyes when the phone rang again. "Natalie, it's Lily." Natalie put down the guitar, swallowed to control her voice, and picked up the receiver. "What's going on?" Lily demanded anxiously. "You found a body?"

"Do we have a Port Ariel town crier?" Natalie asked. "How did you find out?"

"Your neighbors across the street called my father. Apparently they're afraid they're going to be dragged into something unsavory. They wanted to know if they needed representation and said they wanted the best."

"What a pair of self-involved idiots."

"Why didn't you call and tell me what happened?"

"I didn't want to upset you. I figured all hell was breaking loose in your world already considering the attack on Alison."

"I didn't know anything about it until this morning when I called Dad. He was just on his way to the hospital."

"He didn't go until this morning?"

"Apparently not."

"Viveca called here around one A.M. wanting *my* father to come. I wouldn't wake him because he was wiped out and sound asleep, but I talked with her for a while. She told me she'd asked your dad to come, but he said he had his own problems."

"You think he was unfeeling."

"To say the least. He's supposedly in love with Viveca."

"Well, maybe he's not as crazy about her as he thought."

"Last night was a fine time to decide that."

"What is it with you?" Lily asked sharply. "I didn't know you'd become Viveca's champion. And my father *has* been through a lot. He's nearly reached the end of his endurance."

"I didn't mean to offend you. It's just been quite a morning."

"Never mind." Lily's voice turned oddly flat. "About this body you found. Who was it?"

Natalie stiffened. *About this body you found. Who was it?*

Lily sounded like Natalie had found a stray cat on the porch. She'd gone off on a tangent about her father and Viveca before she even *asked* the identity of the body. "It was Jeff Lindstrom, Lily," Natalie answered slowly. "His throat had been cut."

"Like Tam's," Lily said without expression.

"And Warren's and Charlotte's and Alison's." Natalie waited for Lily to say something else, but she didn't. "Who do you think could have done this to him?"

"You sound as if you honestly expect me to have an answer," Lily said edgily. "Do you think I know more about all of this than you do?"

"No, I thought I was just asking if you had any ideas," Natalie said carefully. "I haven't talked to you since Nick found out Lindstrom was Eugene Farley's cousin."

"His cousin!" This time Lily sounded genuinely shocked. "What on earth was he doing here?"

"He told Nick he was gathering information to write a true-crime novel about the recent murders. Then Nick found out he was Constance Farley's nephew. When he spoke with Constance, she said she didn't know anything about a book and she was very upset that he was in Port Ariel poking around. Then he disappeared on Thursday."

"The day of Tam's funeral."

"Lily, did Jeff ever try to talk to you or your father about Tam and Warren?"

"The only time I ever saw him was that day in the store. You heard the conversation. And I know if he'd tried to talk to Dad about Tam, Dad would have mentioned it. He had nothing to do with Jeff Lindstrom." Her voice rose. "*Nothing.*"

"Lily, what is wrong with you?"

"What's wrong with *you*? You're asking me all these questions about someone who was murdered. You sound like you think my father and I know something. And what's all this with the sheriff? He's *Nick* now? Are you on the rebound from Kenny? Trying to score some points with the handsome young sheriff by doing his dirty work for him, badgering your oldest and supposedly dearest friends about murders?"

"Lily, for God's sake, calm down!" Natalie was stunned by Lily's outburst. "I didn't mean anything—"

"The hell you didn't! Just keep your suspicions to yourself, Natalie, before you do a lot of damage!"

For the first time in their long friendship, Lily slammed down the phone on her. Natalie sat dumbfounded, holding the receiver for nearly a minute as Lily's words played over and over in her head: *Just keep your suspicions to yourself before you do a lot of damage.* But she couldn't keep her suspicions to herself, not when Lily sounded so jumpy, so *frightened* . . .

She called police headquarters. Nick had just walked in. "What now?" he asked in a harried voice.

"Hello to you, too."

"Natalie, if you tell me you've found another body—"

"Don't worry. I'm not setting foot outside this house unless it's an emergency. I'm calling to tell you I had a phone conversation with Lily. She'd heard about me finding a man's body this morning." Natalie paused, fighting down her sense of betrayal. Lily was her friend, but they were dealing with multiple murders. "She didn't know whose body it was and she didn't immediately ask, which was odd. When I finally told her it was Lindstrom, she didn't seem shocked. I asked if he'd questioned her about Tam. She said no and that she'd only seen him once, that day in her store. But when I asked if he'd talked to her father, she got really edgy. She denied it vehemently. She was nervous and belligerent." Natalie took a deep breath. "She didn't sound right, Nick. She's wary and she's scared. *Really* scared."

IV
SATURDAY 1 P.M.

"Mr. Peyton isn't home. I don't know when he'll be back."

A slender woman with salt-and-pepper hair and finely

crinkled fair skin looked at Nick with startlingly beautiful, innocent violet eyes. "May I come in and wait, Mrs. . . ."

"Ebert. I'm Mr. Peyton's housekeeper." She hesitated. "I don't know. Mr. Peyton isn't really up to visitors. This is a very hard time for him."

"Yes, because his daughter was murdered. But I'm the sheriff, Mrs. Ebert. I'm investigating Tamara's death. I *must* talk to him."

Her hand fluttered to her chest. "Oh, no, has something else happened? Is Lily all right?"

"Lily is fine. This concerns other developments, but it's very important. Please, Mrs. Ebert."

He gave her his most ingratiating smile and she answered with a nervous smile of her own. "All right. After all, you *are* the sheriff and this is important. Please come in. Maybe I could get you something to drink? Tea? Coffee? A soft drink?"

"A Coke or a Pepsi if you have it. It's getting warm out."

"Oh, yes it is. Such a lovely day. Yesterday was so gloomy. Please make yourself comfortable in the living room and I'll be right back."

Nick hadn't gotten a chance to study the room after Tamara's funeral. He didn't know much about antiques, but he knew these were valuable. The room was beautiful, although much too fussy and formal for his taste. Above the fireplace hung an oil portrait of Tamara and Lily done when they were about sixteen. Both had golden blond hair brushing their shoulders, both wore pale green dresses that highlighted their hazel eyes. Their bone structure was identical, but no one who looked into their eyes would confuse them. Tamara had a gentle, shy gaze. Lily's eyes looked at him boldly, twinkling with fun. A dove and a peacock. Both beautiful, but so different.

Mrs. Ebert returned carrying a silver tray bearing a glass of Coke and a plate of Ritz crackers topped by thin slices of cheddar and Swiss cheese. "You have the air of a man who didn't have lunch," she smiled. "I could fix some soup if you like."

"No thanks. The crackers are great. You're right—I haven't eaten since this morning." He sat down on a moss-green settee, took a sip of icy Coke, then reached for a cracker.

"I'll just go back to the kitchen while you wait—"

"If you're not busy, would you keep me company?" Nick tried hard to look innocent.

The woman hesitated. "No, I haven't anything to do. Mr. Peyton didn't even eat his breakfast and said he might be dining out."

"He's getting back into the world."

Mrs. Ebert sat down on a wing chair across from Nick. "No, I don't really think he has dinner plans. He simply doesn't want to eat." She crossed her long, shapely legs and pulled her navy blue skirt over her knees. "He's devastated, Sheriff Meredith. Those girls mean the world to him."

"At least he still has Lily." She smiled. "And Mrs. Cosgrove." The smile vanished. "Don't you like her?"

"I don't know her well," Mrs. Ebert said shortly.

"About as well as you'd like, I imagine. I know Lily doesn't like her and from what I've seen, I wouldn't care for her, either. There's just something about her . . ."

"She's overbearing," Mrs. Ebert said promptly. "She acts as if this house is already hers, redecorating, doing away with Mrs. Peyton's things."

"You were fond of Mrs. Peyton."

"She was an angel living on earth. Such a simple, unassuming woman. She considered having a housekeeper a wild extravagance, not to mention pretentious, but she really didn't have any choice because her multiple sclerosis kept her bound to the wheelchair those last few years. My first couple of months here were tense." She smiled again. "I was recently widowed and so lonely. When she realized that, everything changed. We became like sisters. She saved my life—my emotional life."

Mrs. Ebert sighed and looked at the portrait of the twins. "I think she would be horrified by the idea of Viveca Cosgrove becoming the girls' stepmother. Of course there's just Lily now . . ." Her lovely eyes filled with tears. "I never should have talked so much about private matters. I had no right."

"You have every right to your opinion," Nick said gently. "Of course, after what happened to her daughter, Mrs. Cosgrove won't be around here much."

"Now I feel worse. That girl is very . . . disturbing, but she didn't deserve what happened to her. It's horrible!"

Nick reached for another cracker. "But she's alive, not like Jeff Lindstrom."

"Jeff Lindstrom?" she asked blankly.

"His body was found this morning. He'd been murdered like Tamara and Warren."

The violet eyes flew wide. "My God! He was so young!"

Nick had mentioned Lindstrom without expecting to hit pay dirt. He tried to hide his surprise and excitement. "You knew Jeff Lindstrom?" he asked casually.

"I didn't really *know* him." Mrs. Ebert tucked a graying wing of hair behind her ear. "He came here once. He asked to speak with Mr. Peyton and I said Mr. Peyton wasn't seeing anyone, but then he got rather loud and Mr. Peyton came in."

"When was this?"

"Thursday night, after Tamara's funeral. Can you imagine the nerve? Lily was still here. She told her father not to speak with him, but Mr. Peyton did anyway."

Lily had told Natalie she'd only seen Lindstrom once in her store. She'd lied. "He must have had something fairly important to say to insist on seeing Mr. Peyton at such a bad time."

"I excused myself, of course. And then Mr. Peyton demanded that Lily go to her room. The girls' room is just as it was when they were teenagers. She argued with her father, but he was adamant. It was so upsetting!"

"I'm sure. I wonder what Lindstrom wanted?"

"I wouldn't know." Nick looked at her intently and her gaze dropped. He had a feeling he was dealing with a discreet but scrupulously honest woman. "Well, that's not quite true. I did overhear *part* of their conversation. I didn't mean to, but

I'd gone to the kitchen and from there you can't help overhearing . . ."

"I understand." He took a sip of Coke. "I had a talk with Lindstrom once. He was pretty obnoxious."

"He was odious! Loud, rude. I didn't catch every word, but he kept asking questions about Warren. Did Mr. Peyton know Warren was having an affair with Charlotte Bishop? Did Mr. Peyton believe Warren had *murdered* Tamara? Mr. Peyton was becoming extremely agitated when suddenly Lindstrom said—"

She drew a deep breath, frowned, and looked down at her twisting hands. Don't let her stop now, Nick implored silently. But he knew this woman would not respond to pressure. He continued to look at her with interest but not avidity.

"Well, this has been bothering me," Mrs. Ebert resumed slowly. "Lindstrom said something about *exposure* to Mr. Peyton."

"Exposure?" Nick repeated quietly as the word screamed in his mind. "I wonder what he meant by that?"

"I haven't the faintest idea. I don't believe Mr. Peyton has any secrets. He's an honorable man. He was devoted to Mrs. Peyton. That's why I'm surprised by his involvement with Mrs. Cosgrove. She's *so* different . . ." She was wandering and Nick wanted to shout, "Get back to the point!" Extreme will power stopped him. "I wondered and wondered what this Lindstrom character could have meant by exposure," Mrs. Ebert went on. "And I think I have an idea."

Nick was leaning so far forward he nearly fell off the settee. He quickly grabbed the glass of Coke and drained it to hide his agitation.

"Do you need another drink, Sheriff?"

"No, I'm fine. You said you have an idea what Lindstrom meant by *exposure*?"

"I wondered if it might have something to do with Alison. I thought possibly she'd been in some mischief and Mr. Peyton wanted to protect her for Mrs. Cosgrove's sake."

"Alison? Mischief?"

"I can't think of anything else, particularly since I learned she's been going to the Saunders house at night, dressing up, listening to music. It's hard to tell what else she might have been doing."

"I see what you mean about Alison," Nick said. "What happened after Lindstrom made this threat?"

"Mr. Peyton told him to get out or he'd call the police. And Lindstrom left. Afterward I went in to see if I could do anything for Mr. Peyton, but he was quite sharp with me. The first time in ten years. But he was deeply troubled. He drank two snifters of brandy. Took them straight down. I've never seen him do that before."

"And then what?"

"Then he slammed out of the house and drove off. Lily had come out of her room by then and she was terribly worried. She went out, too. Mr. Peyton didn't return until near dawn. I know because I was too disturbed to sleep and I heard him come in."

"Where do you suppose he went?"

"I don't know." She colored slightly. "Perhaps to Mrs. Cosgrove's house. He often stays there quite late."

"And you didn't see Lily again, either?"

"Not that night." Mrs. Ebert rubbed at a shallow vertical line between her eyebrows. "I feel that I've said far too much, but Mr. Lindstrom was a terrible person. The very idea of verbally attacking Mr. Peyton on the day of his daughter's funeral! Not only that, but threatening him with exposure, of all things. It was distressing and ridiculous!"

Nick was quite sure Oliver Peyton found the threat of *exposure* distressing. He was not at all sure the man found it ridiculous.

V

After downing another glass of Coke and a second plate of Ritz crackers with cheese, Nick gave up on Oliver Peyton. "Will you tell him I need to talk with him when he comes home?" he asked Mrs. Ebert.

"Certainly. I can't guarantee that he'll contact you, though."

She looked at him regretfully. "He seems to be dodging people lately. All the stress."

"I understand. But this is very important, Mrs. Ebert. Would you give me a call even if he doesn't? I won't mention your name to him." The woman looked as if she were going to refuse. "Mrs. Ebert, I'm trying to find Tamara's killer."

"All right," she said unhappily. "I'll call."

He felt slightly ashamed as he walked back to the car. He'd enlisted the woman's help by telling her he wanted to find Tamara's killer. He knew Oliver Peyton didn't murder his daughter. He wasn't so sure Oliver Peyton had not murdered Jeff Lindstrom.

He sat in the car wondering what to do next. He's wanted to talk to Hysell about Dee, but Hysell wasn't coming on duty until four because he'd been up all night dealing with the Alison Cosgrove attack, allowing Nick to go home for a few hours of sleep and some time with Paige. He'd talk to Hysell this evening. Now he'd make another attempt to see Dee.

Nick braced himself as he pulled up to the Fisher home. His first two visits had been less than pleasant. He had a feeling his third could provoke an actual physical attack from the frail Mrs. Fisher. He noticed an old Volkswagen in the driveway that had not been there on his previous visits. Maybe it was Dee's.

His question was answered as soon as the front door swung open. A woman of around thirty with curly brown hair stood before him. She wore jeans on a sturdy frame, and her only makeup was a slash of bright pink lipstick. She looked exhausted.

"Dee Fisher?" he asked.

"The famous Sheriff Meredith. Ted talks about you a lot." From her tone Nick guessed Hysell did not speak of him in glowing terms. "My mother has a lot to say about you, too."

"We've had a couple of conversations. May I come in?"

"Why?"

"Because I need to talk to you." Dee continued to stare at him. "If you don't want to disturb your mother, we could speak out here on the lawn." He paused. "Or at headquarters."

"Headquarters!" Mrs. Fisher appeared behind Dee like a small, squawking bird. "I knew you'd gone and done somethin' wrong, Dee. Can't keep outta trouble. Just like your daddy!"

She began to rasp, then to cough. She backed away from the door, hacking forcefully into one hand, swatting with the other at Dee when she came near. "Get away! You only make me worse!" Splutter, gag, snort. Dee turned to Nick, looking utterly hopeless and exhausted. "You'd better come inside. As you can see, I can't leave her."

Nick stepped inside. He knew better than to suggest calling the E.M.S. Dee hovered over her mother who bent double, alternately coughing and cursing, until the siege began to subside. "I'll get you some lemonade," Dee said.

"Beer!"

"Mom—"

"I said *beer!*" Mrs. Fisher quavered. "And get him one, too. He's a beer-drinkin' man. Might put him in a better mood."

"Lemonade for me," Nick told Dee. "I'm on duty."

Mrs. Fisher glared at him. "Coward."

Off to another roaring start, Nick thought as he entered the small, stuffy living room. At least he'd pinned down the elusive Dee.

She returned to the living room with a glass of lemonade and a can of beer. Mrs. Fisher motioned to the plastic-covered couch Nick had sat on the other night and planted herself on the armchair across from him. "Mrs. Fisher, it might be better if I spoke to Dee alone," he said.

Angry light flared in her eyes. "This is *my* house! Nothin' goes on in here that I don't know about and that includes conversations!"

What must it have been like to grow up with this hostile, suspicious woman? Nick wondered. He wanted to order her from the room, but he knew it was no use. Dee was looking at him warily as she hovered near her mother's chair.

"I talked with your mother this morning," Nick said. "She said she hadn't seen you since yesterday afternoon."

"I was out."

"He knows that!" Mrs. Fisher snapped. "Out doin' *what* is what he wants to know, and me, too, for that matter, me here *dyin'* and you not even botherin' to come home all night." She took a slug of beer from the can. "And don't try to tell me you was with that deputy 'cause he called here for you this mornin'. I said you was in church. Hah! Bet he believed *that* one!"

"Ma, *please*," Dee said tiredly.

Nick looked at Dee. "I *would* like to know where you were."

"What's it matter? I don't have to answer to you."

"What is the big secret?"

"There's no *secret*." Dee tried unsuccessfully to laugh. "I just think it's my own business where I go."

Nick stared at her steadily. "Normally I would agree, but you've heard what happened to Alison Cosgrove last night."

"I saw the paper this morning. She got attacked. What's that got to do with me?"

"Do you know what happened to Jeff Lindstrom?"

Dee stiffened. "Who is Jeff Lindstrom?"

"The man Natalie St. John found murdered in front of her house this morning." He paused. "The man who's motel room you were seen coming out of Thursday night."

"I *knew* it!" Mrs. Fisher exploded. "Knew it, knew it, *knew* it! Whorin' around. He's the one!"

"I don't know any Jeff Lindstrom!" Dee's fists clenched. "What are you saying? That I killed this guy?"

"I'm saying he disappeared Thursday and he was found murdered this morning. I'm saying you were positively identified as the woman who came out of his room at the Lakeview Motel Thursday night crying."

"The Lakeview?" Color faded from Dee's face. "Who says they saw me at the Lakeview?"

"The desk clerk. Wade Hanley."

"I don't know any Wade Hanley."

"He and his father were in a car wreck two years ago. His

father died. Wade spent some time in the hospital and met you. He remembers you."

"He made a mistake."

"Then you deny being at the Lakeview Motel Thursday night?" Dee stared at him defiantly. "Ms. Fisher, I have to tell you that you could be in some serious trouble." Nick was stretching things. He had no evidence linking Dee to any of the murders, and only Wade's word that she was in Lindstrom's room, but he knew she was holding back.

"Dee, what's going on?"

Everyone looked up to see Ted Hysell standing in the doorway. "What are you doin' in here?" Mrs. Fisher demanded. "Nobody let you in!"

"The door was open," Hysell said. Nick knew this wasn't true, but the deputy held Dee's gaze. "Dee, I'm going to ask again. What's going on? Were you seeing Jeff Lindstrom?"

Dee's mouth quivered. Finally a tear ran down her cheek. "Honest to God, I don't know who Jeff Lindstrom is. I was at the Lakeview, though. Not just Thursday—a few nights. But it's not what you think, Ted."

"Then what was it?" Nick asked.

Dee sat down on the couch, her shoulders sagging, tears flowing freely. "Ted, you remember me telling you about my niece Maggie that ran away from home? The one that's sixteen?"

"Lou's girl?" Mrs. Fisher asked. "I didn't know nothin' about it."

"I didn't tell you. But I did tell Ted."

"I remember," Ted said.

"She got tied up with this older guy. Supposed to be her boyfriend, but after a few months he tried to put her on the streets. When she wouldn't do what he wanted, he started beating on her. So she came here."

"Wantin' money, no doubt!" This came from Mrs. Fisher.

"Wanting safety," Dee said. "Her mother got remarried after her and Lou divorced and the new husband doesn't like Maggie. He's some big deal at a bank and thinks because she's been in trouble a couple of times, she'll ruin his reputation. Her mother let Lou have her. Lou is my brother, but he's a louse."

"I'll drink to that," Mrs. Fisher said, gulping to prove her point.

"That's why she ran away in the first place, having to live with Lou," Dee went on. "She didn't have anywhere else to go but with this guy, this *creep*. When he tried to turn her out, she had to get away from him. I guess I was sort of her last hope, but she'd told him about me. She was afraid he'd come here looking for her, so I put her up at the Lakeview. You know, hid her away."

"What room number?" Nick asked.

"Room number? Ten. Why?"

"Because Lindstrom's room number was eleven."

Dee frowned. "Was he about six feet, dark blond hair?" Nick nodded. "I remember seeing him. He gave Maggie the eye. I told her not even to talk to him."

If Dee was telling the truth, Wade's surveillance wasn't as keen as he claimed, Nick thought. He'd seen Dee coming out of the room *next* to Lindstrom's.

"So you were going to the Lakeview to see Maggie?" Ted asked, a trace of doubt in his voice.

"Yeah. I put her up there a few days. Cost a pretty penny, although it's the cheapest place in town. But I had to keep her safe till I could get something worked out for her. I wasn't having much luck. Thursday night she said she was going back to the creep. I talked her into giving me just a couple more days, but I was so upset I thought I'd die. I've always loved that girl and I couldn't bear thinking of her being a prostitute, maybe getting AIDS. I guess I was crying when I ran back to my car."

"Where have you been for the last twenty-four hours?" Nick asked.

Mrs. Fisher leaned forward. "That's what *I'd* like to know, me here *dyin'* all alone and you traipsin' around playin' savior to some kid you barely know and what never done a *thing* for you, not like me, your own mother—"

Dee said in a low, distinct voice, "Ma, shut up."

Mrs. Fisher recoiled, spluttering. "Well, well I never . . ."

Dee looked at Ted. "I was trying to work out things with Maggie's mother. She lives in Brantford, Canada. I went there to see her. It's not that far, but far enough so I had to spend the night. Anyway, the husband finally caved in and Maggie's mother came for her today. They're on the way back to Brantford now."

"You realize we'll have to check this out," Nick said.

"Yeah. I'll give you the name and phone number. Could you wait until Maggie's mom has time to get home, though? If her husband gets a call from the police, it could set him off again, make him change his mind about letting Maggie stay. They should be home in three or four hours."

Normally Nick would have been unwilling to wait so long to verify a story, but he thought Dee was a woman of limited imagination and her story was too full of details for her to have invented it on the spur of the moment.

"I think you've answered all my questions for now," Nick said, standing. "I would like to talk with you again, though. Maybe tomorrow."

"Talk to her about what?" Mrs. Fisher asked querulously.

Nick's eyes met Hysell's and the answer hung in the air. Maybe Dee hadn't murdered Jeff Lindstrom, but they still had four other victims on their hands, all children of people who had been instrumental in the destruction of a man Dee Fisher loved beyond reason.

19

"It's your bedtime."

"I don't have a bedtime," Paige answered.

Mrs. Collins put her hands on her hips and glared. "You do now, young lady. After all the trouble you've caused me, you should be glad I don't put you to bed at six. And don't think I don't know your father is only keeping me until he can find someone else!" She drew a deep breath. "Well, I've told my friends I'm quitting this job because I won't waste my time taking care of a disobedient little girl. You might have gotten away with your shenanigans before, but not now. This isn't New York City, you know!"

Paige groaned. Mrs. Collins had been going on and on like this ever since what Paige now called "The Famous Saunders House Incident." It wasn't bad enough that the killer had seen her and that she'd been forbidden to even talk to Jimmy for a whole month. She also had to listen to Mrs. Collins carrying on *all day long*! She was almost glad to go to bed.

"Come on, Ripley," she said resignedly. "We'll go read in bed."

"You'll do no such thing! You will turn off the light and go to sleep immediately. Your father has spoiled you rotten, letting you get by with too much for too long," Mrs. Collins harped, full of noble indignation. "I taught *my* daughter to *behave*. She would never have sneaked out in the middle of the night with a *boy*. Of course, she had a loving mother to watch over her!"

The last statement was issued with an edge of reproach. When Paige turned a stricken look on her, Mrs. Collins realized her blunder. "Not that it's your fault you don't have a mother. It's a tragedy. I could cry when I think of what happened to your mother. Shot by those hoodlums! No doubt she sits up in Heaven every day and weeps her eyes out over the little girl she had to leave all alone and will never see again until *you* die!"

Paige's face crumpled. Everyone else said her mother was in a beautiful place playing a harp (which she hadn't known how to do in life) and singing and watching lions play with lambs in her spare time. Now Mrs. Collins claimed Mommy was unhappy and cried all day and would continue to cry until Paige came to be with her. It was *awful*. She suddenly felt guilty for being alive. Maybe she should die as soon as possible so Mommy could stop crying, but then Daddy would be sad and she would miss him and Ripley and Jimmy *so* much . . .

Overcome, Paige broke into noisy sobs. Mrs. Collins went ramrod-straight, alarm flickering in her eyes. "Now you *stop* that! What if your father comes home?" She was appalled at the desolation she'd wrought, frustration turning up the volume of her voice. "What's wrong? You don't want to go to bed? All right, you can stay up until midnight, just stop that bawling. Lord have mercy, you are the most difficult child I have *ever* known!"

Mrs. Collins marched back to the kitchen, muttering to herself. Paige emitted a few more ragged sobs, then lapsed into hiccups and sniffles. She turned on the television and sat down on the floor two feet away from the screen. Mrs. Collins had warned that if she sat so close, television radiation would blind her, but at the moment she didn't care. She was miserable. Ripley, usually not one for cuddling, butted her with his head a couple of times before curling up in her lap and purring with abandon when she stroked his back.

Paige was just regaining control when the doorbell rang. Maybe that was Natalie, she thought hopefully. Maybe Natalie knew she was grounded and her world was ending and she'd come again with her guitar for a lesson. That would be great!

She gently scooted Ripley off her lap and ran to the door. She swung it open. A figure smiled. "Hello, Paige."

It was dark. It had begun to drizzle. The person had pulled up the hood of a poncho.

"Hi," Paige managed to say, recognition flashing in her eyes. Shock and fear coursed through her, but she smiled and tried to look innocent. "I'll go get my daddy," she improvised. "He's in the kitchen. With his gun."

"Oh, I don't think so." A sigh. "What a shame you had to recognize me."

II

Jimmy Jenkins sat behind the oak tree on the Meredith lawn. He'd dodged through backyards and over fences to reach the house and avoid the cops that had been posted outside his house and Paige's after Natalie St. John told the sheriff she thought the killer had seen Paige at the Saunders house. He was taking a chance, but he hadn't seen Paige since Thursday night. He wasn't *supposed* to see her for a month, which was crummy. Not because she was his girlfriend or he missed her or anything. Just because they'd never gotten a chance to discuss their daring adventure.

His parents were still furious. He wasn't allowed to leave the Jenkins property, but his parents were focused on his little sister Ivy and his little brothers Jason and Joel, who'd caught her cold, so he'd taken advantage of the situation to visit Paige. He had it all planned. As soon as he saw her bedroom light come on, he'd throw little pebbles against the window like always. She'd shimmy down the tree and they'd get to have a good, long talk about Alison Cosgrove and how they'd been responsible for saving her life from the mad killer, even if nobody would give them any credit.

He'd gone out of his house the back way and traveled a circuitous route to the Meredith home, dodging the watchdog cop out front. To occupy his time until he saw her bedroom light, he'd brought a book, *Treasure Island*, which Paige said he'd like, even though he'd never admit to her he was reading it. He'd reached page ten when a cool drizzle started. He hunched up against the tree trunk, protected by the thick limbs.

A few minutes later a blue car pulled up to the Meredith house. He laid the book aside and peered at the person climbing out, but the hood of a dark green poncho prevented him from seeing a face. The person walked up to the cop in the cruiser, said a few words, and the cop nodded, like it was okay for the person to go to the door. At least it wasn't the sheriff returning home, Jimmy thought. That would have sent him scurrying. And it wasn't Natalie. Wrong car. Must be a friend of Mrs. Collins.

III

"Paige, who's there?" Mrs. Collins called as she passed from the dining room into the living room. Paige couldn't answer. The figure stood in the shadow beside the stairs, a hand pressed firmly over Paige's mouth as a sinewy arm held her body like a vise. "If it's that Jenkins boy, your father will skin you alive! You know you're not allowed—"

Mrs. Collins crossed the threshold into the entrance hall. The figure stepped forward. Mrs. Collins's eyes flew wide before a brass plant holder slammed against the side of her head. She stood still for a moment, her mouth a tiny, surprised "O" as she crashed forward onto her face.

"Such an annoying woman. At least she'll shut up for a while. Maybe for good. And now for you."

Paige's rapid heartbeat seemed to shake her entire body. This was it. This was what she'd feared since the night the hooded figure had looked right into her eyes at the Saunders house. Now out would come a knife and slash! She'd been worried about her mother being alone. Maybe she wouldn't be alone much longer.

The figure took a step away from the railing, dragging Paige along. Suddenly Paige heard a yowl and a black missile flew off the newel post onto her captor. A scream of rage filled the entrance hall. The arm released Paige, but she couldn't move when she saw Ripley hurled against a wall. "Ripley!" she shrieked. The cat lay motionless as the arm snaked around her again. "You *killed* him!"

"I didn't mean to." Genuine regret. "He might be alive, but if he is, one of our local vets will have to fix him up." A low, creepy laugh. "I'm afraid Natalie St. John won't be around, Paige, because you're going to help me lure her to her death."

IV

"Ripley!"

Jimmy heard the shriek and jumped up. What was going on? What had happened to the cat?

He wanted to go to the door, but of course he couldn't. Maybe it wasn't any big deal. Maybe Mrs. Collins had just stepped on his tail or swatted at him or something and Paige got all bent out of shape—

But he'd heard the terror in her voice.

Jimmy crept from the protection of the oak tree and slunk along the side of the house. He couldn't go up on the porch and look in the big picture window, but if he remembered from the two times he'd been inside the house, there was a little window that leaked light into the entrance hall—

A little window that was about two feet above his head. "Damn it all," he swore in his best imitation of his father. He looked around. Where was the wooden milk carton always so conveniently present in the movies? While he was pondering this question, he heard the front door open. He shrank against the house, watching while the person in a poncho led Paige out to the police cruiser. The window came down. The poncho person's hand shot out, and the cop's head sagged. Then the person dragged Paige away from the cruiser and made her get into the blue car.

Jimmy's jaw sagged as the car pulled away. For a moment he stood still, stunned. Then he raced to the front of the house, up the porch steps, and in the door. Mrs. Collins lay in the hall, blood pouring from her head. Ripley was a crumpled black lump by the wall. Jimmy dashed for the phone.

"I gotta talk to the sheriff," he yelped thirty seconds later. "It's an emergency, I'm tellin' you. Somebody took his daughter out of her house and drove away with her." He paused. "This isn't a *joke*. I'm tellin' the truth, I *swear*. It was a blue car and the license plate started with 3R." His voice rose and shook in agitation. "Listen, you've *gotta* tell Sheriff Meredith, because this person had a gun to Paige's head!"

V

True to her word, Natalie had stayed home since finding Jeff Lindstrom, only taking Blaine out once when reporters disappeared to file stories. Andrew had called at five o'clock. "There was a three-car pileup. I have two more surgeries."

"Are you the only surgeon in Port Ariel?" Natalie had asked only half playfully. Hundreds of times in her life he'd called to say he wouldn't be home for hours.

"At the moment I feel like I'm the only surgeon within a thousand miles. Keep the doors locked, honey. I have to go."

By nine-thirty she had reread a third of *Wuthering Heights*, Paige having started her on a Brontë kick, washed and dried a load of laundry, and was in the middle of her favorite Saturday night program when the phone rang. She clicked the MUTE button on the television and listened to the answering machine.

"Natalie? Are you there? It's Paige." The young voice vibrated with fear. "Natalie, if you're there, *please* answer."

Natalie lifted the receiver, cutting off the machine. "Paige, what's wrong?"

"I . . . I need you to come get me."

"Come get you? Where? What's *wrong*?"

A tiny sob. "I'm real scared. I think maybe Mrs. Collins is dead." A bigger sob. "And Ripley, too."

"Dead! Paige, are you home?"

"N-no. I'm at this spooky place. It's old and empty and . . . what?" Natalie heard another voice. "It's called The Blue Lady."

"The Blue Lady! What on earth are you doing there?"

"Please come. You *have* to come and you can't call the police and you have to come alone or . . . or . . ."

"Or I'll kill her," a ragged voice said. Then the line went dead.

Natalie sat frozen for an instant. This was *not* real. This was some silly prank Jimmy had dreamed up.

But Jimmy wasn't cruel. Impetuous and reckless, but *not* cruel. He wanted to be like Nick when he grew up. He would never pull such a malicious prank.

She glanced at the notepad on the table beside the phone where she'd jotted down Nick's phone number. She dialed. The phone rang ten times. "I think Mrs. Collins is dead," she could hear Paige saying. At nine-thirty either Mrs. Collins or Nick would be home with Paige, but no one answered.

She dialed 911, asked that an ambulance be dispatched to Meredith's address, gave her name, then hung up when asked to repeat the information. She didn't have time to waste. Next she called police headquarters. A pleasant-voiced woman answered. No, the sheriff wasn't in. No, Ted Hysell wasn't in. Would she like to speak with another deputy?

Natalie hesitated. Going to The Blue Lady alone was dangerous, but alerting a deputy who might arrive with the siren screaming could mean death for Paige. She calmly said she wasn't in need of help and hung up, wondering whom she could call instead. Lily? No. Much as she hated to admit it, she had doubts about Lily. Her father? He was in surgery. Harvey Coombs? Ridiculous.

Tearing through her purse looking for her car keys, she cursed the fact that there was no one to help her. Blaine followed her to the door. "I can't even take you this time," Natalie said. "A big dog might spook whoever has Paige."

But what would she do? she asked herself as she wheeled desperately out of the driveway and headed the short distance to The Blue Lady. She had no idea whom she was up against. And the gun! She'd been so flustered, she hadn't even retrieved her gun from the suitcase. She almost turned and went back for it, but there wasn't time. Besides, what if the killer searched her as soon as she entered The Blue Lady? Finding the gun could spark a violent reaction, and Paige's life was at stake. No, she'd face this without police, without a weapon. She had no choice.

Darkness shrouded The Blue Lady dance pavilion. Over the years, owners of the hotel had hauled in truckloads of sand to create a beach along the lakefront. No one had bothered since the fire in the seventies, though, and now the narrow, eroding strip of sand looked desolate bathed in weak moonlight and cool drizzle. It was almost impossible to imagine this dismal place as a scene of fun and glamour. Natalie had the sudden, chilling impression it had sat brooding here all these years, waiting for something awful to happen inside its rotting walls.

She got out of the car and glanced around. Tattered clouds floated across the moon. Off to the side of the building sat a car mostly hidden by shadows. She could tell that it was blue, but she didn't make an effort to identify it. What was the point? Yellowish light from the sodium vapor lights of the nearby convenience store drifted dimly over the portico of the pavilion. Business was slow at the 7-Eleven tonight. Two cars and nobody entering or leaving. No one to see her go into The Blue Lady. No one to call the police. Maybe that was good.

Natalie had forgotten to put on a sweater or windbreaker. The cool, damp air clung to her bare arms; mist coated her face. She trembled, but she didn't know if it was from the sixty-degree temperature or from fear.

She had no idea what she would do when she entered the pavilion. Maybe her mere presence would be enough and the killer would let Paige go because her purpose as bait had been fulfilled.

But Paige could identify her captor. The chance of the killer letting her go was zero. And what could Natalie do about it? She was unarmed and help was not on the way. The killer had been playing games with her for days. Tragically, Paige had been drawn into the game.

The padlock hung loose. Natalie drew a deep breath and pushed open the door. "Paige?" Nothing. What had she expected? That the child would run into her arms and they could return to the safety of the car? She took two more steps into the cavernous room. Three candles burned on the dais. A voice floated out of the near-darkness. "Close the door behind you."

Natalie stepped back, never taking her eyes from the candles, and pushed shut the door. "Now what?"

"Come to the dais."

The dais with its three candles looked far away. She walked slowly, glancing up at the mirrored ball throwing glittering reflections from the candle flames onto the empty tables and walls. A faint scent of roses floated from the candles. The night she had followed Blaine to The Blue Lady and heard the voice so like Tamara's threatening to kill her, she had smelled roses. But tonight not even the sweet floral aroma could hide the smell of mildew and decay hovering in the abandoned pavilion.

Natalie reached the dais. "All right. I'm here. Why don't you show yourself?"

A low snicker. "I'll be happy to." A figure stepped from the shadows, dragging along a whimpering, terrified Paige. "Good evening, Natalie," Ruth Meadows said.

20

Natalie stood stunned, her mouth so dry she couldn't swallow. She thought she'd been stupefied to come home from school to find her mother missing. She thought she'd been flabbergasted to walk in on Kenny making love to another woman. None of those things compared to finding the bodies of Tamara and Jeff. And even those grisly discoveries didn't cause the immediate, profound shock of realizing Ruth Meadows was a murderer.

"I don't understand," Natalie said stupidly.

Ruth smiled. "Then I did a good job." She wore a dark poncho with the hood down. Her short, silver hair shone in the candlelight. She held Paige close. The child's lower arms disappeared behind her back. Her wrists were tied or handcuffed. "You never guessed who I really am," Ruth said.

Natalie stared at her, images and phrases flashing in her mind. Their gazes met and held, one aqua and glinting, the other dark and steady. "You told me to have golden dreams," Natalie said slowly. "Viveca said Eugene Farley told Alison to have golden dreams. You're Constance Farley."

The silver-haired woman nodded. "Right you are, dear. It's a shame you didn't realize it sooner."

"You *can't* be Constance Farley. Nick talked to her in Knoxville."

"The sheriff talked to a woman who *claimed* to be Constance Farley."

"But the police questioned her neighbors."

"Natalie, you're a bright girl. Use your head. How long has this woman lived in Knoxville? Six months. She introduced herself to her neighbors as Constance Farley. They had no reason to doubt her."

Her voice was so cold, her grip on the child so tight. "Why don't you let Paige go, Constance? I'm the one you want, not her."

"Now you know I can't let her go," the woman who was Constance Farley said in a patronizing voice. "Besides, there's something I want you to do." She nodded at an object on the floor near Natalie. "My cell phone. I want you to call your father and tell him to come here."

"Here? Why?"

"Because he's going to watch me kill you."

Paige whimpered. Natalie stiffened. "I will *not* call my father."

Constance's hand raised to Paige's head. She held a gun. "You *will* call him or I'll shoot her."

"You won't," Natalie said desperately.

"Won't I? Don't forget Warren and Charlotte and Alison and Jeff. And of course your dear friend Tamara." Constance paused. "You know, I actually liked Tamara, but I still slit her throat and left her to bleed to death on a dirt road. So don't tell me what I won't do."

Natalie glared into the unflinching aqua eyes. Had they looked so hard all along and she simply hadn't noticed? Or was the difference that Constance Farley gazed openly at her now, not disguised behind the mask of sweet Ruth Meadows?

Natalie picked up the cell phone and punched in her home number. What if her father was still at the hospital, perhaps in surgery? Would Constance hold her and Paige prisoners until he finished? If so, would Natalie get a chance to overpower her? Doubtful. Constance had a gun to the child's head. Natalie had nothing except her wits, which at the moment seemed paralyzed.

On the eighth ring her father picked up, sounding breathless. "Dad."

"Just walked in the door." He paused. "What's wrong? You sound strange."

She swallowed. "I'm in trouble. Actually, Paige and I are in trouble."

"Trouble?" Andrew repeated. She heard the dread in his voice. "Just tell me."

"First of all, you must promise me you won't call the police. If you do, Paige and I will die."

"Die? *Die?* What in God's name are you talking about?"

"Dad, don't shout. Listen. Do not, under any circumstances, call the police."

He took a deep, shaking breath. "All right. No police. I swear. Now what is this about?"

"The murderer kidnapped Paige. She used her as bait to get me to come to The Blue Lady."

"The Blue Lady!"

"Yes. She wants you to come here, too."

"*She?*"

Natalie's eyes flicked to Constance's. "Dad, it's Ruth."

"Ruth?" he said blankly. "Ruth *Meadows*?"

"Yes."

He emitted a little gust of air. "Natalie, this isn't funny."

"She isn't really Ruth Meadows, Dad, she's Constance Farley."

"Constance Farley? Eugene Farley's *mother*? Someone is pulling a stupid joke on you. I have *seen* Constance Farley."

Natalie lowered the phone and looked at the woman holding Paige. "My father says he's seen Constance Farley."

"Two years ago. I weighed seventy pounds more. I had long, dark hair pulled into a bun and I wore glasses. And he *saw* me for exactly three minutes when he came to tell my husband and me how very *sorry* he was that my son had not survived the surgery."

Natalie raised the phone again. "Dad—"

"I heard her," he said thinly.

"She's standing here in front of me with a gun to Paige Meredith's head. Please get here as soon as possible. I repeat, do *not* call the police." She paused. "And do *not* bring a gun—"

"A gun! I don't own a gun!"

"I know *you* don't." Please pick up the emphasis on *you*, she implored silently.

"That's enough," Constance said. "Hang up."

"Dad—"

"Hang *up*!" Constance shouted. Andrew must have heard her. Natalie clicked off the phone. "Lay it down." Natalie placed the instrument on the floor. "Now we wait."

Natalie looked at Paige's chalky face. "Please take the gun away from Paige's head." Natalie made her voice gentle and respectful. "You're frightening her terribly, and I'm sure she's not going to run away, are you, Paige?"

"I won't move. I *swear*," Paige said fervently.

Constance hesitated. "If I take the gun away, I know *you* won't make a run for it," she said to Natalie. "You're far too noble."

"I'd never make it to the door."

Constance smiled. "That, too. I said you were a bright girl."

The cool drizzle had turned into a lonely rain spattering against the dirty windows of The Blue Lady. Rose-scented smoke drifted out from the candles on the dais. The flames danced and flickered in the musty darkness. "While we wait for my father to come and watch my execution, why don't you tell me what this is all about?" Natalie said.

"You know that it's all about Eugene."

"Vaguely. But I didn't even know Eugene. He must have been quite the son to warrant all this wanton slaughter."

Natalie had meant the statement to be a taunt and it worked. Constance's eyes narrowed. "My son was worth *everything*. And what I've done isn't *wanton slaughter*. It's *justice*."

"Pardon me if I don't understand what in the name of God Tamara and Alison had to do with your son's death."

"They had nothing to do with it directly. But their parents did."

"Innocent children paying for the sins of the father and all that nonsense?"

"It isn't nonsense!" Constance flared.

"Then explain. Dad can't get here for at least ten minutes. We have time for you to describe your brilliant plan. How did you pull all this off, Constance?"

"You're trying to stall me. It won't work."

"Stall you from what? Killing me as soon as my father gets here? I don't think it would work." She shrugged nonchalantly although everything inside her quivered. "You can talk or we can stand here staring at each other with me thinking you are an absolute lunatic for trying to avenge your criminal, suicidal son. It's up to you."

"My son was *not* responsible for what happened to him," Constance said with quiet venom. "His problems started a long time ago. With his father."

"I thought his problems only started in Port Ariel."

"They *culminated* in Port Ariel. They started with Hugh."

"I thought your husband's name was Walter and he had a government job in Washington."

"That was all a lie, the fictitious background of Ruth Meadows."

"Is Ruth Meadows a complete fantasy?"

"Of course not. None of this would have worked if she'd been a complete fantasy." Constance sighed and looked slightly beyond Natalie, seeing another world. "My father was a professor of anatomy at Ohio State University," she said. "If you're wondering where the skull on your bed came from, it belonged to a skeleton he used in class. I kept it after he died."

"Only now it's missing a head."

"No matter." Slowly Constance lowered the gun from Paige's head. Relief flickered in the child's dark blue eyes, but she didn't move. For an eleven-year-old, Paige was showing remarkable presence of mind.

"So your father was a professor of anatomy," Natalie prodded.

"Yes. He was a brilliant man, and everyone thought he was kind and quite refined." She sneered. "In reality he was brutal. He beat my mother and me. And he made us do horrible things. The worst for me was the pigs." The pigs? Natalie wondered, keeping her gaze steady as Constance dredged up memories. "We had a farm outside of Columbus. My father knew I loved animals, so he made *me* slaughter pigs. Wrestle them down and slash their throats. Pigs can be quite vicious, you know. It takes great skill and strength to kill one quickly and cleanly, but he made me do it, over and over, until I became a master at it. All that slaughtering later came in quite handy."

It also traumatized you, Natalie thought in horror. How awful—a young girl who loved animals forced to struggle with pigs emitting high-pitched, terrified squeals as they fought for their lives. Had it been so different for a young Constance than killing humans so many years later?

"I married Hugh when I was twenty," she went on. "He was an accountant, ten years older than I, very conservative, especially where money was concerned. Believed in living on a shoestring. We did have a lovely honeymoon, though. We spent it here, at The Blue Lady. It was before the fire. I thought the hotel was fabulous—my father had never taken us anywhere. I didn't see how shabby The Blue Lady had become by the late sixties. I didn't realize Hugh had chosen it because it was *cheap*." She glanced around the musty, cavernous room. "We danced in this pavilion. There was a perfect red rosebud on our table. The mirrored ball sparked so beautifully."

"You've been coming in here and polishing that ball," Natalie said.

"Oh, yes. *Such* hard work. At first I thought it was ruined, but I was determined to restore it as best as I could."

"Why was it so important?"

Constance looked directly at her and smiled beatifically. "I told you we danced here. I wore pink silk. Blue lanterns hung around the outside, making the place look like a fairyland. The light from the lanterns and the flames from the candles on the tables reflected over and over in those hundreds of tiny mirrors. It was magical. And after we danced beneath that glittering ball, Hugh and I went back to our room and made love." She sighed. "That was the night I conceived Eugene."

Oh, God, Natalie thought. No wonder The Blue Lady held

such significance for Constance. How many nights had she spent in here, polishing that damned ball, recalling, no doubt romanticizing, the night she thought her precious Eugene had been created?

"You did tell me you'd been here before," Natalie said. "That part was true."

"Yes. Unfortunately I told Eugene so much about The Blue Lady and Port Ariel, he decided he might like it here, so he applied to Bishop Corporation. He was hired and he met that *bitch*."

"Viveca Cosgrove."

"Yes. You should have read his letters about her. I knew from the start she was trouble. Older than he was. An executive. Prosperous. He kept saying she'd been all over the world, she was used to the best. I encouraged him to find someone younger, certainly someone without an adult, disturbed daughter. I was worried. Hugh made fun of him. The boy was so much brighter than his father, so much better-looking, and Hugh was jealous. He always downgraded Eugene. He told him a woman like Viveca was only toying with him, that she'd only truly be interested in a man with money. Hugh had great influence over Eugene." She looked meaningfully at Natalie. "*He* planted the seed."

"What seed?"

"Why, to embezzle the money, of course."

"You don't mean he encouraged Eugene to steal from Bishop Corporation!" Natalie exclaimed.

"No, his influence was much more insidious than that. He just kept mentioning how he'd heard rumors about what a slipshod operation Bishop was, how loosely it was run, especially the accounting department. And then he'd talk about Viveca and how interested she is in money."

Natalie stared at her blankly. "That's it? You think those comments were encouragement for Eugene to embezzle?"

"Hugh planted the seed," Constance said stubbornly. "He knew how impressionable Eugene was."

No normal, adult man could be *that* impressionable, Natalie thought. Viveca made plenty of money as an executive at Bishop, and no one but she knew why she'd broken off with Eugene. He had stolen, plain and simple, but Constance didn't want to blame *him*. "Did you kill your husband?" she asked quietly.

Constance's gaze grew distant again. "I didn't cut his throat. I didn't poison him. I just reminded him, day after day, that his son was dead. That his son had blown off his *head* with a .38 revolver. That his son had *still* been alive after losing half his *brain*, and on some level had been aware of what was happening to him on that operating table where your father *butchered* him."

Tears had been welling in Paige's eyes. The child was frightened of Constance and horrified by what she was hearing. Natalie didn't know how much longer the remarkable control she'd shown so far could hold. Enough of grisly details. "What did you do after your husband died?" Natalie asked quickly.

"Hugh had a heart attack. I could have called the emergency squad and probably saved him, but I didn't. I watched him writhe and moan until he was gone." She shook her head. "Then I had a nervous breakdown. I spent nearly a year in a psychiatric ward. At first my sister and her son Jeff came to see me, but only out of curiosity. They thought it was just a temporary little 'spell.' That's what my sister called it. When she realized it was much more serious, the visits stopped. Insanity in the family was embarrassing.

"When I was released, my family would have nothing to do with me. I had to hire a woman to stay with me because I wasn't up to being on my own. That woman was Ruth Meadows. She'd been an aide at the hospital. Her husband had died and left her with a pile of debts. My stingy Hugh, however, had made us live like poor people while he tucked money away. So much money that could have made life *so* much happier for Eugene and me. And there was a large life insurance policy." She gave a brittle laugh. "There I was, all alone, crazy, and *wealthy*. At least wealthy by my standards. And Ruth's. She was desperate and not burdened with any high moral sense. So I made a deal with her."

"To trade identities."

"Yes. When I first dreamed up the plan I thought it could never work. But the more time I spent thinking about it, working out every detail, planning for every contingency, the more convinced I was that it *would* work." She frowned. "*Where* is your father, Natalie? You don't suppose he's gone to the police, do you?"

"No. He knows you're serious about killing us if any police show up. He's probably just rattled, running around looking for his car keys or something, but he'll be here soon. Tell me how you pulled off the identity switch, how *you* became Ruth Meadows."

Constance smiled. "It didn't take a genius to come up with the plan. I didn't have a driver's license, but Ruth did. It was the only picture I.D. we had between us. I'd already lost seventy pounds during my illness. I had my hair cut short, had it colored silver, and got aqua contacts so I'd look as much as possible like Ruth. You know how bad those license photos are, anyway. It was a pretty good match."

Yes, Natalie had always been struck by "Ruth's" eyes. They *were* aqua, a shade she'd never seen in nature but one she'd seen in ads for colored contact lenses.

"The houses in Port Ariel and Knoxville are rented," Constance went on. "That way we avoided any in-depth checking involved with getting mortgage loans. We didn't use credit cards. We stayed in constant contact so that all correspondence dealing with my husband's estate, as well as any other important correspondence, could be forwarded to me, then returned bearing an authentic signature, not a forgery.

"I wrote letters to the few relatives with whom I remained in touch and sent them to Ruth, who forwarded them so they would have a Knoxville postmark. Ruth also made certain to be seen every day by her neighbors. She walked her dog. I *never* appeared in Knoxville. Ruth is the only woman neighbors and business people in Knoxville have ever seen." She shrugged. "There are recorded cases of this kind of scheme being pulled off for years, but I wouldn't have risked it. I only needed a few months, long enough to move here and establish myself before I began my work."

"Your work being the murders," Natalie said flatly.

"Yes, of course. I made a few friends, including little Paige's sitter, Mrs. Collins. We attended the same church, were on the same committee. I was just dropping by some leaflets to her tonight when unfortunately Paige recognized me from that night at the Saunders house. She tried to hide it, but those expressive eyes gave her away."

"You didn't go to the house to get her so you could use her to lure me here?"

Constance gave her a genuinely innocent look. "No. I'd been led to believe she couldn't possibly identify who was at the Saunders house that night. Besides, I thought she'd be in bed, and I only planned to hand the leaflets to Mrs. Collins and leave. I wasn't going in the house."

"But you had a gun."

"I always carry a gun these days," Constance said offhandedly. "Really, this wasn't how I planned things, Natalie. I didn't intend to shoot you. I intended to slash your throat, like I did to the others. But when I saw that Paige recognized me, I didn't have any choice but to make my move."

"Then let Paige *go*," Natalie begged.

"I can't. Not *now*. You don't seem to understand, Natalie, that I'm forced to do things I don't always *want* to do."

"Such as killing Tamara. You said you *liked* her."

"And so I did. But Oliver Peyton had bungled my son's case. Any fool could see that a first-year lawyer could have put on a better defense. So he had to pay by losing one of his children, just like I lost mine. I knew Tamara from the suicide hotline. She even told me about her evening walks. Choosing her instead of Lily was simply a matter of convenience."

Rage, hot and bitter, rushed through Natalie. Gentle, loving

Tamara had been killed because she was a *convenient* target for this lunatic. Natalie wanted to rush at the woman, screaming and clawing, but that would only result in the death of Paige. Instead she clenched her fists and tried to force down her fury and disgust. "And then there was Charlotte and Warren."

"Oh, I had no qualms about killing them. Awful people. The children of awful people. Max Bishop hounded my poor boy over a couple of hundred thousand dollars, as if he'd ever miss it! And that lout Richard Hunt. My husband *knew* him! But he still pointed the finger at Eugene. He could have covered up the embezzlement so easily! But no, he had to show off."

To Constance, everything was personal. Her son had not been brought to justice—he had been persecuted. "I understand why you attacked Alison," Natalie said. "She's the child of Viveca. But what about Jeff? He was your nephew."

Constance smiled. "Exactly. My no-good nephew. He was fired from his job at the newspaper, you know, so he decided to hit up good old Aunt Constance for a loan. He went to Knoxville and found not me, but Ruth." She shook her head. "I'm afraid Ruth didn't handle matters well. *She* should have stopped him, but she has no stomach for killing. At least she did warn me about him.

"Apparently during my early days in the hospital I'd raved about getting back at the people who'd hurt Eugene by hurting *their* children," Constance continued. "And of course the murder of Tamara was in all the Ohio papers. Jeff was bright. He figured it out and decided to find me by tracking the people in Port Ariel that he thought *I'd* be tracking."

Her eyes narrowed and her voice turned vicious. "He found me through you, Natalie. He watched outside your house the night of Tamara's viewing and followed when your father took me home. He did nothing then. I didn't even see him until the day of the funeral. That's when I dropped my purse in the church. Andrew rushed me home. He waited until your father left, then he came to my door, brazen as sin. He planned to blackmail me." She laughed harshly. "He got a nasty surprise. I dragged him to the basement and kept him a prisoner until the perfect time to kill him."

"A time when you could safely leave him in front of my house so I could find the body. Why?"

"Why you?" The gun shook slightly in her hand. Even her voice trembled. "Of everyone who hurt my Eugene, I hold your *father* most responsible. My son could have pulled through that operation. That nurse Dee Fisher said so. But Andrew botched it because he hated Eugene for stealing that tramp, Viveca. And after he'd murdered my son, he came into the waiting room with his matter-of-fact expression and said Eugene hadn't made it. That's it. 'Sorry. We did all we could.' So blasé." Her voice rose shrilly. "There wasn't an ounce of feeling, of *compassion*, in his eyes."

Natalie knew this wasn't true. Her father felt for all his patients, but Eugene Farley's death had especially bothered Andrew. "If he *had* lived, he would have been brain-dead," Andrew had told Natalie sadly. "At least he could have been an organ donor—he wanted to be—but his mother forbade it. Now nothing of that tragic young man lives on except the memory of a stupid mistake and a horrible death."

Natalie heard a crunch of gravel outside. Paige blinked and Natalie knew she'd heard it, too, but Constance didn't seem to notice. It *had* taken Andrew a long time to get here. Why? Were the police with him after all? Suddenly she knew she had to keep Constance distracted.

"You say you held my father most responsible for your son's death," she said. "You must have hated him, so why did you date him?"

"*Date!*" Constance burst out. "I was *researching*! You didn't live here. You didn't even have your own place. I couldn't ask Tamara a lot of questions about someone I'd never met. But your father supplied the answers, and I would have come after you, but you came home first!" She laughed. "Actually, your arrival in Port Ariel is what set everything in motion. It was a sign, you see. All the children were here, ripe for the picking."

"Why didn't you taunt the others like you did me?"

"It would have made everyone too careful. Besides, I wanted to hurt you the most."

The creak of a door. A soft whisper of air. Someone entering the building. "But how did you pull off the things you did to me?" Natalie asked loudly. "The anonymous phone calls, for instance."

"I told you, Natalie, I *knew* Tamara. I've always been good at mimicry. I could imitate her voice. I called you the afternoon you found her body. I have call block—I knew you couldn't call me right back. Then there was the day you supposedly received the call from Lily telling you to come to Tamara's. I simply called your number using my cell phone while you were in the shower."

"You tried to talk me out of going!"

"Natalie, I'd heard enough about you from your father to know arguing would only make you more determined to do as you pleased!" She frowned. "Of course, when I sent you to Tamara's I didn't expect Jeff to be wandering around there, but it was really an added bonus because he frightened you."

"And the night I came here to the pavilion and you hid, saying you were Tamara and threatening to kill me? You couldn't possibly have known I'd be walking along the shore that night."

"That wasn't planned. I was here working. I'd already finished with the ball"—she looked up with pleasure at the sparkling, mirrored ball—"but there were so many other things to do to restore this place. I'd been here for hours, working by candlelight, and I needed a breather, so I walked along the lake. You know I'd made friends with Blaine earlier. She saw me and started toward me. I had no good explanation for being on the shore so close to your home that late at night, so I ran for the pavilion. The dog chased me. I guess she thought it was a game. And then *you* came to the pavilion. I was flustered at first. I was trying to hide when I stepped on something and yelped. In you charged, wanting to help, Natalie to the rescue! So I decided to take advantage of the situation." She laughed again, that awful, brittle sound with a note of hysteria capering underneath. "I never expected to almost get shot!"

"And you broke into our house."

"I let myself in with keys. I'd stopped by your father's office one day. The place was so busy no one noticed me poking through the desk drawers. I had copies of the keys made, then I made another little surprise visit and returned the keys. I went to your house several times before that night."

Andrew had told her Ruth had only been to the house once, but the day Natalie met her she'd referred to the framed photo of Natalie and Clytemnestra in her father's study. And the day she brought the cherry pie, she'd known which drawer the towels were kept. Why didn't I notice these things? Natalie asked herself.

"Anyway, you shouldn't be angry about the night I tore up your clothes and the picture and left the blood and the skull," Constance went on. "I could have hurt Blaine, but I didn't. I told you I love animals. But I'd frightened her. I made a point to never be around her again."

"You were very clever, weren't you . . . Constance?" Andrew said.

She looked up, but Natalie didn't want to make any swift movement that might cause Constance to fire the gun held so close to Paige.

"Andrew," Constance said calmly. "You don't usually drive so slowly. You didn't bring the police, did you? Or were you just considering whether or not you wanted to risk your life to save your daughter?"

"I won't even answer the last question." His deep voice echoed around the huge, empty room. "And I didn't bring the police. Why are you doing this?"

"I already told Natalie. You're going to watch me kill her."

"You're going to kill my daughter because your son killed himself?"

"*You* killed my son!" Constance flared. "You killed him on the operating table."

"I did no such thing. I knew he was a lost cause as soon as I looked at him, but I *tried*."

"That nurse said—"

"That nurse was furious with me over another matter. She was also out of her head over Eugene's death."

"You killed my son, Andrew. My only child. And now you'll know the pain of losing *your* only child. An eye for an eye."

"You're very fond of quoting the Bible," Natalie piped up. "Nice little quote you left at the murder scenes about their throats being an open tomb."

"The quotation was apt. Max Bishop, Oliver Peyton, Viveca— none of them has ever done anything that's good."

"And my father has never done good?" Natalie asked.

" 'Their feet are swift to shed blood.' Your father raced to the hospital to shed my son's blood on his operating table."

"That is a damned lie!" Natalie shouted, suddenly losing control. "You twist the words of the Bible to mean whatever suits you."

"You shut up!" Constance raged. Her arm tightened around Paige and she shook the little girl with such ferocity that her head snapped back. Her *neck*, Natalie thought in horror. She's going to break Paige's neck.

Natalie had not been aware of her father stepping off to the right until she heard him yell, "Constance!"

The woman whirled. Paige swung to the side, no longer providing a shield. Something roared past Natalie's ear and she caught a glimmer of muzzle flash. Constance jolted, her eyes flew wide, and liquid splattered from her right shoulder.

Dad has my gun! Natalie thought in the startled moment before Paige broke free of Constance's grasp and lunged away. She managed two stumbling steps before her feet tangled and she crashed to the floor of the dais. Constance fought to regain her balance, waving the gun before she dropped it from her injured right arm. She kneeled and grabbed for the gun, her fingers curling around the grip.

"Dad, shoot her!" Natalie pleaded. He fired, but the shot flew wild. Constance laughed. Natalie shuddered at the laugh of a maniac.

A crash somewhere in the distance. A male voice yelling "Police! Freeze!" one second before a gunshot blasted through the room. Constance whirled again, gun raised, firing blindly before two more shots hit her. She crumpled into a heap with a soft laugh bubbling in her throat.

EPILOGUE

Natalie and Paige sat at the piano in the Meredith living room. Natalie finished Sarah McLachlan's "I Will Remember You" with a slight catch in her voice. Paige looked up at her. "You were thinking about someone special, someone you won't see again." Natalie nodded, picturing Kenny's handsome face. "Just like I won't see my mommy."

The pain Natalie felt knowing she would never return to Kenny couldn't possibly compare with Paige's pain over the death of her mother. Natalie put her arm around the child's shoulders. "Paige, life is full of good-byes. They hurt. But life is also full of hellos." She smiled. "If I hadn't said goodbye to someone a couple of weeks ago, I wouldn't have met you."

"And you're glad you met me?"

"You bet I am!"

"And Daddy and Ripley?"

"Them, too."

"That's good to know," Nick said.

Natalie hadn't heard him come in. He looked tired after the recent events, but also relieved. "Daddy, guess what?" Paige asked excitedly. "We just got back from Dr. Cavanaugh's and he says Ripley gets to come home tomorrow!"

Natalie smiled. "Ripley is doing fine after his surgery. He hurts, and he'll need to rest in a cage for at least a week. Before you know it, though, he'll be jumping off the newel post again."

"Oh, great," Nick groaned. "That's one particular trick of his I could do without."

Paige beamed. "I'm gonna go call . . . some friends and tell them about Ripley."

When she left the living room, Nick motioned toward the couch. Then he sat down close to her. "Hard to believe that forty-eight hours ago Paige was in the hands of that maniac. You'd think nothing had happened to her."

"She's resilient but not indestructible. I think there might be repercussions."

"That's why I'm taking the week off. We need to be together. Also, my ace babysitter is in the hospital."

"I hope when she's released she won't be coming back to work here."

Nick rolled his eyes. "No way in hell. I've been talking to a few women who might work out. Before I hire one, though, I'm going to learn a lot more about her than I did Mrs. Collins. I'd like to have someone who would actually watch over my daughter, not tie up my phone all day."

"Well, I know Paige will be glad to see the last of Mrs. Collins. She'll also be delighted to have you to herself, and this is one week when you won't worry about her."

"I'll *always* worry about her, especially after everything that's happened. I don't want to be her jailer, though. She'll start to hate me."

Natalie smiled. "And that's why you've decided to let her talk to Jimmy again. You know that's who she's calling."

"No kidding?" He grinned. "I guess Jimmy's not so bad. Besides, if it hadn't been for him, I would never have known where to find Paige that night." His face grew serious. "After dispatch let me know she was missing, I went tearing to the Saunders house and I would have ignored the report of a disturbance at The Blue Lady by that guy at the convenience store if they hadn't said a blue car was parked outside. Jimmy had described the car she was taken away in."

"That officer posted outside also might have bled to death if help hadn't arrived so fast."

"Yes, and he has a wife and two kids. I don't know what they would have done without him."

"So Jimmy has redeemed himself."

"Partially." Nick frowned. "Of course, Paige wouldn't have been in any danger to begin with if he hadn't talked her into sneaking out—"

"Part of Jimmy's trouble is that his parents are so wrapped up in the younger kids, they don't give him the supervision he needs," Natalie interrupted. "I think that situation will change now. I also think both Jimmy and Paige have learned their lesson."

"Then they're the only ones who got anything good out of this tragedy," Nick said. "Richard Hunt lost a son, and the Bishops and Oliver Peyton each lost a daughter."

"Oliver might have lost two. When Alison regained consciousness and told her mother she'd listened to Oliver and Max Bishop talking on the phone—"

"About how old Max had paid Peyton to do a lousy job of defending Eugene Farley?" Natalie nodded. "I don't get it. Peyton *has* money."

"Not as much as he claimed. He's in debt and he needed the bribe money Bishop offered. That's what Alison was raving about the day of Tam's funeral. I remember Oliver looking like he was going to have a heart attack. He knew that *she* knew what he'd done. I wonder why she sat on that information—but then, Alison has her own incomprehensible reasons."

"Do you think Viveca will stay with him?"

"Lily told me she's already bade him a crushing farewell. I guess Viveca has higher standards than I gave her credit for. Lily is also badly disillusioned. She's not speaking to her father. I believe she'll forgive him, but not for a long time." Natalie sighed. "And then there's *my* father. I think he's sworn off women for good. First Kira, then Viveca, then Ruth . . . I mean Constance."

"God—what a shock. She had everyone fooled."

"Except Jeff, and look what happened to him."

"Yeah," Nick said slowly. "I thought of something a few hours too late to be of any use. Lindstrom's driver's license said his name was Jefferson. The woman in Knoxville called him Jeffrey. I should have picked up on that."

"It's a pretty small detail and there was a lot going on. What will happen to the real Ruth Meadows?"

"She's missing. I think my phone calls spooked her. Then Constance probably missed a couple of phone calls and Ruth decided something had gone wrong. When the Knoxville police got to the house Sunday morning, her clothes and personal effects were gone. She left the dog she'd walked every day so she'd be seen. One of the neighbors is taking it in."

Natalie smiled. "Just like you're taking in Constance's cat Callie."

Nick tried to scowl. "It wasn't my idea. When Paige heard there was a homeless cat, she decided Ripley needed a girlfriend."

"You could have said no," Natalie said innocently.

"I couldn't and you know it. So now we'll have two cats."

"And I have a dog. No one answered the ad for Blaine."

"To your tremendous disappointment," Nick laughed, then sobered. "So what are you going to do with her in Columbus?" he asked softly.

Natalie looked down at her pearl ring. "Have you seen that empty building on Dawn Street?"

"The little brick place beside the park?"

She nodded. "I think it would be a great place for a clinic with boarding facilities. The dogs could be walked in the park each day."

"Natalie, what are you trying to say?"

"I'm going to buy it." She glanced up. "I believe there's room for another vet in this town."

Nick's dark blue eyes widened. "Are you joking? You want to stay here and open a clinic?"

"Yes. My life in Columbus is over."

"I thought you had someone there. Someone you cared about."

"I never told you that."

"I did a little investigating." Natalie raised her eyebrows. "Not for personal reasons. There was a murder investigation and—"

She held up her hand. "It doesn't matter. There *was* someone, but there isn't anymore. I've already told him. And the funny thing is that I'm not all that upset about it. I suddenly realize I haven't been happy for quite a while, and not just with my personal life. With my own clinic, I can give more personal care and run the place exactly as I please. And in Port Ariel are my father, and Lily, and . . ." She smiled. "Well, I just believe it's time to come home." She paused. "I might be making a big mistake . . ."

Nick reached out and ran a finger over the curve of her cheekbone. "Then again, you might not," he said gently. "There's only one way to find out."

IN THE EVENT OF MY DEATH

There were once six teenagers in Wheeling, West Virginia. They called themselves the Six of Hearts. They knew how to have fun, and get into trouble. One night things went too far and a girl died. The rest swore never to speak about what happened.

Thirteen years later one of the remaining Six is murdered. When Lauren receives a terrifying message, she fears she may be next. She knows the killer is watching her, and she's running out of time. But to stay alive she must question everything she thought she knew, and suspect every friend she thought she had.

HODDER

TONIGHT YOU'RE MINE

Fifteen years ago, Nicole and Paul had the perfect life. She was a university student, and he was a concert pianist. They were deeply in love, and passionately happy. Until one violent night changed everything.

Although Nicole managed to build a new life for herself, the past continues to haunt her. Paul was reported dead in a car crash, but Nicole can't shake the feeling that he's still alive and out there, somewhere.

Then Nicole thinks she sees Paul at her father's funeral. When this is followed by a series of mysterious murders of people somehow connected to her past, Nicole begins to wonder if Paul has returned, and if he's protecting her, or saving her till last . . .

HODDER